Books to watch for by Gerald D. Johnston

Shakespeare's Dead (Summer '13)

∞

Series Collaboration (Spore Press)
(With Lucia Adams, Paul Freeman, and Sharon Van Orman)

Season of the Dead: Book I (Spring '13)

∞

Dropcloth Angels

Gerald D. Johnston

Freakshine Press

Within the novel, there are brand names used which we should give mention to. Any and all omissions brought to our attention will be corrected in subsequent editions. Excerpt from Lewis Carroll's *Alice's Adventures in Wonderland* (©1865). George Carlin – interview quote. The traditional Jamaican version of the nursery rhyme, 'Einey, meenie, minie, moe' appears – author unknown. The Lord's Prayer – God. The brand name 'Froot Loops' ™ is owned by The Kellog Corporation. McDonalds ™ is a trademark of The McDonalds Corporation. Volkswagen Beetle ™ is owned by Volkswagen. Tylenol ™ is owned by McNeil Consumer Healthcare, a division of Johnson & Johnson. Wikipedia was the jump-off point for several tidbits of information including, syphilis, its causes, effects, treatment, past sufferers, etc; electronic door locks; mental institutions and a few medical issues; non-medicinal pharmaceuticals (or street drugs); and laws of extradition. Other research material: 'The Argyll Robertson Pupil' – JM Pearce (Journal of Neurology, Neurosurgery & Psychiatry;Sep2004, Vol. 75 Issue 9); New York Times Reporter, William Buehler Seabrook, *Jungle Ways* (1931). New York: Harcourt, Brace and Company.

Published in the United States by Freakshine Press
New York, New York
www.freakshine.com

Back cover author photo by some random chick
ISBN-13: 978-0-9868202-0-5

Caveat for the Leery or Unaware

This is a work of fiction, not a confession of inside information. While there exists secret societies such as those described within the novel, I've taken certain liberties in creating fictitious criminal organizations, shady peoples, and landmarks of ill repute.

Several recognizable cites or towns have been mentioned, but permission was not asked for/not given for their use. I expect that those effected will understand. If not, it won't be the first time I've pissed someone off.

There are several fictitious places mentioned herein, but their locations have been obscured. For example, The Paradise Valley Institute has never existed (to my knowledge) in St. Louis – but there is a Paradise Valley campground near my city of birth. ☺ The Mud Vein Lounge is entirely fictitious, but wouldn't it be cool if it wasn't?

All of the characters in this novel are fictitious creations, birthed through the fingers of yours truly. Any resemblance to persons, living, dead, or existing in some alternate dimension that lies between a fart and a fat man's undies, is purely coincidental.

This work is not meant to glorify the following: the wanton murder of innocents, recreational drug use, sensationalism within the media, sex for money, or even sex with a slipper.

Remember, without darkness there can be no light. Straddle the twilight and read on.

Gerald D. Johnston

For my mother & father, with all the love a delinquent son can muster; for my beautiful wife, Jennifer, and two little nose miners, Jacob & Katie; and, for believing (or not) in me, my five brothers & sisters.

Last, but never least, a heavenly shout out to Spike (a.k.a. The Cringer): Playing dead was the only trick he eventually mastered.

ACKNOWLEDGMENTS

My list is long. I wish I could name all of the readers who've helped Zoe & Zane make it to this point, but that would be another novel. Here are the beta readers whose input was greatly appreciated. Without their aid I wouldn't be writing this: Barbara Elsborg, Shana Raywood, Courtney Johnson, Ginny Fralick, Donna Kawarthy, Jan Malera, Jane Alexander, Genevieve Graham, Steve Troster, Sheila Hillman, Nancy Grondin, and a very special thanks to Amanda Leck for the eleventh hour edits and fresh insights on a troubling chapter one (which is no longer chapter one).

You peeps rock.

Gerald D. Johnston

Part I

Unstoppable Force Meets an Edible Object

Once upon a time, there lived a girl of worth. Here is her story, give or take a lie or two.

Gerald D. Johnston

1

WORTH

Zoe Beaupre stood at a crossroads.

She was lost, but standing at an intersection of two forgettable Toronto streets had nothing to do with this pressing issue: in one hand, she held an empty bottle of Percocet, complete with her name on the label, like an honest-to-god prescription she *actually* needed. The other clutched a very old, recently stolen pocket watch.

The Percs had been a gift from a gentleman doctor of her acquaintance back in St. Louis. Knowing she couldn't pass a customs search with her drug of choice, she'd asked for and received—for a favor that *still* hurt when she tied her shoes—a prescribed solution to carry her through the week long stay she'd planned with her sister. *Should* have, but didn't. She dropped the bottle back into her purse, just in case. You never know when you'll need an empty pill bottle, complete with your name on it.

Zoe dangled the watch by its chain and it rotated lazily, trapping arcs of sunlight that shone like butter against the tarnished casing—and she suffered a momentary pang of guilt. The watch wasn't *exactly* hers to sell. While searching for a pair of earrings in her sister's jewelry box, she'd rescued it from an encroaching mass of cheap trinkets.

"That's right, bitch," said a voice from within her head, *"Do it. You're already going to Hell. What's a little theft gonna hurt?"*

She should've known she wasn't going to make it through the morning without *him* speaking up. *"What's it to you, Monkey? Is it yours? No, it's not, so shut the fuck up."*

"One monkey, shutting up." The purple monkey materialized on the sidewalk at her feet, holding one fuzzy hand over his yarn stitched mouth and flipping the bird with the other.

This didn't compute. Monkey never gave up so easily. *"That's it?"*

Purple Monkey nodded his head earnestly.

That's weird, she thought. He'd usually not stop until she'd torn him to pieces or tossed him out a window.

"What's weird?"

"I thought you were gonna shut up?"

"I am. Let your conscience be your guide, yada yada." The monkey shrugged and hitched a ride on the back of a passing dog.

Zoe stared after him. About ten feet away he turned, winked, and disappeared.

The word *weird* had taken on a whole new meaning after he'd invaded her head. A doctor had run several tests, but they came back negative for a tumor or any physical reason for his presence. A Psychiatrist, on the other hand, asked if there'd been any changes in her life lately; had she been taking any new prescriptions...any *other* drugs?

He'd known about the heroin. How could he not? He *did* have the results of her blood analysis in his meaty little claw. Upon leaving his office that day, she'd decided to forgo another appointment or a second opinion in favor of self medication. A quack couldn't help her, not even if they knew the *whole* truth about Monkey.

Truth was, the monkey wasn't exactly new to her. His previous existence had marked a very pivotal point in her young life, a time of growth and discovery. In appearance he was all she remembered him to be, but that was the sole similarity. *This* Purple Monkey—this invisible monster—wasn't cuddly and soft, he was vulgar and rude.

Bought as a pair when they were children, purple for Jeanne and pink for Zoe, the stuffed monkeys became the main attraction of The Sisters Beaupre private circus. Though seen as nothing more than a broom under a bed sheet by their mother, the circus was their own secret fantasy land. A world in which the sun shone its smile all day and all night; a world where a girl could be a star, take charge—living on cotton candy and pretzels—and thrive without parents who would leave or yell about Jesus all the time: Two girls and their monkeys against the world.

During a return bus trip from one of Jeanne's chemotherapy sessions, Zoe had been so caught up with the fog art she'd been painting on the window that, when her mother dragged her away, she left Pink Monkey behind on the seat. Later, her mother had called the bus line, but the monkey hadn't been turned in to their lost and found. Pink Monkey was gone forever and so was Circus World, at least for Zoe.

Three days later while she sat cross-legged on her bed, staring miserably out the window at the rain as it pelted the road with tears the size of golf balls, Jeanne brought Purple Monkey to her room and tossed him on the bed. She told Zoe the monkey wanted to be with her now – that it was tired of Jeanne and liked her better. Zoe gladly accepted her sister's offer and immediately pitched the Big Top. She felt sad for Jeanne, not having her own monkey anymore, but she could thereafter be the audience neither one of them ever had, someone to laugh and enjoy the show.

At first, Jeanne watched all the time, but then the cancer came back and her visits to the Big Top grew shorter and further apart. Soon she stopped watching at all; not even Purple Monkey made her smile anymore. Circus World was never the same after that. Zoe tried to understand her sister's lack of interest, but couldn't help hating Jeanne and her cancer for giving up on Circus World. After a while the illusion died and Zoe also gave up on the Big Top. By the time she turned seven it was just like her mother had said: a bed sheet and a broom, nothing more. That didn't mean she gave up on Purple Monkey. After all, he was still her best friend.

Zoe remembered dragging the stuffed carcass of that violet simian to school, the dentist's office, and the beach—literally *everywhere*, including the bathtub. Eventually there wasn't much more than patches and a lingering aroma of unwashed socks left of him, but she didn't care. He was more than material, stitches and button eyes. To Zoe, he was a connection; a conduit to that sunny place where fathers didn't leave, mothers didn't scream, and sisters didn't get cancer.

One day, while Zoe was down the street at a friend's pool, her mother tossed Purple Monkey out with the trash. Upon finding the monkey missing, Zoe was inconsolable, nearly tearing the house apart in her search for him. Her mother couldn't understand the tantrums, especially when they continued past the first week. And, subsequently, neither did the therapist Zoe was sent to see over the affair.

It wasn't until Zoe came across a wonder drug named heroin at a house party some thirteen years later that the same monkey—odd colored button eyes, clumsy patchwork and all—returned. He walked right up to her in the middle of someone's trashed living room and said, *"Hey, Bitch."* Just like that.

She knew it wasn't *real*. She was older and knew better then. Grownups, at least sane ones, didn't *have* imaginary friends. But that little fact didn't stop it from talking, or, for that matter, from acting like a complete dick.

And why should Monkey care about a stupid watch? Why should I? Besides, if Jeanne had even cared a little bit about the damn thing, she should've taken better care of it.

At times, Zoe found guilt as easy to sidestep as an oncoming turtle. She dropped the time piece into a pocket and waited for the light to change. She was left-handed, so she went right.

Penniless after only two days, she'd sorely underestimated the price of a good time in Toronto...hence the watch, hence the pawning of said watch. If needed, one or more swinging egos could be milked for the rest of the cash, but only as a last resort. She was on vacation after all. For lack of a pill, she popped a breath mint.

Two blocks up, she found a pawn broker.

~~oOo~~

"Fifty dollars, no more," was the pawn broker's first and final price.

"What do you mean *'fifty dollars'*?" Her words lashed like a cool mint scented whip across the mixed odors of the cubicle sized entry. "The fucking thing is gold, you asshole."

For his part, it was clear the pawnbroker had played this game many times before. In response he grunted and found his bellybutton with an index finger.

Zoe sensed she was going about this all wrong, and wished her last words were spaghetti so she could suck them back in one long strand.

"I'm sorry, sir. I've been under a great deal of strain lately and recently lost my plane ticket home to St Louis. My finals start tomorrow and I need to get back. What do you say about eighty bucks for a poor student?"

The pawn broker, a dark little East Indian man wearing a shirt too short for his paunch, eyed the grouped track marks below her rolled up sleeves and flexed the wrinkle between his brows. "I say fifty dollars." He picked up the magazine he'd been reading when she entered and proceeded to flip through the pages, ignoring both watch and woman.

After a few fanned pages, he smoothed a few wisps of hair across a forehead so high he'd need a telescopic handle to comb past the crown, and said, "Let me show you something, please."

The man laid the magazine face down and left the counter. He returned with a dusty shoe box, pulled off the lid, and set it atop the magazine for her to see.

In the box a Timex rubbed faces with a Rolex, whose strap was slid through the buckle of a very feminine pearl backed number, which sat on the face of another, and so on. The gangbang of jewelry in the box was very impressive and all looked very expensive to Zoe, but she *could* see his point: This was a buyer's market.

Damn.

As this new failure spread through her like a stain on a takeout bag, she wondered if Jeanne would give her another loan.

"You see, my friend," said the smelly man, "I have many, many watches—more, probably, than I could ever sell. Yours is a very fine watch, a pretty watch. But, young lady, if I cannot sell it, how much do you think it is worth?"

Again, she saw his point, but the way he spoke was really beginning to irritate her. "Okay, whatever. Take it and give me the fifty bucks."

Zoe sighed and leaned back in the small entrance, tapping the wall with her head.

The watch had belonged to her father. When he left the last time, he'd pulled Jeanne aside and given it to her. He must not have seen his younger daughter in the hall as he bent and kissed Jeanne before leaving. Zoe hadn't received that same farewell. Actually, she'd received *no* farewell whatsoever, so she felt almost nothing by the loss of the watch.

A hand emerged through the bars and set a slip of paper on the counter. "Please sign your claim ticket. There is a pen to the right."

From where she stood the hand reminded her of *Thing* from *The Addams Family*. She pushed away from the wall, plucked the pen from its cradle, scribbled *Morticia Addams* in the signature box, and slid the slip back through.

She was going to be short, way short—especially if she planned to have any fun while she was there. Before giving up, she decided to play her only remaining card. Zoe tilted her head and tapped her fingers on the counter to get the man's attention. "Hey," she said, low and gentle, inwardly cringing at what she contemplated.

The pawn broker looked up from writing her information

into a ledger, and his massive forehead wrinkled into rounded steps as his eyebrows came up. "Miss?"

She glanced out the door, then forced a smile to her lips. "Is there anything we could work out for, say, another eighty bucks?" A stab of revulsion flowered in the pit of her stomach at the thought of him sweating over her. No stranger to doing what needed doing for the cause, Zoe succeeded in diffusing the rebellion with a silent burp.

"Maybe back there?" she said, pointing over his shoulder to the rear of the shop.

The little man didn't miss a stroke with his ballpoint. Once finished with her claim ticket, he ripped it off and approached the window. Sliding it through, along with enough body odor to fumigate a square block of roach infested houses, his face loomed within inches of the bars.

"Whatever it is that has you, young lady, you must fight it. It is not my place, for certain, to speak to you so boldly, but you started it." Every consonant hit her like a sledge hammer.

He leaned across the counter and ran his fingers along the cluster of needle marks on Zoe's arm. "My dear son, Senji, was taken by the drugs two years ago." His fingers trembled as his arm receded back through the gap in the bars.

Zoe's skin tingled in the wake of his touch. Her eyes found the floor and stayed there as she took the fifty from the counter and stuffed it into the front pocket of her jeans. Before leaving, she mumbled, "Thank you," then walked out.

Once on the sidewalk, she took a deep breath as she unrolled the sleeves of her shirt—sleeves she didn't recall rolling up!—and buttoned them at her wrists. Feeling more than a little dirty, she drifted into the flow of pedestrian traffic and allowed it carry her where it would. After a while she began to feel an old familiar itch.

Damn monkey.

2

PAINT BRUSHES & OTHER NEEDED INGREDIENTS

Beaver Creek (80 kilometers north of Toronto)

"Annie?" Zane Ellis stood over the hogtied hitchhiker, a bucket of warm water in one hand and a sponge in the other. She was awake, but her soul was somewhere else. Her eyes, swollen almost shut, were two pairs of veined lips, so dark they seemed poisonous. As he watched her, he wondered where she was, where *all* his victims escaped to in that space of time between capture and death. He also wondered if he could go there too. He had his own place, a secret room in his head, but was their escape, their refuge, any better than his?

Wherever it was, he would've loved to paint its landscape.

He nudged the girl's bare leg with the toe of his shoe. "Annie, it's time to get you cleaned up. Wake up, sugar."

The girl's head swiveled like a punch drunk boxer's. Then, after a whistled intake of air, reality leaked through a crack under the door to her safe place; her eyes opened and she jerked against the thick ropes holding her to a pole in the middle of the shed. Around the ball gag in her mouth, her incoherent cries were hoarse and guttural—slobbery, even.

Zane stepped back and allowed her to vent. He wasn't mad, didn't feel the need to silence her. He'd be pretty miffed if he woke up naked and tied in a strange place too. But he also didn't want her to stain his clothes with her sniffles and snot, so he decided to wait until she'd finished. Annie didn't seem as strong as some of the others had been, so he guessed it would be only a few minutes before she'd see her situation for what it had been building up to since birth: hopeless. He'd use that time to slip into something more suited to the task, and maybe make a pot of coffee.

He stepped out of the shed just as the sun met the sky. It spread across the horizon like a fresh paper cut awaiting the day's first bead of blood. This was fitting. This was an omen.

He left the door open so the girl could see what he saw, witness one last beautiful sunrise before eternity took her. He felt it was the least he could do.

His eyes fell to an old axe-stabbed stump, caught in relief by the sun's first rays. The profiled axe called forth an image of things to come. He turned and regarded her one last time before heading for the house. Although fortuitous, their meeting had been largely disappointing. She'd been standing at the side of the road with her thumb in the air, holding a sign that read "Going that way", accompanied by an arrow pointing *up* instead of forward.

An idea began to percolate as he pulled to the side of the road in answer to her waggling thumb. Her presence had introduced an opportunity for a 'practice round' for his upcoming show and he had every intention of pursuing it.

Granted, the 'hitcher and the dark road' was as cliché as a meeting could get, but whose fault was it the girl had snubbed any motherly advice she'd ever received in regard to strangers and deserted roads? Surely not his. Plus, it wasn't as though he'd been actively searching her out.

He nonetheless considered her a gift horse, a bonus of sorts. As the memory of her hustling after his brake lights brought a smile to his face, he mused over the *real* direction the arrow had been pointing: up.

Up was where the angels sang.

One punch as she leaned into the car was all it took. That had been the most disappointing part. Add that to the fact she was standing alone on a dirt road near dusk, and he might have rethought his belief in the Chaos theory in favor of the flowery notion that everything happens for a reason.

But that would be madness.

At about eighteen years of age, the girl was too stupid to live and too old to unlearn all that had brought her to this point in her life—to that dirt road in particular—so Zane had decided to help her out. More, he was going to help her "up". And since she would only be exercise, a warm up, Dr. Gideon wouldn't need to know about her. The old man would only want the video feed for the kill planned for the main event, and this girl was definitely *not* main event material.

As he stared into dawn's amber yawn, contentment faltered, and then faded, as an image of his benefactor surfaced. Four hundred miles by air, a whole country away, and Zane *still* fell under the greedy man's shadow. A fact he shouldn't have found surprising, considering Dr. Gideon owned the chalet and the forty acres it rested upon.

The doctor was a constant irritant, but his wealth and connections were extensive, which was why Zane hadn't killed him yet. He smiled as he imagined a not-so-distant future in which Gideon was no longer needed.

The doctor wasn't happy about lending him the chalet, but relented and gave him two weeks.

Two weeks didn't leave much time for nuance and preparation, but Zane would be free to create *his* art, *his* way, without the old man looming over his shoulder, uttering suggestions regarding lighting and camera angles, or screaming for a premature but enduring money shot. Short sighted quick thrills were all the rage among the clientele who purchased the doctor's movies. All brutality, no vision.

Zane had vision, but his creative nature was something for which Gideon held little humor. Through his art, he intricately mapped the secrets and struggles, the birth and death rattle, of all humanity, one canvas at a time. Where Gideon saw dollars and blood on a drop sheet, Zane saw divinity; a gleaning of the pattern within the chaos, rendered in the purest color of the spectrum. Maybe someday his genius would be recognized, but likely not by Gideon.

The single missing item for his upcoming video drama was a co-star…someone *special*—and not that too-stupid-to-live hitcher. She *was* going to be a part of the show, but would serve in other, less visible, ways.

He'd taken most of her hair the night before, while she was still unconscious. At the moment, her mouse-brown locks were in the kitchen, soaking in a shallow pan of bleach and conditioning solution. Later, he'd require a much larger sacrifice. Her hair would make fine brushes, but a paintbrush wasn't a paintbrush without a handle.

~~oOo~~

Zane recalled Gideon saying he rarely visited the chalet. He could have guessed without being told as he rummaged through the closets for something disposable to wear; there was nothing that would've fit the doctor's lanky form. Judging by the sizes, Gideon's parents could have taken jobs in a travelling circus as a pair of chubby midget clowns.

If he went back to the shed wearing any of Gideon's father's old clothes, Annie might think he was crazy, or some inbred Jethro type axe murderer. If only he'd stuck with his original plan and gone into town for clothes and Froot Loops, this situation might have been avoided.

Upon searching the garage, he found a pair of vinyl coated rain pants, but, oddly, no matching coat. Beneath the pants was a pair of rubber boots that would fit, but then he thought if he wore the pants and boots together with no shirt, Annie might suspect him of being some homicidal Mr. July from a Fireman's calendar.

He decided to have a cup of coffee first, then figure out what to wear…maybe go into town for a box of Froot Loops and clothes. Then he could relax on the patio and work on his tan until lunchtime.

At a growl from his stomach, he amended the thought of leaving her alone to rousing her right then. The sun would always be there, fresh and new every day, but *she* wouldn't.

Besides, breakfast *is* the most important meal of the day.

Twenty minutes later, he stood in the doorway of the garden shed, coffee in one hand, and axe in the other. In lieu of clothing, he'd decided to dress as he did for his shows. He was naked.

After setting the axe down, he took a sip of coffee. It was good. He'd have to remember how many scoops he used. And he'd been right about the girl; she *was* calmer now. She still sobbed and snotted as she shook like a palsied rabbit, but at least she'd settled.

Annie was dirty, slightly overweight, and sat amid a muddy lake of her own bodily excretions, but Zane saw the beauty beneath the mud and tears and planned on savoring every second they spent together. Before she could slide back into another eye rolling convulsion which might delay him further, he shushed her.

She quieted, but shot fearful glances at his naked form. He followed her eyes to their target, and sighed. "I'm sorry for that, I really am. Listen, I know we've just met, but please believe me when I say to you that sex is the furthest thing from my mind. I'm not that kind of guy."

His eyes wandered from her to a shelf cluttered with all manner of tools, and his gaze settled upon a dust covered saber saw. He smiled, and then squatted in front of her with his forearms resting on his knees. "That was the good news."

She didn't seem relieved. This was going poorly. Annie wasn't being very receptive at all, and Zane couldn't help but feel partially responsible. If he'd only gone into town first for something to wear, this awkwardness over his nudity may have been avoided.

He soaked the sponge, squeezed it, and began to wash her, starting with her face. "I don't think you want to hear the bad news, so I'll tell you this instead: You and I, Annie, are going to make beauty come alive. Together we'll create a masterwork, blood and bone, that will make the heavens weep. Won't that be nice?"

Annie blinked and shivered, sobbed and snotted.

As he circled, searching for a good starting point, he spoke into her ears words of assurance, words to soothe: "I just need your bones, but have no fear, sugar. Nothing is wasted, never with me."

The soothing words didn't work—they *never* worked—but the screams weren't so bad, and didn't usually last very long. Surprisingly enough, Annie's did. She howled along with the rusty saw, in a jack-hammering crescendo, until he was halfway through the second limb. She was a real trooper.

Before pulling it out, Zane stared into her eye for a very long time. Annie wasn't in there anymore and he hadn't heard her leave. She'd gone back to her happy place and could stay there forever. Zane felt at peace. Peace for her, peace for him.

Maybe it was the coffee, could have been the beautiful day, likely a mixture of both, but he was happy right then and began to whistle while he worked.

3

THE FEED

Aside from their apparently diminutive size, Zane knew little about Gideon's departed parents. One thing he liked about them was their decision to mirror every wall in the spacious living room. Zane loved mirrors. He found himself to be as beautiful as others must also find him to be and could while away an entire day studying his flawless self. In addition to the captivating view, it was within the realm of mirrors where his secret room lay, beyond the glass and before the glaze, and only for him.

At the moment, the mirror was only a mirror; he admired himself and nothing more. At thirty he could pass for twenty five, younger if he dressed right. According to his mother, he was the very image of his father, with his sun streaked blonde locks and slender muscular form. The only difference, his mother had said, was that his face, although like his father's, was something more than extraordinary. It was a gift from an angel. He could never fault her observations. His face was wonderful to behold. He'd never met his real father or seen a picture, but he must have been a handsome man indeed.

Aside from birthing him, his mother's only real legacy was a tattoo that stretched across his back and down the side of each arm. The artwork depicted two large black, birdlike wings interlaced with arcane markings that, in all the years since, he'd not been able to decipher. Could have been his mother was truly inspired from above and it *was* angelic script. More likely, though, she was insane. "From an angel, to an angel," she'd repeated as she poked at him.

Meant as a gift—one of the few she'd ever given, and a fact that made it all the more special—his mother had created a masterwork upon his skin with nothing more than a sewing needle, two bottles of ink, and a stone's quantity of patience. She'd finished the wings approximately twelve hours before his eighteenth birthday. Eleven hours before he killed her.

Without being aware he'd gone there, Zane found himself staring into the living room from the other side of the mirror, from the doorway of his secret room. This was good. He could think there, be alone there. Maybe add a window at the back...maybe see Annie on the other side, see where she went.

But he couldn't. There was much to do. The show would be his time to shine He could come back then. He could come back with an angel...his drop cloth angel. Slowly, as though wading against a current, he stepped toward the door, toward himself.

He passed from his room with the force of a fired bullet; the rejoining staggered him as he became whole again. After a moment of blinding white that circled his head like a hurricane sized halo, he looked up. The face in the mirror was bleeding, bleeding from the mouth. He'd bitten his tongue again. He didn't like the taste of his own blood. It was bitter. Not sweet like some of those he'd known, known and tasted. His mind began to wander...to faces, to places...

But, the show.. the show must go on, and he was the star; Cannibalangelo was the star. *Practice*, he thought. *Practice makes your good better and your better best.*

He wiped his mouth, took a deep breath, and then lowered his arm to hang at his side. Once relaxed, he began to practice being human. Practice for him began with tears: crying on demand was a talent he'd so far found impossible to master without the use of props.

With a finger he traced the dry eyes and frowning mouth of his mirrored partner, leaving behind a sweat smeared outline on the glass. Moving on through his routine, he cleared his throat and spoke to his endless image, "Me? My name is David. David Jackson. I write fluff pieces for music magazines...I'm in sales...an insurance claims adjuster...a friend of your uncle's..."

Then he tilted his head and whispered, "Yeah, I don't believe me either." He spat at his reflection.

On the coffee table there was a remote that controlled everything from the blinds on the windows, to the thermostat. He pushed buttons until the stereo lit up. *You sure do have all the toys, Doc,* he thought.

From speakers secreted somewhere in the high ceilinged room, an eerily luminous keyboard chased lightening and waves as they crashed and Jim Morrison crooned.

Wailing along, side-by-side with the lizard king, Zane rode the storm.

From underneath the music there came an unfamiliar annoying ringing. Zane spied the telephone on a stand across the room but made no move to answer it. He left the call to the answering machine, killed the stereo, and then entered the kitchen.

The machine picked up and his own voice said: "Hello..? Hello..? Is there anyone there?"

At least Zane thought it sounded like him, but different, like a close impersonation. Maybe it was him, maybe it wasn't.

Zane smiled as he waited. "Gotcha," said the machine, "I'm not available to take your call right now. Busy, busy. So leave a message and I'll call you back."

Beeeep.

"You've changed my greeting. That was not entirely intelligent of you. Very funny, though, Zane," was Doctor Gideon's tinny, not-very-amused response. "Listen, call me as soon as you get this. We need to talk."

Zane grabbed the extension from the charger on the kitchen counter and thumbed the talk button. Sighing theatrically into the phone, he said, "Kinda busy here, Doc. And the name's David, at least for now. You know that. You say Zane again and I'm hanging up. Two weeks. You gave me two weeks. Say what you have to say and make it quick."

Zane held the phone away from his ear as the doctor spoke. He opened the refrigerator and peered in. "Hi, Annie," he said, and pinched her bloodless cheek. Aside from the head, there was a lonely cluster of condiments and a pitcher of water. *Great.*

Against the protest of his grumbling stomach, he closed the door and sat down at the kitchen table. He'd put all the leftovers in the freezer and didn't feel like thawing anything for later. Also, he was getting kind of sick Annie. What he really wanted right then was a big bowl of cereal.

No cereal, no milk…he was normally more prepared. He'd been on his way to get those, along with a change of clothes, when he'd met Annie. *Damn Annie. Damn boring tasting Annie.*

As he half listened to the doctor, Zane leafed through the flyers he'd brought back from his premier foray into Toronto. Surely his angel could be found somewhere among them.

"Zane, I'm only thinking of your best interests. I can't help you from here. If anything goes south on you, my boy, you're on your own. We don't cross borders. It's just not done."

"David—and it looks to me, Doc, like I just did cross borders, so drop the jilted bitch routine. I'll be back in a couple of weeks. Besides, I'm hot and ready to rock at this end," he said, referring to the video cameras he'd installed the day before. "Wanna do a check? I'll send you the link and do a visual."

"Yes, I suppose. Say, you're not going to skin an Eskimo or bite the heads off any penguins, are you?"

"You're not very PC are you, Doc? It's not Eskimo, it's Inuit—and *no* penguins. I heard they taste like chicken, and you know how much I hate chicken." Zane blinked at the small computer screen, having a hard time focusing at first.

"I thought we were doing fine here in Chicago, but this…"

"This what? This project that you have no control over?"

said Zane. As he typed, he pictured that safe little man sitting in his cozy little den, tasting the dark side one teaspoon at a time—sipping the violence vicariously through Zane and others like him. *Fucking Jerk.*

"There," said Zane, clicking send. "Oh, by the way, I've brought that table in from the foyer. You remember, the one you bought from that Scandinavian sadist in Florida, the one with all those body piercings?"

"No. Definitely not. I—"

"Well, I can't work without a table, can I?"

The phone sighed, "Never mind. Just be careful with—"

"Thanks, Gideon. I'm touched you care."

"My table, Zane. Be extremely careful with it. It's priceless."

"Yeah and where'd you get the money for it?"

"You, Zane…among others, but mostly you."

"Now, was that so hard? Come on, Gideon. I feed, you get the feed, and the viewers get to watch. Only gonna be one loser here and she won't be in a position to care."

"Jesus, your optimism never ceases to amaze me."

"And you're *not* optimistic?"

"No. I'd consider myself to be more of an *opportunist*. That said I still believe this venture of yours is nothing short of insane. Will you even be ready by Thursday?"

Zane left the computer and headed for the dining room, and he began to feel dizzy—something that had begun the month before, and had since become a daily occurrence. He'd come to recognize this hostile takeover as a battle with a demon. He was sure of it. It manifested itself as an absence of self, a draining force that supped at him from inside his mind.

Sweat swelled across his stomach and down the backs of his legs like a pair of dead mice, and Zane knew he was in for more than a mere skirmish. Next, he could expect the flickering blackness; the struggle for his eyes, his brain, and fragments of his past. Then, there was the pain. Oh, the electrifyingly magnificent pain. The demon truly was a worthy adversary.

The attacks had taken on a frantic nature lately, which led

Zane to believe he must be winning. What other explanation could there be? Gideon didn't know about the demon, and Zane would never tell. How could a man like Gideon ever presume to understand?

"Yeah, Thursday," Zane said, focusing his will upon ignoring his invader, "Have you ever known me to miss a shoot?" Then, his mouth said something he didn't know it was going to say, but thought was funny nonetheless. "You know, you can be a real crotch crust sometimes, Doc—a real cunt." The demon may have been his enemy, but he sure spoke the truth.

The demon was closer, grasping for him from the inside—scratching, pulling. Zane swayed, willing it away as a child would a persistent bogyman. Through the oily black vortex swirling ever larger, he said, "Look, I gotta go. We good?"

Pain flared in his skull, racking him with a body shudder. Gideon might have said something, but he wouldn't have heard. Zane had a hard enough time keeping his fingers closed on the phone. "I said: Are we good?"

"Are you deaf, boy? I just told you."

As drool began to seep from his mouth and run down his chest, Zane walked to a corner of the room and slid down the wall. "Must be the phone. Sorry. So, what did you say?"

"I need you to come back to Chicago this weekend. There are some papers here for you to sign."

"Papers?"

"Saturday afternoon. I'll see you then."

"Sure." Zane forced the needed air through his vocal chords. Cradling the phone in both hands like a pet scorpion he waited, and would as long as he could. "Your minute's been up for a while, Gideon. Plans to make, people to bake," he mumbled into the receiver.

"Don't worry," said Gideon, "it's nothing bad."

Nothing bad. Check. "'Kay, bye," Zane mumbled. *Weekend. Check. Go see Gideon. Check.* He keyed END, let the phone fall from his fingers, and collapsed onto his side. He wanted to dig a hole through his skull—free himself, expel the pain. But he knew that's what the demon wanted; it wanted free access, a doorway in. Zane was smart, Zane was wise; he wouldn't be fooled by any damn devil. This war would be won in inches. There was nothing he could do but wait. Wait for either victory or defeat. Zane clenched his teeth, tucked himself into a ball, and rode the storm.

~~oOo~~

The sun had tripped over its own shadow and fallen behind the couch sometime before Zane pushed himself away from the floor; the darkness outside the Chalet absolute. Even the stars shied away from him for reasons only another star could fathom. Could have been, he mused, they were embarrassed for the beautiful naked man laying in a pile of his own feces and felt he needed privacy. Maybe it was simply cloudy with a chance of empathy.

He quickly checked his face and hands for blood, then breathed a sigh. He stank, but remained unblemished. Rolling away from the puddle, he plodded in the direction of the laundry room to find a mop and some plastic bags.

After cleaning his mess and showering, he returned to the kitchen and stood by the table, staring down at the flyers he'd been leafing through earlier while talking to Gideon. Eenie meanie miny moe, he thought, then lifted one away from the rest. The lucky winner read:

National Cancer Society of Canada
Memorial & Fundraiser

Tomorrow.

It wasn't perfect—cancer victims were creepy—but chance had spoken.

He was happy again. Not even an image of cancer-tainted meat could bring him down. Like peas and carrots, he could eat around the bad parts. His spirits were on the mend and the pain receded. He'd won. The demon was gone.

So what he couldn't remember the name of his old high

school or how to do long division. The demon was more than welcome to keep that shit. "My name is David," he said to the flyer, "and I'm gonna make you love me."

They always did.

4

SWEETS

Every town and every city, no matter the size or population, had an underbelly. It was a place set aside for the trade or purchase of anything a mind could imagine, and even more it couldn't. To Zoe, this was a certainty right up there with death and taxes. Whether that place was something as inconspicuous as the men's room stall of a roadhouse in Buttmunch Nowhere, or spanned whole city blocks, she *always* found it. Like found like; she belonged there. In a sprawling, culturally diverse Mecca like Toronto, she didn't need to walk far down its treasure trail to find the goods.

Zoe spotted a woman who looked as though she might be able to help. She stepped in front of the woman, and said, "I got a baby to feed, girl. You seen a paperboy around here?"

Translation: Excuse me, kind lady. I have a small hankering for a little heroin and was wondering if, by chance, you might hold knowledge of where I could meet a supplier of that particular narcotic?

The kind lady to whom Zoe spoke, whose sapphire spangled skirt fell dangerously short of hiding her black lace underwear, looked Zoe up and down and made a tsk tsk sound. Then she produced an index finger with a two inch nail—smartly color matched to her skirt—and hit Zoe's pause button. "Bitch, you need to get the fuck outta here."

Zoe understood. She'd have said the same thing, although, maybe with not the same flair as the slender, busty, black woman. She also understood that there was nothing to be gained for the woman in speaking to her except a pimp-slap for *not* doing her job, and talking to someone who wasn't there to buy what she was selling.

Zoe was there to buy, but it wasn't sex she was looking for. And she wasn't there to steal her away to another pimp, either—which was likely why the girl was giving her the heave.

Her own pimp, Cherry Charles, was pretty good to her, so she'd never done it, but it's a common practice for hookers to move from stable to stable like a roaming pack of Alzheimer's stricken mares. Ladder climbing businesswomen at heart, hookers followed the sugar. Or maybe, but only sometimes, they'd leave for the simple reason that the next pimp might not slap as hard for not producing.

Such is the life of a good thoroughbred.

Zoe couldn't imagine the statuesque woman presently waggling her fingers in her face ever allowing herself be run by *any* man; she was lean and sharp featured, so majestically black she was almost blue, and carried herself with a drop forged demeanor that belied the demure coo's and coy looks she tossed into passing cars. But every whore answered to *somebody.* That's just the way it was.

"Girl, you stand there much longer and motherfuckers gonna think we're a tag act. Go on now, keep walking, Dorothy. You ain't gonna find Oz here." Eight painted nails clicked like a tap dancing spider as she shooed Zoe away with both hands.

"Look," Zoe said. "I know you're busy, but all I'm asking for is a nod in the right direction. If you could help me out, I'll give you five bucks for your trouble."

"Does Jessica Sweets look like she needs your money, honey?" the hooker asked. "Watch Jessica's finger, baby; Jessica's only gonna show you once, so pay attention." She pointed over her shoulder as she spoke, "You see that parking meter down there, the one with the yellow tape and the doggie turd right beside it?"

Zoe looked past the woman, "Yeah, so what?"

"Go drop some money in it—the meter, honey, not the turd—and then wait." She gave Zoe a body shrug laden with unknown portent and seductively swiveled back to the slow procession of lonely drivers. "You wait around... could be you'll find what you're looking for." She blew a kiss at a plus-sized suit in a station wagon. Then, through the side of her mouth, as she pushed her breasts together for a balding pink man in a late model Audi, she added, "Now, piss off."

Zoe stepped past the working girl and headed for the marked parking meter. Along the way she pulled the contents from her pocket to find some coins for the meter. She found: two American quarters, three Canadian pennies, and, covering the entire handful, a generous clump of lint shot through with cat hair.

Fucking Mr. Moto. She really hated that goddamned cat. Her sister, Jeanne, treated it as though it were a child, and let it get into *every-fucking-thing.* Zoe had even found the little shit sleeping in her knapsack the first day she arrived from St. Louis.

She blew the mingled hair from her mismatched coin collection and walked on. The meter didn't take pennies and she was pretty sure the American quarters wouldn't fit, so, like the actress-in-training she'd been for all of three semesters, she faked it. *Damn thing looks broken anyway,* she thought, as she twisted the knob on the meter. After stuffing the change back into her pocket she sidestepped the pile of dog shit and backed away from the meter to wait.

No more than a few seconds passed before a teen waddled over and stood near her. He wore a pumpkin colored hoodie and a pair of matching sweat pants so large she could have slid in with him and had room to spare. A black ball cap, just a shade darker than his skin, sat at a skewed angle on his head. The brim of the hat was so flat it must have been ironed. From beneath its band, short tight curls peeked out, glistening like wiry strands of black gold in the mid day sun.

He gave her a once over and nodded toward the meter. "You couldn't even throw a dime in it? Sure is nice to have a dime when you need it." He pulled a cigarette from behind his ear and lit it. "I got a dime for you, if you need it. Do you need a dime?" His once over slid back up for another go and lingered just south of her neck. This act didn't go unnoticed by Zoe.

"Yeah," Zoe said. "I've been waiting for my uncle Harry for thirty minutes, and I don't want him to get a ticket."

"You might be waiting forty," the teen threw back. He pinched the cigarette in a Buddhist's meditation grip, first finger-and-thumb making an O, and flicked ashes into the air, which sent them back at him to settle on his orange sweat shirt. He brushed them away, and then flicked more ashes. "Times are tough all over, little sister."

Zoe moved close to the young man and bent to whisper in his ear, "You're telling me all you got is forty dollar bags? Do you think I'm fucking new, buddy, 'cause I'm not. What have you got for forty?"

"A fingernail."

"Are you kidding?"

"See you 'round, sister. You talk too much." He turned but made no attempt to leave. As he stood huffing double hauls from his cigarette, the youth thumbed his lighter open and closed—over and over: Sproing, clack, repeat.

Things just didn't seem to be going Zoe's way at all. In her mind she could hear her sister saying, "Zoe, you're great at everything. No matter what, always remember that. You're bigger than any obstacle in front of you...." She was pretty sure Jeanne didn't have situations like this in mind when she gave her the old college prep talk, but Jeanne didn't know then that her baby sister would drop out of college and end up a heroin-whore—or, *chemically assisted escort*, as Cherry jokingly called his girl, Candace. But Zoe figured if God, with his penchant for mockery of the human condition, gave her a half decent body, then the only *right* thing to do would be to use it.

She rolled her eyes, took a deep breath, "Say, kid. I was—"

"Kid?" He turned, still puffing like the little engine that could. "I look like a kid to you, lady?" He gave his chest two piston-like taps with a balled fist. "I'm eighteen, bitch. Are we doing business, or what? 'Cause if no, I gotta go."

"I didn't say that. Look, it's not like I know your name or anything. How about I call you, oh, I don't know…Brown Sugar." She clasped her hands behind her back, knowing it would push her shirt open enough for the teen to see a little lace. Business was business, and she'd been around long enough to know that men sift most *business* decisions through their one-eyed brain.

"That's better, girl. I like that." He leaned against the wall beside her, tilting his head in her direction as he eyed the street. "My boy's in lockdown and I'm covering his route 'til he's out, so take it or not, what I got is all I got." The teen bent to watch a car roll slowly past, and waved to three youths who catcalled and shot a stream of friendly obscenities at him. Following the car with his eyes, he said, "We could probably work a little something out if you're short."

"You want *all* this for forty dollars?" She pulled up close to him, and slid her hand down the outside of his pants. "How about this," she whispered her lips across his ear lobe, "I take care of you, and you take care of me?"

He stood with his eyes closed for a few seconds, possibly, Zoe guessed, discussing the venture with his cock broker, and then nodded. "I got a place. Follow me."

Brown Sugar's "place" was a third story apartment in a building that looked from the outside as though it should have been condemned. The inside was a totally different story. It was much worse. He shouldered open a warped, graffiti tagged door, and said, "Wait here a sec. I gotta see what time my moms is gonna be home."

At the word "moms," Zoe suddenly felt kind of gross, and old—older than her twenty one years anyway. She mouthed the word 'moms' back to herself in the form of a question and wrinkled her nose. "Eww." From within the apartment came the heavy machine gun fire and explosions of a video game, and a chorus of young voices yelling above the din. After a moment, Brown Sugar opened the door.

"Ok, c'mon in. But we gotta be quick 'cause my moms is home in a half-hour."

She followed him into the apartment. "Oh, I don't think we'll need that long," she said, then waved an arm down the dingy hallway. "I like what you've done with the place. Is that a Warhol?" She pointed to a body sized gap in the plaster.

"Huh?"

"Nothing. Lead on, candyman."

"Oh, right."

He led her to a room with a set of bunk beds pushed against one wall and a three foot high pile of dirty clothes in center of the floor. Zoe shut the door behind them. "Why don't you show me what you got before we get started? I don't know you."

He yanked at the drawstring on his pants. "Right, right, I get you, baby."

Chuckling, she said, "No, Brown Sugar, the smack. I'm pretty sure I already know what *that* looks like."

"No, baby. I stashed it in my shorts, see?" He fished out several bags of heroin and assorted pills. "I got you covered."

Always one to save another's feelings, Zoe raised an eyebrow and tactfully said, "Are you seriously that fucking stupid?" She couldn't believe what she was seeing. He'd been standing out in the street with all that shit, carrying it in the very first place a cop would check, and he seemed fine with it.

"What?" he asked, confused by her anger. "What else I'm supposed to do with it? Leave it here around my little brothers? Hell no. My moms'd beat the black off my ass, she found this shit."

Zoe waved an arm in the air to dismiss his comments, and shifted into Candace mode—her superwhore alter ego. "Forget it. Just give me my stuff and drop your shorts." She threw him a condom. "C'mon. Let's go."

"Okay." He tossed one of the bags from his lap to her and

pushed the rest onto the floor. "But can you turn around for a minute?"

"What? Oh, sure," she said.

Purple Monkey appeared on the floor before her and peeked around her leg at the young man sitting on the bed. He brought his index finger and thumb together and squinted at his measurement. *"You can really pick 'em, eh whore? Better tie a knot in that jimmy hat for him or he might lose it in your meat wallet."*

Zoe lifted her shoe and brought it down on the monkey, squishing imaginary stuffing out his mouth, ears, and every seam. *"Shut the fuck up and let me work."* Stepping on him wouldn't make him go away for long, but it felt damn good to stomp his ass once in a while.

In Zoe's experience as an escort, men always assumed the worst, like you were going to steal their fake, five-dollar Rolex, so they'd hide their wallets and watches. But surprisingly, when Brown Sugar told her she could turn around again, the assorted goodies were still scattered at his feet, and his wallet—which had fallen out of his voluminous pants—lay open in an upside-down V near his left shoe. All that had changed was that he'd dropped his shorts and pulled on the condom. A chuckle rose, but Zoe met it half way and shushed it. His battery pack barely filled half the rubber and, from where she stood, it looked fully charged. *Poor Brown Sugar. God wasn't very kind to you, was he?*

"Now, you just sit back and relax," she said, squatting down in front of him, "and let Candace take care of you."

But Brown Sugar *didn't* relax. He looked like he was having a stroke. His eyes were squeezed tight and the cords in his neck looked close to bursting. Zoe understood immediately and felt silly for not realizing earlier how innocent this so-called 'player' was. This all felt very wrong. The right thing to do—if there *was* a right way to do anything in a situation like this—would've been to give the kid forty dollars for the smack and leave with her stuff…and self respect.

But Zoe wasn't that *right* kind of girl—and forty bucks was forty bucks—so she lowered her head and went to work.

Exactly thirteen grunts—she'd counted—and a Klingon

war cry later, she walked out of the room with two forty-dollar bags of heroin, one bag of assorted pills, his cigarettes and lighter, and one black wallet. She most definitely, beyond a glimmer of a shadow of a doubt, was *not* that right kind of girl. But she also figured she was probably doing him a favor. After having been ripped off by her, he might quit trying to be something he wasn't and go back to school. *Maybe; it could happen*, she thought.

When she hit the street, she was still trying to put the whole experience into perspective when she heard a familiar voice: "Just who the fuck do you think you are puttin' my boy out on the street, selling your shit?"

Zoe glanced sideways at the hooker she'd met earlier. The woman faced away from the sidewalk, speaking animatedly into a cell phone. Zoe slowed to listen to the woman's end of the conversation.

"You goddamn right I'm mad." There was a short pause, then, "Yeah. I saw him half an hour ago down at that broken meter pretending he was some kind of hustler." A pause, then, "Fuck that, Orlan. Donald's only fourteen years old!"

Zoe lowered her head and picked up her pace. At the next mailbox, she lifted the cash out of the wallet and dropped it in, then patted herself on the back for acting as such a Good Samaritan. As she walked back to her sister's apartment building, she decided this was one chapter that was *definitely* going to be left out of her autobiography. She shucked a cigarette from Brown Sugar's pack, and thought of Jeanne and how she was making out at her Cancer lecture thingy.

5

SMITTEN

A pamphlet brought Zane to the cancer survivors' general assembly, but a chance encounter kept him there. He'd sat through seven mind numbing testimonies, each an after school special in the making, but failed to find his "IT" girl. After three speeches he would have settled for a man. After four he would have settled for a fucking dog, as long as it was cute.

Just as he'd thrown in the towel and left the building in search of a cab to take him back to his car—left four blocks away in an underground garage—a leggy blonde stepped out of the very cab he hailed, then hurried past him into the building. Waving the cab away, he turned and stared as she disappeared through the turnstile. It was brief, but something alien had stirred within him as she passed. That "something" would not go unexplored.

Twenty minutes of staring at her profile from across the auditorium, wishing she'd face toward him—and allow her to bask in his beauty as a return favor—was rewarded as she stood and took the podium.

He'd be able to watch her now without the need to look away if their eyes met, which they inevitably would. What else was she going to look at, the rest of the doe eyed, slack jawed masses? No, not with him there to feed her eyes.

She'd been cancer free for going on three years, etcetera, ad nauseum. He couldn't help tuning her out at first. Everyone has a threshold when dealing with the self-indulgent whining of strangers, and he'd passed his personal limit two sermons back. Her name was Jeanne. He didn't catch the last name—not like it mattered—but he could always get it later. After the show she'd have another name anyway.

Zane didn't remember most of what she said so much as how she said it, how she moved her body. She had the fluid grace of a prima donna. Her slender fingers, so delicate, so expressive, wove a visual tale of sorrow for him. That it was only for him, he had no doubt; each time she looked up from the podium, she found his face. She felt the connection, too. That was good.

By the end of her speech Zane could already imagine himself with her, much the same way he'd felt for all of his angels, but different—which only served to reinforce his belief that he'd create his masterwork this time. There; with her; with Jeanne.

She would be his feast, his Venus for the show.

Following her speech, which was also blessedly the conclusion of the conference, Zane retrieved a small piece of onion from his vest pocket, mashed it between his fingers and rubbed it across his eyes. He squinted through the sting of onion as he made his way to the front of the auditorium. Positioning himself close to the stairs she'd need to descend, he pretended to study various crayon drawings and finger paintings of sunny meadows done, presumably, by children with cancer.

At the bottom of the stairs, the blonde woman was immediately engaged by a group of elderly people, a fan club who held her up to say how inspiring her story had been. *Hello, people. I'm inspired, too. Beat it*, he thought; hoping the girl would linger long enough to hear him speak after she was done with to the rest of the moo-sayers.

Zane stood behind her, nearly touching her shoulder, and faced a poster depicting some of the many souls lost in the battle with cancer during the year. There were an awful lot of faces there. Cancer put up the kind of numbers a man like Zane could respect.

Well, here goes, he thought. "We seem to find just enough light in our darkest moments," he said, loud enough to intrude, in a tone laden with pain and his eyes brimming over with onion induced tears.

The young woman turned at the comment, and then noticed the tears in his eyes. She excused herself from the fan club and placed a hand on his arm. "You couldn't be more right." She studied him for a few seconds, concern showing on her face. "It's pretty bad, huh? Would you like to sit for a minute?"

Zane smiled through his tears. "Thank you. You're very kind. It's just that your words—I wanted to tell you how much I enjoyed your speech, that's all." He swiped at his eyes with the back of one hand, then went on, "They struck a very.... My daughter would have been six this Sunday. She's—she's with her mother now." He cried, unabashed and totally remorseless. He could've been mistaken, but he would swear that there were real tears mingling with the false. No one was there to gloat for him, so he did it himself: And the Oscar for overacting goes to Zane Ellis in "To Catch the Long Pig". First contact was, without a doubt, his favorite part of the pre-meal, pre-show courtship.

After forty minutes of skirting a mutual attraction, he proposed they continue their chat over coffee. They walked to a café around the corner, ordered two cups, and sat down. She may have been easy on the eyes, but this girl, Jeanne, really liked to talk. He stayed silent as she regaled him with a testimony of the support she'd received from her mother and sister, Zoe, and of her long road to recovery. She never mentioned a father, and he wasn't about to ask.

Some of this was just a retelling of her speech, but, against his nature as a predator, he didn't mind. Nodding sympathetically, he fell into a well used pattern of asking the right questions at the right times, and soon—to his astonishment—he not only respected cancer, but also grew to hate it. Hate it for how it could have hurt her as it did.

He would be her dark knight. Right then and there, he made a silent vow to her: *That evil will never have you. I'll give you the dignity it never would.*

As loathe as he was to end their time together, there was an issue of secrecy he had to address. Discretion and paranoia had been his armor and shield for many years and, together with what he regarded as a kind of karma within the chaos, had serviced him well in the past; it was long past time to go. He gently began to steer the conversation toward another meeting.

"I'm heading to Chicago on business later today, but I was wondering if we could have dinner sometime? I haven't felt this way in a long, long time and was hoping we could see each other again." He paused for a moment to check her body language. Nothing had changed in her posture or demeanor except for one thing: A small expectant smile touched the corners of her mouth.

Her eyes dipped to his naked ring finger as she picked up a paper napkin and began twisting it. "Oh, well, I don't know…"

"Ah," he said. "You're with someone." She wasn't, but she was nervous. And why shouldn't she be?

"No," she said. "It's not that. It's just that I haven't dated since, well, since before the cancer." She held onto a shrug and lowered her eyes to the napkin in her hands. "I sure wasn't much to look at while the big C was eating me from the inside out." She wrapped her arms across her chest and affected a bitter smile. "I couldn't even get a date for my prom."

They had that in common. Zane had never gone to a prom either. Funny how the educational system frowns upon eighteen year olds who eat their parents.

Zane reached into his vault of appropriate responses and praised himself for finding one so fast. "There's beauty in strength of will, Miss Beaupre. Anyone who couldn't see then what I see now wouldn't be worth dating. I don't believe for one second anyone could ever say you were ugly. Some people just fear what they don't understand."

As he studied her, her smile vanished, maybe lost in some past sorrow. Quickly, he said, "I mean, don't get me wrong. You are beautiful, but that's just one small slice that makes up the pie that is you." He raised his cup to cover his smile. A quick glance at the clock on the wall told him he should have been gone long before then, but some unexplainable phenomenon said, "stay." Maybe it was some kind of trick—some last ditch effort by the demon to turn the tide in his favor.

She blushed as she leaned across the table to squeeze his hand in both of hers. "That was one of nicest things anyone's ever said to me. Are you some kind of sadist who just likes to make a girl cry?"

He wondered if she felt that, felt the same spark he did as their hands touched.

"I would never make you cry. And thanks for the compliment. I actually work for Hallmark as a writer."

"Shut up. Really?"

"No, but I'm a big fan of their Snoopy collection."

She squeezed his hand. "Oh, you're terrible. So what do you do for a living, Mr. Jackson?"

"I de—sales. I'm in sales—but I dabble in a little bit of everything." The blunder was definitely a wakeup call. He needed to leave before he said anything really stupid. *Yeah, I deal in priceless antiques. Whoops. That was last time. Oh, and did I forget to mention that I'm a Leo, with very particular diet? Dummy,* he chided himself.

Get out. Now. Grasping for a reason to leave, he thought of the stray dog he'd caught burrowing into the trash back at the chalet. "Oh, I almost forgot about my dog. I should have been home an hour ago." he said.

"You have a dog? I have a cat. What's its name?" She ran her fingers through her short, pale blonde pageboy hair and leaned forward.

She was an apparent fan of animals. His beauty notwithstanding—no wonder they were connecting; he'd been thought of as an animal a time or two.

"Rusty," he replied, recalling the blunt edge of the axe he'd used to split the dog's skull. "He's a scamp. But, sadly, he's a one-trick doggie. All he can do well is play dead. So if you see him, try not to razz him about it. He's a very sensitive guy."

"I'll keep that in mind for when I meet him."

Zane was sure she couldn't blush any deeper than she already had, but her cheeks darkened to violet. She was in awe of him. He should have seen this, but then he never usually spoke to any one woman for such a length of time.

"May I call you, Miss Beaupre? I haven't felt like this in a long time and would love to do this again." Urgency steadily rose in him; there were too many people around, people that might remember seeing him, seeing them together. This time the smile reached past her mouth and made it all the way to her eyes.

Is that guy over there looking too hard at me?

"How about you call me Jeanne, Mr. Jackson?"

"David," he said. "No, I meant: may I call you sometime?"

"Why would you want to call me sometime? My name is Jeanne," she said, as a little line of confusion drew her brows together.

She looked serious. Zane sat staring, his cup halfway to his mouth, not really knowing how he should respond. He didn't want any clarification he made to seem condescending, so he'd need to choose his next words wisely. She couldn't be that dumb.

Before he could speak, she did.

"That was a joke," she said, mischievously. "I made a funny—and, yes, I'd love to see you again. This is nice."

Her smile was so genuine Zane couldn't help but return it. "I agree. Maybe we could—"

"You know," she said, setting her coffee down and leaning forward, "my mother told me you could tell everything you need to know about a man just by studying his eyes."

She leaned closer—so close he tasted her true scent under the perfume, and the cinnamon gum under the coffee. Large before him, her eyes were a clear, brilliant blue, and they held him. They were mirrors. He was already a part of her; he could see himself—twin Zanes—right there in the limpid shine of her eyes.

"I should really be—" he started, wondering at her beauty, but wondering more at why she was doing what she was doing.

"Shh." Her face was no more than a foot from his. "Your eyes are the stem of your soul."

"Oh, really now," he said. This was a joke. She couldn't really see his soul...could she? In the back of his mind, he knew her little display would bring a few looks. Fear of exposure nagged like a sliver and his neck burned with imagined stares, but he couldn't remove his eyes from her.

Tick tock. Yes. He had to leave.

A hint of coffee and cinnamon hit him as Jeanne said, "You have strange eyes, David, but they're pretty."

"Pretty?" That one word broke the spell, and he flicked his eyes to all the tables in his periphery: cows chewed cud, chewed pie, cows guzzled coffee. All was well. Pretty? A flower or a summer dress is pretty. Try magnificent, majestic...even godlike. But not pretty. Did she say *strange*?

She must have noted his displeasure, because she amended "pretty" to "handsome."

"Okay, so what do my handsome eyes tell you?" Other than the fact that I am your final destiny.

She moved closer, her nose scrunched in mock concentration. "Can't tell. My mom never showed me how." She released his hands and sat back. "How long have your eyes been like that, you know...one pupil bigger than the other?"

~~oOo~~

From the personal notes of Dr. Bartholomew D. Gideon, Psychiatrist

Re: Case subject #11901

STATUS-ACTIVE, OUT-PATIENT

Entry 39: December 12/07

"Argyll Robertson pupils ('AR pupils') are bilateral small

pupils that constrict when the patient focuses on a near object (they 'accommodate'), but do not constrict when exposed to bright light (they do not 'react' to light). They were formerly known as 'prostitute's pupils' because of their association with syphilis and because of the convenient mnemonic that, like a prostitute, they 'accommodate but do not react.' They are a highly specific sign of neurosyphilis."

~~oOo~~

"Uh, what?" Zane lifted one hand self-consciously to his face, then dropped it back to the table. Pupils? Immediately, he knew what the problem was: The demon. "Oh, that. I had an eye appointment today and he used this stuff to dilate my pupil to get a better look at it." It was that goddamned demon playing tricks on him. How petty.

Time to go.

Jeanne leaned forward and touched his arm. "Oh, I'm sorry. It's not noticeable, really. It's just that I couldn't help but see it. Really, it's not that noticeable."

"Is it very gross?"

"Not even. It's cool, like David Bowie."

"So, what do you say? Drinks with a half-blind man?"

"Maybe," she said, posing with one finger under her chin as though thinking it over. "Okay, but I buy the drinks. It's the least I can do. Just not this week; my sister's in from out of town until Monday."

That worked for him. He was gone for the weekend anyway. She wrote her number on a napkin, and he handed her a business card.

"Just use my cell number," he said. "I've written it on the back. The number on the front is my old one."

Jeanne patted the pocket where she'd put his card. "Like I said, my sister Zoe is staying with me and I really should be going. She'll kill me if I don't take her shopping before she goes back to school. I'll talk to you soon."

Your sister sounds like my kind of girl. "Monday? Sounds

good to me."

She twisted the tattered remains of her napkin, wringing it like a soaked cloth. After she'd managed to tear the napkin in two, she dropped it on the table. Maybe he shouldn't have pushed for Monday. It's possible he was going to have to do this the old fashioned way and catch her sleeping. Another option would be to find someone else, but why? She was perfect. She was pure.

Jeanne nodded and shouldered her purse.

"Monday-ish it is then." Good, he thought. If he had to pull her from bed and drag her to the chalet, what kind of date could they hope to enjoy? Not to mention it would likely ruin the show.

As corny as it may have sounded, right then he really loved his job.

He peered nonchalantly around the room, wondering if they'd be remembered there. He made sure to pick a table away from the window, away from the ceiling camera—and no one had seemed overly curious of them. His name didn't matter; the next week it might be Joe or Walter, but a face was harder to change. He'd remained longer than caution dictated, but, weighing the risk against the prize, Jeanne was worth it.

Although she was gone, the residue mixture of her cinnamon gum and perfume—something jasmine, he guessed—clung to every inch of the space they'd shared. After filling his nose one last time, he turned dreamily on his heel and left by the back door.

Reveling in his olfactory delights, he experienced an unfamiliar tingling; a tightness in his loins, one he was not entirely comfortable with. He'd never been sexually aroused by one of his victims before and felt slighted by the minor mutiny. To shoo this sensation away, today's David, tomorrow's somebody else, began to formulate a mental list of items and preparations; he wouldn't be caught without like he had with the last one, Annie. He and Jeanne would share something truly poetic and he wanted every detail to be perfect, not just for him, but for both of them. Whistling softly now, he produced a mini recorder from his pocket, and pushed STOP.

6

EVEN ON AN ANGEL, DESPERATION IS AN UGLY GOWN

Zoe had been mellowing somewhere between Tingling Toes Ave and a street that sounded like O when the keys jingled in the lock, effectively deflating her buzz…somewhat; it would take a lot more than Jeanne's arrival to kill it entirely. She'd soaked in the afterglow of a needle induced state of detached bliss for about an hour, so she'd be conversationally functional. Maybe not the brightest or wittiest companion, but functional.

She received her sister with an up nod of her chin. Sitting cross-legged on the floor with a bowl of cereal in her lap, Zoe attempted to make sense of the cartoon she'd put on earlier.

Jeanne dropped her coat and purse as she passed a chair, twirled once like Doris Day, and plopped down onto the sofa.

This in itself wasn't an un-Jeanne-like thing to do. She was bubbly by nature and couldn't help herself. What *did* turn Zoe's head was the un-Jeanne-like look on her older sister's face. The look manifested itself in a slight color in her cheeks and a guilty glint in her eyes, but it was enough. That, and the fact she didn't automatically ask Zoe whether or not their mother had called while she was out—which she *always* did—was a dead giveaway. Something was definitely up, and it looked an awful lot like guilt.

If Zoe knew anything, she knew guilt. She'd defined her entire existence from beneath guilt's ten ton shadow. *Speaking of,* she thought. "Mom called."

"Guess what?" Jeanne said.

"Said she'd call back later. She was going out with the rest of her coven to find some babies to strangle in their sleep."

Jeanne waved the message away as though it was a pesky fly. "That's nice. I'll call her later. But, guess what?"

On the television, a little yellow bird had just pulled a three-foot baseball bat from a two-inch pocket, and caved in the skull of a black and white cat with a speech impediment. "Or maybe she's just gonna bathe in their pure baby blood to keep her looking youthful and—"

Jeanne snatched the remote from the coffee table and killed the television. "Come on, Zoe. Mom's not that bad. She'd do anything for either one of us and you know it."

"Or *to* us."

"See? That's just the attitude I'm talking about. She really does miss you, you know."

"Yeah," Zoe managed around a mouthful of Cheerio's. "I know. Her love shimmers along the blade of every cackled insult. Can you turn the TV back on? I was watching that."

"You could've watched television at home, and I'm *not* mom, so stop being so difficult. You came to see me, remember? Your loving sister…best bud?" She tossed a throw pillow at the back of Zoe's head. "Pay attention to me, darn it. *Ask me.*"

Zoe set the bowl on the floor beside her and wiped her chin. In the dead screen of the television, Jeanne stared at her back, waiting for the one thing Zoe *wasn't* in the mood for Conversation. "Alright, spill it, Jeannie. Something happen at your cryfest? Or was there a half price sale on pleated pants at Sears?"

Jeanne glared, and then said, "I'll forget you said that because I know you really don't mean it. Now, guess what?"

"Didn't we just do this? I already asked you what happened

today." *Please don't be anything that's gonna kill my buzz.* Still somewhat foggy from her own day, Zoe swiveled to face her sister. "Keep in mind I'm sensitive. If it's bad, creepy, or cancer related, keep it to yourself."

"I met a man today," Jeanne blurted.

"You met a man." Recalling her own meeting that day, Zoe inwardly cringed. "That's it?"

"Yup. He's so nice. His name is David. Too bad you couldn't have been there to meet—"

"I'm sure he must be fabulous," Zoe said. Then, noticing the dreamy gaze, she began to get the impression Jeanne must not date very often. She tried to recall her ever mentioning a man before this, but couldn't, and felt a pang of guilt for never noticing.

She wanted to ask Jeanne how long it had been since she'd been on a date, but if she broached *that* particular subject, the results might ruin her sister's mood, or set her off into another conversation. Neither of which idea seemed overly appealing, so, instead, she said, "That's awesome," hoping it didn't sound as phony as it felt to say. "So, is he going to call?" she prodded, believing it to be the next logical question—and also might expedite their "chat" to the part where they got to stop talking. She *did* have a cartoon to get back to.

Jeanne nodded. "Or I could call him. Whatever."

"Huh," Zoe mused. There were seven 'o's left in her bowl. Five had clustered together into a tight raft—possibly plotting some daring escape—and the other two 'o's had already made a break for it, having climbed halfway up the side of the bowl. When she looked up, Purple Monkey had joined them and presently stood on the coffee table, humping the pillow Jeanne had thrown. Caught off guard, Zoe barked a laugh, but quickly covered it with a cough.

She cleared her throat and nodded sagely at whatever it was Jeanne had just said, and then returned to the conversation. "Is he cute?" she asked, as she leaned forward and pulled the pillow out from under the jack-hammering monkey. Monkey shot her a one-finger salute, rolled off the table, and vanished before hitting the carpet.

"He is cute. Very. But what's more important is that he's really nice—a nice guy who wants to be happy again. He's a widower." Sadness descended over Jeanne, possibly remembering things the man said, or how much of a loser she was for never dating.

"A widower? Really?" Zoe's eyebrows shot up, in spite of not wanting to care about some anonymous john. *How very morbid and very gross! Wow. Just how desperate are you, sis?* "So...Um, how old *is* he?"

"I think he said he was twenty-nine. Does age really matter?"

Duh. Heeell yes. "I guess not." Zoe flashed on some of the fossils she'd had grunting over her in the past eighteen months, which brought forth a shudder. Twenty-nine was only three years older than Jeanne, so Zoe guessed that wasn't so bad. "Is it cold in here, or is it just me?"

"Maybe you're coming down with something. You do look a little peaked. I could make tea—"

"*Your* tea? No thanks. Your tea sucks big sweaty donkey balls. I'll pass." *A widower? Come on, chick, as pretty as you are, you should have guys clamoring to get a peek at those granny panties.* To Zoe, Jeanne had always been more than simply human, and she couldn't understand why Jeanne held herself back.

"So why don't you tell me how you really feel about my tea?"

Jeanne was beautiful, honest, and giving—and those were just the qualities she *hated* about her.

The expectant look on Jeanne's face said she was waiting for Zoe to say something supportive, but if that was the case she was talking to the wrong person.

Again, guilt struck Zoe. This time its spear plunged deep into the belly of her buzz and killed it: killed it deader than the bulk of her brain cells. *Fuck. Oh well. That's what I get for not being a better sister. As far as dating goes, why shouldn't I show her some support? Just because I hate men and everything that smells like them, doesn't mean she doesn't deserve to be happy. And if being happy means banging some dead woman's leftovers, then so be it, right? Whatever get's you off, right?*

As tender as those notions seemed, their sentiment may have been lost on Jeanne. Zoe was wandering into uncharted waters: The Touchy Feely Triangle. She'd been so long away from normalcy that simple give and take conversations like this seemed alien to her. She flicked the two escaping 'o's back into the milk and forced the muscles in her cheeks to rise. One dimple...two dimples. There. A smile was better than anything she could've said.

"So what do you think? Should I call him tonight?"

Even on an angel, desperation is an ugly gown, Zoe thought, which spurred a potentially promising change of venue for their chat: The mall.

Zoe tilted her head and smiled. "Do you have anything to wear on a date?" At least clothes were a subject they could both enjoy.

"Sure. I was thinking I might wear that pantsuit mom gave me last Christmas."

"Gay."

"But I really—"

"Gay."

"Stop that. I happen to think it makes me look nice. Why can't I wear it?"

"It's *your* date, sis, not mine. I'm just here to help."

"Funny—you don't seem very helpful to *me*."

"Come on, *really*? Listen, you *could* wear the pantsuit if you want him to think you're some kind of tight assed bore. I just think you'd make a better impression if you showed off your tits."

Jeanne reddened. "I am not a tight...bore. I'll have you know that people find me very outgoing."

"Yeah, like who? Work people?"

"No. Well, yes. There are people at the advertising firm that think I'm fun, but I have fun all the time. Ask anyone."

"I didn't ask if you had fun. I asked whether you wanted this David guy to think you were a tight assed bore." A funny thought suddenly occurred to Zoe. Funny only because it was something else she'd never noticed about Jeanne: Zoe had never once heard her sister swear. In all of their conversations, long hours of painful chemo treatments—during every fight they'd had over a hairbrush or the bathroom—Jeanne had never cussed in her presence.

"Say ass for me."

"Huh?"

Zoe put her elbows on the coffee table and propped up her chin with her palms. "Ass," she repeated. "I want you to say it."

"Why?" A small, confused smile tugged at the corners of Jeanne's mouth. "Just because I don't swear like a trucker, I'm a bore?"

Zoe smiled.

Jeanne narrowed her eyes and leaned past the coffee table until only a foot separated them. "Ass," she whispered. "A-S-S, ass." At seeing Zoe's eyes widen, she smiled, and with a devilish grin, she added, "fuck, shit, goddamn, pussy!" The bravado in her voice did nothing to arrest a fresh blush from spreading across her face. Zoe fell backward, roaring with laughter.

"Okay, okay," she said, between fits. "You're a trucker's dream. I give."

"See? I'm not a prissy bore." Jeanne smoothed her unwrinkled pants, and then waggled a finger at Zoe. "I simply choose *not* to dumb down my speech with vulgarities, the way *you* do."

"You sounded like mom there."

"Shut up. Really?"

Zoe sat up, nodding, "Yup. But I won't hold it against you." She stood and said, "C'mon. Let's go."

"Go where? I just got here."

Zoe grabbed Jeanne's purse and threw it to her. "Shopping."

"Oh, yeah." Jeanne palm-smacked herself in the head. "Sorry. I almost forgot I said I was going to take you out. Do you hate me?"

Zoe stopped. "Oh, you're still taking *me* out, but you're going to treat yourself, too. My pick though, 'cause your short hair and church lady pantsuits make you look like a lezbo talk show host."

Jeanne shrugged, obviously hurt, but said, "Sure."

Zoe ushered her sister out the door ahead of her. "Maybe even find some sexy underwear and a nice pushup bra..."

As she closed the door, the phone rang. Jeanne was at the elevator, pushing the button, and didn't hear it, so Zoe locked the door and left the call for the machine. If it was their mother, calling from Sarnia, Jeanne could call her later.

Mommy dearest, Zoe thought darkly. If the buzz hadn't already been gutted and dressed by the revelation that her sister was a full blown prude, thoughts of her mother would have driven a straw right through its heart and drained it like a heroin flavored juice box. *Bitch.*

~~oOo~~

As the phone attempted a connection with Jeanne Beaupre, Zane leaned against a pillar in the boarding area at the Toronto Airport, watching planes take off and land. After five rings, a recording of her voice proclaimed that "Jeanne and Mr. Moto are out..." Blah, blah. He hated answering machines, especially ones with cutsie messages, for all of the same reasons *everybody* hated them, plus one: Leaving a message left one more mess to clean up.

Beeeeep.

"Hi," he said, as he slid into his persona. "It's David. Please don't think I'm a kook for calling so soon. Okay, maybe I'm a little kooky, but only in a good way, honest. But here's the thing: While I was packing I came across a couple of tickets for a show playing next Thursday night; a French circus or something. I'm told it's very artistic and super chic. I guess that means it's cool. A client gave them to me last week, and I'd just put them in a drawer thinking I wouldn't get the chance to use them. We could make a night out of it. Again, not a kook, just a little kooky. It could be fun. Call me."

He spied an empty seat in the boarding area next to a young girl and took it. Leaning back in the chair, he pressed his palms to his temples to squeeze back the mounting pressure behind his eyes. The flight to Chicago would be the third of many check marks for the day, and yet he felt like he was in the twentieth hour of a dance-a-thon. As always, the flight would offer no respite. If anything, the altitude would compound the growing pain between his temples. *Fucking Gideon*, he thought. *Always gotta have the last word, exert control, show me that he's the boss of me; like I can't take care of my own self. Well, fuck him. I'll show that crusty old bastard what art really is. Then, maybe I'll make him the star of his own movie; show him the other side. Yeah.*

His head throbbed like a struck thumb, and the pressure leached down the back of his neck and stiffened every muscle in its path. When he opened his eyes, there was a fluffy brown bear dancing just below his nose and—sprouting like a pink tail from the bear's back—a child's arm led to the seat to his left.

"Whatsamatter, mister?" inquired the child, attempting to sound growly and gruff. "You tired or something?"

Zane smiled, gave an exaggerated yawn, and then spoke to the bear, "Yes I am, Mister Bear. I've had a very busy day."

"Baloo." She pulled the bear to her chest and made it wave to him. "His name is Baloo, and I'm Katie."

Zane loved *The Jungle Book*. Affecting a lisp, he said, "Well it'sss a pleasure to meet you, Katie, and you too, missster Baloo." He shook her hand, and then the hand of the bear. "My name isss Kaa, and I'm a ssssnake." He received her expected response; the girl giggled. In his own voice, he said, "You know, Katie, you should never, *ever*, talk to strangers. Didn't your parents ever teach you that? Where's your mommy?"

"She's over there." The girl pointed to a line of people at the check in counter "Getting bored passing those people so we can get on the plane. See? There she is." She waved at the back of her mother's head. Katie lifted her purse until it was touching Zane's nose. "We have matching purses. See? My mommy says that it's coolio-to-the-max. I don't know who Max is, but there's this kid at my school who's got an older brother named—"

"Yes, that *is* a very pretty purse. I think you mean boarding passes, Katie." He tried not to show the anger he felt toward the girl's mother for leaving the girl alone. In his opinion, certain people should *never* be allowed to procreate. People like this stupid cow of a mother. He'd love nothing more than to pay the self-involved bitch a visit if he had time. "So, Katie, where are you going in Chicago?" he asked, scratching the bear under its chin.

"Hi mommy," Katie said, bounding out of her chair to hug her mother. "You took forever, but me and Baloo stayed right here, like you said."

The woman squatted to talk to her child, but looked over her daughter's shoulder at Zane. "Who's your friend?" she asked. She scooped up her daughter and held her chimp-fashion.

Before he could respond, Katie pushed away and pointed at his nose. "His name is Kaa, mommy. He's a snake—like this," she hissed, and lunged playfully at her mother's neck.

Katie's mother put her down and kneeled in front of her, "Now what did mommy tell you about talking to strangers?" She looked up at him and mouthed, "*No offence*," then looked back at her daughter. "Didn't we talk about this before we left home?"

Zane gave the mother a shrug, and said, "It's not her fault, ma'am, it was mine. I saw that cute little bear and just *had* to know his name." He stuck out his hand and introduced himself, "Rob. Rob Browning." He was still beaming a wide smile at her when he added, "Next time take her with you. Anything could happen. This *is* a busy airport." He held her gaze for a few seconds, hoping his point had been taken, and then he winked at the girl.

"Well," the woman said, as her hand slid away from his. "Okay. We should get on that plane, kiddo. What do you say?"

Her eyes never left Zane as she spoke. "Say goodbye to your friend, honey."

Holding her daughter's hand, she hustled her away. Katie grinned over her shoulder and waved. Zane stuck two fingers in front of his mouth and hissed—eyes crossed, chin tucked in—then Forrest Gump-ed a wave back. After Katie turned around, he glowered at the back of the mother's head. *You're one lucky bitch, lady.*

Then they melted into the crowd.

Zane sighed, realizing he was being irrational and, quite possibly, a little too sensitive. To avoid seeing them on the plane he loitered until most everyone had gone, and then he boarded. No matter how much the woman needed a lesson, one she may not live to appreciate, he had a job to do and needed to keep his eyes on the prize.

~~oOo~~

After a painfully boring flight and a short line at Customs in Chicago, Zane hurried from the airport and slid into the back seat of a yellow cab. As he smiled at the man from whom he'd just stolen the cab, he noticed the little girl he'd met in Toronto before boarding the plane. *Katie,* he thought, pulling her name from memory. She stood alone by the taxi stand. Alone, unless he counted true blue Baloo, and he didn't. Katie held the bear in a five-fingered vise. A scan of the area around the girl showed her mother had abandoned her. *Again.* His heart would have gone out to the little girl if he had one. Righteous indignation was about the best he could do. There was a split second in which he almost told the cabbie to stop. This girl could do better, and he could kick start her search for a more diligent mommy with a flick of his wrist. Of course, he could never make the woman one of his special angels but he could sure hasten her journey to the next plane...and he didn't mean the plane to Baltimore. The entire thought process lasted only seconds, but in those seconds he'd followed them to their destination and showed the woman the error of her ways.

Two eyes squinted into the rearview mirror from beneath a pair of wild, caterpillar-like eyebrows. "I said, where are we going, buddy?"

Zane pulled his shoulder bag onto his lap. "I don't imagine there's room for *you* where I'm going, but for now *we* can head downtown. I need to see a man about a girl."

The cabbie dropped the car into drive and shook his head. "Whatever, buddy. It's your world."

Zane checked his watch then closed his eyes, giving his silent response. *It sure is.*

7

LOVE/HATE RELATIONSHIPS REALLY SUCK

Upon entering Gideon's office, an opening jibe directed at the doctor shriveled on Zane's lips. The old man's number one Dog, Otto Gruber, lounged on the couch in the corner of the room with his booted feet up on a coffee table. At the sight of the big German, the very picture of a modern day Frankenstein's monster, Zane's heart skipped a beat. Otto's presence was unexpected, to say the least. So was his knife.

Also, when he'd entered the outer office, Gideon's secretary wasn't at her desk, and all of the offices he'd passed were similarly empty. Not surprising in itself, being the weekend, but uncertainty blossomed as he placed those facts together with the scarred giant sitting on the couch digging dirt from beneath his fingernails with a buck knife.

He'd had a hell of a flight and was hoping to vent; the doctor was always good enough to take any insults Zane threw his way. But Zane decided it would be prudent to play nice this time. He wasn't scared, really, just being smart. Great things awaited Zane on the other side of death's veil, but pain was something else entirely. That's where the idle giant at the other end of the hunting knife came in. He'd seen Otto Gruber at play on more than one occasion, on camera and off, and had witnessed the deft mastery of his sausage sized fingers. Otto had a *gift*, a talent for keeping his victims alive and screaming for a very, very long time…sometimes for days. Zane had no intention of seeing how long *he* could sing under Otto's knife. Besides, he couldn't die yet. Too much left to do.

"Hello, Doctor Gideon." He smiled. "Otto," he added, nodding in the direction of the big man, who grunted in response without raising his eyes from the self-manicure.

"Please," Gideon motioned to one of a pair of chairs in front of his wide oak desk. "Shut the door and have a seat."

"Sure," said Zane. He closed the door but couldn't bring himself to release the knob. "But if it's all the same to you, I'll stand."

"Suit yourself, my boy, but don't let Otto's presence be the reason. I just thought that, what with the limp, you might want to sit."

"What limp?" Zane said, as the thought echoed in his head. "I wasn't going to ask, but since you've brought him up, what's with the muscle? You losing your faith in my abilities?"

"Who? Otto?" When the old man smiled, his eyes twinkled in the most disarming way. "If you think I called you here for the purpose of doing you harm, Zane, you can put that idea right out of your head. Why would I steal money from my own pocket?" He waved again at the chair. "Please. Let's talk."

Zane remained motionless and, after a pause, Gideon continued. "Do you see a painter's cloth or any other means of arresting your fluids from staining the floor? You're standing on three-thousand dollars worth of carpet, my boy. Please." He motioned again. "Forget he's here. He came to help me with something else entirely."

Yeah? I bet he did, you fucking weasel.

Zane turned the chair so it faced Otto, then sat. From his shoulder bag, he pulled the bio he'd put together on the girl, and passed it to the doctor. The Doctor would add it to the Web page; knowing a victim's middle name or the cereal they preferred seemed to add a dimension of familiarity that their viewers loved.

Gideon placed the envelope on the center of his blotter, adjusted it, drummed his fingers on it, and then said, "Just because the Jews in La La land call Canada *Hollywood North*, doesn't mean you should go traipsing up there to shoot snuff. Who's going to help with the cleanup? And what if you get caught?"

And there it was. What if you get caught? Zane knew exactly what Gideon was implying: that Zane might blab about Gideon and his entire organization if he were caught. Wholly understandable: Zane didn't trust *him*, either. Across the room, Otto had finished with the first hand and moved on to the other.

Otto or no Otto, Zane was pissed. "Are you kidding with all this shit?"

"What particular "shit" are you referring to, Zane?"

"Hmm," Zane put a finger to his lips, pretending to be thinking. "For one thing, you got that big fucking kraut fiddling with a knife over there in the corner, and I just travelled over four-hundred miles to hear you whine like a fucking baby about Canada. Did you forget that I'm doing this one for free? Please tell me I didn't just spend two hours pinned to an armrest by a three-hundred pound sweat factory named Hank, for *this* shit. Why the hell am I here?"

The Doctor barely blinked during the outburst. From his desk, he pulled some papers and leafed through them, then dropped his glasses on the desk. "A lawyer from New Orleans contacted me last week. It's regarding your mother's will."

Zane's eyes narrowed. "Why wouldn't they just contact *me*?" *New Orleans*. That had hit him like a frozen fish in the balls. "And why would it be about my...*her* will? She's been gone for a long time." Images floated up, bloated and bleached, memories of that last night, the night his future found him and set him free.

That's true," said the Doctor, "but there was a trust set up for you after the, ah, death of your parents."

"Parent." Zane stabbed his index finger onto the desk to

punctuate his point. "That motherfucker she was banging wasn't my father. And you don't have to be so delicate, Doc. They didn't die, I killed them."

Gideon could have just stepped out of a Norman Rockwell painting. "Stepfather, then. I'm truly sorry, my boy. In any case, it seems the lawyer would like permission to liquidate the house and all of the assets. He's been contacted by an interested party whose offer is twice the property's market value. The lawyer contacted *me* because he couldn't locate you through your birth name. It was me who signed off at your sanity hearing. He says it's probably the best offer you'll see for the house and, given the current trend, I agree. He needs a signature before Tuesday to move forward with the sale, and that's why you're here instead of waiting until after the shoot. I know this is hard, but I didn't think you'd come if you knew the reason. I understand what you must be feeling, and that is why I'll take care of everything for you. Just sign on the dotted line and you won't ever have to think about New Orleans again."

"No way," Zane said. "Everybody needs roots and, good or bad, mine will always be in the Big Easy." As much as he wanted to get rid of the house and all the horrors buried under its skull of peeling plaster and rotted pipes, if the Doc thought it was a good idea to sell, then Zane thought he would love nothing more than to *keep* the worthless piece of shit.

"Zane, that property is worth a small fortune, even *with* that rotting hulk of a house on it. The flood damage was quite extensive."

Zane shook his head, "Nope. Not gonna happen." He glanced at his watch: one-thirty-five. His flight was scheduled to leave at three-thirty. "I have to make the airport by two, so if that's all you needed, thanks for wasting my fucking time. I'm gonna go now. I still have one more stop to make."

"Suit yourself, my boy. You always do."

Zane stood and walked to the door, but stopped with his hand resting on the doorknob. "I've been thinking about making Jeanne one of my angels," he said quietly.

"No, you don't. Not this time, Zane."

From the couch, the nearly forgotten Otto Gruber wheezed with laughter, apparently finding humor in Zane's statement. "They are my favorite, these angels. Do it, my friend." He stopped shaking long enough to nod his head solemnly, "You are an artist. Do not let Herr Doktor stifle this."

Gideon snapped his fingers at the German. "That's not really helping, Otto. Please keep your opinions to yourself."

"What?" Otto shrugged. "I like his pictures."

Gideon threw up his hands, "Fine. Well, Zane, when you've finished with the canvas, you'd better continue on and paint a big target on your head. But, by God, don't expect me to bail you out of this one."

Zane didn't register the doctor; he was busy processing the ogre-like German's compliment. "Thanks, Otto. That's very nice of you." He didn't care if his reply sounded sappy. He was touched by the ugly giant's praise.

As he was about to shut the door after himself, Otto spoke again.

"I am very glad I did not have to kill you today. Go be happy, Zane. He pronounced the name Sane. Zane had always thought it was cute how he did that.

Unable to come up with an appropriate response to Otto's statement, Zane gave the man a thumbs up and shut the door. So Otto *was* there for him. That was disturbing.

~~oOo~~

After hearing the outer door close, Gideon turned to the big German. "Do you think Zane is sane?"

Otto wiped his knife on a pant leg and grunted, an action that moved his entire body. "Sane? Insane?" He shrugged, settling his rheumy gaze on some invisible object in the center of the room. "How would I know, Herr Doktor. I am as crazy as a one legged dog with fleas."

"There is always that."

~~oOo~~

Jeanne was in a silly mood. Like a cold, Zoe felt the symptoms too. Together they pushed through the apartment door, stumbled to the couch and collapsed beneath an avalanche of shoe boxes and plastic department store bags.

Without knowing exactly why, Zoe pushed through the bags and wrapped her arms around her sister, settling into a long, tight hug. It may have been the brief respite from her other life or, perhaps, it was Jeanne's heart-on-her-sleeve dorky attitude rubbing off. Either way Zoe didn't care.

Jeanne welcomed the embrace and didn't ask why. She sighed, and said, "I'm so glad you could come."

"S'okay, bitch," Zoe murmured into her shoulder. "I was bored and wanted to know how the lame people lived." Tough words for a girl with tears in her eyes and a snot bubble the size of a marble hanging pregnant from one nostril. She would have put this day right alongside some of the best she'd ever had...well, except for that kid. Okay, so it was one of the best *afternoons* ever. Whatever. Right then, right there, she was happy.

No doubt about it, Jeanne was definitely her second favorite drug. But like all habits, there were times when you couldn't do without it and times you hated it more than hemorrhoids.

The cancer had a lot to do with that.

Jeanne's cancer stole the better part of Zoe's childhood from her. Everybody was all about poor Jeanne and her cancer, and never had time for Zoe. Their mother had focused the brunt of her own frustration at Jeanne's cancer upon young Zoe. Jeanne was a saint. When Jeanne was healthy, she'd do volunteer work with the homeless, serve dinner at the church on Thanksgiving and Christmas.

Zoe did all that stuff too, but nobody ever called her a saint. One night when she was twelve Zoe broke a window at the church with a rock. No reason. Just picked up a rock and tossed it through a stained glass Mary, right through her arm as it reached for Jesus. Jeanne was a fucking saint; she took the blame for the rock. Zoe loved her and hated her for that.

Jeanne wasn't punished over the "rock" fiasco. "Accidents happen" was what their mother had said. The very next week, when Zoe tripped and dropped a turkey on the floor during the church's monthly fundraiser, she got her ass beat by their mother, the accident's happen lady—once in the car, and again at home.

Of course, Jeanne had gone to bat for her, reminding their mother that there had still been plenty of turkey to go around, but her words didn't make sitting any easier after the pair of world class spankings Zoe received. Natalie Beaupre had told Jeanne to hush and smiled at her.

The only time Zoe had ever seen a smile head on from her mother was when it was coming from a picture. If asked, she could've told someone, with perfect clarity, how her mother's smile looked from the side, when it was leveled at somebody else...like Jeanne, for example.

Zoe's memory of her younger years was rife with disappointments. She was a backboard for her mother's many frustrations: A deadbeat husband, a daughter with cancer, and another daughter (Zoe) who she very possibly thought was the Antichrist. While she put on a brave and caring face to the rest of the world, Natalie Beaupre had needled and nitpicked, neglected, and knowingly negated her younger daughter's need for maternal support to the point that it seemed more a vendetta than mere mother/daughter strife. Zoe could do no right.

Yeah, she kinda blamed that on Jeanne, too: Jeanne and her cancer.

When Zoe turned sixteen, the only person *not* preoccupied with Jeanne's condition was Jeanne herself. She'd given Zoe the only gift she was to receive for her sweet sixteen. They shared a hospital issue cupcake, complete with a matchstick candle to top it off. And, with the help of a nurse, Jeanne had made her a braided leather key chain. It was the clumsiest, most left-handed attempt at a craft Zoe had ever seen. She loved it and told her sister as much with tears streaming in streaky blue mascara lines down her cheeks.

It was easier to cry then. Teens are more or less at the mercy of their hormones.

Attached to the lopsided mass of leather was an oversized steel ring with the keys to Jeanne's bright orange Fiat—for her to borrow until Jeanne was out of the hospital. "Not to keep, silly," Jeanne had said, "Unless, well, you know."

Zoe knew.

Five years later, Zoe *still* used the keychain and mended it whenever it threatened to unravel, but she never did drive that car. After five misfires with the Young Driver's Test, her mother had stepped in and bought Zoe a bus pass.

At the time, Zoe believed she may have cured Jeanne's cancer with the aid of a splendid and wordy recap of the five failed attempts to navigate an empty parking lot. After adding in that the poor little man who'd drawn short straw all five times had finally run screaming from the car, Jeanne was in tears. She laughed so hard the bed literally shook under her emaciated eighty-five pound frame. The monitor hooked up to the numerous patches pasted to her body had begun stuttering in an alarming Morse code. Jeanne collapsed back on her pillow, and gleefully shouted, "To hell with the cancer. I think I'm going to die laughing. *Five times?*" Then they both laughed.

Two weeks after the delivery of that animated tale, during a review of Jeanne's latest test results, the cancer was going, and Zoe was sure she was the reason. After eight weeks, it was still going. And after twelve weeks, it had gone back to whichever layer of hell it slithered from, with its barbed tail tucked between its legs. Jeanne's Thyroid gland was, once again, an unblemished butterfly.

Their mother thanked the Lord for His blessing and praised His name. Zoe believed she should have been praising *Zoe*, but never said so.

Natalie Beaupre had redecorated Jeanne's bedroom and planned a huge party. She invited everyone she knew, and they all came, casserole dishes in hand, clucking all about the good

Word. Natalie allowed Zoe help with the decorations; she'd be in charge of the "welcome home" sign.

Still too weak to walk, when Jeanne was pushed into the house and everybody started cheering, Zoe unfurled the sign she'd spent the better part of the day creating. Instead of the welcome home party that her mother called it, the banner read: Cancer Can Kiss My Creamy White Ass. Zoe thought it fit better than a boring old "welcome home" sign. Besides, the gaping fish look her mother shot her with was worth the after party ass beating she could look forward to.

Her mother was not amused, but, like the rest of her gin soaked cronies, she came around after a few drinks. After the party there was no spanking or yelling, there was just a happy (if slightly dysfunctional) home. Natalie Beaupre was even *nice* to Zoe for a week or two.

Recovery or no recovery, Zoe found herself in a constant state of turmoil over whether she should hate her sister or love her. The verdict ended up a hung jury so she settled for *Have*, which rhymed with save: half hate, half love. She wasn't proud of her feelings, knowing full well Jeanne was blameless, but neither could she stop them.

Before she'd left to study theater in Saint Louis, Zoe jokingly told Jeanne of that word, *have*, and together they'd laughed it off as teen melodrama.

Before Zoe boarded the plane, Jeanne hugged her, and said, "Don't forget: You're bigger. Oh, and I love you."

To this Zoe had responded, with a confused, wounded whine, "And *your* short hair makes you look like a boy."

Jeanne had barked a laugh at her sister's insult. "No, no. Not you, silly. You're bigger than any *problem* you meet. Now go make me proud."

"Oh, right. Bye, bitch. I *have* you."

And that was the last time she'd seen Jeanne for two years...until this week. Right then, Zoe wondered how proud her sister would be—whether she'd even be hugging her if she knew Zoe was a hooker, that she was the failure their mother always said she'd be.

Of course she'd hug her. Jeanne was a saint.

"If you let go I'll make us some dinner," Jeanne said. "I was thinking, a nice chicken tetrazzini, a homemade bruschetta and a caesar salad. Sound good?"

"I thought we were having macaroni?"

"We are, but you'll be happy to know that I *do* have a lot of wine."

"Great. While you're preparing that feast I'm gonna go wash my pits. I smell like the inside of a boxing glove."

"Thanks for that mental picture. Knock yourself out."

Zoe rummaged through her bag until she found her kit, deftly palmed it, and slid it up her sleeve with the ease of a veteran card shark. She waited until her sister was busy in the kitchen, and then locked herself into the bathroom. She needed a fix so bad her skin ached. *Just a taste.* She stood at the sink and unzipped her kit, and was startled by what she saw in the mirror. There was tightness around her eyes that sucked in the surrounding skin, pulling it toward the center of her face like a black hole. Maybe it was the lighting, but she'd never noticed that look before.

Recalling the first hit she'd taken from Brown Sugar's stash, she frowned at the spoon in her hand and then sifted half of the powder back into the baggie. She might have been a junkie, but not a hopeless one, and Jeanne wasn't stupid—naïve, maybe, but not dumb. *Yup, just a splash to take the creak out and give the monkey a snack.*

The monkey, after appearing from under the vanity, nodded gravely, tapping his head to signify how smart she was, how wise she was, how *hooked* she was. She watched as he produced an impossibly huge syringe from behind his back. He stuck it in his fuzzy purple arm, then crossed his eyes in mock ecstasy and convulsed for a few seconds before crossing his arms and feigning death.

"You have to be the lamest fucking monkey ever to darken a junkie's back, do you know that?" she said aloud.

Always the method actor, Purple Monkey stuck his tongue out the side of his mouth. *"I can't answer you 'cause I'm dead, but if*

I could, I'd say: Go fuck a green banana, skeezer."

Zoe stepped on him and kicked him under the claw foot tub. He'd go on forever if she let him. *"Bye bye."*

Within two minutes she was tapping the air from the chamber of a plastic syringe. Another twenty seconds, and one of her socks was stretched into place near the top of her thigh. Then…

Slap, slap, jab… magic.

Heat cascaded through her like a warm cotton ball meteor shower. The rough, rocky edges of reality slid away, softening, rationalizing it down to the spongy pulp of its core. "Jeesuss C-christ," she whispered into the ethereal fog that swirled around her, warping her vision, the whole bathroom, into a fishbowl.

She sprawled on the toilet like a rubber stone. The skirt Jeanne bought for her had flipped inside out and was bunched above her waist, and the forgotten sock she'd used to raise a vein lapped at the toilet water like a cotton-tongued dog.

She didn't want to, but as soon as she could stand, Zoe smoothed her skirt and washed her face in the sink.

Holy shit, that was… She fought to find the right word, but came away lacking the vocabulary to pay proper respect to her current state of cozy goodness. Stealing from the sixties, she slurred, "Groovy." *Groovy? Yeah. Why not,* she settled. The word slid from ear to ear, then back again as a pulsating rainbow of colors—each letter adopting a shade for its very own. The rainbow raked across her mind like the tumblers of a player piano, zinging out a zong of pure thought and musical color, bathing her, drowning her, monkey and all, in the visual flavor of surrender.

Brown Sugar, you little chocolate god! That shit was worth every stroke: all thirteen of them. She floated near the door long enough to sober up, then left the fishbowl and swam in the direction of the kitchen.

Jeanne was draining the noodles when she entered, and motioned with her elbow at the wine bottle on the counter. "Our feast is just about done, why don't you open the entree."

As Zoe fumbled to wrap her mind around the physics

involved with the use of a corkscrew, she smiled at her sister, probably the last twenty-something virgin in Toronto. "So tell me about your geek. Is he some kind of lame-o, or what?"

"There's not much to tell really, and he's not lame, thank-you-very-much. If you knew what that poor man has been through, you'd cry," said Jeanne. "Just the fact that he's been able to move forward after losing his wife and daughter..." Her face took on a wistful expression, and she afforded a small smile. "And funny—him, not his loss. He's very charming," she paused. "And did I mention that he's *hunky?*"

Hunky? Who says that? "I'm sure I will." *willwillwillwillwillwillwill.* According to the flash image that slapped Zoe's cerebellum with the force of creation, the word "will" was apparently the color of a newborn's first cry, pink and full of promise. *Oh-i-took-too-much.*

Jeanne nodded. "Oh, by the way, he called while we were shopping."

"Do you have a corkscrew for this?" Zoe began opening drawers, oblivious to Jeanne's last statement. *Hunky's a weird word, but then, I did say groovy...*

"Um, it's in your hand." Jeanne raised an eyebrow but didn't pursue the issue. "And since you asked—*not*—he said he wants to take me to that new *Cirque du Soleil* show downtown. Isn't that great?"

"Got it," Zoe said triumphantly, dropping the cork on the counter. "Hunky's not such a bad word," she said as she presented the bottle, successfully opened. "I say silly words all the time."

"Are you even here?" Jeanne frowned at the deadpan look she received from Zoe. "You could be a little happier for me, you know. I'm nervous enough as it is."

The backlog of Jeanne's words, albeit slowly, eventually plodded through to Zoe's heroin-clogged server. Understanding tardily pushed its pointy cursor through the bog that hindered reception and began to download. Seconds passed, then her eyes widened as she rounded on her sister. "You haven't dated since high school, have you? Holy shit,

Jeanne! I'm right, aren't I?"

"Well, there was this guy from accounting…" Jeanne said, weakly, and then paused to think of more. "Oh and… Yup, that's about it." Her face couldn't have been more crimson if she was standing naked in the middle of a football field at half time.

"No way." Zoe broke into a chortling laugh. In between wheezing, heroin enhanced guffaws, she threw in an, "I'm sorry," and a, "one guy?" Still giggling, she decided to sit down at the table before she fell on the floor.

Jeanne turned on her then. "I'm sorry I didn't have everything handed to me on a silver platter so I could pee it away like it didn't matter! That's right, I know you haven't been in school."

The laughter died in Zoe's throat. "Where did you hear that? Mom?"

It was Jeanne's turn to laugh. "Ha! Heck, no. If Mom found out, she would have gone down there to Saint Louis and dragged you home by your big lying lips. And you can thank me for not telling her by not lying to me anymore!"

"What? What the hell have I lied to you about? I've been at school all goddamn year, busting my ass," Zoe shot back. Okay, so she lied. But at least she was right about the "ass" part.

"See? There you go again. I know you haven't been in school."

"Well, if it wasn't mom," Zoe spat, "then who? Who the fuck would say that?"

"Does the name Sissy Houlahan ring any bells? She called here wondering what she should do with all the stuff you left behind."

That bitch! I told her I'd come back for it. "Oh, right. Sissy," Zoe started, trying to back away from the pit bull she was cornered with. "Yeah, she probably called here spreading lies because I slept with her boyfriend." This was partially true. She *did* sleep with her former roommate's boyfriend, but was relatively sure Sissy never found out.

Jeanne faltered at the notion of Zoe having sex, then she glowered at her. "Stop lying. Is that all those acting classes were good for? Lying? Someday you're going to have to grow up, Zoe."

Zoe's eyes shot wide as she let loose on her sister, "Grow up? That's really fucking rich coming from a virgin who hasn't even dated within her own sub species since she was fifteen. Get a life and stay the hell out of mine." She stood up fast, knocking her chair over, "I don't have to sit here and take this shit from you. I'm not a fucking kid any more, Jeanne, and you're not mom. I'm going out. I'll be back for my stuff later."

She nearly tripped over Mr. Moto in the doorway of the kitchen as she stalked out. The cat had apparently come to see what all the fuss was about and inform the guilty party they'd roused him with their screeching. He raised his nose to Zoe then sauntered over to Jeanne's leg, where he circled like a fuzzy, one pony carousel. In Zoe's heroin addled state, his unintentional feline snobbery succeeded in feeding her misplaced anger. "Fuck you too, cat," she said, as she strode out of the room.

Tears didn't come until the apartment door closed behind her.

She leaned against the wall and lit a cigarette to settle her nerves. *What the hell am I gonna do now?* She puffed and thought, thought and fumed, until inspiration's bulb—in the form of a neon sign—flickered to life in her head. She needed to find a bar. *A drink,* she thought, *or two, or ten. Then, first thing in the morning, I'm so outta here.*

As she stalked out into the night, she suffered an epiphany: Love/hate relationships really suck.

8

STRANGERS IN THE NIGHT

A bar stool probably wasn't the best place to meditate, but Zane figured it wouldn't hurt to try. He'd walked by Jeanne's apartment and the lights were on, so she was home; likely curled up on a chair, cat at her feet, thinking about him. Since he was planning on one more walk past her building before heading back to the chalet, he decided to kill an hour at a bar he'd passed on the way from his car.

There was much to do, much to ponder before Thursday, and the list seemed to grow without end. If he could've only found his room, the one in his head, he knew he'd have an easier time sorting things out. As it stood, he couldn't concentrate long enough to tackle one problem, let alone all that was before him.

A mirror hung behind the bar. In it he saw a handsome man, but not the room. The mirror was just a reflection and the man was just him, a fact reinforced by the dingy dark of the scene at his back. He wanted to blame the bar and its inherent distractions for his lack of success, but knew the bar *wasn't* the problem. He hadn't been able to find the room in the bathroom mirror on the plane ride back from Chicago, either.

Three biggies topped a list of problems that were as numerous as they were varied.

First, there was Jeanne. Had he called too soon? If he scared her off, he could always force her to participate, but that would ruin the mood, not to mention all of the preparations he'd made with her in mind; he'd made new brushes, and spared no expense with the drop cloth. He'd briefly considered using canvas instead, but recalled how poorly blood blended on its surface. He'd ordered flowers, found a great new recipe, and was presently fasting until that meal, some five days away—the success of which hinged solely upon whether she returned his phone call.

Second, there was Gideon's mutant troll doll, Otto. His presence at the private meeting and later cryptic remarks left Zane feeling anxious and more than a little cantankerous toward the old psychiatrist. Zane had been flattered by the beefy kraut's praises for his drop cloth paintings, but then he had to go and dribble that little stinker of a statement about killing him. Not cool.

Third, there was the business with his childhood home. Gideon had blindsided Zane so thoroughly with that memory he'd thought of little else since leaving the doctor's office and subsequently suffered a very real in flight nightmare involving his dead mother and step-faggot, Elias. In the dream, the half eaten corpse of his stepfather stood at the top of the stairs, beckoning and wiggling his bloated erection at him—"C'mere, boy. Give your new daddy a hug,"—while his dead mother, face half gone and grinning like a smashed pumpkin, pushed him up the stairs.

When Zane bounced against his seatbelt, wide-eyed and sweating, his seatmate, a flabby granny with an obvious love for the free peanuts, patted his arm. She'd said, "You poor dear. That must have been just horrible..." Apparently Zane talked in his sleep. He found that good to know. Or, it could have been the demon. Either way, he'd need to watch himself from then on.

Theft of airline peanuts aside, Zane had liked the woman. Her smile was genuine and she had the healthy, meaty looks of a latter day Liz Taylor. He'd thanked her for her concern then ignored her as he thought about home…about New Orleans.

And the big three didn't even include that fucking demon, which would've easily made the top three if the rest of his life wasn't so screwed up. *Jesus,* he thought, as he dragged a hand through his hair. *Stockbrokers think they have a high pressure job. They should try and meet deadlines like mine. Pussies, all of them!*

He eyed his watch for the fourth time in half a minute: Ten-oh-four. Still. He was beginning to fidget, and nothing short of the Hubble telescope could ferret out his secret room, so he gave up and turned his thoughts to Jeanne.

Where he'd failed with his room, he succeeded with her. So much so, in fact, that he began to lose himself in her memory, leaving behind all the sickness and filth reality had to offer, sinking lethargically into her eyes, tasting her skin, her tears, reaching to…

…answer his cell phone.

Again, there was the hard, slightly wobbly bar stool. And again, there was a handsome, if startled, fellow gazing at him from the looking glass. In his pocket, his phone vibrated, blaring out *The William Tell Overture.*

"Jeanne," he said. "I was just thinking of you."

"Hi, David. Is it okay to call so late?"

Zane didn't like her tone. She seemed upset. *At what? Me?* "Late? No, it's never too late for you." *Nice job, Mister Needy. Did you knit her a sweater too?* His eyes dropped to his tented pants. *Again?* he chided himself. *Twice in one week?* Unimpressed with his body's lack of couth, he wanted to punch the offending flagpole. "I guess you got my message then?"

"I did. Thursday night."

Her answers were too short, too clipped. "Is there something wrong?" He pulled off concerned pretty well. Not exactly a stretch for him. He *was* concerned…about keeping his schedule. Art waits for no one.

"Oh, no," she assured him. "Family stuff; I had an argument with my sister."

"That would be Zoe," He said, proud of himself for remembering.

"That would be her. She's been going through some problems at school and I don't know how to help her, or even if I should."

"That's a relief," he said, and meant it. "Not that your sister is having troubles. It's just that I thought you might have been a little put off by my call." That much was true. "I'm sorry. That must sound selfish."

"Not at all. But I didn't call to cry about my silly problems. Forget I said *anything* about her. I called about your message, about the show Thursday night. I wouldn't dream of missing out on a chance to see the *Circe* perform. And I guess," she sighed theatrically, "since you *are* the one with the tickets, you might as well come too."

Zane picked up a slight slur in her speech. If she'd been drinking, this might work to his advantage.

"You're too sweet for mere words," he said. "Does that mean I get to sit with you, too?"

"Sure does, but no footsies."

She *was* drunk. "Are you okay?" he asked. "Have you been drinking?"

"Just some wine. I'm alright."

"Uh oh."

"Uh oh, what?"

"You're gonna be mad," he said, and then paused as he winked at the handsome guy in front of him.

"How do you know? Mad about what?"

"I just remembered that I have clients coming in from Hong Kong Thursday afternoon—a last minute meeting that I couldn't reserve the boardroom for, so they're coming to the chalet. I was going to cook dinner." Another pause, then he said, "Hey, I've got an idea. Why don't you come over too? Our business should be done by dinner time, and I'm sure they won't mind. Actually, it might be nice to have a beautiful woman there to help them forget I may have claimed to know a little Cantonese. A little arm candy is never a bad thing at a sales meeting."

Her laugh tickled his ear and sent a thrill through him.

"Very funny, but I wouldn't want to intrude. That doesn't mean that you couldn't pick me up here after they leave. If it's not too late, we could probably still make the show."

"No. You know what? I insist. It'll be great, I promise. Let me have you for dinner?" His easy tone belied the cold sweat that slicked his hands. He wondered if he'd gone too far too fast.

"Have me *over* for dinner?"

"What a great idea. I should have thought of that myself. So?"

"Hold on a minute here, bub. Are you the kind of guy my mom warned me about?"

"What kind of guy is that?" he asked, unshaken.

"I don't know." She giggled. "She never told me."

"Do you want to bring her along? She could fill me in on how to be that kind of guy."

"Are you kidding?"

"Yeah. I only have four place settings, but she could always eat with Rusty."

"Hardy-har, funnyman."

"Sorry, couldn't help myself. Well?"

"Deep subject."

"Uh huh. I meant about dinner?"

"I know. I'm thinking."

"Am I going to need a drum roll?"

"You wore me down, champ."

"Great," he said, attempting to sound easier than he felt. "I'll send a car for you."

"Listen to you, mister big shot: You'll send a car. I have a car. Where do you live?"

"It's a little far. That's why I mentioned sending a car. So then you wouldn't have to come all the way back here after the show to get it. I could drop you at your place afterward."

"By car, do you mean like a limo or something?" she teasingly asked.

"If that's what it'll take." He could always have Gideon send someone up to drive. "Of course, you could take a cab if it would make you feel better, but either way it's up to you."

Please pick the cab. He could track them through a receipt, and wouldn't need to feel like he owed the doctor for anything.

"How's this? I'll split with you on the cab."

"No way, lady. I couldn't take your money. I'll pay the driver when you get to my house. If you get a receipt, I can write it off."

"Okay," she said, but sounded as though it wasn't.

Two beeps from his phone told him the battery was nearly dead. "How about I call you later, give you directions." It was just as well his phone was dying; it saved him from finding an excuse to hang up.

"Leave the directions on my cell. That way I won't screw them up."

"Great." *Fuck.*

He copied her cell number onto a bar napkin and stuffed it into his pocket, then they said their goodbyes just in time for his phone to die. *Your timing is impeccable, sir,* he thought, nodding to his friend in the mirror.

"Bartender," he said, "Me thinkest I doth needest a remedy for mine parched tongue."

With only Zane and two old-timers near the pool table to contend with, the bartender lounged on a stool behind the bar with his nose pressed tightly to the pages of a paperback novel. The barkeep lifted his head away from the book to offer Zane a tight lipped grin.

"Huh?"

"A drink, barkeep, and get one for that handsome devil over there." Zane pointed into the mirror.

"Oh, sure," said the bartender, and then gazed around, puzzled. You wanna buy *who* a drink?"

"Him," Zane pointed again.

"Ha ha," said the bartender, "Very funny."

"Yeah," Zane said slowly, then grinned. He waited until the man lost himself back between the pages of a Christopher Moore novel before he leaned across the bar and whispered, "I'll get you one later."

The handsome fellow across from him smiled and gave the tiniest wink.

~~oOo~~

The sign over the door *said* it was a bar, but a cursory look in the dirty window didn't lend it much credence. It seemed the type of place where a leper would think twice about using the toilet. On the other hand, Zoe had walked three blocks and found nothing open, so it was either there or nowhere.

The small pool table near the back must have knocked a quarter off the occupancy limit. Seated in the corner of the tiny bar, two old men—a snoozing Methuselah and his kid brother Bob, if Zoe's guess was right—sat nursing a pitcher of beer.

The sleeper was shocked awake by a not-so-covert slap from his friend. "Lester. Hey, Lester. Looks like the scenery just got a little sweeter in here. Lookie," the slightly less decrepit man said, hitting the older drunk one more time for good measure.

"Yup," the slapped man said sagely, as he slurped back the drool headed for his shirt. Then, apparently figuring he'd said it all in that one word, he dropped his chin and once again nodded off.

Five, twenty, or seventy, they're all the same: little boys, Zoe thought.

She walked past the third customer and dropped her purse on the counter. She leaned over the bar, looked left and right, and then swept the small room. "Where's Waldo?" Zoe asked the man two stools down, who studied the bottom of his empty glass most intently.

He didn't respond, so she snapped her fingers. "Yoo-hoo, hey, buddy. Do you speakie the English?"

When the man looked up and saw her in the mirror over the bar, his head whipped around, and he stared into her eyes long enough to be considered rude or mentally challenged.

His face relaxed as he spoke, "Sorry...I thought you were someone else."

"I am someone else. *You*," she said, pointing at him, then at herself, "*me*. See? Someone else. So, have you seen the bartender around, Mr. Oblivious?"

"I think he's back there," Two Stools pointed to a door on the other side of Zoe. "I'm sorry for hitting you with a cliché so early in our relationship, but do I know you? I know how that sounds, believe me, but you look like a woman I know."

"Is she hot?"

"Who?"

"This woman you think I look like," she said, rationing a cigarette from her pack.

"Oh, yes. She's extraordinary. Are you from around here?"

In his eyes, Zoe saw hunger. Nothing new there, but *his* hunger seemed different; like a dangerous kind of different. She definitely would have remembered meeting him before. He was creepy—cute, in a young Robert Redford kind of way, but a little prettier and a whole lot stranger. Without knowing how she knew it, Zoe could tell this man was a bad mamba jamba. "Are you for real? Why the hell would I tell you that?"

Just then, the kitchen door flew open and the bartender strode into the room with a case of beer over each shoulder. He set the beer down, walked over to her, produced a lighter, lit her cigarette, and said, "Sorry, you can't smoke in here." Then he placed an ashtray on the counter in front of her.

Zoe was about to stub it out when he stopped her. "Go ahead, I'm just supposed to tell you 'no' so if a cop comes in it's on you, not me. Get it?"

"Then how are you gonna explain the ashtray, Einstein?"

The bartender shrugged. "I'll tell him you brought it."

Zoe blew plumes from her nostrils. "I can live with that."

"What can I getcha?" While he listened for her response, he pulled open the cooler doors and began cramming the contents of a case into the fridge. Over his shoulder he said, "How about you, buddy? Want another one?"

"Screwdriver," Zoe said. "Short glass, lotsa ice."

"You got some I.D?" the bartender asked over his shoulder as he straightened his rows of frosty brown soldiers.

"Why didn't you ask me that first?" she snapped, and produced her Missouri driver's license.

"American, eh?" The bartender shrugged, then handed the identification back and poured a vodka and orange juice.

Two Stools said, "Let me get that bar keep. It's the least I could do for a fellow American—and I'll have a Poisoned Peach." The bartender shook his head, not wanting to voice that he had no idea what the man was asking for, so Two Stools told him.

"Sounds like a hooker's drink." Zoe pulled out a five to pay for her screwdriver.

"Ouch," the man said, wincing. "My dear departed mother used to swear by them; said they were nothing less than a peek at the pearly gates. Try one, I insist."

She'd been hoping for a quiet place to stew over the argument she'd had with Jeanne, but saw that it wasn't going to happen with Two Stools chewing on her ear like a wad of bubble gum. Zoe relented. "Sure," she said, "hit me, bartender."

When the drinks were in front of them, Two Stools picked his up and took a long slug. "Dis da shit, boy. Let me tell you dat," he said, with a perfect French quarter cadence. "Well, take a sip. *Then* tell me it's a hooker's drink."

Zoe found it to be as tasty as he obviously did, but foresaw the makings of one hell of a hangover. "Not bad," she said, and raised her glass. "Please allow me to amend my previous statement by informing you that no self respecting hooker would ever drink this. It's way too sweet and fruity. But, yeah, thanks. Live long and prosper and all that, but do it over there."

She lit a cigarette from the stub of another, then slouched down and turned away. With any luck Two Stools would take the verbal ear cuff for a hint and leave her alone.

She knew Jeanne hadn't fallen for the feeble lie she'd improvised before storming out. Zoe was going to have to tell her *something* about leaving school, but not all, for sure. Or, she could just leave in the morning without saying anything.

"Jarvis," Two Stools said, breaking in. Again. "Jarvis Baudelaire." His hand stretched out over the expanse between them.

Barely able to mask her irritation, Zoe swiveled to face him. "Look," she said. "Jarvis, is it? You seem like a decent fella, but I'm not interested." She stubbed out her cigarette and lit another. "Why don't you go hit a night club or something? You're cute. You could probably pick up there no problem. I'm here to sort some stuff out and I don't appreciate the background noise."

He faced her, but looked at his finger as he drew patterns through the sweat ring left by his glass.

The mention of Baudelaire sparked in Zoe memories of long nights hitting the books. She'd written an essay on the outspoken French poet Charles Baudelaire for a philosophy course the first semester she was in St. Louis.

Watching him play with his water drawing, she couldn't help feeling a little guilty for her outburst. A glance down at the bar in front of him showed a balloon head with a sad face. It even sported a puffed out bottom lip—quite the accomplishment, considering the medium.

She snorted smoke through a laugh she wasn't expecting. "You don't give up, do you?" she asked, squinting through the thick cloud. "Candace." She shook the proffered hand.

"My pleasure," he said, but, for some reason Zoe didn't think it was. His eyes seemed so cold. For a minute there, she almost forgot he was creepy.

"Is that a tattoo, Chuck?" She nodded at his wrist.

Jarvis pulled his hand away and tugged down the cuffs of his shirt. "It's not Chuck, it's Jarvis."

Zoe looked him over and rolled her shoulders. "What kind of relationship could we have if we start off with lies? You see this nose?" She pushed her nose up like a piggy and snorted. "It is to bullshit what a divining rod is to water, and right now it's pointing at you, Chuck. You don't look like a Jarvis, if a Jarvis could even have a signifying look. And also, when you said your last name, your eyes moved off to the left. Left being the direction lies are snatched from during thought process and oral delivery, I can only surmise that, by now, your pants must indeed be on fire. But if you want to call yourself Batman or Jesus Christ, you go right ahead...*Chuck*."

His face slackened for the tiniest fraction of a second, a wave that displaced something dark and brooding, primal and terrible, and then his smile returned. So fast had the flicker been that stop motion photography might not have picked up on it, but Zoe did.

She went on before he could respond. "Lying is a sin, Chuck. And, as everyone knows, sin is evil. I don't need any more evil in my life." She drained her glass and shook it at the bartender.

As she waited for the refill, she eyed Jarvis in the mirror. There was something decidedly unsettling about him but she couldn't place her finger on it. Maybe he was a cop.

Zoe leaned toward him with her legs parted slightly, allowing her skirt to ride up a little. "Are you a cop, Chuck?"

Again, his features shifted. *Predatory*, she thought this time. *This dude's a hunter, but definitely not a cop.* It was time to leave. Smart girls learned fast who to walk away from, and when to run. Right then Zoe wished she'd worn sneakers.

"Me? A cop? No way." His eyes traveled down as he spoke. "Why—?" he started, then understanding dawned. "No, I'm not a cop." His eyes lingered on her legs, then he motioned to the bartender, "Drinks, barkeep. One for me, and one for my new friend."

Zoe quickly stood. "No thanks. I gotta go, but good luck with the hunt."

"Hunt?"

"Yeah. You know, for a woman."

~~oOo~~

Outside the bar, Zoe picked up her pace. She didn't look over her shoulder until after turning the corner.

Back in St. Louis, roughly six months earlier, she'd been

sent to do a bachelor party at the Adams Mark Hotel. It was a job she'd done many times before, and would likely do another hundred times, but this time had been different. While standing at the door to the hotel room, with her hand already balled to knock, an unprecedented feeling of panic had washed over her so completely that she broke out in a cold sweat and her knees buckled. Zoe heeded that feeling of dread and lowered her hand without knocking.

From the lobby she called her boss, Cherry, and told him she felt sick and had to go home. He hadn't been happy, but sent another girl to do the party in her place; a busty, platinum blonde woman who'd fashioned herself after Marilyn and called herself Fantasia.

The day after the party Fantasia hadn't called in or stopped by to see Cherry, so he took two of his boys around to the hotel to see if she was playing house whore on his time. The room was empty.

Whether the girl had found love somewhere between the sheets and bubbly—unlikely—or had come to a foul end—very likely—would be left a mystery. Cherry tipped a bell hop a hundred dollars for the name on the credit card that paid for the room only to learn the card had been reported stolen that morning.

Believing he'd shown a pimps prescribed amount of due diligence in his search for one of his missing mares, Cherry washed his hands of the affair and cut his losses. After all, Fantasia *was* in her thirties. She wouldn't have been around much longer anyway.

Sure, Zoe lost sleep over the missing Fantasia, if only because it could have just as easily been her who'd gone missing. She wondered about the panic attack that probably saved her ass—and so did Cherry. After he'd returned from his extensive two-hour investigation, he'd taken her aside: "Candace, you're either one lucky mutherfucker, or you got the ESP goin' on. Whatever it is, girl, use it but don't abuse it."

After that day, Cherry would sometimes pull her aside and quietly ask for her take on this player or that john. Zoe thought he was nuts, but never said as much. He was good to her, in all the ways a pimp *could* be good to a whore, so she did as he asked without hesitation.

Zoe was rarely wrong back then, and sure didn't think she was *now*. That guy from the bar was kreepy...kreepy with a capital "K".

She doubled back at the next block and headed for her sister's apartment. If Jeanne was asleep, Zoe could sneak in, collect her things and call a cab. Once at the airport she could have one last party with Brown Sugar's beautiful shit and then flush the rest. With any luck she could catch the redeye to St Louis and take a nap before the afternoon shift.

Jeanne was asleep when Zoe tiptoed into the apartment, so she could make a clean escape. Then Zoe saw the note on the coffee table. Nine words written on a plain white piece of paper in her sister's large, round schoolgirl script: "I'm sorry. I love you. Just stay with me."

She kicked off her shoes and, still holding the letter, walked to the bedroom door and watched her sister while she slept. *I guess I could hang out for another couple of days,* she thought. *What's it gonna hurt?*

When she slipped into bed beside Jeanne, her sister rolled over, sighed, and draped an arm over her. To Zoe, it felt like warm socks on a cold day. "I love you, too," she whispered, low enough so as to not disturb her. She closed her eyes and pulled Jeanne close. When sleep found her a short time later, Zoe dreamed of dark angels and light, a long dead French bard, and Jeanne.

~~oOo~~

The girl—Candace?—had wished him luck. Wished him luck with the hunt.

Zane watched until the girl passed the window. Of course, he had no intention of following her, especially not after she'd wished him luck. Any attempt to rekindle their conversation would end badly, he just knew it.

Both achingly familiar and tantalizingly different from any woman he'd ever met, the fair haired beauty had a tongue that cut like broken glass and a chip on her shoulder wide enough to tap dance on; she was *marvelously* rude. Like him, she was a child of chaos.

Also, there was *something* else…a certain sensation for which he had absolutely no reference, other than his mother. Having thought of women as nothing more than meat for as long as he could remember, Zane couldn't tell a crush from hunger pangs. Either way, he wished her well.

"Do you think she was a whore?" The bartender had come to the end of the bar to watch her exit. Judging by the dreamy look on the young man's face, he'd also found her intriguing.

"Uh uh," Zane said. "She was an angel for sure."

9

SCAR TISSUE & BRAIN CELLS

"See?" Jeanne posed in her dress before the mirror. "I'm not such a prude."

Boredom aside, Zoe wondered about this date of Jeanne's. Her ability to read people—her "Gift", as Cherry called it—was useless to her with Jeanne's date, but there was something not quite right. Then again, she'd never met this David guy. He could be a perfectly *nice* dweeb.

She chalked it up to an overactive imagination and returned to the task at hand: looking interested. After a few moments she drifted off and fell into mumbled affirmations mode.

When next she looked up, Jeanne was standing with a hand on her hip, staring down at her.

"Uh-nh," Zoe mumbled, having lost the thread of conversation. "And so, like, you're taking a cab out to the middle of nowhere on a first date? Makes perfect sense to me."

"Second date. And it's hardly the middle of nowhere. He'll drop me off here after the show. What's wrong with that?"

"Nothing, I guess." Zoe eyed her older sister with a mixture of envy and mockery. Envy because of Jeanne's virtuous anticipation. It had been a long time since Zoe had looked at men as anything more than a necessary ride that ended in candy land. As for mockery, well, that flowed from somewhere deeper in her soul, but for approximately the same reason.

She couldn't remember her own first nervous fumbling, and the feather duster hand that squeezed your stomach just before that first kiss; the kiss that said you were meant for each other and nothing else mattered. Being together was perfect for a while, but then you grew to know each other. The cute little noises made while in the throes of passion turned from adorable to annoying, then to just one more thing to add to the long list of other teensy-weensy things you hated so much about them that you wanted to choke them in their sleep.

Chalk up one emotional scar, then another, and another. Soon you're just one lumpy mass of scar tissue searching for Prince Charming in the fogged up windows of a Chevy van in a truck stop. Zoe felt that *love*, in all of its various disguises, was merely a voiced contrivance invented by a lazy caveman so he could get laid without having to work very hard for it.

"Fuck 'em all but the breeders. Let the rest pay for it," was Zoe's Amazonian answer to the dominant male monkey.

"He's a dog lover, Zoe. How dangerous could he be?"

"Hitler had a dog."

"You were all gung ho about this the other day at the mall."

"You're right. I'm sorry." *Man, I can't wait to meet this loser.* "He sounds nice."

"It's alright. How do I look?"

Zoe would have been lying if she said anything other than stunning. The low cut red dress fit Jeanne as though it had been made for her alone, and her legs were gorgeous, which kind of pissed Zoe off. But beauty had never been an issue. It was everything else in Jeanne's life that screamed soon-to-be-spinster-cat-lady.

"It'll do," Zoe said, then smiled anyway. "This guy's gonna bust a nut when he sees how hot you look. I mean it."

"Are you sure about this dress? I feel like a whore."

Hey! "Believe me: you're not dressed *anything* like a whore." *That dress would take too long to get out of; it stains too easily; whores don't wear pantyhose...*

Jeanne tugged on the hem of the dress. "Are you sure this

isn't too short?"

Zoe plopped down onto the bed. "Hell, no. It almost covers your knees as it is."

"I'm a tramp."

Zoe rolled her eyes. "Prude is more like it."

"Maybe, but at least I've never had to shave my legs."

"Okay, now that's just gross."

"What? It helps keep the pantyhose up."

Zoe stared at her sister, thinking, *who are you?* Something had to be done. She felt it was her sworn duty to squash this budding cat lady persona and rescue her sister from the clutches of Sears and J.C Penny. First things first, though. She needed to boost Jeanne's self-confidence and subtly build up her ego in such a way that she didn't see it coming.

"You're so fucked up. You need help, big time."

Jeanne turned, just in the process of finding a long unused hole in the back of her ear with an earring. "Did I forget to tell you how glad I am you came? You're such a shining beacon of hope that I don't know how I was able to manage without you."

"Now you're coming around, lady."

"Lady of the *evening* is more like it; my boobs are gonna pop right out of this dress. By the way, I was being sarcastic. Could you try to be a tiny bit more like a real sister?"

"Didn't I wade through fifty iron elbowed hags during a red light sale to find you that kick-ass bra? If that's not love, well then I don't know what is. Tell me you don't love that bra."

"Okay, okay. So I love it. Thank you. Your love falls like rose petals into my dreary life."

"More sarcasm? Jeannie, I think there may be hope for you yet."

"You're impossible. Pass me the phone book. I need to call a cab."

"Hey, I was thinking. Why don't I just drive you there in your car?"

"You can drive now?" Jeanne raised a freshly plucked eyebrow.

"Yeah, apparently you just need the right teacher. I met this guy in St. Louis who taught me a lot." And he did, too. Cherry had taught her more about stick shifts than she could have picked up from a stunt driver—but that was another story.

"And you have a license?"

"Yup. Wanna see it?"

"No...I believe you," Jeanne said, then chuckled, "Well...maybe you should show me."

~~oOo~~

The drive out to David's chalet consisted of long periods of silence, broken occasionally by some inane remark about the scenery. Zoe could see Jeanne was half out of her mind with anticipation. For a woman normally verbose to the point of being irritating, Jeanne had withdrawn into a foggy shell of perfume and hairspray.

Nerves, that's all.

Okay, if that's the case, then why the hell am I so nervous? And why is that goddamn monkey riding the hood like it was a fucking surf board? Zoe could easily put a face to why *she* was edgy—she needed a fix—but was clueless when it came to any courtship ritual that didn't start with a menu of holes you couldn't put that dirty thing in.

She hadn't been high since the night they argued about school, and her craving was presently parked on her chest like a truckload of scrap metal. The quiet was definitely okay. Zoe was in immediate need of self-medication and nothing this side of hell would do except for that *one* thing. Every so often her hand stole into her bag and settled on the reassuring oblong shape of her kit. She fought the urge to hiss, "My precious," and let it loop through her head instead. *Are we there yet?*

Purple Monkey had grown bored with hood surfing and perched on the dash like a bobble head Jesus. Zoe split her time between watching him dance, and keeping her lunch in her stomach.

"Hey bitch, you know what?"

Zoe snuck a peek at her sister, oblivious to all but the road, and then narrowed her eyes at the monkey. *"Oh, not now you little prick. Leave me alone."*

"You should really be paying attention."

Zoe snatched him up by the ear and tossed him out the window. He opened his mouth to speak, but disappeared before hitting the gravel.

Jeanne glanced over, and then craned her neck to look in the passenger mirror. "What was that all about?"

"A bug."

"Oh?"

"Yeah, a purple one."

They turned onto a gravel road, and Jeanne said, "Okay. Two roads up and it should be the second driveway on the right."

"Uh huh."

"Are you paying attention?" Jeanne asked. "You have to find your way back."

"Yeah, I'm watching. I'm a steel trap. Do your thing, but try to do it a little quieter."

Jeanne glanced at her. "Are you okay?"

"I'm okay." Zoe wiped sweat back through her hair and flipped the visor down to look in the little mirror. "Maybe I'm coming down with something."

"Whatever it is, you look like crapola." Jeanne slowed the car to check the numbers on a mailbox. "1190...it must be up ahead a ways." Then she frowned, "If you're too sick I can cancel. It's no biggie."

"No, you deserve this. Shit, you *need* this. Really, I'll be fine. I'll drop you off, then go back to your place and take a nice long bath." *Please shut up! Shut the fuck up and get there! I can't take much more of this...*

Jeanne loosened her fingers on the steering wheel and flexed each hand in turn. "Sorry, I'm a bit nervous."

"No, duh." Zoe fought nausea and mopped her brow. She wondered how fast she could open the door if she had to puke, and then double checked her seatbelt. "Don't be. I bet he's in his house right now, still not believing his luck. Hey, is that it over there?" She pointed at a chalet set far enough back from the road that it was barely visible.

"Hold on." Jeanne pulled up close to the mailbox at the road. "The number's right, but there's no name on the box." She let out a low whistle, "Holy moly, Zoe. Check this out."

"I'm looking." Zoe perked up for the first time during the journey. Her material side, always at the forefront, said *jackpot* "What did you say this geek did for a living?"

"Sales, I think."

They pulled up to the house and parked beside a Lincoln with rental plates and Jeanne got out. "That must be his clients' car."

Zoe slid across the seats and leaned out the door, "You want me to stay for a minute? I don't want to just dump you off at a stranger's house and leave. What if he isn't home?"

"Look who's a mom all of the sudden."

"Funny. Want me to come up and meet him?"

"His clients are in there—and I'm not a kid, Zoe. I can handle a doorbell all by myself."

Jeanne was right; she wasn't a kid and Zoe wasn't her mother, but she'd still feel like shit if she just left Jeanne there by herself. On the other hand, Zoe wasn't sure she'd be able walk all the way to the door without falling on her face.

"Why don't you call him, make sure he's there."

Jeanne shrugged and walked a short distance from the noise of the engine and spoke into the phone as she paced. After a broad smile, she giggled and closed the phone.

"Well," she said, walking back to the car, "He's home, and from the sound of it, burning our dinner as we speak. He said I should get a receipt from you and let myself in."

"So go get the money and I'll give you a receipt." Zoe was only half kidding. He wouldn't miss the cash, and she happened to need some.

"I'm going to take that as a joke and send you on your way. It's fine."

"So how come you're choking your purse?"

Jeanne loosened her hold on her handbag. "I never said I wasn't nervous. Go, I'll be fine. Take care of yourself, and I'll call if I'm going to be late." She emphasized the word *late* with an overdramatic wiggle of one eyebrow.

Jeanne *would* be fine. She always was. Zoe was a different story. If she didn't get out of there, get some wind blowing in her face, she might pass out right there in the laneway.

As Zoe backed up to turn the car around, she called out the window, "Try to come home with your underwear, whore." She laughed and Jeanne blushed, and then she sped down the long drive. One last look in the rearview and Jeanne was gone.

10

TO BE YOUNG & IN LOVE

When she'd spoken to him on the phone from outside, David said to come on in, that he was in the kitchen attempting to avoid a fire, and she could grab a drink from the bar in the living room. That was all fine and dandy, but the fact remained that she didn't feel right about walking into someone else's house without knocking. Upon opening the door, guilt washed over her like a spring shower.

Immediately inside the entry, there were two idols of some black aromatic wood. The statues faced each other, identical, mirrored like a pair of four-foot bookends. She could have studied those two alone for the rest of the night, but there was so much else to take in. *My God*, she thought, *I feel like I'm in a museum!* David hadn't mentioned he collected antiques.

In the center of the room, a waist high pedestal held only a pestle and a stone bowl. There seemed to be nothing exceptional about them other than that they looked very old.

On the wall and in glass covered cases, there were tribal masks, ritual instruments, and pieces of art from cultures she'd never known existed. This was the collection of a very well off person. Suitably impressed, she imagined her mother and the happy dance she'd do after meeting this man. *Oh, you're so bad, Jeanne.* But she *was* right. Natalie Beaupre would love this man at 'hello' and be picking out china patterns before the tea was served.

They'd arrived on time, but on time to Jeanne meant they were ten minutes late, and she couldn't help feel guilty. She was about to call out to let him know she'd let herself in when she saw him enter the living room, wiping his hands on a dish towel. His eyes widened at seeing her.

Jeanne's face fell when she saw David's cable knit sweater and charcoal grey crew pants; he was casual and she was dressed for a night at a singles bar. *What was I thinking, letting Zoe pick out my clothes?*

Feeling more self conscious than ever, she said, "Sorry I'm late. I couldn't find anything to wear."

"Are you kidding?" He pushed a full glass of wine into her hand and kissed her on the cheek. "You look amazing. Red suits you; it really brings out your eyes. I feel sad for my clients that they'll miss out on meeting you."

"They're not here? You should've called to let me know. We could've eaten in the city."

"And miss out on having you all to myself? No way, lady."

Jeanne gazed past him. In an attempt to deflect his compliment, she said, "This is a beautiful house. I can see why you decided to live outside the city. I know people who'd kill for a property like this."

He shrugged. "The property belongs to a business associate." He nodded toward the twin wooden statues near the front door, "I see you've met my bodyguards."

"Quite the odd collection your friend has."

David nodded, and was just about to answer, when he was preempted by a smoke alarm from the back of the house. Dinner was burning.

In answer to the alarm, he started toward the hall. "I'll rescue dinner. Feel free to hang out and peruse the art. Oh, and don't forget to take the money for the cab. It's in that dish on the little table."

At his mention of the money, she gazed down at the pedestal she'd passed and, sure enough, two fifty dollar bills lay under a tube-like rock rounded at one end, like a helmet. Upon closer inspection of the six-inch rock, she was struck by its soft curves, mushroomed head… *Yuck! Is that a penis?* She chuckled and nudged it with a finger. *Funny what some people considered art.*

Leaving the great entrance behind, Jeanne set off to see if she could help with dinner. When she reached the dining room, she rapped on the wall. "Knock, knock," she said, peering into the room.

From behind her, a hand touched her shoulder. "Oh, I loved these when I was a kid. Who's there?"

Jeanne spun around. "Judas Priest!" she squeaked.

"Judas Priest, who?"

"No, silly." She slapped his chest. "I said that because you scared the fudge out of me."

"Oh, sorry. Some of the sauce spilled over onto the burner; dinner's fine. Okay, who's there?"

She rolled her eyes. "Forget it, funnyman. Do you have that bottle of wine handy?" She was 'first date' nervous and very conscious of, well, everything about herself. Right then she wished she'd brought a sweater. The wine helped.

"More wine? Sure, but while I get it, I've got a joke for you."

"Sure."

"Okay. A cannibal was walking through the jungle and came upon a restaurant operated by a fellow cannibal. Feeling hungry, he sat down and looked over the menu… Broiled missionary was ten dollars, fried explorer was fifteen, and there was a choice of grilled republican or baked democrat for one-hundred dollars. Shocked by the pricing, the cannibal called the waiter over and asked, 'Why so much for the politicians?' And the waiter replied, 'Have you ever tried to clean one? They're so full of shit, it takes all morning.'"

David filled her wine glass and set the bottle on the dining room table. Then he turned to her with a wide, mischievous smile, "Now that's comedy."

"That's comedy," she echoed. As she set her glass down on the long, narrow table, she noticed it for the first time since entering the room. The table was the most intricate piece of furniture she'd ever seen. There was a series of swirling grooved valleys cut into its surface, which connected at the center and followed one path straight over the edge. The grooves gave her the impression of gutters. Covered by a tarp of sturdy transparent plastic, it reminded Jeanne of her mother's couch, the one piece of furniture saved for the "good company". She sipped her wine while David brought the food from the kitchen.

"So, what was it you said happened with your clients?"

"You're not mad, are you?"

"You're forgiven, but no funny stuff, eh. I'll karate chop you." She mimicked a chop at him. "Hi-yah." *Okay, I'm a dork.*

"Duly noted." He placed a hand over his heart. "I promise to be a perfect gentleman."

"This table…" she began, not exactly sure what she wanted to say. Her fingers followed the patterns and swirls around the surface. It didn't seem to have the royal look of a banquet table, nor would it have been wide enough for diners to be seated along the sides. Two chairs were pushed up to the table, one at either end.

Jeanne looked up as David pulled a chair away from the table for her. "Why thank you, kind sir. What is that, lamb? Whatever it is, it smells wonderful."

David set a plate on the table. "Just a little something I picked up during my travels. It's called hitcher stew." He walked around the table, lighting candles on the way. As he passed the doorway, he flipped the light switch off. "I'll explain what the table was originally used for *after* dinner. If I told you now it might ruin your appetite. We couldn't have that, could we?"

Jeanne shook her head, and sloshed a dribble of wine down the back of her hand.

"If you ask me," she said, "it looks just plain creepy. Maybe you should keep it to yourself." Jeanne raised her glass to make a toast. Oddly, the long dancing shadows of her arm created what seemed to her inexperienced eye as a penis shape on the wall. *Jeez, kid. You've got wieners on the brain.* "To new beginnings," she said, and giggled as the shadow reached her mouth.

"I couldn't have said it better myself." He took a tiny sip. "To you," he said, tilting his cup, "A rare and radiant beauty worthy of Michelangelo."

"Yeah, but I'll settle for you." *Oh my god, you whore. Where did that come from? Gosh, it's a good thing you can't see my cheeks right now.*

"I'm glad you feel that way. It'll make the rest of the night all the more memorable."

~~oOo~~

"Wow. That was amazing," Jeanne said, a small burp escaping with her words. Whatever was in that stew, it was better than her mom's. "Oops." She tipped her wine glass back to drain it, pouted, and then held out the glass for more. "By the way, I thought you said you had a dog." She panned her head left and right, whistling.

Seated across from her, elbows on the table, fists balled under his chin, he sighed. "There's no dog, sweetie. And that meal you just ate and loved so much was a hitchhiker named Annie...more specifically, her thigh." A toothy smile stretched his face taut, but stopped just shy of his eyes. The flickering candlelight lent a sinister flavor to his expression that hadn't been there before.

"Ha ha, very funny," Jeanne said. But she *wasn't* laughing. Nor did she feel very well. Peering down at his untouched plate and back to his face took all of her effort. The previous glow she'd felt had turned to cold sweat and her eyelids fluttered like the wings of a hummingbird.

She rubbed her eyes with the palms of her hands and tried to stand, but unable to coordinate one straight leg, let alone two, she fell back into her chair. She wanted to scream, but pulling in enough breath for the task was impossible.

"What have you done to me?" She wheezed against the pressure of her tongue as it swelled against the roof of her mouth. Objects around her lost cohesion, and the edges of her vision became fuzzy.

"Done?" he replied, smiling impossibly wider, "Nothing...yet." He stood and slowly walked to her, then leaned in close to her ear. "But before you slip away, I want you to know something: You are," he paused to fill his nose with her, "positively the most intoxicating creature I have ever known and it truly is an honor to be your savior."

~~oOo~~

From the personal notes of Dr. Bartholomew D. Gideon, Psychiatrist, & Hobbyist Voyeur

Re: Case subject #11901 STATUS-ACTIVE

Excerpts from titled: "Dr. Bartholomew D. Gideon, Snuff Producer Extraordinaire"

My Struggle, my Search, my Snuff, my Savior

Entry 13: July 28/07

So what does human flesh taste like? If you've never had human flesh before, think of the taste and texture of beef, or veal, except a little sweeter in taste and a little softer in texture. Contrary to popular belief, people do not taste like pork or chicken (or so I am told).

~~oOo~~

"You..." she began, "you did this...for...sex?" Jeanne grew quieter as she rambled, her breasts rising and falling, struggling against an unseen weight.

Slow...slower.

Distantly, she felt hands on her body, dragging her across the long oak table. Laid out lengthwise, she'd displaced the dishes and silverware, unceremoniously shoved to the side...for her. A gravy boat had tipped and, as its far off warmth pooled at the small of her back, she couldn't help but wonder if the stain would come out or if the dress would be ruined.

David's fingers and nose traced from the soles of her feet up to her knees, then dipped to the inside of her thigh, lingered, then moved on. Paralyzed, and too far gone to register anything short of terror, Jeanne concentrated on the wall, on the shadow play provided by the candles. A bunny...she saw a bunny created by their overlapped shadow...

From the outer reaches of her periphery, a slender blade in David's hand caught the candlelight like quicksilver.

~~oOo~~

"Sex?" Zane asked. "Is that what you think?" He was offended she'd think such a thing. "I could never—" But his thoughts travelled to the tightness struggling for freedom in his pants.

Could I?

In response to the unspoken query, his penis doubled its efforts to be loosed. This was a sign. It had to be! Coming to Canada had been new—and he'd never shared a meal with one of his angels before—so this had to mean something! He wondered if this was what it felt like to be romantic, to live in the moment with someone you wanted to be *one* with.

One. Yes, one. It was all so clear he wondered how he could've ever felt it to be otherwise. This was romance. This was special. Why not share the thing he'd only shared with one other person? Mother had been his first, but why should she have the monopoly?

Using the knife, he sliced the dress from her body. After utterly destroying the garment, he folded it with care and set it on a chair, then stripped off his own clothes and tossed them into a corner—mindful not to cover any of the cameras.

Filled with a new and wondrous hunger, Zane trembled with anticipation as he crawled up onto the altar and parted her legs. Reflected by one of the numerous mirrors he'd hung facing the table, his eyes traced the feathers and lines which comprised the gift of a loving mother to her devoted son; a tattoo that signified all of her hopes for him, and how he'd reach them: on the glorious wings of righteousness.

In his mind, this was his privilege. This woman's life was his by right. He was Cannibalangelo and here on the table lay his muse, his bounty. He leaned back with his hands still resting on her parted knees, and imprinted her beauty in his mind for the portrait to come.

"This is all for you, Jeanne. I've worked so hard to make this night truly special." He paused to run his tongue along her leg, tasting her fear, sampling her salt. "We're almost there, lover. Are you as excited as I am?"

~~oOo~~

Jeanne's mind swam in a vacuous pool that sucked all sensation into itself and left dread in its place. David's face hung like a harvest moon above her, blank and cold. Try as she might, she was denied the final retreat of closing her eyes against his face. Unable to even move her eyes anymore, the only shadows visible were those cast on the ceiling—an imagined spider, an imagined fly: a very real end.

Then, mercifully, her vision faded to a blurry negative, making light into shadows, and shadows into a death shroud. Numbed, but not fully, his touch grew steadily surer, more urgent. Abruptly, he lowered himself to her, trembling as their bodies met.

As he entered her—from across eons of space—her own body vibrated sympathetically with the tremors that ran the length of his body, racking him as though electrocuted. His breath labored near her throat, became bestial, accented by sobs of pain and whimpers of delight.

~~oOo~~

Softly at first, Zane dared himself deeper into her, and arched his back as the demon took him. With eyes wide with wonder and fear, primal hunger and agony, he surrendered. His demon lowered their shared mouth to meet her throat. They were simultaneously ecstatic, furious, and alive with pain and loss. That was the very second Zane fell in love with the notion of romance.

Pumping with the aided fury of his demon, Zane laid her throat open and supped on his Mona Lisa.

~~oOo~~

Over the roar of the void, Jeanne heard David's guttural cry, felt a far off tug at her throat, then, mercifully, she drifted away.

~~oOo~~

A blue-green wall of smoke filled the distance between the monitor and its viewer. With the exception of the screen, no other light burned in the large two story house. A forgotten cigar smoldered idly beside the keyboard as Gideon immersed himself in his edit of Zane's show.

He alone controlled the master feed and, after editing on the fly, sent the best shots and angles out as one file to the website. Cameramen he had, but would never trust Zane's feed to them. Also, it was cheaper to do it himself. His personal credo was "Only the best," and no film school flunky could capture the true essence of Cannibalangelo's craft better than he could. The fact he was too cheap to pay them only entered his mind as a benefit and not as a contributing factor for his hands-on approach.

Even after all the years, he remained fascinated by the utter brutality of Zane Ellis…and of mankind in general. Gideon recalled their most recent conversation. Zane's self control was slipping; the fact that Zane was engaging in intercourse with his dinner was a perfect example of that. There was but one solution for this development: Zane would soon need to be put down.

However, for all his talk of disposable army and damn the weak ideology, Gideon loathed to give that order. His reasoning had nothing to do with allegiance or anything resembling pathos. What it *did* have to do with was Gideon's love of the almighty dollar. Each time Gideon found himself wrestling with this very eventuality, he returned to the same argument: Zane Ellis was to killing what Elvis was to rock and roll. Gideon's fans absolutely loved him. Sooner or later, however, he was going to have to face the fact that Zane was going to get lazy, make a mistake, or go off the deep end altogether. When that happened, things would get...complicated. Gideon couldn't allow that.

It was for this eventuality he kept others on his payroll, men of a slightly *different* ilk. They called themselves cleaners. He called them his dogs.

In the bottom corner of the computer screen he noted the number of clients currently logged on to purchase Cannibalangelo's latest feast; the numbers greatly exceeded Gideon's expectations. And it hadn't cost him one red penny.

He settled deeper into his chair and fished the forgotten cigar from the ashtray. As he watched his creation piston into the woman and rend flesh from her right arm with nothing more than his mouth, Gideon thought if an Oscar could be given for this dark, high octane performance art, then Zane Ellis, with his near perfect attention to pace and detail, would have won. Tonight's performance would keep Zane on the right side of the dirt for at least one more show.

~~oOo~~

Zoe had every intention of waiting until she made it back to the apartment, she really did, but need put up an argument she didn't mind losing. The argument went like this: As out of it as you are, you could cause an accident, maybe hurt some poor soul unlucky enough to be near the road. And what about *you*? You could hurt yourself. One tiny hit and all of the pain would go away; safer for them, safer for you. Safer for *everyone*.

Purple Monkey listened to this mental exchange as he dangled upside down from the rearview mirror, swaying with each bump in the road. When he saw she'd made up her mind, he dropped down and climbed onto her purse.

"You just can't fucking wait, can you?"

"Now's not a good time, monkey. Leave me alone."

"Always something, eh?"

"Like you care."

"I don't, but you should. Do you even know where we are?"

"If you're so fucking smart, you drive."

"You're fucked."

Instead of being dragged down the "I-know-you-are-but-what-am-I" path, Zoe turned at the next small dirt road and skidded to a halt at the side of the lane. The kit was in her hand before the dust settled.

Sometime later euphoria (and a need to pee) spit her back onto the graveled road. Stoned, she spun rocks out in a wide wake worthy of a hang ten. The only problem was, where to? She couldn't remember which direction she'd come from. Eventually, after crossing the same side road four times, she came to the conclusion Toronto had most likely followed Brigadoon into the mist.

Three hours later, Zoe angled into an open spot below Jeanne's apartment. *So much for a twenty-five minute drive,* she thought, and half expected to find Jeanne sitting on the couch, having beaten her home *after* her date. But, no; her mystery man would likely want to spend as much time with her as possible. *Ah, to be young and in love. Stupid fucks.*

Zoe's well weathered soul couldn't fathom the need to have someone always hanging around, in the way, and to not be complete without a man to make up the other half of you. She *could* understand the need for physical contact; everyone needs to blow off steam at some point. But those needs could easily be met with a visit to any adult toy store. *Need, need, need.* As she patted her purse on the way through the door, she wondered why people couldn't be more like her: any need she had could always be filled by one generic prick or another.

11

CATNAPPED & BAMBOOZLED

After a long bath and a snack, Zoe decided to call Cherry. It was kind of nice just being Zoe for a change, but the world kept turning with or without her, and eventually she'd have to catch up and get back in line. Cherry wouldn't be pleased she'd decided to linger in Toronto longer than the week she'd planned, and the longer she stayed the less happy he'd be. She speed dialed his number and he picked up after the first ring.

No "Hello, Candace" or even a "wassup, bitch," just straight to the meat: "You better be calling from outside my front door, baby."

"Sorry, Cherry. I ran into a small problem up here. My sister needed me…" She let her statement dangle in the air long enough for him to make his own assumptions.

After a short pause in which he bellowed for someone to "turn down the mafuckin' music", he said, "Aw, girl. Did the cancer come back?"

Cherry wasn't like most pimps she'd met, and for that matter he even hated the title. He considered himself a procurer of pleasant company—something Zoe had always teased him over, saying, "A rose by any other name is still pussy, Cherry." His aversion to the "pimp" label was odd, but stranger still was the fact he actually cared about a few people.

His girl Candace was one of them.

She sensed the change in his tone and mentally gave herself a high-five. "Yeah, we had a little scare, but I think she's gonna be okay. I'm real sorry I didn't call 'til now."

"So you can owe me, baby."

"Thanks. You're a peach, Cherry."

"Fuckin' right." He deflected the remark. "You stayin' clean?"

"I've been a good girl all week." She crossed her fingers, legs, and eyes. "It's been hell, but I've been loading up on sweets instead. I'll talk to you tomorrow."

"Sweets, huh? Well, you take care of that *sweet* little white ass of yours." He hung up.

She pushed END and immediately keyed in the number for the airport to check the flight schedule. Her talk with Jeanne about school would have to wait; it was time to get back to work. Besides, she was starting to get the itch, and not for heroin. Men were scum but they still had their uses. Unlike some hookers, Zoe was still quite fond of a good fuck every once in a while. A look at the bedside clock said it was 12:13 am. She started packing.

Upon finishing, Zoe stared down at the last two items on the bed: the kit and the drugs. Neither would be making the flight.

Mr. Moto had joined her in the room while she was on the phone with Cherry, and now he lay next to the kit, luxuriating in a slow tongue-scrubbing of his fuzzy beans.

"Shoo, cat." Zoe said, and waggled her fingers at him.

Mr. Moto dropped his leg and shifted into Caligula mode. He graced her with a look used only by Queens of England and asshole cats: *You there, serf. Scratch my belly. It's not going to scratch itself you know.*

"Fine, fuck you. But keep your eyes off my stuff," she said. "Ain't no catnip here. This is people nip."

As she wondered if she should hide the stuff somewhere in the apartment until her next visit, she heard a noise outside the bedroom. She quietly turned toward the bedroom door, toward a man's whisper.

Zoe let out a breath she didn't recall holding and relaxed. *Oh, Jeanne. You dirty bird,* she thought. *Go on, girl, work that moneymaker.* She smiled to herself, guessing her sister had invited David up for a coffee...or more.

Excited for her sister's leap into womanhood, she strained to hear them. Again, she heard the man's voice, but no Jeanne. Then the beam of a flashlight danced passed. *Oh shit!* Zoe was about to be burgled, or buggered—maybe both.

She slid the backpack over her shoulder, then stole a look out the door before slipping into the hall. The burglar was bent down in the hall closet, shoveling the contents behind him like a dog digging for a lost bone.

Zoe was no ninja, but had studied ballet for eleven years and thought the two seemed pretty much the same...well except for the knives, throwing stars, and any knowledge at all that might save her. Okay, they were nothing alike, but she could be stealthy when the need arose. She eased away from the open door and stayed close to the wall. Her heart pounded in her ears and she couldn't escape the sudden rising need to pee.

The man babbled to himself, just low enough that Zoe couldn't hear the exact words, but she sensed he was searching for something in particular. Soon he gave up on the closet and strode into the kitchen. She knew leaving now was her only chance of getting out before he found her, but she just couldn't convince her feet to get with the program. *Move, goddamn it!*

Zoe ducked out into the hallway, hugged the inside wall and sidestepped toward the front of the apartment. From the sounds of it, the thief was either speed prepping a cake or turning the kitchen upside down, so there was little worry he'd hear her leave. It was roughly fifteen feet to the door and she'd be in view for the last seven. That's eighty-four inches; the favored height of an NBA center; the length of Duke, her roommate's albino python that died after falling off the balcony back in St Louis.

Yeah, seven feet was pretty fucking far.

An image flashed through her mind of a Christmas show she'd seen as a youngster, "*Santa Claus is Coming to Town*", and a scene in which the winter warlock and a young Kris Kringle sang a song about 'putting one foot in front of the other.'

She started to push away from the wall, putting one foot in front of the other, knowing it was now or possibly never, when his form retreated from the kitchen in front of a swinging flashlight.

Frantically, Zoe's head shot around, searching for anywhere to hide. Her gaze slid past the hall closet, where a certain monkey was doing a soft shoe dance atop a particularly hideous green dress. She headed toward the bedroom door, then stopped. *The closet!* She took a step in the direction of the closet and tripped over Mr. Moto, who'd come out of the bedroom to chastise his belly scratcher for shirking her duties or, possibly, to see who'd messed up his closet and tipped the litter box.

Zoe sprawled into the opposite wall, and quickly picked her way through the cluttered closet. She pushed past Halloween costumes and old bridesmaid dresses, reached the back of the closet, and pressed herself firmly against the wall. Then her heart skipped a beat as Mr. Moto rubbed against her leg. *NO!* her mind shrieked, feeling like she was seconds from having her head spontaneously explode. *Oh god please get away you motherfucker I promise I'll rub your belly and scratch your chin just get the fuck away!* The realization that she didn't have to pee anymore came distant second to the sound of approaching footsteps, accompanied by a voice that seemed oddly familiar.

"What have we here?" said the burglar, separated from her by only clothes and a cat.

All that kept Zoe from screaming as his hand brushed her coat covered leg was the residual effects of the heroin she'd taken on the way back from dropping off Jeanne. Scream or no scream, she was unbearably close to hyperventilating. Mr. Moto let out a startled meow as he was lifted away from her leg.

The intruder's arm passed through a thin sliver of view afforded by a lace-lined dress and Zoe caught a quick glimpse. The tattoo caused total recall to splash through her like a polar dip.

I know that tat! Where did I see it? Then it all came clear. *Aw fuck,* she thought, *I knew it. I fucking knew it.* It was the kreepy-with-a-kapital-K guy.

"In you go," she heard him say. His footsteps receded, moving toward the bedroom, but Zoe's plans of leaving had already left. She was going to stay planted like a mighty fucking oak until Kreepy was gone.

Not that she really gave a shit, but she couldn't help but wonder what Kreepy wanted with a cat—a mutt cat to boot. She took a few deep breaths and managed to dislodge her heart from the back of her throat and get it slowed down to a stuttering thump.

After an eternity of strained breathing, the front door snicked shut, but she counted to thirty before leaving the safety of the closet to slide the locks home.

She crossed the living room and pushed one slat up slightly on the vertical blinds; no one yet. *A camera,* she thought. *Where did Jeanne put that..?* There! On the small table next to her left hand! "Gotcha," she whispered, and snatched it up. *Smile, prick,* she thought, as a nervous giggle slipped past her lips. She fingered the power button, thumbed off the flash and raised the blinds enough to get a decent view of the street below. About ten seconds later a man in a dark coat and baseball cap emerged from the building carrying a satchel over his shoulder. One after the other, she snapped pictures until the man turned the corner.

Zoe was already digging for her cell phone as she let the blinds drop. When the emergency operator picked up it was like a dam had burst inside her and she began to cry and gibber until, after three attempts, she could finally give the woman Jeanne's address.

Offering up that tiny bit of information sapped the last of her strength. She plucked a tissue from the box on the coffee table and collapsed onto the couch. After laying a half decent duck call down into the tissue, Zoe let her head fall back and she closed her eyes. The police would be right over.

Immediately, her eyes flew open again. "My stash!" she squeaked, and bolted toward the bedroom.

~~oOo~~

She hid her kit along with the stash of drugs in her backpack, and returned to the living room to wait for the police.

There was a short rap, then a man's polite voice, "Metropolitan Police. Open the door, please."

When Zoe opened the door, it was the female officer who spoke: "Are you alone, Miss?"

"Just me and my monkey."

"Monkey?" Both officers echoed.

"Nothing. You wanna come in?"

The female stepped to one side. "Would you step out into the hall for a moment, please?"

"Sure." Zoe glanced down at the stain on the front of her pants.

The second officer brushed past and searched the apartment while his partner stayed with Zoe. When the male officer rejoined them he shared a look with his partner, and directed them to follow him inside. Zoe asked them to have a seat, but they declined and stood while she recounted the events of the evening, and to a certain extent, the conversation she'd had with the creepy Baudelaire guy at the bar. The female police officer relayed the description of Marvin or Jarvis Baudelaire over her radio.

"You said this is your sister's home, Miss Beaupre. Where is she now?"

"On a date with some guy she met last week." Now that the danger had passed, Zoe wanted nothing more than for the police to leave so she could scrub the pee out of her shoes and have another bath. *If only monkeys could fly.* "Can I go change my clothes now?"

The male officer put up his finger. "Just one thing, Miss Beaupre. Were you packing for a trip? I noticed a bag on the bed in the other room." His pen hovered over his note pad.

She couldn't match his Jedi stare for more than a couple of seconds. "Yeah, I'm heading back to St. Louis in the morning."

"So that is, in fact, *your* luggage on the bed?"

"Why?" A greasy fist tightened around her stomach. "Did you open it?"

The male officer squinted up from scrawling in his pad, "It fell open while I was checking the bedroom. Are you diabetic, Miss Beaupre?"

Zoe was outraged; guilty as charged, but still pissed off. "You know fucking well I'm not. You can't just go through my stuff like that."

"Well, you did call *us*, Miss Beaupre," he said.

Zoe stood with her mouth hanging open like a mailbox waiting for a pickup, and then said, "Seriously?"

"Beth, will you go with Miss Beaupre so she can change her pants?"

The female officer gestured toward the bedroom, *'after you'*.

Then Zoe did something very out of character for her. She did as she was told. She wanted to scream and ask why they were doing this to her when the real criminal was out *there* somewhere, but instead all she could muster was "Okay."

After changing pants and borrowing a pair of her sister's shoes, Zoe was led back to the front door. It seemed the police were leaving, but they weren't leaving alone.

"Zoe Beaupre. You are under arrest for possession of an illegal substance, do you understand? You have the right to retain and instruct counsel without delay. We will provide you with a toll free telephone lawyer referral service, if you do not have your own lawyer. Anything you say can be used in court as evidence. Do you understand? Would you like to speak to a lawyer?" Once finished, he retrieved a set of cuffs from his belt.

Zoe closed her eyes and wondered if Jeanne was having any

better of a night than her. However her date went, Zoe hoped it had been worthy of ballads. Maybe then Jeanne wouldn't be pissed off when she had to go down to the police station and bail Zoe's skinny ass out of jail.

12

MIGHTIER THAN THE SWORD

Four days and two hours, almost to the second, and it seemed the more Zoe tried to ignore it, the louder and more demanding the clock became, jangling her nerves right down to her brain stem. She let her gaze wander around the interrogation room, paused at her reflection in the one-way glass, then returned to the video camera to her left. An attempt to stare down the lens recording her every movement left her with only a morbid thought: *All we need is a couple swinging dicks and a fluffer and we could make us a movie.* She needed a smoke. She needed a hero. But mostly, she needed the smoke.

They'd brought her in for possession of a narcotic, then kept her for questioning after recovering a blood flecked dress and Jeanne's cell phone from the kitchen table at the apartment. "Suspect evidence", she'd heard one officer call it. She had another name for it: A big old fucking frame-job. This was her sixth visit to this room, and they were no further ahead than after the first session. She laid her head on the cool metal table and closed her eyes. *Come on, Jeanne. Joke's over,* she thought, praying, not for the first time, her sister had done something reckless and dumb like take off to Jamaica with her new geek.

"Miss Beaupre?"

Zoe jumped at hearing her name. Squinting against the overbearing whiteness of the room, she peered up at a pair of blurry suits. She'd cried so long and hard she'd given herself a headache, and her eyes were swollen like bee stings.

"Yeah?"

"Do you remember us?" asked the older of the two suits.

"Yeah." She sniffed. "You're Ernie, and he's Bert."

"Close, but we're not homos," the older cop flung back without smiling. "I'm Detective Jenks, and this is my partner, Detective Coulter."

"I know who you are." She blew a stray lock of hair from her face. "Jenks," she pointed at him, "and Detective Billy."

"Coulter."

"Whatever," said Zoe. "The point is: I'm not stupid, just sick. And where's my sister?"

"We were still hoping you'd be able to shed a little light for us there. We've been literally grasping at straws here, miss Beaupre, and anything you might be able to remember, no matter how insignificant you think it is, could be the break we need. Again: anything missing from the apartment? Money, jewelry, any personal items?"

"A cat."

"We're already aware of the cat. It was picked up around the corner from your sister's apartment building by Animal Control late yesterday afternoon. Anything *else*?"

Zoe sniffed. "Nothing I haven't already mentioned like thirty goddamned times. Besides, how the fuck should I know? I was just visiting."

They spent the next hour grilling her over every minute detail of the events leading up to the break in: from Jeanne's meeting with David something, the trip to the mall, and everything that happened right up until the time she called 911. She even told them about shooting up right after dropping her sister in the country. That's how freaked she was.

Detective Billy leaned back in his chair and studied her as he rubbed the back of his neck. "And you can't remember anything about the drive there, nothing that stood out at all? A barn? A picket fence? A crossroad? Nothing?"

Zoe couldn't meet his gaze. She shook her head.

The younger detective was frustrated and it was beginning to show. He ran a hand across his face and slumped in chair. "It's not like she's a set of keys or a pair of sunglasses, Miss Beaupre. How could you lose an entire person? The word 'convenient' comes to mind."

When Zoe used her mental translator, she found "*convenient*" meant bullshit.

Always the devil's advocate, she understood their apprehension in believing her. Her only contribution in aiding the police to find Jeanne had been a vague recollection of the house belonging to her sister's date as being "somewhere in the sticks", a sort-of memory of a tattoo she couldn't fully describe, and a camera with nine grainy photos which could've been just about anybody. Yeah, she'd been a great help.

"Come on, Billy. Ease up a little," Jenks said, then took over. He aimed a fatherly frown at Zoe and dropped his bulk onto the chair beside her. "Look, I know we've been over this before, but there's got to be something you can remember. It's been four days, Miss Beaupre. Aren't you worried for your sister?" He left her to ponder this statement as he stood and walked across the room.

"That's right," the younger detective said. "See for yourself." He placed a newspaper in front of her. Instead of waiting for her to 'see for herself', he stabbed a finger onto the paper. "You should see what that sneaky reporter put in there about *you*."

"That's enough, Billy."

"Yeah, Detective Billy," Zoe batted her eyes at the red-faced man, "You should really lay off the Red Bull." Over his shoulder, Purple Monkey mimicked the young detective, pointing at her and scowling. She looked away before being sucked into a smile she knew she didn't deserve. For the life of her, she couldn't understand why the monkey was so jovial. She hadn't had a fix in four days. *Since the day Jeanne...* She left the thought unfinished, and peeked up at the clock: Four days, three hours and a bit. *But, hey, who's counting?*

She was.

Zoe dropped her gaze to the paper. On it, there was an older picture of Jeanne, a high school yearbook photo. She willed her hand to stop shaking long enough to touch the smiling face, then flipped the newspaper so she wouldn't have to see it anymore.

Jenks cleared his throat. "This morning we interviewed one of your sister's neighbors, a Mrs. Angelo from 3C across the hall. Said she'd definitely heard the sounds of an animated argument two nights before the claimed break-in. Is there anything you'd like fill in on your end regarding the fight?"

"Argument."

Jenks shrugged. "Sure."

"Not a fight, got that?" Jenks nodded for her to continue. "Okay. But it's got nothing to do with this, really. She said she found out I hadn't been going to school and we had a…an argument about it. I left, got drunk, came back later. The next morning we talked about it and everything was peachy." She lied about that last part, about everything being peachy, but they didn't need to know every little detail about her life. "Did that nosy bitch across the hall say anything about *that*? And what about the bartender at that shit hole? Did you even talk to him?"

"The bartender, a…let's see here," Jenks said, as he flipped through his note book. "Ah, here he is. A Victor Dimaggio, age twenty-seven, yada yada, ya… Ah, here. He said there was a guy there, but didn't remember much about him. He sure remembered *you*, though."

"Well? What did he say about the other guy that was there?"

"Not much. He said something about a recipe the man had given him for a drink. Said he made one for you, too. No real description of the man, other than that he thought the guy looked harmless enough."

"Sure, that's what they say about all the—New Orleans!" Zoe blurted. "That guy said he was from New Orleans!" She divided her triumph between the two detectives, expecting them to jump up and chase down the lead. Thing was, they didn't seem as thrilled as she was about this new fact.

Jenks opened his mouth to speak, when his phone started to ring. He shucked it from his pocket, glanced at the screen, and frowned. "Jenks." he said, holding his finger up to mark his place with Zoe. He was silent for a few seconds, and then the color drained from his face. "Where?" He stood and left the room.

Detective Coulter waited until his partner had gone, then leaned across the table and shut off the video camera. "I was just reading the file we received from the St. Louis PD. This isn't your first arrest is it? Of course not, silly me. But prostitution is a far cry from..." He shrugged, likely because he didn't have anything on her yet, but was hoping. He glanced at the door. "So tell me, just between you and me and these four walls, what do you go for...fifty, sixty bucks?"

You wish, jackass. She bit her tongue and slouched in the steel chair, feeling hopeless and alone, unable to even lash out at the asshole for his blatant insults. Everything he'd said was true.

She was so tired.

Just then, Jenks leaned in and beckoned his partner into the hall.

Zoe could see the younger detective's profile through the Judas window in the door. He might have been cute if he wasn't such a douche. His eyes went wide at something said and he shot a glance through the window at her. *What now?* She lowered her eyes to the newspaper and flipped it over. *One of them will come back and say it was all a misunderstanding. Yup...No they won't. There's something wrong. Jesus Christ, Jeannie, where are you?* She dropped her gaze back to the paper and began to read.

Mysterious circumstances surround the disappearance of local woman...

Zoe was getting to the small section of the article pertaining to her, when the door opened. Detective Billy stepped through alone and palmed the door shut. He'd checked his swagger and his eyes were no longer filled with indifferent haughtiness. In place of that was a mixture of excitement and angst. Without a word, he crossed the room, unlocked her cuffs and took a seat. He produced a pack of cigarettes, toyed with his lighter for a few seconds, took out a cigarette and slid the pack over to Zoe. She watched his Adam's apple bob a few times before he spoke.

"Let me start by apologizing for my earlier remarks." He lit his cigarette and took a long drag. "Go ahead." He motioned to the pack, chuffing twin plumes from his nose. "It's okay. What are they gonna do, arrest us?" Then he affected a smile that slid right off the side of his face.

Zoe was confounded. She flicked her gaze between him and the pack, back and forth like the offer was some kind of trick. Finally, she picked up the pack and took three cigarettes. Even before she lit one her nerves settled. The detective continued to apologize, repeating the same shit fifteen different ways. His lips moved but she couldn't give a damn what came out of his mouth, unless it was: "*You're free to go. Your sister is outside waiting for you.*"

She could only wonder at their abrupt departure, and then the five star treatment from the man who'd wanted her strung up by her toes not five minutes before. Apparently, men weren't just assholes, they were fucked in the head too. And that was her professional opinion. *Five dollars please.*

She had a customer back in St. Louis who had this thing for ice cubes. He was basically harmless and tipped well, so she put up with his exploration of her body with the frozen probes. Zoe wouldn't have admitted it, but she actually liked it most of the time—except when he'd slowly run a piece up her spine. And that's how she felt right *then*, like detective Billy had taken up where Frosty the Ice Cube left off.

"What?" she asked, as she fought off a phantom shiver. "Is this the part where you play good cop? Your buddy gonna come back in with a tire iron and some lube?"

The detective flicked an ash toward his coffee cup, missed, and then dragged it off the table with the side of his hand. "Actually, Miss Beaupre, uh…we believe we may have found your sister."

~~oOo~~

The crowd parted for Jenks' tan sedan, but not without considerable cajoling on his part. "Get the fuck back!" seemed to work pretty well. Before the car came to a complete stop he was already shouting orders at no one in particular through the window. "Get out of the way! Can't you see the flashing light? Move it!" This was *his* crime scene and he wanted to make sure everyone in the cheap seats knew that. His gaze swept the perimeter of the yellow taped area surrounding the parking lot filled with police cars, and finally settled on the donut shop at its nucleus. "Fanfuckingtastic," he mumbled under his breath, feeling it was anything but. Most of the police officers at the perimeter of the crime scene held a steaming cup in one hand, which really pissed him off because now he wanted one *too*.

"What the hell are those people doing in there? Somebody get 'em out, now!" He stopped a passing patrolman, "Officer Toms. Have the witness statements brought to me." Before the man could take three steps, Jenks called him back. "And Toms?"

"Yeah, Jenks?"

"Find somebody to get me a coffee."

Seven-hundred and sixteen: That was the magic number of days left until his retirement checks would be postmarked to the sunny state of Florida. If he had his way, he'd already be picking sand from between his toes and bitching about peeling shoulders, but his wife, "the boss", had said no, claiming they may still have too much life left at the end of the money. His answer to her had been a diplomatic, "Fine. Fuck it, but three more years and that's it." And he meant it too. That is, unless she didn't want to. After all, she *was* the boss.

Once upon a time, he thought he'd have to be prodded into

retirement at the end of a sword, and only relinquish his shield and gun after having them beaten out of him, but times-they-were-a-changing. The only work he now looked forward to was the tan lines he'd *work* on compliments of a genius named Speedo.

Someone handed him a pair of neoprene gloves, a mask and some booties, as he stepped into the circle of uniforms that surrounded a police car. There, dead center of the car's hood, a severed head lay atop a folded, blood-soaked sheet of some sort. A shiver ran down his spine, and his breath hitched at a whiff from the car's direction.

It's just a head. We all have them. Hers just happens to have nothing below it. After donning the gear he circled the area, then turned his attention to the police car's hood. *Oh, God.* This was no spur of the moment garbage toss. Whoever did this had staged every detail. Jenks flipped open his note pad and scribbled his preliminary assessment, noting first, the smell: The odor of mango hung like a tropical aura around the bodiless head. His mind wandered back to the list of possible missing items from the victim's apartment, things that might, under normal circumstances, go unnoticed: Shampoo, conditioner, a makeup bag and a bottle of perfume. He wondered if the mango was hers or the killer's. Up until that very second, he loved the smell of mango; it carried him off to Florida and the image of reaching up to pick one for breakfast any time he wanted.

Right then he wasn't certain if he could ever eat one again.

The hair had been washed and, from the looks of it, styled. The makeup was fresh. He leaned closer, as if to impart some secret meant for just the two of them, and sniffed again. Under the fruity aroma emanating from the hair was a very subtle fragrance—lamb chops was the closest he could guess, but knew that wasn't it. He'd smelled it before, but couldn't quite recall where. He underlined this scribbled line twice.

There was no blood visible anywhere on the head itself, which made the cloth beneath all the more confusing. It was a large, loosely folded drop sheet. Several smears and blotches of dried blood on the sheet seemed inconsistent with the overall tidiness of the rest of the setup. Jenks began separating his initial findings into sub categories, and attempted to piece together some reason for the daring calling card. He'd always been good with puzzles, but this one stumped him; to start with, it didn't even have enough pieces.

Even as that thought crossed his mind, he cursed himself, recalling the picture of the girl, retrieved from the apartment. She'd been pretty. Not for the first time that night, his temperature rose in anger. This was more than the mere frustration he'd felt with the younger Beaupre sister. Her, he could deal with, but this…this was monstrous.

He'd been so focused on his thoughts, he didn't realize until he was nearly done with his notes that the squad car beneath the head was still idling, and the driver's door stood ajar.

As he turned, he dropped the mask under his chin. "Who belongs to this squad car?" He could have left the mask up, but how would they know how pissed he was without noting the severity of his scowl?

A young policeman raised his cup in cheers. "It's mine, sir. I called it in."

"Great. Do you want to tell me why it's still running, super cop?"

"I…uh…didn't want to mess with the crime scene, sir."

Jenks nodded his head impatiently, noticing the officer wasn't wearing a portable. "Uh huh. So where did you call it in from?"

"Oh." The officer's ruddy face turned a deep pink. "I'll shut it off then."

"You do that," Jenks said to the back of the young man's head, then raised his voice and asked if anyone knew where the rest of the woman was. As warm as the night air was, he felt as cold as his words and didn't really like himself right then.

The officer he'd first seen as he pulled up, Toms, spoke. "That's it, Jenks. What you see is all there is. We've got men out scouring in a ten block radius, but so far they've found nothing, bupkis." He passed Jenks a cup of coffee and nodded toward the hood of the car. "Who does that? I mean, where's the rest of her?"

Jenks shrugged. What other answer could be given?

He dropped the mask into his pocket and stepped away from the car, pulling Toms with him. "Thanks for the coffee, old buddy, but I didn't mean for you to get it. You could have sent one of the kids."

"That's okay, Ed, I wanted one anyway. But that's not why you pulled me aside. You think he's here?"

"I would be, if I were him. Could you get one of the crime scene guys out there with a camera?"

Toms turned toward the crowd. "Already did."

"You're the man."

Toms nodded, "Been around the block a few times, Ed."

Jenks waited until Toms walked away, then took a calming breath and closed his eyes momentarily before reaching into his pocket for his mask.

~~oOo~~

Zane let himself be herded out of the way along with the cattle, but there was no way he'd miss the final act of his own show—even if it hadn't been planned.

Up until he'd read the morning paper he had no idea the little vixen from the bar was Jeanne's sister...or that she was the sole suspect in her sister's disappearance. In retrospect, it figured though. He remembered first seeing the girl in the mirror at the bar; he'd almost fallen off his stool, thinking it was Jeanne. And the only thing that stopped him from guessing they were related was that she was, he assumed by her driver's license, American. Any other time, he'd have to say this couldn't have gone any better if he'd planned it himself, but the girl was blameless. He felt obliged to do *something*. He *did* murder her sister.

That was why he staged this little show—to absolve *her* and receive the well deserved credit for himself. And since he didn't leave his calling card often, he liked to make it a memorable experience for all those involved, especially the doctor, who'd moan for hours on end over the paintings. *I win twice*, Zane thought, as he melted back into the crowd.

As he politely excused himself and squeezed past the cattle, there was a flash from the corner of his vision, and again, and again. He raised his hand reflexively to the side of his face and turned to peek through his fingers at the photographer; he was ten feet away and snapping pictures in Zane's general direction. *Shit*, he thought, *Should have seen that coming.* Not feeling he was going to need it, he'd left his disguise in the car.

Amid the fear of being found out, he noted it wasn't even his good side.

He turned away and circled back through the crowd until he was behind the man, knowing he'd soon leave the bunched in crowd to snap pictures of the flow of people who, after getting an eyeful of nothing but black uniforms and strobe lights, were leaving for home. This would isolate the photographer somewhat from prying eyes, or at least Zane *hoped* it would. Catching the man away from the herd was the only way he could separate him from the pictures and still hope to get away. If he tried to snatch the camera and run right now, he'd be seen by anyone nearby, and that would be a very bad thing. He'd wait. Good things come to those who wait. He kept pace with the man and waited for good things, waited for his opportunity to kill him.

Soon, the photographer found interest in a leather clad skinhead. As an added bonus, the punk didn't seem fond of having his picture taken. The skinhead stepped away from the herd and strode down the street at a brisk walk. Zane ran a hand through his hair—which came away soaked in sweat—and let out a breath he'd been holding for about the last ten minutes. *Go get him, Spot*, he urged, watching as the cameraman broke from the crowd and headed after the punk. *Atta boy. Get 'em. I'll be right with you.*

After a quick glance over his shoulder, Zane exited the crowd. All attention remained upon the rumored *head* in the parking lot. *Moo.*

He slowed to allow a gap to develop between them, and shadowed the man from half a block back. Up ahead, the punk slid behind the wheel of a long, black, heavily dented Cadillac and left half an inch of rubber by way of a farewell. The photographer snapped pictures of the vehicle until it swerved around the corner, then let the camera fall to his chest. He flipped open a note pad and scribbled a line before stowing it in his pocket. Then he turned and took his first steps toward the last minute of his life.

A sword, Zane wished, after remembering that, along with his disguise, his knife lay useless under the seat of his rental car. *My kingdom for a sword.*

He stood on the sidewalk at the mouth of an alley, his cell phone pressed to his head, and waited. He was good at waiting. When the photographer's shadow passed over his foot, Zane patted his pockets, and said, "Hey, pal. You wouldn't happen to have a pen, would you?"

~~oOo~~

Jenks heard a single, low budget style horror scream from the direction of the street, and followed a pair of officers past the barricades to investigate. Try as he might, he couldn't keep up with their full out sprint; age and too much of the boss's good cooking left him sucking shoe leather and dust after the first thirty feet.

He caught sight of them about fifteen seconds later, as one frantically pushed a tightly packed mob away from the sidewalk, and the other screamed into his portable for an ambulance and backup. Jenks bore down and ran the last twenty yards.

When he arrived it was pandemonium. People jostled each other, knocked one another down, and stepped on those unlucky enough to have fallen. The two officers were literally being swarmed by a wall of bodies. A flash here, a flash there—and soon it was like neon popcorn.

After several screams had drowned out the curses of the

fallen—banding together into a chorus of outrage that seemed closer to the sound of a car being crushed into a cube—Jenks, along with several officers who had followed him, quelled the minor riot. Once things settled down he called for a sweep of the surrounding blocks, then turned to see what all the ruckus was about in the first place.

The ruckus, as it turned out, was caused by a body, leaned against a garbage can. A body who, aside from the three inches of a cheap ballpoint pen protruding from one eye and a slender trail of seeping blood, could have been a vagrant, missing only a sign that might read: Will play ded fer a doller.

But that wasn't the case at all.

As a hot queasiness stole through Jenks' stomach and an unseen hand squeezed his heart, he walked slowly over to the lifeless body of the lead forensics tech for the night watch, Dan Marshall; a man he'd known nearly half his life. Jenks almost forgot himself, almost fell to his knees right there beside his friend...*almost* trampled a crime scene.

Suddenly, he whipped around, glaring from one officer to the next. "Find him! Find him! Find that bastard!"

In the aftermath of his outburst, he stood wiping spittle from his chin and laboring to catch his breath. As he did, he was afforded a closer look at the pen's entry wound. Slow and steady, the wound trickled like a faulty draught spigot or a terminal case of pinkeye, wending its way to pool in the man's lap. A piece of paper had been stabbed onto the pen, barely visible beneath clotted layers of blood. Though it had soaked through, the black ink under scarlet easily read: NICE TRY

Dan's camera had been smashed and emptied of film, and his carrying case stolen, but a used roll of film had been recovered from the sidewalk near the base of the garbage can, between the crushed remains of a Chinese takeout container and a dented pop can.

Jenks shook his head, attempting to put this new personal development to the back of his mind, to act like a professional, but couldn't seem to wear that face. *How could I hope to do that? Dan's been my friend for longer than I care to remember. Used to be,* he

119

amended. Used to be, he would trounce Jenks' ass on a regular basis at everything from bowling to cooking the perfect steak, and, like the great guy he was, Dan had never once gloated. Jenks sniffed but caught himself before he cried; he pretended to sneeze instead. *And this is how it ended for him? Stabbed through the goddamned eye and left to die in the street like a stray dog…with nothing more than a two word eulogy to send him off?*

"Awe, Danny." He sighed. "What did you go and do? Heroes are for TV."

He watched as the roll of film was placed into a bag marked 'EVIDENCE'.

"You treat that film like it was the god damn Arc of the Covenant, you hear me?" he said, too loudly to be considered friendly. Too late he checked his tone, and added, "I'd like copies of those photos as soon as they're developed, please. It's Jenks. Write that down. Detective Ed Jenks."

"Yes, sir."

At Jenks' back a million phone cameras sparked and clicked pictures of the body. "Could somebody find something to cover this man, please?"

Within seconds he'd played the entire night back. Jenks hated to think it, but couldn't help but admire the boldness of the perpetrator of the surreal blood painting back at the donut shop, and then this second crime. He felt the killer's actions here showed a level of commitment you just don't see any more, and that made him one dangerous person indeed.

Gazing down, he thought of Danny's wife, Magritte, and what he'd say to her. She had a smile for every occasion, good or bad. Which smile would she wear for this? And Jenks' own wife, Libby…what about her? Maybe after hearing about the murder of her best friend's husband she'll reconsider waiting those seven-hundred plus days, and say "Let's get the hell out of Toronto right now."

As he waddled back toward the remains of the Beaupre girl, Jenks realized that being a homicide cop wasn't much fun anymore.

13

FREEBIRD

Zoe's backpack and other personal effects were waiting for her when she was released from custody, minus, of course, her kit and assorted pharmaceuticals. She didn't expect to have them returned, but hope was like a flower in that it needed fertilizer to bloom. As it stood, the heroin wouldn't be able to dull the sharp edges of her present reality.

Jeanne was dead. No mere monkey stood a chance against that kind of pain: Pain that sat on her, suffocated her like a four-hundred pound gorilla.

Jeanne was dead. No star winked out to mark her passing, no wall of wailing mourners. She was simply evicted from life like a squatting vagrant. No notice, no waiver.

Jeanne was dead. Zoe had even been robbed of the "take me instead" speech she prepared as a teen, when Jeanne had been really sick. Back then, imagining that talk with God eased her mind, but now that Jeanne was gone, really gone, nothing she could say or do would change the fact that her last words to her sister were, "Try to come home with your underwear, whore." *Very classy.* She hated herself. She hated the police. She hated God. It was the perfect trinity of hate: All for one and fuck you.

The sole force powering her feet was the knowledge that

her mother would arrive shortly, which made Zoe want to be anywhere but there. She wouldn't stand a chance against her mother's soul piercing glare, or the blame that would surely ride that same beam straight through her head. No way. Better to be gone.

She was two blocks from the police station before realizing she hadn't a clue where she was going. There was really only one place she *could* go, and she still had the spare key to get in.

Two blocks from the apartment, she passed the bar where she'd met Kreepy, the probable burglar and likely murderer (at least to her). She stopped and peeked in the window, half expecting to find him awaiting her return. The place was open but empty except for a girl behind the bar. In lieu of her drugs—which were long gone—she figured a drink would be the next best thing, so she went in and sat down.

"What can I get you?" asked the girl, who seemed genuinely happy to see her. Probably would have been just as happy to see Satan or Bob Marley's moldy corpse come strolling in, just as long as *somebody* did.

"Screwdriver," Zoe said, taking up the same stool she had the week before. Gazing around, she noticed how drab and plain the room was when you could actually see the floor. On the up side, she was alone; no music or murderers there to keep her company.

"Hey," the bartender said, placing the drink in front of her, "You hear about that chick?"

"What chick?"

"You know, the chick with the head. You kinda look like her picture."

"Huh?" Zoe said. She felt like the girl had punched her. *You little bitch.*

"I mean, fucking Jeffrey Dahmer or what, eh?"

The muscles in Zoe's stomach flopped. If she opened her mouth, she might scream. If she screamed, she might never stop. She dropped a five on the counter and left the bar.

Once outside she leaned against a parked car and emptied her stomach, then stayed hunched over in case there was a more. To any passerby, it might look like she was reading her future from the pattern of splatters on the white wall tire. If that was true, her future was headed for the gutter.

She pushed away from the car and aimed for anywhere.

One foot, then another, and another. That's all she could do, really. Forward was the only direction left. There was no going back. Jeanne was dead.

~~oOo~~

The phone woke Zoe the next morning. She answered it before she was fully awake.

"Yeah?"

"Miss Beaupre?"

"Yeah," she said slowly, now fully awake and wishing she'd said no instead.

"Good. Your mother expected we'd find you there. This is Detective Jenks." He sounded down, like somebody had stolen his morning box of donuts.

"Uh huh." She pulled a pillow over her head. It smelled like Jeanne and that made her feel a little bit better. "What do you want?"

"I was wondering if I could stop by this morning and speak with you. There's something I'd like you to see."

She recalled the last time she'd invited cops into the apartment and was about to say no, but Jenks sounded so pathetic she thought he might cry if she did. Also, she couldn't imagine what he could have that she'd care to see. Trying to sound mistrusting, but yawning instead, she kind of said, "Ya, la whahhhn."

Apparently the detective was fluent in yawn. "I'll show you when I get there. How does half an hour sound?"

"Like nine-hundred ticks and nine-hundred tocks."

"What?" His tone seemed to question more than her statement—maybe her sanity, too.

"I said it sounds a little ambitious. You know, early?"

"I'm sorry."

"Of course you are. Never mind," she said, "I'll put some coffee on."

"Oh, that won't be necessary," Jenks said, distantly.

"I know. I was kidding." She hung up on him.

Zoe was still in bed when the knock came twenty-six minutes later. She answered the door in an oversized tee shirt and nothing else, and was suitably satisfied when both men found something totally engrossing on the tops of their matching penny loafers. Her first smile in six days. Too bad there was no joy in it.

Four eyes burned her backside as she sashayed ahead of them across the living room. Zoe told them to have a seat and excused herself. She washed down five extra strength Tylenols, then returned and plopped down onto the couch to wait for them to bite.

She sat cross-legged and gazed between them, daring them to peek. Detective Jenks ignored her antics pretty well—he seemed pretty bummed about something anyway—but his partner, Bobby, snuck a peek every time he believed she wasn't looking, which was never.

Everyone deals with pain in their own way. Some weep. Some build an emotional barrier around themselves. Zoe's way was a bastardized form of the latter. She wanted everyone she came into contact with to feel as insecure and uncomfortable as she did.

"Miss Beaupre, I'd like you to take a look at some pictures," Jenks said, then laid out half a dozen eight by ten photos.

"Oh no—" She looked away. "Bastard." *How could they do this?* As much as she loved her sister, she didn't want to see her like *this*.

"Relax, Miss Beaupre. These are photos of the crowd at the...scene. There were pictures taken that *somebody* didn't want seen, and we believe they may be in there somewhere. Take a look, would you? Please?"

Her eyes were immediately drawn to a blown-up eight-by-ten of an arm circled in marker. It was blurry, digitized to the point of being almost unrecognizable, but the markings were unmistakable. It was a good thing the Tylenols had blossomed; instead of screaming, she raised a hand to her cover her mouth. "That's him."

The 'tough bitch' barrier she'd erected cracked, then shattered, and she felt foolish and underdressed. Before looking over the rest of the pictures, she excused herself to put on some pants.

The remainder of the morning was spent at the station with a police artist, perfecting a drawing of the man she'd met at the bar. She'd already done this once, but apparently they thought her Kreepy guy was more important now. She tried to help with the tattoo, but had no luck with the artist. The crowd photo of the tattoo was better, and even *it* wasn't that great.

Even when she'd seen the tattoo, she hadn't seen the whole thing. And without knowing what it should look like in its entirety, she could recognize but not replicate it. The whole ordeal left her flustered, and the artist's incessant needling over details she couldn't recall only served to compound her frustration.

That afternoon and most of the next morning she spent in the company of the two detectives, scouring the countryside around Toronto and leafing through pictures of houses; anything was better than sitting around. She remembered little of the house, except that it was huge, and there was a rental car in the driveway.

Barely able to mask his frustration at their lack of progress, Detective Jenks dropped her at the apartment. He woodenly thanked her for her time, and then sped away before she could respond.

His final look had said what she herself was now thinking: Stupid junkie. Out there somewhere an animal was laughing; laughing at the stupid forgetful junkie.

~~oOo~~

The night before the token funeral, Natalie Beaupre stopped by the apartment to see Zoe.

"I suppose you'll need a ride back to Sarnia." She craned her head past Zoe to look into the apartment, possibly believing she'd catch her stealing the television, or blender.

"You know that I do, mom."

Natalie Beaupre pursed her perfectly penciled lips and glared through her daughter. "I'll be leaving tonight. Ten o'clock sharp. Be downstairs by five-to or not at all." She stole another look over Zoe's shoulder, stepped back from the door and headed for the elevator.

Zoe leaned against the doorjamb, staring after her. She believed her mother when she said she'd keep going. As rigid as wrought iron, Natalie Beaupre had a heart to match. *How can you still hate me so much?* Zoe wondered after her.

Upon doing a hasty mental check of her finances, she called out as the elevator doors opened, "I can take the train if you don't have room, mom." *Okay, that sounded lame. How the fuck could she not have room? Come on, Zoe, you can't be a wimp forever.* "I mean, it's okay…"

"It's fine." Those two words, sharp as twin scythes, cut deep into Zoe's spirit.

She'd never prayed for an elevator cable to snap before, but this had been a week chock full of firsts. She closed the door and lit a cigarette, then put on her thinking cap. The police had taken all of her drugs the night of the break in, so if there was any chance of living through the three and a half hour drive to Zoe's hometown, Sarnia, she was going to need to be creative. She needed to medicate to capitulate. Otherwise it was gonna be a long fucking ride.

Standing before the medicine cabinet, she realized she'd never opened it before and couldn't understand why not. It was usually the first place she plundered when faced with a new environment. Before coming face to face with her own sunken eyed penance stare, she yanked open the vanity mirror.

Roxanol 100 (morphine), Tylenol #3's with codeine, and a full bottle of no name antidepressants: that was some pretty heavy duty shit for an outwardly plucky twenty-something with no apparent emotional baggage. *Oh, Jeanne. I'm sorry I was never there.*

She swiped the cabinet's contents into her purse and poured herself a glass of water. After taking two of each pill, she retired to the couch to wait for ten o'clock.

After a few minutes of watching the second hand plod through its orbit, the drugs hit her—left jab to the chin, uppercut, uppercut, body blow. In retrospect, Zoe thought it may have been prudent to read the label on one or two of those bottles.

From the table beside the sofa she picked up a framed picture of Jeanne taken two years earlier, and ran her fingers over the glass. "I'm so sorry, Jeannie. I tried…I really did, but I couldn't help."

She didn't know what she was apologizing for more—allowing Jeanne to be murdered, or not remembering how to get back to the last place she'd seen her alive. With the hem of her t-shirt, she wiped tears from the photo, and then hugged it to her chest as she spoke to an empty room. "This isn't finished. I'm gonna make it right. I promise."

Zoe meant every word, she really did. But promises uttered and promises kept, seldom met. Nevertheless she needed a crutch, however improbable, and a vow gave her a sense of purpose, a shield to hold back the pain.

~~oOo~~

The image of a young woman filled the entire surface of Gideon's computer screen. The photo did the young woman no justice at all, but mug shots rarely did. This was the girl who claimed to have seen the man who murdered her sister. Recalling the sister and the photos Zane included with her dossier, the resemblance *was* very close. If not for the dull eyed stare, sunken cheeks, and much longer, slightly darker blonde hair, this younger sister could have been a twin. Gideon mused over the possibilities of a sequel to Zane's latest work as he picked up his telephone.

~~oOo~~

Sarnia, Ontario

The day of Jeanne's funeral came and went like a dragonfly, speeding by in spurts, only to lag at the most inconvenient times, and then linger long enough to leave a scar before soaring off again.

It had been a long dry summer and the grass had been the worse hit, and it whispered like crisp linen sheets under the assembled mourners as their feet shifted during the service. Even the trees had tightened their bark, adding leaves and far reaching lower branches in hopes of soaking up any sun or rain they possibly could; the dappled sunlight that filtered past the branches played along the purple and chrome casket at the center of the gathering, leaving the mourners to the shadows.

Because many of Jeanne's friends expressed their desire to speak at the funeral, Natalie Beaupre had limited those allowed to speak to three, and Zoe wasn't one of them. Her mother forbade her from the lectern, stating, "It simply wouldn't be proper."

Zoe had relented, consoling herself with the fact that she couldn't think of anything to say anyway—which was a bald-faced lie. There were many things she wanted to say. Of course, now that she'd been denied the word well had gone dry, and the eulogy she planned to give had been shuffled to the back of her mind. It disappeared somewhere between the library book she forgot to return in the fifth grade and her first lover. The power of self delusion was a great and awesome weapon indeed.

After the service Zoe stood like a dime store Indian beside her mother, politely thanking the strangers' faces that made their way past the closed casket. Some stared, some looked away, but they all murmured their condolences. A few even went so far as to lean in for an uncomfortable hug before moving from her to slip into a tight embrace with her mom, the frost queen. Zoe felt safe in her belief that she'd never felt so unwanted in all her twenty-one years.

Her mother didn't speak to her until the casket had been lowered into the hole and the crowd broke off into smaller groups.

Her mother hugged her, and Zoe returned the squeeze but felt more like she was squishing a doily-wrapped bag of dried out bird bones than a human being. As her mother's tears smeared the side of her face, she whispered in Zoe's ear, "I want you gone in the morning. I've already bought your train ticket home."

Zoe pulled back from her mother and silently turned away. *Home? I thought this was home.* She waited until her mother walked away, and then let out the sob she'd been holding in.

"Zoe?"

She felt a hand on her arm. It was the reverend who'd given the service. She didn't turn.

"Zoe? Are you alright?"

She took a deep breath, then faced the man who'd baptized her twenty years earlier. "Thank you, Reverend Tom, I'm fine."

"So you remember me. I didn't think you would."

She smiled through her tears. "How could I not remember the man who talked me to sleep every Sunday for seventeen years?"

Reverend Tom chuckled, but then grew solemn. "She doesn't hate you, you know. She prays for you every day."

Zoe sniffed, smiling ruefully at his words. "Then I guess I never want to see what it would be like if she actually hated me."

She hugged him and stepped back. "Thanks, Reverend Tom. You've always been nice to me."

He deflected her words with a shrug. "That's my job. Do you have a ride back to your mother's?"

She noticed he didn't say 'home'.

The last cars were leaving cemetery. The only remaining vehicle was Reverend Tom's rusty blue pickup. "Thanks, but I'm gonna hang back here for a while."

"Are you sure? I can wait in the truck if you'd like to be alone for a few minutes." He nodded toward the casket. "To say goodbye, I mean."

"No, you go ahead, really. I'm good."

After he'd gone, Zoe walked back and sat next to the grave. She didn't speak. There was no need.

A mild breeze picked up, trading the stale air for a fresh breath, and a bouquet of assorted flowers fell from the podium and rolled to a stop at her feet. Zoe bent to pick it up. As she did, a pair of flowers fell away from the rest. Two roses landed on her foot; one red, one white. *For unity*, Zoe remembered. Jeanne had told her that once. She lifted her face to the sky and smiled. "I *have* you, Jeannie," she said, and walked away. She kept the roses.

Purple Monkey caught up to her as she started down the street. "*So whose brainstorm was it to use a whole coffin, anyway?*"

Zoe's back stiffened but she wasn't about to give the little prick the satisfaction of letting him know he could get to her. She couldn't kill it, whatever it was, but she sure as hell *could* ignore it, so she did—but not before pre-punctuating her intended silence with a "Fuck you, monkey. That's too rude, even for you."

"*Could have used one made for a baby, don't you think? A teenie, tiny coffin? Sure would have made more sense, wouldn't you say?*"

Lip securely clenched between her teeth, Zoe settled in for a tirade of lewd comments. She could feel it coming as sure as she knew life sucked ass.

"*And did you hear the sound from inside the coffin when they pulled it out of the hearse? Kinda reminded me of the disappointing sound you get when you shake a box of Smarties and find out that there's only one left. Almost made me cry…*"

She picked up her pace, but there was really no outrunning him. She knew that. He was as much a part of her as her own hands. *Sure would be nice though, even for a little while.*

"*What would?*"

She screamed so hard she felt her jaw click. "Leave me alone! Please, could you just shut the fuck up?"

For once, he actually did as she asked and remained quiet for the rest of the night. Miracles can happen if you know how to read them...or don't expect them to be very big.

They plodded along in silence, a slouching girl bundled in a lead cloak of sorrow, a rose clenched in each fist like velvet cudgels, and one threadbare monkey, silently picking at a loose string dangling from the end of his nose.

Part II

"But I don't want to go among mad people," Alice remarked.
"Oh, you can't help that," said the Cat: "we're all mad here.
I'm mad. You're mad."
"How do you know I'm mad?" said Alice.
"You must be," said the Cat, "or you wouldn't have come
here."
--Lewis Carroll

14

HOME IS WHERE THE WHORE IS

Zoe didn't return to her mother's house that night until after her mother's cronies left to haunt their own houses. Casserole dishes clenched firmly in their claws, they'd receded to their recorded soap operas with downloaded recipes of candied yam or some other artery clogging treat. She'd instead toured her old neighborhood to see if anything had changed.

There on that corner, she'd received her first real kiss from a boy; she'd been nine and he was ten. Unable to recall his name, she *did* remember his breath smelled like wet leather and his lips tasted like peanut butter. The tall blue house down the street, the one with the overgrown lawn, was where her best friends, Cara and Charlene, used to live; identical twins, their mother clothed them alike until they were twelve. They hadn't kept in touch with Zoe after high school, and, to be truthful, Zoe couldn't recall their face anyway. *Is this the way it's supposed to be? Will I forget Jeanne's clear, perpetually amused gaze, or the way she made me feel like everything was fixable?*

It had only been a few years since Zoe's departure for fame and fortune but nothing was the same. Or maybe *it* was, and she *wasn't*. Everywhere she looked it seemed smaller, like a diorama of what home used to be.

She stood under a large elm tree at the end of the driveway for an extra fifteen minutes after the last light winked out, then entered the house and tiptoed up the stairs. *Just like old times,* she thought, recalling countless late night rendezvous' and midnight parties. She even remembered the creak pattern of the stairs: one, two, four, six, eight, and ten. Just for good measure, she stepped back onto eight and was rewarded with the sound of two pine trees, mid-coitus.

When she pushed open the door to her childhood room, Zoe discovered it had been converted into a sewing room. Her mother didn't sew. She closed the door and walked down the hall. She stood outside the closed door to Jeanne's old room for a moment before retreating back to the main floor. The living room sofa had been made up for her and a note rested upon the pillow. It read: "Train leaves at six. I'll wake you when I get up." That's all. No "love mom". Straight to the point, that was the mother she knew.

The next morning, mother and daughter arrived at the train station in Detroit exactly one half-hour before departure. They hadn't spoken more than a few syllables during the seventy-six minute drive *after* crossing the border into the U.S. Zoe had painfully counted off each passing minute.

When she shifted into park, Mrs. Beaupre held the steering wheel, ten-and-two, and stared out the windshield at the trains—or a smoke plume, or maybe nothing.

A sideways glance at her mother revealed something Zoe believed she'd never see. Her mother looked beaten. Her shoulders were a little rounder, her hair a shade greyer than yesterday. She was a china plate that had been smashed and repaired with scotch tape. God knew Zoe didn't want to pity her, but couldn't help herself. The events of the last week were more than enough to put her mother into an early grave and the woman seemed to be running on autopilot, saving the act of feeling *anything* for another time; maybe until after Zoe exited the vehicle, or when she was back in Sarnia, but probably never.

Zoe opened the passenger door and, with one foot on the ground, placed her hand over her mother's. "Take care of yourself, Mom. I love you." She moved to step out of the car when her mother's free hand closed over hers.

"Goodbye, Zoe," Mrs. Beaupre said, with a fast squeeze of her hand. "Don't be a lost cause. Hurry up now, you'll miss your train."

"'Kay."

It wasn't a Hallmark moment, but they parted on better terms than the day before. That was a start.

~~oOo~~

Zoe shared an apartment with another of Cherry's girls, Katrina, and she called her after switching trains in Chicago. It wasn't because Zoe shared any kind of emotional bond with the girl, but it was either talk or think, and thought can get a person into trouble.

She could've called Cherry but wanted to put that conversation off until she was back in St Louis. Not that she was going to lie to him (very much), but he didn't need to know every goddamn thing about her either. He was still a man after all.

Kat picked up after four rings. "Yello," came the familiar, nasally, adolescent sneer (at least it sounded a lot like a sneer), then a tiny squeak, like a goosed a mouse, followed by a muffled, "Keep going, honey. You're doin' fine."

"Kat?" Zoe raised her voice. "Can you hear me? I'm on a train."

" 'Course I can hear you, Candy. Where the fuck've you been? Cherry's been bubbling over for days now; he's ready to shoot the next motherfucker says candy." She whispered something unintelligible, and then moaned. Returning to Zoe, she asked, "Guess what I got in me right now?"

Zoe chuckled. She didn't feel deserving of one, but there it was. "Are you with someone?"

"Yeah, and guess who?"

"Don't care. Say, listen—"

Kat obviously didn't care that Zoe didn't care because she went right on talking as if Zoe *did* care. "Glenn Simms. We're dating."

Zoe would never have guessed that her roommate and fellow hooker—a girl so shallow you could wade through her and barely wet your sneakers—could *ever* surprise her, but, *again*, there you go. "Glenn Simms, the *cop*? Are you fucking insane? Dating? Cherry know you're giving it up for a cop?"

"Cherry's got nothing to do with it. It's my body and I'll do what I want." The young girl paused for a moment, then asked, sweetly, "You're not gonna tell him, are you?"

Zoe studied the translucent ghost of herself in the window for a few seconds before responding. From the earpiece came the unmistakable groan of well pounded bed springs being pushed past their factory rated limit.

"I'll make you a deal, *roomie*. I won't tell Cherry about your cop, if you don't tell him I'm gonna be back today. Deal?"

"Deal," Kat said. "Cross my heart and swallow a fart."

She might have said more, and probably did, but Zoe ended the call and pulled the protesting Purple Monkey into her lap. She had a lot to think about and needed the specialized comfort only a stuffed animal could offer—even if it fought her affections like a cornered coyote and swore like a sailor.

Lately, she'd had her fair share of cops, and now her roommate was playing house with one? Zoe didn't like the idea of a cop hanging around the apartment at all.

Dumb.

Fucking.

Luck.

That three word mantra coddled her into dreamland but must have mugged her of any dreams on the way out, because when the train lurched to a stop in St. Louis, she brought nothing away from the nap but bloodshot eyes and a sore neck. Purple Monkey sat shivering at her feet like a recent prison rape victim; he sighed loudly every once in a while to inform her he was still pissed off over the invasion of his personal space.

Cherry was standing at the platform as she stepped from the train.

Her mentor smiled down at her as he pulled her into a very un-pimp like, fatherly hug and kissed her on the top of the head. Then, with a noise seemingly scraped from the bottom of an oil drum, he chuckled. "And here I thought you forgot all about me, Candace. Shows how stupid I am, huh?" Cherry snapped his fingers and his driver stepped forward, took Zoe's back pack, then speed walked ahead of them through the terminal and out to Cherry's limousine.

Cherry waited to speak until he'd poured a drink and lit a cigarette. Zoe's instincts told her he was going to cuff her in the head, mash the cigarette on her forearm or, at the very least, toss the drink in her face. It's what any other card carrying pimp would have done, but not Cherry. He was an island all to himself. He didn't even look pissed to be there at the station, especially after what Kat the cop-sucking rat had probably told him.

It was for this reason she found his calm demeanor all the more unnerving. He'd never been physically abusive with her, but then he'd also never had a *reason* to hit her. She'd seen Cherry lose it on more than one occasion and the mess was more than a mop and bucket could handle. He was as vicious as he was large, and had a difficult time halting himself even after the object of his wrath lie bleeding and twitching in a puddle of their own fluids. Zoe couldn't remember if he'd ever struck a woman before, but harbored no desire to be the first.

"You ever step in dog shit, Candace?" he finally asked.

"Yeah, I think everybody has."

"Of course they have. And you know what?"

"What?"

"It don't matter how careful you are in the cleaning, you just seem to spread that shit around, gettin' it on everything, see?"

"Yeah, shit stinks." Zoe wanted to give him a chance to explain himself. He had the soul of a philosopher caged in his massive chest, but didn't flower his words or beat a particular topic of discourse to death with sleep inducing displays of pontification. Instead, he used the world he knew, barbaric and bleak as it was, to make his point. This by no means meant he lacked the vocabulary to convey his stark perceptions; he didn't need it. Cherry could explain Tolstoy's *War and Peace* while spinning a yarn involving three rats, a cat, and a dumpster full of maggots covered in soy sauce. No shit.

"The point is," he said, "no matter what you do, shit sticks with you. All you can do is keep walkin'. Eventually that shit's gonna mix with all the other stuff, good and bad, that falls under those shoes. After a while that shoe's gonna smell more like an old taco or a piece of berry-berry chewing gum. Get it?"

"So is this your 'shit happens' speech?"

"I guess it is." He shrugged. "But it's more than that. You'll see."

"So you're not mad?" she asked.

"Course I'm mad, bitch, but what did I just say?"

"Shit happens?"

"Ed Zachery, baby."

Right then Zoe realized Cherry knew everything. "So you know what happened in Toronto." It was more a statement than a question.

In answer, he said, "Zoe Amanda Beaupre."

"That's my name," she mumbled. "Don't wear it out."

"Don't worry, Candace. That's the first and last time you'll hear it from these lips. Cross my heart."

"And swallow a fart?" she asked, and tilted her head as she twirled a lock of hair around a finger. "Just for squirts and giggles, boss, how exactly did you know I was coming back today?"

His answer told her she had someone to feed a fart to.

This didn't mean Zoe was going to renege on her half of the deal. If Cherry found out about Kat's cop, it wouldn't be from her. Zoe would steal her roomies last dollar, or man— well, maybe not the *current* one—but she was nobody's rat.

After she let herself out of the backseat, he called after her,

"I can set you up tonight if you're up to it."

"Yeah? Who?"

"I got two of yours and a new one. Take your pick."

Without a second thought, Zoe said, "Bring it." Purple Monkey slapped her in the head.

"That's my mare."

As she passed through the double doors of the apartment complex, Zoe couldn't shake the feeling she was being watched. Quickly dismissing it as just another symptom of withdrawal, she filed it and hit the elevator's 'up' button. The monkey slapped her again, and twice more before the elevator doors closed on the sight of a man in sunglasses sitting just outside the door.

~~oOo~~

Kat was gone from the apartment when she entered; presumably, she left sometime after the Judas act she'd pulled on the telephone. With only two thoughts on her mind, Zoe doffed her clothes to take care of the first: a long, hot shower. The other she'd deal with after she was clean—or *later*, if she could wait for a fix that long. *Maybe never if I can be strong.*

But who was she trying to kid?

Once clean, Zoe emptied her back pack and picked an outfit from a double-wide closet known affectionately to her as 'The Whore Store'; tonight she was going schoolgirl.

Her eyes strayed toward the telephone many times. It was that pesky second thought of hers…more of an image, really: an image of a man named Kelly, Pretty Kelly to his friends. Zoe called him P.K. She felt no man should call himself nor allow others to refer to him as pretty, especially if he was as ugly as an orphanage on fire, which he *was*.

P.K. also carried the singular distinction of being the last tie Zoe had to her former life as a student. Their convenient relationship had spilled over into her new life and she'd never seen fit to change it. P.K. was a dealer. More to the point, he was Zoe's dealer and always had what she needed. As ugly as he was, there wasn't one person she could imagine wanting to see more.

She'd made an unspoken promise to Jeanne—or the memory of her—to stop. Just stop. Two flowers had sealed her promise and she'd kept them as a reminder.

However, to get through this she was going to need help. There were numerous saviors ready to lend a hand without asking who, what, or where. They carried such noble titles as Dramamine, Gravol, and a new personal hero called Percocet. Of course they were *also* drugs, but sometimes you had to fight fire with fire.

And so it was with a full belly of her new personal saviors she met her first regular client, then dreamily slid under the second. It wasn't until the third date of the evening that things got out of hand.

If the battle for her addiction hadn't been raging so loudly in her head, distracting her from all else, she might have heard her little voice protest in alarm. Its warning cry fell far short of the din, and failed to stop her from getting into the car with number three.

Three: a number only slightly overshadowed by seven as a sign of luck or good things; The Holy Trinity, a threesome, matching symbols on a slot machine, third time's the charm—all threes and all good things.

Number three for the night was neither good *nor* easy. "Simply Bob" was how he'd introduced himself, but simple wasn't how the evening unfolded. Zoe's heroes had won the day by keeping at bay the great horse that would otherwise consume her, but left her rear flank exposed to other dangers. Dangers like Simply Bob.

And his gun.

~~oOo~~

Gideon stood up from his desk, pulled a pair of cigars from his breast pocket, and offered one to Zane. "Let me just start by saying you've done it again. Pure gold, all of it: the girl, the dinner, and even the sex. Everyone loved it. It's all they can talk about on the web site."

Zane blinked. "I'm touched…but?" He could tell there was one coming.

"That angel thing you do," Gideon said peevishly, like a father chastising a child for leaving his crayons all over the floor. "Did you have to leave one there?"

"Yes, I did." He clenched his teeth to hold back what he really wanted to say. This conversation could end many ways, but Zane didn't want to kill Gideon yet so he bit back a retort. "Anything else?"

"Just one loose end and we can move on to bigger and brighter things. We have to get rid of the girl."

"And which girl is that?" Zane knew exactly which girl. He also knew the doctor would have to have been deaf and blind to not have seen the news coverage—even as far away as they were now, in Chicago. Severed heads did that. And the discovery of another drop cloth angel had crossed the border faster than a dyslectic draft dodger.

"I don't know, Zane," the doctor shot back sarcastically. "The girl who claims to have had drinks with you two days before you bit her sister's fucking head off? The same girl who hid in a closet while you ransacked her apartment and stole her cat—"

"Her sister's apartment, her sister's cat."

"Whatever. My point is this: She needs to go away, period."

"I won't kill her. I like her."

"Fine, I'll make a call."

"You do that and I'll bury the parts of you I *don't* eat right beside her."

"She's a whore."

Zane smirked. The stunned look on Gideon's face alone would have been worth keeping her alive. "You say tomato, I say—"

"No, Zane. I said whore, not tomato. What is it about her that gives you the right to mess with the good thing we've got going for us?"

Zane shrugged. He hadn't really given it much thought, but figured he might as well give the ranting old fart some kind of bone to chew on. "Because I like her style. The chick's got moxie. Bottom line: She lives or you die. Good enough?"

Gideon looked away, then slowly shook his head. "Yes. I suppose ...for now. But Jesus Christ, my boy, she *saw* you." He pulled a police sketch from under the file on his desk. "See for yourself. This sketch was added to the FBI's international database yesterday morning and tagged to those damned angel pictures of yours. You're flouting the only cardinal rule of our business. I'm afraid it may come back to bite all of us!"

Zane turned the picture and studied it for a few seconds before pushing it away. "It's close, sure, but I was wearing the latex chin, and the ears and hair are all wrong. Where did you get all this stuff, anyway?" He motioned to the thick file and pictures.

"You're not my only friend, Zane, but I may be *yours*—so take this advice: Stop. Just stop for a while. Take a vacation. Have sex, for god's sake, but don't kill anyone. You might even want to think about a new face."

"Never."

"Give it some thought. I know someone, and he's very reasonable. By the way, how are those headaches? I can write you a script for something to kill the pain, if you like."

Zane cringed at the mention of his demon's handiwork, as though thought would call it forth. "My head's fine, my face is fine, and neither requires your assistance."

15

LUCK BE A LADY

As numb as she was from the drugs, Zoe could tell number three was a hard man, but not the good kind. He didn't smile or try to fill uncomfortable silence with inane conversation the way most johns did. When he picked her up, there was no fumbling for the door in an attempt to be a gentleman.

He'd rolled the window down and barked at her like she'd just missed roll call. "My name's Bob, simply Bob. Get in."

She did.

She twisted in her seat to get a better look at him, wondering if he was as hard as his first words indicated, but he turned and said, "Eyes front. I'm a man. Isn't that good enough for you?" Her head snapped back as he stomped on the accelerator.

Asshole, she thought. Number three was apparently a control freak. She'd seen the type before and wasn't happy. Guys like that always reminded her of her mother.

"Yeah," she said, unsure how to respond, or even if she should. "Did I do something wrong? You're really creeping me out with that steel gazed, flat-topped, army sergeant shtick. You can let me out, you know, and keep your money." She felt him sizing her up, and it was only then she sensed the familiar warning bell. As loud as it was, she was surprised to have not heard it sooner.

"Right here's good." She fumbled for the closure on the seatbelt. "I can walk back."

Unable to pop the catch, panic surged through her like jolts from a battery post. "Stop the car, Ben, or Bill, or whatever the fuck your name is. This date's over." She repeatedly jammed her thumb on the power window button to no avail.

Zoe whipped around to him with acid in her glare and a string of obscenities all loaded up and ready to go, and then deflated when she saw the silencer equipped pistol lying across his lap, pointing right at her.

"Eyes forward and hands together," he rumbled, an octave lower than the grumbling V-8 under the hood. "Be still and I'll make this easy."

Zoe started to speak and he raised a gloved finger. "But if you don't keep your trap shut..." he said, licking his lips and cracking his first smile of the evening, "then you may make this gig a little more entertaining."

The fine hairs on the back of Zoe's neck stirred and her throat felt like it was trying to strangle her tongue. The pins and needles she'd felt earlier were back and singing like the Vienna boys' choir, and her heart dropped through the floor of her ribcage.

In a panicked wheeze, she said, "Okay, okay," then slammed her lips together and faced forward. When Zoe's hands met, her first instinct was to drop her head and pray but she couldn't stop her mind from stuttering back to the image of the fatheaded pistol long enough to formulate a proper plea. *Stupidstupid!* She screamed into her head. She should have seen this.

Ohjesus-ohjesus-mygod-ohjesus to the tenth power. Or that's how long she would've let that banner fly through her mind if Simply Bob left her to it.

"I'm impressed, Zoe," he said. The use of her real name and not "Candace," sent a fresh shock from her toes all the way through the top of her head. She risked his wrath and turned to face him as he continued. "Any other girl would have been screaming her face off right about now."

Zoe swallowed. *Did I imagine that?* It took some effort to find enough saliva for the task, but once she did, she cleared her throat, and said, "Would it do any good?"

Simply Bob smiled into the traffic past the windshield; an elastic tribute that snapped like a slingshot. "No, but the radio doesn't work, so you're gonna have to be the entertainment."

"Mind if I ask what I did? I don't even know you." Not wanting to plead, she kept her tone steady and level. She had a feeling groveling was what he craved, and vowed to not give him the satisfaction. "If it's about the money, don't worry. You can have me. For free. I'll put the money in and not say a fucking word. On my mother's soul, I swear."

"Funny you'd mention your mother, Zoe—"

"Wait a minute. You called me Zoe. I—"

"Slow down there, chickie. You interrupted me. Don't do that. I can't begin to tell you how much that scrapes my nipples, but if you do it again you'll sure as fuck find out. Tell me you understand that."

Tears welled up as she nodded. When he cocked the gun, she blurted, "I understand, I understand! Okay? I'm sorry."

"Good," he said, as he relaxed his grip on the gun. "Now, as I was saying, pull your skirt up."

"What? You didn't..." She let the rest of the words die on her tongue. She unclasped her sweaty hands and laid them, palms down, on her thighs.

"What are you, shy all of the sudden? Are you a whore or not? Pull up the skirt and drop your underwear."

Zoe knew what she was, but it felt like a twisted knife coming from him. She wiped tears from her face and tugged her skirt up under the lap belt, then slid her thumbs under the band of the underwear and guided them to the floor. This was normally a task she delighted in taking her sweet time performing, arousing herself more than any man could, but now all she could feel beneath the growing dread was confusion: *He knows my name.*

"Good," he grunted. "Now hand 'em over."

Zoe complied. He raised the panties and pressed them to his nose, inhaling deeply. "Ah, nineteen-eighty-six: My favorite year." Then he stuffed the panties in his pocket. "Now, my little chickie, roll your bean for me. Pretend your life depended on it. While you keep yourself busy I'll tell you a little story."

"You know, if you open this seatbelt I can give you a better show."

The look he gave her said he didn't think so.

"What?" she asked. "Isn't it a time honored custom for P.O.W.'s to try to escape?"

"Yeah, chickie, but you ain't no soldier."

"A girl can try, right?"

He smiled again. Zoe hoped that was a good thing.

As she raised her feet to the dash and slowly parted her legs, a thought occurred to her. *If I could get a cop interested enough in what I'm doing in here, he might pull us over!* With a plan forming, she relaxed and smiled. She watched for his reaction as both of her hands travelled seductively down the inside of each thigh and back up to the moisture she was surprised to find.

She was no stranger to the fine instrument between her legs; playing lead cello was one of her specialties. With a finger, she woke the conductor and began.

"Once upon a time, in a land far, far away," Simply Bob began, as his eyes roved between the road and Zoe, "there was a girl who saw things she ought not to have seen. Saw someone she ought not to have seen. Know what the girl's name was, chickie?"

So focused was she on the task in hand, she'd drifted off, hearing him only in the most basic sense—having always been more of a method actress, she was dangerously close to orgasm. Sometime during his monologue she'd begun to buck her hips and slide up, then down as far as the seatbelt allowed, slamming into her talented hand as the crescendo rose. "Wha...?" was her breathless response.

"We got to stop. If you keep that up we're gonna have an accident."

"Nobody's watching," she said, hiding her disappointment.

"I ain't talking about that. If you keep that up I might get excited and shoot you by mistake." Then he turned another smile on her. "You, my chickie, are truly one of a kind." From under his seat he produced a set of handcuffs with an extra cuff. He pulled over and parked in the deep shadows of an abandoned warehouse's entrance. "Put 'em on, one on each wrist, then raise your arms over your head."

Nirvana left her like air from a balloon as he shook the cuffs in her face. She wiped her wetness on her skirt and took the cuffs. After snapping a bracelet onto each hand, she lifted her hands over her head and closed her eyes.

Simply Bob secured the third cuff to the headrest. "I was told about you and what happened to your sister. Haven't seen the video yet myself, but I hear she put on a hell of a—"

"Don't you talk about her, you fucking pig," Zoe screamed into his looming face. She lunged forward and surprised him with a head butt on the side of his face. A muzzle flash lit up her vision as the gun coughed, followed by the sound of a pebble striking a tin can. Momentarily blinded, she cringed backward in her seat. As she squeezed her eyes shut, a hand closed around her throat and the barrel of the gun was tapped against her closed mouth.

"Oh, you little bitch." His grip tightening on her throat and he grunted with the strain of choking her with one hand. "You put a hole in my car. Open up," he said, still tapping on her teeth with the fat silencer. "Open that pretty mouth. I got something for you."

It must have been then that he realized he was still choking her, and he let go. When he did, she opened her eyes and mouth at the same time. As she gasped for a breath, he shoved the barrel into her mouth. "Now close it." She did. "If that gun falls out of your mouth, I'm gonna forget my orders and blow the back of your head out. Nod if you understand." She nodded and pursed her lips around the gun's barrel.

After leaving the iron pacifier to her oral ministrations, he dropped her seat back, and unzipped his pants.

"I wasn't going to do this, but your offer made me think

twice. Open says me." he said as he laid a hand on her knee and the other back on her throat. "Now don't you start jerking around, chickie. If that gun goes off, there'll be tiny bits of you all over me."

Simply Bob spit onto his hand and rubbed it along the length of his shaft. He centered himself before her, cursing the lack of leg room, and then pulled her hips toward him. He entered her hard and fast, and paused at the end of each deep thrust. All the while, he squeezed her throat, and likewise, never stopped talking. "To make a well interrupted story short...ahhh. You saw a man—uhh— you should not have seen. Your instructions are simple—stop crying, you're ruining this for me—forget him, forget me, and everything you think you saw. Oh, yeah..." Once he'd finished what he needed to say, he picked up speed and force as his fingers tightened on her neck. The car rocked beneath his swooping thrusts, and he slapped his other hand to her throat, throttling her, stabbing into her body as though he intended to pin her to the seat.

Starbursts flooded Zoe's vision and a storm raged in her head. Oxygen starved, her strength waned as his breath quickened. She'd done nothing more than he asked. She believed him when he said he would shoot her if she moved, having read that much from the dull glint in his eyes. She held the gun in her mouth for as long as she could stay conscious, but just as his hot liquid painted her insides, she faded. The gun slid from her mouth, giving a moist "pop" as the suction was broken. The bitterness of failure had no time to hit her before she slipped away.

She awoke to the sharp pain of a slap to the back of her neck. Before she could react, another followed. Pain radiated in waves from her whole body. Her eyeballs felt two sizes too big for their sockets and her head had a heartbeat all of its own. She was now sitting in the empty parking lot, still naked below the waist, but alive and outside the car. Simply Bob hunkered over her, holding her up by a fistful of hair. She guessed it hadn't been long since she passed out, and that he'd dragged her from the car in a hurry, because his trousers were still bunched around his ankles. She wanted to bend forward and bite his mushroom off, but instead leaned to the side and vomited. Whether by blind luck or a subconscious fear of renewing his wrath she missed his shoes.

He cursed and stepped away from the puddle, pulled up his pants, then bent and unlocked the handcuffs. "Wow, chickie. Was that intense or was that intense? You gave me quite a scare there." He walked over to the car and dropped the cuffs on the seat, came back with her purse and tossed it into her lap. He squatted in front of her, pushed hair out of her face, and held her by the chin. "Who am I?"

Zoe could hardly speak above a squeak, but answered as best she could. The thick aftertaste of gun-oil and metal soured what little saliva she was able to muster. She had no intentions of making him ask twice. Her mouth formed the word, "Bob." She cleared her throat and tried again. "Bob," she whispered.

"Who?" He put a hand behind his ear as though he hadn't heard her.

"Nobody." She coughed, then spat to the side.

"Good." He released her face and wiped his hand on her shirt. He retreated to the car and slid behind the wheel. "Now for the important question: What do you remember about the fellow up in Toronto?"

She didn't look up. She couldn't. "What fellow?"

"Good girl." He shut his door and started the car, then rolled down the window and pointed at her with a glove-sheathed finger. "But, chickie, if you fuck me, you won't be my first stop, get me? Maybe you love your mother, maybe you don't, but I'm thinking you do. So if you screw around, I'm gonna go all the way up to Canada and cut her fucking head off and bring it back here just to beat you to death with it. Do you believe that?"

"Yes." She nodded, but couldn't hold back the mixture of anguish, fear, and hatred any longer. Unbidden, a scream tore from her throat. When it died away, she waited for tears that didn't come. There were no more left to give.

His parting words were a whisper. "Shhh. Hurry home now

and lock your doors. Don't forget: mum's the word." He started to back out, then tapped his brakes and stuck his head out the window. "This is much larger than you could ever imagine. Consider yourself lucky." Then he was gone.

Zoe watched his tail lights, mesmerized at how stark they were against the sooty background of the warehouse district. After his car turned a corner, she looked around, realizing how dark it was, and also how very alone she was. She picked herself and her purse up off the ground, smoothed her skirt, and headed for the street.

As was her custom, she was left handed so she picked 'right' and started walking. Soon, she came to a street that, about half a block down, was lit up by a sign that promised fresh coffee. The coffee sounded nice, but what she craved more than anything at that moment were people, lots of people and lights.

A bell sounded over the door as she entered the diner, and it startled her. She flinched, and muttered, "Fuck," before she could stop herself. A few patrons lifted their heads, but when they saw her puffy eyes, disheveled clothes and hair, they quickly went back to their meals or menus. Zoe didn't mind. She wanted nothing from them except their presence.

From the waitress, she ordered a coffee; she was going to need something to wash down the copious amount of drugs needed to calm her nerves. After the waitress returned with a steaming mug, Zoe downed a handful of pills, refreshing the troops. Even heroes needed reinforcements.

16

THROUGH THE LOOKING GLASS

Zoe didn't remember leaving the diner, but vaguely recalled someone yelling into her face, someone with a name tag. The hours that followed came in fragments; pieced together scraps that may or may not have been hallucinated. Somehow, she managed to articulate her address to a cabbie, and made it all the way to her front hall before that old trickster, gravity, kicked her feet from under her and slapped her in the face with the floor.

The bright side of lying on the floor was that it was *her* floor, in *her* home. A home she shared with a Kat; not Mr. Moto, but a Kat she cared for just as little.

The cold tile soothed her bruised cheek. Behind her, the door stood like an open invitation but there was little she could do about it. Until the moment she landed face first on the floor she'd been able to retain that sense of need to push on, to stay the course. Stoned but coherent, mobility and activity had held the swaying sickness at arm's length, but not anymore. Prostration had seen to that. The simple act of moving her foot six inches to kick the door closed sapped the rest of her strength and left her a panting, sweaty mess.

Sometime later, as the moon illuminated a pale landing strip on the living room floor, she mustered the strength to crawl to bed. The sleep which had been within inches but unattainable until then, found her and kicked her past dreamland into the place where nightmares fed...

She was in the front seat of Jeanne's car, parked in front of the house: *His* house.

Jeanne was at her side—or at least a misty form representing her corporeal self. Through the windshield the sky seethed like Van Gogh's "Starry Night" and the house suckled from the stars, breathed the stars; drawing them in and feeding on their very essence.

In the heavens, white shapes fled before the house's mighty intake, dodging and hiding where they could. Zoe saw these dimming forms as wings and muted light. They were dying; the angels were dying. Here, she knew inexplicably, nothing shined for long.

Jeanne's voice sounded in her head: "I'm sorry." Then the spirit was impossibly in three places at once: sitting behind the wheel smiling at her; drifting toward the bulging chalet; and standing at the front door.

"Jeanne! No!" Zoe screamed and groped for her, but found only air.

For the same reason all things happen in dreams—just because—Zoe found herself outside the car, facing the house. A warm sticky breeze picked up and pushed at her back, prodding her toward the house. The second ghost dispersed before the wind's touch, leaving only the apparition on the steps.

Fear held her feet, but, as though tethered to that last ghost who waited patiently at the threshold, the dream moved her once more. In a blink she stood inside the house. The interior was so utterly devoid of light that nothing save the open door gave the space any depth at all. As dark as it was, the form of Jeanne, lit by an iridescent glow, was plain to see. Both alien and familiar, the ghost emitted a small but resolute smile, one Zoe had seen many times before, and then it moved further into the black.

Suddenly, whatever force it was that brought her there to

stand beside the shade no longer pushed her. The abrupt lack of its pressure gave no relief, nor was it reassuring. Something had scared it away...something stronger.

The doorway stood mere steps away, but Zoe's limbs were planted; both charge and retreat were stolen as a shape began to coalesce from the gloom beyond Jeanne's specter. From the gobbled stars and unfortunate night flyers sucked down the chimney, the shape grew and took on the rough form of a man. Its darkness enveloped the celestials and bled them out, devouring them without incorporating their former glow.

Before the transformation was complete, Zoe knew him. Before the skull sprouted its fiery eyes and slashed a mouth, she knew him. She had no *real* name for him, but she knew him. He was Kreepy.

Zoe watched in horror as the creature lifted an arm to greet the ghostly form that coasted obliviously toward him. The fiend's claw found purchase and pulled Jeanne close as it raised its smoldering gaze to Zoe.

She couldn't bring herself to look away. His eyes stayed with her as his mouth travelled to the bared throat of Jeanne's ghost.

Bones popped and sinew stretched as the beast's lips parted. His eyelids drooped as he bit into her, slurping and sucking as he chewed.

After parting the ethereal head from its neck, the creature favored Zoe with a lupine grin, tiny pieces of ectoplasm dripping in gobs from his chin. As he did, the body and separated head became solid. The discarded the body fell to the floor with the finality of a dropped book.

"What do you think Baudelaire would write about this, whore?" said the darkness surrounding her. The creature's grin flashed again as he dangled the head by the hair. "You've seen enough. I think you better head out now," it hissed, then hurled the head at Zoe.

The weight hit her like a cannonball, and drove her back out the door. She fell past the steps, through the ground and toward the oblivion of Hell. The screams previously stolen from her throat, now ripped free and vibrated as something visible and alive, billowing around her like a broken parachute.

She couldn't see the ground, but sensed it…rushing to meet her, to crush her. While she plummeted, Jeanne's head kept pace, turning lazily as it bobbed in the breeze; its open, damning eyes found her with each rotation. She swung both arms at the tumbling head, but it weaved under and around each swipe like a dancing bee.

The ground was coming: the heat of Hell's fires, the sulfur and the screams of the tortured. She could see, smell, and hear her own damnation in the wind. Touch was all she lacked, but it was coming. The ground was coming.

And the head loomed before her ear. "Candace," it said, and then an arm sprouted like a tentacle from the stump of its neck. The arm found her shoulder, fingers digging in.

"No!" Zoe swung and beat at the floating head with both fists, screaming, "No, no, Nooooo!"

The landscape bled away as the head shifted and flew away from her, changing shape as it screamed. The head and arm grew a body. A body that soared back, back…

…and into Zoe's dressing mirror, exploding it on contact.

The foggy residue of the nightmare receded from her vision at about the same time a second form took shape in the bedroom doorway. The hazy silhouette moved toward her as she struggled to sit up. She caught a glimpse of Kat, sprawled in the jagged remains of her full-length mirror, before a ring clad fist connected with her chin.

A few seconds before consciousness left her again, she heard a man's voice. "Oh my god. Kat? Are you alright? Don't move. I'm gonna call…" and then Zoe lost the voice under the wail of another's screams. Then she lost those too.

"Wakey wakey, eggs and bacy."

What?

"I know you're awake, bitch," came a voice she could place

to a face.

There was a bandage around her head. Judging from the pain she felt just opening her eyes, it was needed. Upon attempting to raise a hand to the bandage, she found she was strapped to the bed. *Am I in a hospital?*

The face belonged to Kat's current boyfriend, Glenn Simms.

"Where's Kat? Is she okay?"

Glenn snorted. "Oh, so you remember almost killing her? You're a lucky bitch, you know that?"

"So I'm told," she said weakly. "How is she?" Scraps of memories came to her in large enough pieces to scab together what must have happened in her bedroom. Enough, anyway, for her to realize she'd really fucked up this time, fucked up *bad*.

"Scarred," he said. "I should probably thank you for that. Her career as a hooker is over now, that's for sure."

"That bad, eh?"

He jammed his hands into his pockets and stared past her. "Is a hundred and sixteen stitches bad? Almost took one of her fingers right off."

"I'm sorry," Zoe said, knowing it meant little to him.

"Sorry? No, not yet, but you're sure as shit gonna be. And that's a fact, bitch." He walked to the bed and sat beside her, running his fingers over one of the straps holding her wrists in place. "You know what I just did?"

She wasn't sure if she wanted to know.

"I signed a piece of paper that's gonna keep you here, right there in this bed, strapped up for the next five days. Right now that probably doesn't sound all that bad to you, but by tomorrow that addiction of yours is gonna be chewing its way right through your dirty little guts. Yeah, I know you're a junkie. Did you really think you were fooling anybody?"

"You can't make them keep me," she said, unsure of whether or not it was true.

"Oh, but I can. I'm a cop, bitch. It's within my right." Then he leaned close to her, and whispered, "I told them you were screaming that you wanted to kill yourself, and wanted to take Kat with you 'cause you're a sick fucking lezbo slut. And do you know what the doctors said?"

Zoe shook her head.

"Not a god damned thing. With the amount of shit they pumped out of your system, they believed me. Why wouldn't they? I'm a cop. So you lay there and ponder that while the bugs crawl up those pimpled fucking arms of yours. Rot in hell," he said, then left the room.

Later in the morning a public defender paid her a fruitless visit, and informed her there wasn't really anything he could do. She'd be evaluated by her doctor and a psychiatrist. Her fate rested in her own hands. His only advice was to be as forthcoming as possible and under no circumstances be confrontational with the doctors. She'd thanked him for nothing and dismissed him by closing her eyes and turning away.

Purple Monkey stopped by in the afternoon to pay a visit. He liked the hospital so much he decided to stay.

During the interview with the hospital appointed psychiatrist, withdrawal interrupted, channeling insults and rude comments, which did nothing to secure the good doctor's confidence in Zoe's ability to care for herself.

Regardless of her phantom purple poltergeist, she hated the doctor's tie and told him as much right before she spat at it. She missed, but guessed he got the point; he snapped his clip board shut and stalked from the room. She called for him to come back, saying, "the monkey made me do it," but he kept walking, huffing and clicking his pen.

"Thanks, dickhead." She blamed the monkey. "Thanks to you, they're gonna think I'm nuts."

Purple Monkey, on the other hand, thought the session had gone smashingly well. "But you are nuts, bitch."

Zoe began to hum. He hated when she hummed.

The monkey tugged at a loose seam on his leg. "Say, you wouldn't happen to have a needle and thread lying around, would you? I'm falling apart here."

"Me too," she said, and continued to hum.

~~oOo~~

Two long days later, Zoe's possession was complete. The monster named Withdrawal had peeled back the remnants of her humanity and devoured her soul like a ripe banana. She halfway believed—in her more lucid moments—the next visitor to enter wouldn't be a doctor, but a priest there to perform an exorcism. In the brief periods she was awake, the pain was so great that she screamed herself hoarse, or until a nurse came with the next dose of valium.

Prince Valium: defender of the lost, the downtrodden, the junkies.

Zoe never stood a chance. By day five she was nearly catatonic and babbled nonsense to any who passed...or to the monkey, who'd given up trying to drown her out with bawdy limericks and finally pulled cotton from his own butt to stuff into his ears.

~~oOo~~

"Doctor Gideon?"

The doctor put down his pen and keyed the intercom, "Yes, Erica?"

"Two things: There's a note here from Dr. Cargill. She wants to know if you will sit in for her on Tuesday."

"Which group is it this time?"

"The W.T.C., sir."

"Women Taking Charge?" Gideon recalled the last time he'd sat in on that session. The women had wept more than a mesh umbrella during their incessant bleating. As the only male in the room, Gideon found himself the sole focus of their channeled rage. The experience had left him feeling guilty for having the audacity to be born with a penis, and greatly in need of a drink. There wasn't a steak's chance on a fat man's plate he was going to put himself through that again.

"That's the one, sir."

"Tell her I'll be painting my toenails on Tuesday."

"Doctor?"

"Tell her I'm busy. What was the other thing?"

"There's a gentleman named Bob for you on line two."

"Excellent," he said. "Please put him through."

He dispensed with any type of formal greeting and jumped straight to the point. "Will she talk?"

"Hi, Doc. Me? I'm fine, thanks," replied Bob. "And to answer your question: no."

Gideon hated Zane for making him do this. The girl was a loose thread in the fabric that cloaked Zane, him, and his entire operation, and it was a major breach in protocol to not simply have killed her. He was *still* baffled by the whole affair. One conversation. One simple conversation with a whore in a bar had caused all this trouble.

"How do you know she won't talk?" he asked, a tad more anxiously than he'd planned. "She could tell her mother or a friend. God damn that Zane and—"

"It makes sense to me, why he'd let her live. That little chickie sure does have something about her that makes you...I don't know...feel *something*."

"Jesus, not you too?"

Bob chuckled. "Calm down, Doc. You're gonna give yourself an analism."

"Aneurism."

"No, Doc, I meant *anal*. She's not gonna talk."

"And you know this *how*?"

"Because as we speak she's being shipped to the nut ward. Even if, and that's a mighty big if, she decided to talk, who's gonna believe her there?"

"Nut ward?"

"Yeah, I lifted her chart from the nurses' station at the hospital. She's going to a place called Paradise Valley."

"What did you do to her?" Gideon knew he should've had Bob bring a camera.

"Not much, really. I sure gave her a good stiff talking to,

though. I think it was more the drugs she was taking than anything I did. She ain't gonna talk. 'Nuff said?"

"Well," Gideon said, relaxing for the first time since Zane pardoned the girl. "That changes everything. Thank you, Bob. Your services were excellent, as usual. I believe I can handle it from here."

"That's good. Because if you were planning on doing her, I was gonna tell you to get yourself another man. I don't kiss and kill."

When the line went dead, Gideon cradled the phone believing he was the last sane man left on the planet. From his bottom drawer he pulled the three eight-by-ten photos of the girl. He flipped them front to back, back to front, studied them, and couldn't for the life of him understand what was so special about a junkie that would warrant such odd behavior out of not just one killer, but two.

He dropped the pictures back into the drawer, then picked up the receiver and dialed a number. Two rings connected him to a man named Remy, who'd done odd jobs for him in and around St. Louis.

"Well, if it ain't good old Gideon. How's the twins?"

If Gideon didn't know the man better he wouldn't have understood the "twins" remark. Remy was obsessed with his own genitalia. "Still there, last time I peed. Thanks for asking. Say, Remy, I was wondering if you might be able to help me out with something. What do you know about The Paradise Valley Psychiatric Facility?"

"The one here in Saint Louey?"

"That's correct."

"Me? Nothing. But I got a buddy that works there, a fella I play cards with."

"Do tell. This friend…is he like you?"

"Ain't nobody like me, Doc, but if you're asking if he's cool, then yeah. Why?"

Gideon hated outsourcing. He closed his eyes and licked his lips. "Do you trust him?"

"Jesus, Gideon, I don't even trust my granny. Look, if

there's something you need done, I can do it."

"This friend," said Gideon, "what does he do there—janitorial, yard maintenance?"

"No, man. He's muscle for the freak show; he's an orderly."

"You don't say..."

17

TACO STAINS & GUM WRAPPERS

Zoe awoke in a small room, strapped to a gurney. She was unsure if she was still at the hospital, or the mental health clinic the doctor had told her about. Either way, their drugs were free, so she had no complaints...yet.

Other than the fact it was white, the first thing that struck her about the cubicle sized room was the smell. The acrid odor of bleach barely covered the musty stench of urine and mold. White walls, white ceiling, white sheet; she couldn't see the floor, but guessed it was white too. The only visible respite came from a partially burnt out fluorescent bulb that strained with the effort of a particularly painful bowel movement to keep up with its obviously younger counterpart.

The sound of a bolt being thrown back caused her heart to skip a beat. A middle-aged woman with the beak of a sparrow entered and clucked a greeting not dissimilar to an Australian bushman.

"Good. I won't need to pinch you." Before Zoe could respond, she added, "I'm kidding, of course. My name is Adebelle, but you may call me nurse Adebelle. Welcome to Paradise Valley Psychiatric Facility. This is the first day of the next twenty days or so of your life. I say 'or so' because, if you screw up and don't stick with the program, 'or so' may be much longer. Any questions or concerns?"

"Yeah, what's that smell? It reeks in here."

"You'll get used to that." Nurse Adebelle called out the door to have an orderly move Zoe to her room.

Before bustling out the door, the nurse placed a slender hand on the muscular shoulder of a smiling man wearing an outfit that closely resembled a dentist's smock. "This is Tony. He'll fill you in on the rules and take you to your room. Hospital policy dictates you be brought there in a wheelchair, but we can't seem to spare one at the moment. You'll remain on the gurney instead."

Tony was a stocky brown man with a ready smile and large droopy eyes. He nodded as the nurse passed, and waited until she'd gone before speaking.

"Don't worry about her, honey. She's not as lame as she seems." He wheeled the gurney out of the room and down the hall as he rhymed off the rules of the house. "Number one: No smoking. Number two..."

Zoe allowed him to drone on as she took in her surroundings. Robe clad, blank faced people with varying degrees of bed head passed, staring, likely as curious of her as she was of them. Some babbled or drooled, many did both, but one thing most of them had in common was the heavy lidded gaze of the perpetually pacified.

There were patients strapped into chairs and beds. Some read books upside down while others answered themselves. A woman played hopscotch with a plant and complained to a chair that the fern was cheating.

As they passed a room with the door opened wide, Zoe said, "Stop."

Tony's face came into view upside down above her. "I don't like the rules either, but you gotta know them."

"No, not that. Go back to the room we just passed."

Curious at her command, Tony backed the gurney up to the door. They both looked inside and then at each other. Tony rapped on the open door. "Try and not rip that one, Meat. I don't think they'll give you any more." The orderly pulled the door closed and continued with Zoe to the next hall.

Zoe's look of wonder met his flat stare. "Was that guy just busting a nut into a slipper?"

"Who, Meat?"

Zoe couldn't recall ever seeing a member that big on a human being in her life, and she'd seen plenty. "Is that his name? It fits. Was that a slipper?"

"Sure was. Welcome to your new home," he said with mock flourish, and unbuckled her straps.

"Finally," she said, rubbing her wrist. "I have the worst itch."

"Why didn't you say something? I could've scratched it for you."

"Not if you knew where it was."

~~oOo~~

"Oh, my." Gideon cradled the phone after speaking to the orderly. The man was going to work out just fine. He worked the nightshift in the mixed ward where the girl had been sent. He smiled as his secretary entered his office with a cup of coffee and set it on his desk. "Fortune truly does favor the prepared mind. Don't you think, Erica?"

"What, sir?"

"Nothing. Say, why don't you take the rest of the afternoon off? Go buy yourself something pretty."

Erica was out the door before he finished speaking.

Gideon settled into his chair, closed his eyes, and smiled. Things were going to be just fine.

~~oOo~~

Zoe recalled rule number seven: "NO visitors and NO phone calls for the first week."

This was hunky dory with her. Who'd want to talk to *her*?

To keep her mind off the monkey, who'd been wandering aimlessly around the room, singing some lame country song over and over, Zoe took up reading: flyers, newspapers, the little tags on the mattresses, her own mind—then she recalled Tony saying something about a library.

The illustrious library...

In the common room there was a modest five tiered milk crate book shelf containing about twenty books. Most were missing several pages or were heavily scrawled upon by some crayola Picasso, but after a quick search through the tattered tomes she found a book that, although well-read, was otherwise fully intact. She flipped it to read.

"Still Life with Woodpecker," she read aloud, then thought, *Sounds gay.* Nonetheless, she tucked it under her arm and retreated to her room.

On the way, she kept her eyes on the tiles at her feet. One-hundred and sixty-two steps brought her to her door. Zoe wasn't afraid of her fellow lodgers, but had no interest in speaking with them, touching them, letting them touch her, having them sneeze on her, blink at her, or masturbate later to her memory. She'd seen *Silence of the Lambs* and was still creeped out by any she considered to be 'not right in the head'. If crazy was a bug—and she wasn't saying it *was*—she didn't want it biting her. They were *nothing* like her. She didn't belong there and was going do whatever it took to be out of the institute in the promised twenty days. Then she could get back to work, score some H, and get on with living her version of Barbie's dream. All she had to do was stay cool and speak to no one.

Easy enough: Stay cool, check. Speak to no one, double check.

Unwanted or not, conversation found her in the form of the horse-cocked slipper pounder, Meat. She'd barely passed the first chapter of her novel when the young man entered her room, sat down in the corner, and erupted into a conversation he must have begun sometime before entering.

She placed a finger in the book and stared at him as though he were a puddle of semen on a silk dress. She had no idea why this man had been detained, so she decided to allow diplomacy to govern her words. "What the fuck do you think you're doing? Do you think you know me? Because you don't, and that's the way it's gonna stay. Beat it, hammerhead." Then, satisfied he'd get the message, she lifted the book and continued reading.

"Tom Robbins," Meat said. "That's the book Elvis was supposedly reading on the crapper when he died."

"This very copy? No wonder it was damp."

"No, probably not that copy, but the same title. And it's not true."

"What's not true?"

"That he was reading it; he died before it was published."

She set the book down and sighed. "Thanks for clearing that up. So, is there something you need, Hammerhead?"

"Meat."

"Whatever."

"Or Mickey. Everybody calls me Meat cuz I have a big tool."

"I saw. No amount of scrubbing will ever erase that particular memory. Thanks for that."

Solemnly, he said, "My gift, my curse."

Zoe giggled in spite of herself. "I imagine in the wrong hands it could be deadly."

"Truly."

Not wanting to give him the wrong idea, she buried her nose in the book, but couldn't erase the image of him doubled over with a slipper in his lap. "We all have our burdens to bear, but apparently some weigh more than others." She shifted her gaze to his baby maker.

"What are you here for?" He asked the floor, then pulled off his slipper and peered into it as though the answer to his question might be at the bottom.

"It's a mistake," said Zoe, "one that'll cost me twenty days, but whatever." She shrugged and went back to reading. Meat stayed, watching her read about a woodpecker, but didn't interrupt again, so she ignored him. After a few minutes of silence she forgot he was even there. An hour later he stood and walked out.

The next morning after pills and breakfast, he returned, but this time he brought a friend along, introducing him as Danny. Zoe attempted to *not* linger on the massive burns covering most of the newcomer's exposed skin, but was drawn to them each time he moved; his taut, shiny, skin looked ready to rip like crepe paper if he sneezed. Her peeks apparently weren't as covert as she thought. Danny smiled at her obvious discomfort. To put her at ease, he said, "It's okay to look, Zoe. They're just burns. I don't care if you don't."

Zoe continued reading without comment.

Meat and Danny spoke between themselves, only including her if she asked a question or laughed at something said. They'd answer the question or clarify a detail, then go on chatting. Zoe thought their presence should bother her, but, by noon, as they stood to leave, she stopped them. "Where are you going? You didn't finish your story about your mother's salad tongs and the pregnant Doberman."

Meat lingered long enough to answer. "It's lunchtime." He patted his groin. "This animal doesn't run on batteries you know. You coming?"

"Yeah." She was surprised at how easy it was to be nice. "Save me a seat."

Over a bland meal of a grainy grey meat smothered in gelatinous, lukewarm, gravy and an even *greyer* creamed corn, Meat pointed out patients to her and offered his opinion of them. Zoe interrupted after Danny left the table.

"What's with the burns? Was he in a fire or something?"

Meat nodded as he watched his friend walk away. "He was burned while trying to save a man."

"Brave kid," Zoe said, "but why's he here?"

"Because he believes he's a phoenix. He started the fire; burned down a whole fucking school."

"Holy crap. Were any kids hurt?"

"You gonna eat that?" Meat pointed to her untouched meal.

She stabbed her plastic spork into whatever meat it was,

and slid it to him. "You didn't answer my question."

"Nope, no kids. It was nighttime," Meat said around a mouthful. "Only one there was a janitor. Danny swears he didn't know the guy was in there. He just likes the way the fire 'speaks' to him." Meat added little bunny ear quotations with his fingers.

"Oh," she said, instead of *'what a fucking loon'*.

Zoe looked up when Meat said, "Fry," guessing he was still talking about his firebug friend. "Frye, come here. I want you to meet somebody."

He wasn't still talking about Danny; he was speaking to a young buck just entering the cafeteria. The man looked to be in his early twenties, but could have passed for younger. He had a boyishly handsome face, and if Zoe was right, given the loose swagger and athletic build, played some kind of sport, like football or hockey. Their eyes locked as he reached the table.

"Zoe. This is Steve Frye. He breaks stuff," said Meat.

"Well, Meat. You just summed up my life in three words." Frye held out his hand to Zoe: "Nice to meet you."

Zoe wasn't much for touching, but she took his hand; he was cute.

"So what's your malfunction? You seem okay to me," Zoe said, dropping his hand.

"Great," Frye replied. "I'll just head on home then."

After swallowing a mouthful of the daily special, Meat spoke. "Steve's a quarterback for Michigan State. He was moved from Detroit because his father didn't want the media to find him."

"Ooh," Zoe enthused, "a plot rife with mystery. What'd you do? Kill somebody?"

Frye glanced at Meat and they both fell silent.

"Oh, God, I'm so sorry," she said, mortified. "I wasn't thinking...I..."

Both young men burst into laughter, then Frye said, "Nah, but almost. According to my doctor I had a nervous breakdown brought on by stress. What landed me here instead of jail was the fact that my coach was able to jump out of the way of my dad's car before I could hit him with it. Too fucking bad, if you ask me."

Just as he'd finished, a girl with black hair and blonde roots stormed over, and loomed over Zoe. "Oh, aren't you just so fucking special. You just got all the boys wanting you, don't you? You...you slut!" The girl slammed a tray of food down onto their table and stalked away, muttering.

Meat wiped potato from his eyes. "Hi, Mary. Bye, Mary." Then he turned to Zoe. "That was Mary."

"So I gathered." She brushed a dollop of pureed meat from her robe and wiped her book on a pant leg. "What's with the Jerry Springer reject?"

"Who knows," said Frye. "But I think she really likes you."

"And me without my prom dress."

Danny returned to the table and surveyed the mess. A smile stretched crookedly along his waxy cheeks. "What'd I miss?"

Meat scooped a handful of potatoes and mashed them into Danny's hair, and said, "Nothing now."

Danny took it in stride, laughing, and they joined him. Silly, but somewhere during that outpouring of mirth, Zoe realized she was going to be okay. These three men (or, two men and one teen) had, for the briefest of moments, extracted her from the quagmire she'd slipped into and helped her to stand. She was beginning to understand Cherry's "shit happens" speech and related it to her present situation: Meat, Danny and Frye were the first of many gum wrappers and tacos that would make the shit stink a little less than it did the day before.

Oddly, she hadn't seen fuzz-one from Purple Monkey since her arrival at the clinic and began to wonder whether he really existed at all. *Maybe he's found a new friend to pester,* she thought, then discarded the notion; she couldn't be so lucky.

That night at lights out, she met the night orderly, Bud, for the first time. The alarm in her head sounded at his approach. It told her the only thing she needed to know about him: he was bad mojo.

Zoe pretended to be asleep when his flashlight found her

face. She imagined him leering as the light travelled the length of her covered form. *Fucking letch.*

The flashlight clicked off after a few minutes and the door swung silently home. Then the electronic lock sounded and she was once again alone. Sleep came, but much later. Each time her eyes drooped, she started awake, warding away an imagined hand at her throat—remnants of her date with Simply Bob. In the end, it was Jeanne's memory that rocked her to sleep. Good old Jeannie.

~~oOo~~

As day seven approached, Zoe knew, if not for her three new knights, she wouldn't have made it through what was aptly known as Hell week. Of course the methadone helped. She avoided Scary Mary when she could, but the slender Goth girl was relentless. It seemed Zoe had been singled out by the black haired bitch as the bane of her existence. Zoe wanted nothing more than to confront her, to beat the fake right out of the cunt's wannabe Goth color, but common sense stayed her hand and tongue.

The orderly, Bud, returned nightly to watch her sleep. She hadn't spoken of his visits to her new friends, but each of them mentioned she looked tired.

Her response was always a vague dismissal. "You know, new bed and stuff." Having only recently acquired the ability to make friends, she wasn't sure of the protocol involved in revealing secrets.

Late in the morning of the seventh day, Zoe awoke with the stiff muscles of the oxygen deprived. The sleepless nights were getting to be more than her body could handle. She'd wanted to report the strange nocturnal visits to Nurse Adebelle, but a feeling told her holding her tongue would be prudent. Zoe had no desire to see how Bud would react if information of her knowledge of his visits came back to him in the form of a reprimand.

Tony, the rule reading orderly, came to see her shortly after she'd brushed her teeth. He informed her she could now make phone calls and have visitors between eleven and two. He laid a prepaid phone card on her desk and told her where to find the payphones. As he turned to go, he stopped and snapped his fingers. "Oh, yeah. A Mister Jonas was here a few times to see you, and your mama called seventeen times. She sounds like quite a handful—scared the shit out of little Sandy up at reception. Just so you know."

Cherry came? "Thanks," she said to his back. *Mom called seventeen times?* She all of the sudden felt like a child again, overflowing with all the guilt and anxiety that peppered her youth. *Shit*, she thought. *How the hell did she find out? I'm twenty-one! I'm an adult, goddamn it. I'm gonna call her back and tell her to mind her own fucking business. Yeah, that's right. I'm a woman now, mom, and you can kiss my ass.*

Even as the rant formulated, she knew she could never *say* things like that to her mother. But thinking them made her feel less like a lost little girl, and more like the hardnosed woman she wanted to be.

Zoe picked up the phone card, wondering who she would call. Her prospects were few, having only two possibles in her short mental phone book: the Bitch and the Pimp. Both choices held little promise of pleasant conversation, but she had to call *somebody*. She decided on Cherry. Besides, she really missed the big lug.

Three steps from the door, it opened and in walked Cherry holding flowers and a foil "I heard you were sick" balloon. Two steps behind him, and puffing from an obvious run to catch up, was Tony. The orderly placed his hand on Cherry's arm. "Sir, you were told earlier that you had to be announced. And you can't have those flowers and balloons in here. There's rules. Hell, you can't even *be* in here. Why don't you come back to reception and we'll see if we can—"

"You wanna lose them fingers, little man, keep 'em there. If not, you best get the fuck out." Cherry shrugged at Zoe's disapproving look, then faced Tony. "Please."

Tony removed his hand, looked at the towering man in

front of him, looked at Zoe, gulped, then said, "But you can't be in here. I could get in a lot of trouble for this."

"I can't be here, huh? Well, brother, let me drop a little Nietzsche on that for you: I mutherfuckin' stand here, therefore I mutherfuckin' am. Got that, mutherfucker?"

Zoe didn't know if it would do any good, but thought she should say something. "Come on, Tony, he's a friend. We'll be fine. You can wait right there for him, okay?"

Tony's hand hovered briefly over his radio, and then slipped to his side. "Fine, five minutes, Miss Beaupre, but next time maybe your friend could meet you in the visitor's room, *after* it's been okay-ed." He turned to Cherry. "I'll wait outside and show you out when you're done. And you'll need to take the balloon and flowers with you."

Cherry glowered down at him. "You still here, mutherfucker?"

As soon as Tony left the room to take up his post outside the door, Zoe let out a squeak and jumped on Cherry, wrapping her arms and legs around him—effectively crushing the flowers and sending the balloon up to bob against the ceiling. "Oh, Cherry, it's good to see you. I was just gonna call you." She kissed his cheek.

He carried her to the bed and dropped her, then smoothed the front of his suit. "Now you know these rags cost me eight bills, girl. How you gonna go jumping on a brother like that?"

"Not that it's a bad thing, but what are you doing here? I thought I'd be the last person you'd wanna see right now."

Cherry stretched his back as he gazed out the window at the city below. "A lot can happen in two weeks, Candace...or should I call you Zoe here?"

"Whatever." She hugged him again. He set her on the bed again.

"Alright, Zoe it is. Like I was saying, I had a busy two weeks. I knew that cop mutherfucker of Kat's was spouting shit the second he said you was trying to off yourself."

Zoe nodded.

"Oh, yeah. I know about that punk cop and what he done

to you," Cherry said, without censoring himself for Tony. Cherry never said anything that *everybody* couldn't hear. "It took a little persuading, but he got real talkative after I took off the little piggy that cried wee wee wee." He paused and rubbed his shiny, domed head. "Let's just say you won't ever have to worry about him ever again, and we'll leave it at that. Okay?"

Zoe scrunched her nose at him. "His toe? You took his toe?"

From the hallway, there was an audible gulp. Then Tony said, "I'll be down the hall, Miss Beaupre."

"Sorry, baby. I didn't mean to tell you that part. Just slipped out is all," he said, then snapped his fingers. "I almost forgot. I brought you something." From behind his back, under his jacket, he produced her purse and grinned.

Her face fell when she saw it. Then she blushed for entertaining thoughts of the drugs in the side pocket. *Damn it, Cherry, why'd you have to bring that? I was doing so well.* "Thanks, Cherry," she said, her chin held high, "but I don't need that in here."

"No, baby, I dumped all your shit down your squatter and repacked the purse with other stuff. You know, makeup, money—shit like that." He smiled and opened the purse to pull something out. "Look. Remember these?" He wiggled a pair of granny underwear under her nose.

Zoe snorted with laughter. She definitely *did* remember the underwear, but couldn't for the life of her figure out how he did. He was hammered when he bought them during a three day trip to Mexico. She'd accidentally drunk a little water by mistake while brushing her teeth.

After two hours, she'd ruined four pairs of underwear, so Cherry went off in a drunken search for new ones. He found only one store in the resort that carried underwear, and only in *one* style; the kind with a waist band that reaches the underside of the bra. Even in her sickened state, Zoe found the humor in his find, and ruined nine of ten pairs in the pack before the end of their stay. She kept the final pair as a souvenir; her little memento of Montezuma's revenge.

"How did you find these? I didn't even know where they were."

"Contrary to your own high opinion of yourself, girl, you're not that hard to figure out."

"Says you."

"Yeah, says me." He smiled, then grew serious. "There's something about your sister in the newspaper. It's in the bag. So are those pictures I found in the bottom of your back pack. That a sketch of the dude?"

Her skin prickled at the memory. She nodded. "That's the dude."

All of the sudden there seemed to be nothing left to talk about. They stood in silence, nodding their heads in thought.

"Listen," Cherry said. "You know me—I fuckin' hate hospitals. I just put mutherfuckers in 'em, that's all. I'm gonna go." He jabbed a thumb over his shoulder as he backed toward the door. "You gonna be okay this time?"

"Yeah," she said, and meant it. She felt better than, well, ever. "I think so." She wanted to tell him about her new friends, but decided not to. Instead, she said, "But thanks for coming. I mean it."

"If you need me," he said, pointing at her, "Just call—for anything. Hell, even to talk. Got that?"

"Sure do."

As she listened to Cherry berate Tony as they walked down the hall, Zoe wondered if she should have told him about Bud. A quick image of a set of pliers and a certain nine-toed cop said it probably wouldn't be such a good idea. Bud was probably harmless. She pulled the phone card from the pocket of her robe and set out to find a telephone.

~~oOo~~

For the first time in her life, Zoe met her mother just the way she said she would: head on. After the initial pronouncements of, "What will my friends think?" and "How can I ever show my face in church again?", and the like, Zoe calmed her mother down enough to have an actual conversation.

During the long walk to the telephone, she'd made a decision, a decision to let truth be the armor of the new and (hopefully) improved Zoe Beaupre. By exposing it to the light, she would free herself from the life she'd lived in the dark. She told her mother everything; bad or worse, she laid it all out for her mother to chew on, and either spit or swallow at her own discretion.

She'd prepared for the obvious responses from her mother—a violent verbal flaying, disavowing ever giving birth to a whore—but after a long pause at the end of Zoe's confession, her mother was crying.

Just when Zoe was about to say her name, wondering if she'd put the phone down, her mother sighed, and said, "I'm sorry."

There was no "but" attached, only an epic poem of lost years summed up in two words. Words she hadn't prepared for, but welcomed as the acceptance she sought.

"You're not mad?"

"I never said that, Zoe. I'm mad, confused, so disgusted I feel like I need a bath, but you're my daughter. When I told the reverend what I thought you'd been doing, he—"

"Aw, Mom. You told reverend Bill? What did he say?"

"He told me to do as Jesus would."

"Yeah, and what's that?"

"He didn't say, but I think I'm doing it right now."

When asked how she'd found her, her mother said she'd "received a phone call from a man named Charles Jonas who'd informed her Zoe was okay, but—"

"Wait a minute," said Zoe, cutting her off. "Are you telling me Cherry called *you?*"

"Is that what you call him?" Her mother sniffed. "He's a very outspoken fellow, this Charles of yours."

"He certainly is." Zoe choked back a giggle.

"I don't believe you've mentioned him before. He seems to care very much for you. Is he a boyfriend?"

"Yeah, mom, kind of. It's complicated. Say, I should probably get going."

"Wait, Zoe. I'm not very good at this so bear with me. I had no idea...you always seemed so strong. Well, what I'm trying to say is...I'm sorry if I drove you to this...this, ah, state you're in."

"Missouri? No, mom. You just paid for the train ticket."

"You know what I meant."

"I know, mom. I'm sorry too. Old habits die hard. Look, it's not your fault. You might have given me the keys but I was behind the wheel the whole time."

After cradling the phone, Zoe leaned against the wall and smiled. "Fucking Cherry." *Well, it fits,* she thought: *Who better to bring two people together than a pimp?*

18

A FAMILIAR KICK IN THE HEAD

Zoe was alone 'til it started. She remembered that much.

She'd been sitting by the only window in the common room, a steel mesh covered bay window overlooking downtown St Louis, reading her woodpecker book that *still* had no woodpecker—but was engrossing nonetheless—when the girl affectionately known to her as *Goth Bitch* strode over and slapped the book out of her hands. The woodpecker book soared up and up, found no wings, and crash landed in the corner.

She should have stood, retrieved the book, and returned to her room. God and Zoe both knew this would've been the wise thing to do—mostly anybody would. But Zoe was Zoe, which translated to this: she could take a little shit, but had a limit when it came to crazy bitches, especially if she outweighed them. Goth bitch was a waif.

Her knee jerk response to Mary's input regarding her choice of reading material was to kick the girl in the box. One "Bitch" led to a scratch, then a handful of yanked hair. Soon they were caught up in a cartoon-like whirlwind, with feet and fingernails flying as fast as the screamed insults. A small crowd formed and shouted taunts and jeers, alerting the nearest orderly. The orderly, Zoe spied from the corner of a bleeding eye, was none other than her nocturnal peeper, Bud. And he looked pissed to have been interrupted from his crossword puzzle.

She'd heard a few things about Bud from some of the more talkative inmates. The general theme of their collective remarks was that he was a very cruel, very stupid man. But she already knew that. Another fact, one more pertinent to her present situation, was that he knew just where to hit, pinch, or poke without leaving a mark.

One thing they'd neglected to add was how fast he was. Bud's foot connected with Zoe's chest, then he grabbed a handful of Mary's fake black hair and judo-chopped the girl in the throat, sending her choking and rolling to the floor. Then he reached for Zoe, who dodged his hand to get at Mary, who was still rocking and clutching at her throat.

When Zoe rolled and kicked Mary, Bud grabbed Zoe's shirt, reached beneath her robe, and squeezed her breast so hard Zoe thought he might be trying to tear it off to keep for a souvenir. She fell away from him, reeling from the starburst of pain in her chest. Frantically, she groped along the floor, searching for something to hit him with.

Opportunity presented itself as he reached for her. A pencil Bud must have been using for his crossword puzzle (or to doodle boobs onto newspaper pictures) fell from behind his ear and landed on her robe. She closed her fingers on it and lunged upward, stabbing at him with all the pent up rage she felt towards him, that bitch on the floor, her monkey, this fucked up situation, God's blind eye, but mostly just him.

Bud raised his arms just in time to be skewered through both hands as they overlapped in front of his face. Zoe's grip on the pencil was so tight that it snapped off as he toppled backward, leaving two inches of wood and the eraser in her blood-soaked fist.

Bud dropped like a dead tree. Unable to pull his hands apart to catch himself, he sat down hard on the checker tiled floor. He eyed the pencil protruding from the back of his hand in disbelief. As blood found its way past the pencil, his lids fluttered and a strained mewling whimper pulsed past his lips with each visible rise of his chest.

Zoe was still bouncing her eyes from the wheezing Bud to a writhing Mary when the second orderly arrived. He hauled her into a bear hug and held her tight as a nurse spiked a needle into her arm.

Now there's a familiar kick in the head, she thought as the ice travelled through her veins... and travelled through her veins... andtravelledthrrrrrrrrr...........

~~oOo~~

Zoe woke with a champagne headache and a nose full of disinfectant. She was back in the little white room she woke up in on her first day. *Great, right back where I started.* There was no window or clock in the former janitor's closet, so Zoe had no idea how long she'd been unconscious, but the scarcity of sound outside the locked door told her it must have been sometime after lights out. She'd been out at least four hours.

The inside of her mouth felt as dry as a wool mitten as she circled it with her tongue to count her teeth. *All present and accounted for.* Against the shooting pain in her neck, she raised her head to peer down the length of her body. The fact she was strapped down to the bed didn't faze her. She'd expected no less. *Whatever happened to a good old fashioned straight jacket and a rubber room?*

She'd made a very dangerous enemy today. Bud worried her first in the dark—which in retrospect seemed like a premonition—but now their relationship had been kicked up to a different level altogether. His retribution would be swift and mean. The idea of being tied down when his retribution came sent a shiver up her spine.

In an attempt to divorce Bud from her thoughts, she hummed while she counted the tiny holes in the ceiling tiles. Soon she was softly singing to herself.

She was still singing when the door opened and Bud entered, smiling dreamily and favoring her with a glazed stare. He was stoned.

"Well, aren't you the little songbird," he drawled, his voice dripping with honey. "I'd clap, but…" he raised his bandaged hands, "you know." He stood above her for a moment, then tilted his head. "Wow. I can see why you guys cry for these pain killers. They're fucking awesome. Guess what?"

Zoe closed her eyes and turned her head as he neared.

Her eyes shot open again when he jumped up and sat on her legs. As terrified as she was, she was not going to throw more fuel on his fire by crying out. The weight of his body on her knees was agonizing, but she refused to let him see her pain.

"I'll tell you what. I am so fucking jacked right now it should be illegal. Can't feel a damn thing, and *that's* a shame." His finger traced the contour of one breast under the sheet. "Because after that show you and that other chick put on back there in the common room, I was so hard I could've shot my load through a bulletproof vest."

Zoe cleared her throat. "Is that what you want?" *To lose your job?* "You can have me. It's okay." She stretched a photocopied smile, and then winced as it reopened a cut on her lip. "I've been watching you watching me," she said. *That's it motherfucker. Climb on up here for a ride. Do it, you prick. And when you get those pants peeled back from that shriveled stack of dimes you call a dick, I'm gonna scream my fucking head off. We'll see if you can get your pants up before somebody comes. Then it's sayonara Bud, and hello good night sleep.*

He stood with his mouth open for a few seconds, and then shook his head, "No, I can't. I was told to go home. Besides," he grinned, "the man told me to watch you, not to touch you."

Zoe felt the room close in. "What did you say?" She suddenly recalled her time spent with Simply Bob, and his final warning before driving away.

"Oh, nothing. I should go. You hold that thought, you hear."

He told me to watch you, not to touch you.

Bud fumbled with the door handle, cursed, then gave up and used his wrists. "catch ya later," he whispered, and then left.

~~oOo~~

Her confinement in the White Room ended after two days. Meat and Danny were sitting on the floor outside the small room chatting quietly when she walked out, followed by Nurse Adebelle. The monkey was there, too.

Zoe walked over and kicked the monkey down the hall, then turned toward Meat. "How long have you two been out here?"

"Since the pill cart came," said Meat. "I think we missed breakfast." He pouted at the half-mast outline of his member. "We'll get you fed later, buddy."

Zoe shook her head. "C'mon. I think the cook will give us something. Wouldn't want to starve the python, would we?"

As they neared the hallway intersect that would bring them to the cafeteria, their way was blocked by a stocky, fiftyish man named Arnold.

Although she hadn't been properly introduced to the jowly man, he waved at her each time their eyes met, and Zoe waved back. His childlike demeanor and wave were always *so* insistent that she found herself immediately disarmed and liked him without knowing him. She'd asked Meat about him during lunch once and he'd told her that, on the outside, before losing millions for several customers, Arnold had been a stock trader. The strain of the loss had spurred an attempted suicide.

Although Arnold obviously hadn't succeeded, a glancing blow with a bullet caused irreparable brain damage. He'd uttered two words since the shooting, but with them he described every emotion or action he made.

At that moment, he used them together, and pointed enthusiastically down the hall: "Margin call! Margin call!"

"What's a matter, Lassie?" Danny joked. "You say Timmy's stuck in the well?"

"Don't be a jackass, Danny," Meat said, then smiled at the chubby man: "Everything okay, big man?"

"Margin call," Arnold said ominously, and pointed at Zoe.

She stared back without comprehending what he was attempting to convey. "Me? My room's down there, but—"

At her statement, the former trader clapped and pointed again, serving up his apple pie grin. "Margin call," he delivered one last time, then stepped past them, and shuffled down the hall.

Zoe decided to make a detour before heading to the cafeteria. When the three of them rounded the corner, she saw the clutter outside her own door. A scream from within the room stopped them in their tracks. They all shared a look, then broke into a run, sliding to a pileup at the doorway. Amid the mess, half covered by the scant contents of Zoe's in-house wardrobe, sat Scary Mary.

Distantly, as though waking from a dream, Mary focused her eyes on Zoe, Meat and Danny. "I...I...I'm—"

"A fucking idiot," Zoe finished for her, and stalked over to stand before her.

Mary shrank back, gently set the picture down, then scurried sideways. "I didn't know. I'm sorry," she said and darted from the room.

She surveyed the room. Not even the sturdy metal bed frame had escaped the Goth girl's attentions. The purse Cherry smuggled in for her lay open and empty, its contents poured into a pile on the floor.

Zoe picked up the sketch Mary had been holding. It was the police artist's rendering of the man she'd met in the bar. But there was nothing in the drawing or photos that should have reduced Mary into a screaming puddle of nerves. *Unless...*

She turned to Meat, who was with Danny, flipping the mattress onto its frame, and said, "Where's her room?"

When Meat turned to speak, she noticed his bulging erection. "Aw, come on Meat. That's gross."

His look turned sheepish and his ears reddened, which must have been something akin to a miracle, considering the amount of blood it would take to sustain his perpetual state of sexual readiness.

"What? I get excited sometimes."

"Where's her room? I need to talk to her."

"First door before the women's showers—but don't you think you should leave it alone?"

Danny nodded in agreement.

"No, now come with me."

"You want a repeat of what happened the other night? You're already gonna have to tiptoe around that fucking Bud as it is."

"No," Zoe said, firmly. "Let's go."

"Fine, have it your way," Meat said, then turned to Danny: "Go get Frye in case they start scrapping. He'll wanna watch too."

Before leaving, Zoe stooped and gathered up the pictures and the police sketch to bring along.

19

QUITE CONTRARY

Zoe stood in the girl's doorway for a few seconds watching her, wondering at the possibility that Mary might know something about the man who killed her sister.

Meat leaned close to her ear and whispered, "C'mon. Let's go. Leave her alone."

Zoe shook her head and walked into the room. "Mary, can we talk?"

Mary was curled up in a fetal position on her bed, facing the wall. "Is he your boyfriend or something?" she said.

"You mean Meat?"

Mary snorted into her pillow. "No. You know who I mean."

"I do…the guy in the picture. That's actually why I'm here," Zoe said. "You seemed like you've maybe seen him before and I was hoping you could share. He's not a friend, if that's what you're scared of. He's a very bad man." She swallowed back the pain as an image of Jeanne floated to the front of her mind. "He killed my sister."

Mary rolled over. "So how'd you meet him and live?"

"He didn't know who I was at the time."

Mary sat up in the bed and favored Zoe with a haunted look. "I've seen him close up."

Zoe shuddered. "Me, too," she said.

Danny and Frye arrived, and Zoe waved them into the room. Then she sat on the edge of the bed. "How could you even tell it was him from that drawing?"

"After I saw the news clipping about the murder, it just clicked; the markings on his arms...the weird tattoo. I...I'm sorry." Mary shivered and turned away.

Zoe didn't really know what the "sorry" was attached to, so she shrugged. "It's alright."

"I can't imagine what it would be like...."

Zoe didn't answer. She waited.

After a few minutes, Mary took a deep breath. "First off, I don't know his real name. I only know what Clive called him: Cannibalangelo."

Cannibalangelo. The term made Zoe's skin crawl. A police artist's sketch of the painting—a sketch which was 'mysteriously' leaked to the newspapers—left with Jeanne's...with Jeanne, was a depiction of a three-quarter view of an angel, wings outstretched, one arm reaching toward the heavens. Mary could have been lying, but Zoe was ready to listen to what she had to say. For the time being, she kept the knowledge of the painting to herself.

"I'm listening. Tell me everything."

"I saw that dude at a party my ex took me to."

"A party?" asked Zoe. "What? Like a house party?"

"Well, yeah, sort of. But let me just say I had no idea where Clive was taking me, or how sick he really was. We'd been seeing each other about three months and, to be honest, I thought the fetish he had with nibbling on me was kinda erotic, you know? Not like we had sex or nothing while he was doing it. He just licked me down there and I took care of him with my mouth.

"At the time, he was all I wanted, so I overlooked the weird shit he did with his friends. You know, everybody fucks around, but these guys were sadists, man. Get this: We were headed to school one morning—me, Clive and two of his buddies—when his one buddy runs over this cat. Almost took us into a fucking tree to get it, too!

So anyway, we stop just past the cat, and the guy driving—I don't remember his name—well, he walks back to the cat and stands there, staring at it, watching it bounce and twist like he was witnessing something holy. I know, fucking bizarre, but get this: He yells for Clive to come over, so he did. And this is how we got the invite to the party right here. He says to Clive, 'Clive, if you eat a piece of that pussy, I'll talk to the man about getting you into Spankie's.' You'll have to forgive me for staying after that, but I was kinda caught up in the whole "kink scene" and trying to be different. And *that* shit was definitely different.

"I didn't think he'd actually do it, and I had no clue what the fuck Spankie's was. I'm not gonna go into detail here, but Clive scooped up something that'd shot out the cat's mouth, and swallowed it. I puked, and thought he would too, but he didn't. He turned and howled like he was insane, pounding his chest, screaming, "Yeah! Yeah!" I know. I'm sorry. I should have left him right then and there, but a little part of me wanted to stay. I've always been like that. I looked at things one way then: like, I'm bored/what's next?"

Zoe knew the girl was going somewhere with the stroll down gross out lane, but wondered what any of it had to do with the guy in the drawing. "The picture, Mary: what about the picture?"

"I'll get to it. I'm telling you the whole story so you can see what kind of man the dude in the drawing is—fuck, for that matter, what kind of guy *Clive* is now. Alright, where was I? Oh, the party. Well, Clive was literally beside himself for the rest of the week, randier than a two-peckered billy goat, but we didn't have sex then 'cause I wanted at least that much to be special. You know what I mean, right?"

"Sure." Zoe shrugged instead of laughing.

"Spankie's: The big fucking whoop-dee-doo. Clive comes up to me one day at school and starts acting all weird. Said he got the nod and I was allowed to come too, if—and this part really got me going—if I swore never to speak of it. Or else."

"So now I just *had* to go, right? I probably would've burst if I didn't. I was thinking something like *Fight Club* or some shit like that; I didn't know I was gonna see what I saw! It was just me and Clive going in his daddy's car, the other two guys took the one guy's pickup. You know—the one that labeled the cat? All the way out to the sticks, Clive is wound up so tight. There he is, squinting through the window, chin practically in front of the steering wheel, and it wasn't even dark yet! I swear if I'd farted, he would've blew right there. Exploded, I mean.

"He didn't say shit the whole way there, but when we pulled up to some ratty old farm house and parked on the grass with about thirty other cars, he says, 'Whatever you see in there, you don't say fuck all, you just smile, got it? This is big for me, so please don't screw this up.' That's what he said, then he kissed me; a deep, sloppy kiss that stroked my back teeth.

"I was kinda disappointed when we got inside. It was an awful lot of hype just for some fuckin' house party. It didn't strike me as anything he should've been all primed up over, but I stuck on his arm and kept my mouth shut like the good bitch I was. Besides him and his two buddies, I didn't recognize a face in the crowd of fifty or so, so I stayed put. One thing that struck me at the time was how eglegecic—eslactic—fuck! What's that word for a whole bunch of different things all together?"

It was Frye who spoke up. "Eclectic."

"Sure. Thanks, stud. So there was guys in suits, punks, rednecks, and cool people like me—all in this house like it was natural, mingling with each other and having a great old time. Yippee, I thought. Big Whoop. This is *secret*? Then I looked at one of the televisions they had scattered through the house. They all had horror movies on them, real *Faces of Death* shit. But it wasn't. Now I know better. Those sick pricks were watching real people getting snuffed. Real fucking people! One of the guys, the one on the big screen with this great big tat on his back was chewing straight through some chick's stomach while all these assholes stood around cheering. It was about that time I started to get a feeling for what was really going on, and I was thinking like I was gonna toss my dinner up. I told Clive I was going to the bathroom, said I had to tinkle, and he said, 'Yeah, whatever, Mary,' without even looking at me. He was just plain juiced and had eyes for one thing: The nude dude on T.V.

"When I get to the bathroom, the door is cracked open a little and the light's on. I should've knocked, but I didn't. I pushed the door open a little to see if it was empty, and that's when I saw the dude with the tattoo in the reflection of the mirror over the sink—yeah, I was shitting in my pants. I managed to keep from tossing my lunch long enough to get back to Clive, who was busy talking it up with some dude in a suit; the same kind of dude he would have spit on or kicked the shit out of any other time.

When I got back to him, I knew the only thing that could get him to leave the party was one thing: my pussy. I knew, well, I hoped he would take me up on an offer, so I acted all bitch-in-heat. It worked, too. He left with me. I sure had to play it up, let me tell you.

"When we got close to the front door, and Clive was saying goodbye to some of his...I guess I'll call them *friends*—but fiends is more like it—I spied the dude from the bathroom. He's coming out the door like a returned hero and shit, wiping his face with a big old towel, and everybody's whooping it up like he's the second coming. That's when I leaned close to Clive and asked him who buddy was. I know I didn't need to know, but I wanted to be able to put some sort of name to the nightmare I knew was coming that night. He says, 'Cannibalangelo'."

"That's it," Mary said, looking around the room at the collective jaws hinged open.

"One question," Meat said. "What did you do about Clive and your promise?"

Zoe shot him the stink eye. "Show a little class, horn dog."

"What? It's a valid question. I want to know how she got away from him. Come on, Mary. You went this far."

"'S'okay," Mary said to Zoe. "I don't mind. You should

hear this anyway."

"We left the party, and Clive still had that look in his eyes. We were only driving for five minutes when he pulls off to the side of the road and shuts the engine off. He turns in his seat so he was facing me and got all serious like he did on the way in, and asks in a deeper voice than he had going into the freak show, 'You cool with all this?'

"'What?' I ask back, like it ain't no thang but a chicken wang, even though it sure as fuck was. He says, 'You know, the stuff at the party.' I told him it made me so horny I just had to get him alone or I was gonna pop, 'cause I knew that's what he wanted to hear. I really didn't plan on putting out. The minute I saw his future in that fucking mirror in the bathroom, I wanted him gone from my life for good. Shitty thing about that is this: what you want and what you get are usually never the same things. I was stuck.

"Let me tell you: if insanity has a smell, he was fucking drowning in it. He came at me, all mouth and hands, telling me he loves me. I got all deflecty-like and asked if we could go somewhere else just to put him off, but he wasn't having it. He fumbles at my shirt while he's humping the side of my leg like a dog, and yanks my bra right over my head. Then, instead of putting in a little leg work with what he had to play with, he dove straight for my jeans, while he slobbered back and forth on my boobs like he was taking the Pepsi challenge—"

It was at this point Zoe lifted her head to switch channels. Mary only continued on with the rest of her story because it drew the attention to her and no one else. A tactic that, although done for selfish reasons, worked out nicely for Zoe; it left her to her thoughts. None of the rest of the story was going to interest her. And instead of Mary answering any questions, her story only posed *more*.

She left the boys to hover and drool over the Goth girl's tale, while she decided on a course of action. What she wanted to do was call the police. Then she thought of Bob and his last words: "This is much larger than you could ever imagine". She was quickly becoming a believer.

"…so, right when he's about to cum, he bites down on my shoulder. 'Fuck you,' I screamed at him, and pushed him out of me so fast his hip hit the gear shift, making him twist so he pasted the gravy portion of his load all over the radio. He apologized, saying he wasn't really gonna bite me, but I don't know. He actually broke the skin.

"I flipped the visor down and checked the marks in the mirror. Sure enough, he did, so I said, 'Fucker, you left marks on me! If this scars, you're so gonna get it. My brothers are gonna beat your ass.' He didn't know it at the time, but that was gonna happen anyway. My brothers were just itching for a reason to tool him from the first time they seen him.

"When he dropped me at home, I told him I didn't want to ever see him again because he was a horrible lay. I figured he'd take that better than the truth—that I thought he was fucking nutso… *and* he was a horrible lay.

"He stalked me for a little while after that, and called all the fuckin' time, but then my brothers made it pretty clear he should piss off, and I haven't seen him since. My new guy, Spider, he knows how to treat a girl, and, god, can he wiggle his tongue."

"Let me get this straight," said Meat. "You left Clive for a guy named Spider?"

"Yeah, Spider's a one of a kind softy."

"With a name like Spider, how could he not be?" Meat tossed back sarcastically.

"Can I ask you one more question?" said Zoe, and then continued after a nod. "Why the hell have you been on me since I got here? Why'd you pick me?"

Mary shrugged. "Hell, I don't know—because you have pretty blonde hair? My doctor says I have anger transference issues. He could be on to something."

Zoe stuck out her hand. "So, truce?"

Mary eyed her hand for a few seconds then gave it a brief shake. "No, but now that you know all my secrets and whatnot, I guess I can't hate you."

Zoe raised her eyebrows. "Sounds fair."

20

THE INFAMOUS "THEY"

An almost impossible obstacle lay before Zoe, and she could either sit down and turn her back on it, or dig in and climb. But moving forward meant more decisions. The "How" spread its own many limbed branch. Should she call the authorities? If so, which ones? Detective Jenks back in Canada, or the St. Louis police? Was Simply Bob blowing smoke up her ass when he said 'they' were watching? Was *Bud* part of it?

Amid the scattered items on the floor she came across the folded news article Cherry had cut out and left in her purse. The American newspapers lumped Jeanne's death in Toronto together with a series of murders that, until then, had all been carried out in the northern heartland of the U.S. As much as Zoe wanted to know who and why, she couldn't bring herself to see the news article as true. Their words cheapened Jeanne's death to the point that her identity and all that made her special were generic traits shared by mass-produced, mass murdered Barbies: ***Another Drop-Cloth Angel***, The headline read.

Another.

It was as though the singular brutality of her murder had been watered down by the repetition of its execution and pompous display. Jeanne Beaupre would not be just another file, or number seventeen in a long list of women and men butchered like cattle for their meat.

Zoe's mind and course were clear. And, as she tore the news clipping into tiny pieces and threw them into the garbage, an old saying scrolled like a ticker tape through her mind: 'Let justice be done though the heavens fall'. As much trouble as she may find, she needed to see this through, whatever "this" even was. She was angry now. Damn angry. At everyone and everything that had ever stepped on her spirit. She'd give the police one more chance to listen.

She brushed past Danny in the hall, and he looked up from whatever it was firebugs did while alone. "Where ya going?"

She stormed past, saying, "To grab a tiger by the tail and bite it off."

"Oh," Danny said absently. "Well, don't fill up. It's Jell-O day."

Zoe was five feet from the bank of pay phones when Nurse Adebelle stepped in front of her.

"Miss Beaupre?"

"What?"

"Doctor Kirby would like to see you."

"Can I make a call first?" Zoe shifted from one foot to the other.

"You do seem to possess all of the required equipment for the task—but, *may* you? No. He'll only be in the ward for the next hour. Let's go." Her tone didn't allow for debate.

She left her anger to simmer and fell into step with the nurse. "I didn't start it, you know. I was reading and that bitch came at me out of nowhere. If it's any consolation, we've worked things out. It won't happen again."

"How wonderful for you. I'll make sure to tell that to the orderly you skewered through the hands with a pencil that everything is fine now. I'm sure he'll be ecstatic. Let's go, Miss Beaupre. We don't want to keep the doctor."

Doctor Kirby was a planet of a man with the pinched features of a losing general in the battle of the bulge. Beside Zoe's modest file, a mountain of much fatter files awaited his expertise and perusal.

"Miss Beaupre, please, won't you take a seat?" he wheezed, like he'd just eaten Alfred Hitchcock.

"Call me Zoe," she said, then skipped the pleasantries. "Listen, Doc. Like I was just telling nurse Adie here: It was an accident; the pencil thing with that guy."

"Mr. Hawkins?"

"Yeah, If that's his name."

"Really? An accident, you say?"

"Yeah, really. I don't know where the pencil came from—must have fallen from his pocket, then he fell on it. You know, it all happened so fast, like, snap snap—*that fast*—but I could be wrong." She managed all this without breaking eye contact once.

The doctor sucked in a huge breath, as though he planned to blow her right back out the door, then wheezed most of it out in the form of a yawn. "Look, we could go in circles all day but I'm very busy. So here it is: I know the altercation wasn't your fault. I've already seen the video feed from the common room security monitors, so your embellishments were unnecessary." He was sweating now, quite possibly from the effort of trying to seem stern.

"So you saw that it was an accident, right?—as in totally not my fault."

He held up a beefy hand for silence. "Before you waste your energy and my precious time on another story, let me say something, okay?"

"Sure."

"I witnessed how you were dealt with by the orderly. It was entirely inappropriate behavior, and on behalf of the hospital I would like to offer my sincerest apologies and assure you that he has been suspended for the remainder of the week, and, quite possibly, longer—pending a review, of course."

"No shit?" Zoe flexed an eyebrow.

"Quite."

She waited for the doctor to catch his breath, and then asked, "We done?"

He locked his fingers together over his expansive middle, and rocked back in the overstuffed office chair. "Yes. By all means, carry on, Miss Beaupre."

"What about the pencil?"

"As far as I can see it was the result of a series of poor decisions. Good day, Miss Beaupre."

As she made her way back to the pay phone, Zoe smiled to herself at the small but relieving victory. *Score one for team whore.*

~~oOo~~

After three false starts, she was able to connect with the detective in Canada who'd handled her sister's case.

"Jenks. Go," he said, all businesslike.

"You may not remember me, Sir, but this is Zoe Beaupre." She recalled his final disgusted look before driving away.

A pause, then, "What can I do for you, Miss?"

"Before I start, let me tell you that what I'm about to say may seem a little farfetched."

"O-kay," Jenks drawled, now half bored, half befuddled. "Is there something you've remembered from the day of the incident?"

"Not exactly. This is going to sound totally crazy, but—"

"Funny you should mention crazy, Miss Beaupre. I was under the impression you were in a hospital. Is that true?"

"Um, yeah, but I met a girl in here who's seen our guy." During the short silence that followed, Zoe held her breath.

There was a loud rush of air from the ear piece. "Okay," he said. "What the hell. What have you got?"

Zoe related most of Mary's story to the detective, and he interrupted occasionally to ask for clarification or the spelling of a name, which seemed promising. Why would he need details if he thought she was wasting his time?

After taking down her story he remained unconvinced.

"*Really*, Miss Beaupre, don't you think it's possible the girl made it up?" He sighed heavily, *just* like a man whose time was being wasted. "Or maybe you've misconstrued some of this girl's statement?"

Zoe didn't answer. He continued. "All the same, I'll put this in the file and see what we can turn up."

"You don't believe me."

There was a pregnant pause before he answered. "You're calling from a mental facility, Miss Beaupre. Would *you* believe you?"

"I don't know, but I'd at least give me the benefit of the doubt." Not only had she not made a dent with him, she didn't even scratch his paint.

"And so I shall. Leave this with me and if I need to speak with you, I'll leave word with…what's the name of the facility again?"

He knew. He was just fucking with her and wanted her to say it. "Um…" Hope, if there was any in the first place, began to slip away, and her cheeks reddened. "It's called Paradise Valley Psychiatric Clinic."

"Right, I'll also pass this information on to the St. Louis P.D. They'll want to interview you, as well as your new friend." Sounding a little too silky for Zoe's taste, in lieu of goodbye, he said, "Take care, ma'am."

Well that didn't work out so well.

"What did you expect? You're in a loony bin, bitch. Count yourself lucky he even took your call."

"Fuck off, Monkey. And another thing: Why the fuck are you only around for the bad shit? Why can't you be there when something goes right for me?"

He didn't answer. He never answered the important questions.

She dialed the second number with less gusto than the previous one. Things seemed like they were going to turn out fine. *Who are you kidding? It sounds nuts.*

Maybe I am.

"That's a possibility."

"Shut up, I'm on the phone."

The reporter from the Toronto Sun was quite receptive, and grew more excited the longer they spoke…all the way up until he asked if he could quote her in the article. If Simply Bob hadn't just been trying to scare the shit out her—which she didn't think was true—her name was the last thing she'd allow to be printed. A steadfast "No" from her was where the second conversation went sideways.

"Cannibals? Snuff?—where have you been all my life, lady?"

"Just no names, got it?"

Zoe didn't like the way the reporter said: "Sure, kid, wouldn't dream of it." He'd sounded a little too slick, too obliging—like a kindly ferret who'd taken a job as the night watchman at a chicken ranch. Whether for good or ill, the damage was done by the time they said goodbye.

The conversations left Zoe both emotionally and physically drained. Her earlier vision of Justice, as it cut a path of righteous retribution through the ranks of her enemies, had slipped somewhere in the dark and fallen on its own blade.

She was beaten and she was tired, but she was also resolute. There *would* be a reckoning, but it seemed she'd be moving forward as she'd lived: alone.

Now all she needed to do was find someone to *help* her so she could do this all by herself.

~~oOo~~

That night, unfettered from Bud, her night watchman, she enjoyed eight hours of blissful surrender. The next night passed in much the same way. But her peace was short lived. On the third night, he came back. She awoke long before his squeaky tennis shoes carried him to her door...then on to her bedside. Previously, he'd never come all the way into her room, but this time he did.

As always, she pretended to be asleep, but when his footsteps neared, her breath caught in her throat. Pressure rose in her chest, building with each imagined step closer he came to the bed, and then his trembling hand caressed her exposed shoulder.

She cringed from his touch, an action that disclosed her ruse for what it was, but the hand stayed, and breath smelling of onions and coffee followed as he bent forward. His whispered words found her ear through the inches separating them.

"That's okay. I know you're not sleeping." He walked his fingers from shoulder to hip, then slid his bandaged hand between her legs and caressed her through the sheet.

"No. I'm not sleeping," she whispered.

"Just wanted to let you know that pretty soon I'll be coming back to make a deposit in your honey pot, but not tonight. These pills I've been taking make it damn near impossible to pop a rod—and it ain't from lack of effort on my part. I've been tugging on my dick like a cold lawnmower, and nothing, no prime."

"Gee, that's too bad."

"Ain't it just."

"I thought you'd be gone for a week."

"Huh. I got just one thing to say to that shit: God bless my union brothers: United we stand, dividing those legs; puttin' it to the Man like only the union can. Hospital had to let me come back. Union made 'em."

"Hurray for you," she said distantly.

"Exactly," he agreed, apparently not picking up her tone. "I been thinking about what you said the other day." He made a dry smacking sound with his mouth, and then swallowed loudly, "You remember what you said?"

She wasn't sure if he was dumb or crazy or both, but went along and nodded. The best battle strategy with a man like him was to know when to fight, when to play possum, and when to play along.

She played along.

"I remember," she said into her pillow. Zoe didn't think she'd be able to rein in the scream that threatened to burst from her chest if she faced him. "But what do you think *they* would say if we were found out?"

"Shh, shh," he hushed her, smoothing hair back from her

face with a bandaged hand, "It's fine. I got a deal worked out with the night nurse. We sleep in shifts, see, so nobody would ever know." He added pressure to the hand on her head, pushing her into the pillow. "That is, unless *you* said something…" He let the statement hang and then removed his hand.

"No, Bud. I didn't mean the hospital staff," she said, rolling over. In the faint light of the fingernail moon, his eyes shone with a fevered glow. There was nothing more frightening than a stoned, stupid man, unless the stoned, stupid man was also insane. Zoe was no psychiatrist, but the voice of her Gift cried "cuckoo" and she wholeheartedly concurred.

After the split second diagnosis of her bedside patient, she took a stab in the dark. "Them," she said mystically. Holding his gaze was like trying to keep a fistful of sand. Each time she looked into his eyes, his own flicked down to her breasts.

"Them? Them, who?"

"My *friend* who told you to watch over me," she groped, she hoped, she lied. *In for a penny,* she thought, and continued before he could give the statement too much thought. "What if they have someone watching you watching me? They *could,* couldn't they?"

Bud retracted his hand and leaned past her to peer through the window's cast iron grating.

"Do you think so?" he said, then retreated to the shadows near the door. "He wouldn't do that to me. He trusts me. He said so."

Things were going so well Zoe took it a step further. "And what if they see you in my room every night? We should probably be careful about *that* too."

"Yeah, we need to work something out."

"Maybe when I get out you can take me out for a nice dinner."

"Naw," he said, raising his bandaged hands. "I don't think that'll be happening any time soon."

"Yeah." She grimaced at his twin wounds. "About that: I'm really sorry about your hands," she said, her voice sopping with sincerity. "I freaked and thought you were her."

He turned his hands before his face, as though just realizing they were there. "It's alright. I was mad at first—hurt like hell too—but I got over it. Gotta experience everything once in life, eh? I didn't know then you were marking me, marking me as yours, but it's cool. Besides," he grinned, "it'll be a hell of a conversation starter at parties, looking like Jesus come back from the mount."

Bud stood for a moment, said nothing more, then nodded as though he *did*, and turned and left.

After the door closed, Zoe sighed and sat up. She stared out the window, not really looking, not really seeing. After a few minutes of nothing, she lay down and closed her eyes.

~~oOo~~

The next morning, the once call girl/heroin addict, put her foot down—put both feet down—and took up her own cause.

It would only be a matter of time before Bud stirred himself up enough, and then what? Could she stop him? Would the hospital find out?

No. She couldn't flip that coin.

She recalled Bud saying she wouldn't be "getting out too soon". He sounded pretty sure of himself. *Does he know something I don't? Is there a way for him to make that happen?*

Even as her feet hit the floor, Zoe's gut knew the answers to those questions *and* what she needed to do. It was her brain that was having trouble dealing with it. She needed to escape. Simple and to the point, she had to get the fuck out of there...but how? How was she going to extricate herself from this place, a prison in all but name? She couldn't pull off an escape by herself. Aside from Cherry, the only people willing to help were already here.

And for that matter, how well did she really know *them*? Meat was nice; Danny too. As for Frye, well, he was cute. But were they sane enough? She liked them, sure, but what could they do to help her break out? It'd been a long time since she'd put her trust in anyone, but judging by how well *that* worked out, her replacement knights (as she now thought of them) were *it*.

And so it was that a very determined young woman with a very determined sway to her hips, marched into the games room, B-lined to the ping pong table, and snatched the ball out of the air between two of her three new knights.

"Lost serve," said a sweat-soaked Danny. "The ball didn't get here, so lost serve. Gimme the ball, Zoe."

Zoe tossed the ball to Danny, and then faced Meat. "I need to talk to you," she whispered. "In private."

Meat stood looking at her with delighted curiosity, while Danny served the ball. The ball struck Meat's shoulder and bounced off the table.

"Five-three," piped Danny. "Gimme the ball, Meat."

"You win, firebug. I gotta go talk to Zoe for a minute. Hide the ball 'til I get back."

He caught up with Zoe near the door, and fell in beside her. "What's up, chuck?

"Come on. I have a favor to ask."

"Now you went and did it," he said, without elaborating.

She glanced at his tented robe and immediately understood. "You're so fucking gross it hurts to look at you." But she looked again anyway. It was a sight that could never really get old. "You need help."

"Isn't that why we're here?"

~~oOo~~

Zoe told him everything, and he stayed silent and listened. By the end, his face was streaked with tears.

She almost cried too, when he said, "What are *we* going to do?" instead of what are *you* going to do? She knew she could count on him.

"I was hoping you might have a few ideas. Is there a way out of here?"

"Aren't you only here for another couple weeks? I'm sure

between me, Frye, and Danny, we can keep you safe, at least until you're out. I promise that prick won't ever touch you again." He said it matter-of-factly, but the look in his eyes said murder.

"No way. If one of you got hurt trying to help me…well, I don't think I could handle that right now. And something tells me they don't ever want me to leave here."

"Who?"

"Them," she said, waving her arms in the air. "The ubiquitous 'They.' And if I knew who *they* were, *they* would probably kill me for knowing."

Meat studied her for a couple of seconds, gave her a quizzical look, then said, "I don't know much about *They*, but if you want out of here, I know of somebody who might help. She busted out three times in the last two months."

Zoe leaned forward, "Well? Are you going to tell me, or do you want me to guess? Who is it?"

He thrust his hands in his pockets and wiggled his toes out the end of the gaping hole in his slipper, obviously stalling. He leveled his gaze at her and grinned. "Isn't Karma a hell of a thing?"

21

MISSION POSSIBLE

"Mary?" Zoe yelled the question, caught herself and whispered it again, "Mary, the psycho? Really?"

"Really."

"There's nobody else?"

Meat shook his head. "Not that I know of."

"Well, how come she keeps getting caught?" Zoe asked.

"She doesn't. She sneaks out for junk food or to see her boyfriend, then comes back on her own."

"Huh."

"Exactly," said Meat. "But nobody knows how the hell she does it. I think the orderlies even have a pool going as to how she does it. She just shows up at reception with a big grin on her face, like she's coming home from a date or something."

Mulling it over didn't take long. What other option did she have? "Okay, sold. Let's go talk to the crazy bitch."

~~oOo~~

Zoe didn't know what to expect, or if Mary would even tell her, but laughed herself sick after hearing girl's nonchalant four word response.

"I had a key."

"No, really. How'd you do it?"

"What? I used a key. The elevator doors opened, I left, had fun, then I came back. What the fuck is so funny about that?"

"Nothing," Zoe said. "I just thought it would be, I don't know, more elaborate."

"Elaborate!" Mary snorted. "Do you guys have any idea how hard it is to steal a key, then put it back before it's missed? No, you don't."

"Okay," Meat said. "So where'd you get it?"

Mary brushed past them, checked the hall, then bumped them again on the way back to her previous perch on the edge of the bed. "Not until you tell me why you need it."

Zoe stared at the girl for a long time. Long enough to realize she was going to have to tell her something. "Okay, but you gotta swear this to secrecy. If you tell a fucking soul, I'll...No," she turned to Meat, "I can't. I'm sorry, Meat, but I had a hard enough time telling you, and I *like* you."

"Come on, Zoe. She's all we got," he said. "Just tell her about Bud."

"Yeah, I guess he's all that really matters at this point, huh? Fine," she said to Mary, "I guess it wouldn't hurt."

So she did.

"Well?" Zoe asked the wooden faced girl. "What do you say? Where'd you get the key?"

"From Bud."

Zoe's chin dropped. "Really?"

"Yeah," said Mary. "The prick's so dumb he keeps two— one on his hip, and one in his locker."

"How the hell do you get into their locker room?" asked Meat. "That would be as hard as getting out in the first place."

Mary shrugged and offered a smug look. "Why the fuck would I go to all that trouble when he carries one on his belt?"

Zoe shook her head in disbelief. "You expect me to believe you just walk up and take the keys to the front door right off his belt?"

"The elevator," corrected Mary. "It's the only key you need."

"That still doesn't explain how you get it."

"To answer that," said Mary, "tell me what you have in your pockets—both of you."

They patted their pockets and came up empty. Mary reached into her own pockets and pulled out an assortment of objects.

"How'd you do that?" Zoe asked. She picked up the book, her phone card, and a used tissue. "That was cool."

"I take stuff. It's one of the *other* reasons I'm here."

Other reasons? Zoe couldn't understand how Mary had taken the book from her pocket without her feeling anything. "Fair enough. Can you get his key for me?"

"Yeah," Mary crossed her arms, "Right after you tell me why you *really* need it. After all the shit the other night about that Cannibalangelo motherfucker and the look on your face after my story about Clive, this can't only be about that dumbass, Bud."

Zoe pursed her lips and scowled. Her mother would have been proud.

"Come on, Zoe," Meat urged. "She can help."

Zoe sighed, "Fuck it. Sure." Then, without a once upon a time, she began at the beginning and told her. A quarter of the way through the telling, Danny and Frye joined them. After she finished, no one spoke right away.

Meat was the first to break the silence. "Well," he said. "Can we help her?"

"You want me to break Bud's neck?" offered Frye.

"Yeah," Danny said. "We could get him good. Maybe torch him, or, you know, whatever—just a thought."

These comments gave birth to more of the same, until each of them was talking over their neighbor, all with ideas and opinions that soon turned into a free for all forum in which nothing seemed taboo.

And so began the first meeting of what later became known among them as the "Retribution Club".

Zoe sat back at one point during the "meeting" and watched. Mary had jumped into the fray, having been dragged into the mob mindset that sprouted among the testosterone spewing males of the group, to lend a woman's perspective.

Unsure of whether it was the sleight of hand the girl was so gloriously adept in or the ease in which Mary fit in with "her" guys, but, astoundingly enough, Zoe was beginning to like the little bitch.

~~oOo~~

Over the next week, Zoe's merry band of mental patients tacked together quite an intricate plan to extricate her from the sticky situation in which she currently found herself stuck. There were call signs, hallway stakeouts, hoarded sundries, and a mountain of crayon drawings.

Danny recorded staff break times and reported back to Meat, who documented and cross referenced those times with...

Wait a minute, thought Zoe. *Didn't Mary just sneak out when nobody was looking?* She decided not to mention this fact to the rest of her group; they seemed to be having so much fun playing spy she couldn't bring herself to ruin it for them.

The sole other member not caught up in their elaborate plan was Mary, who, having voiced her opinion regarding the redundancy of their collective actions—often swearing profusely at the three young men as she did—finally gave up and focused on the important things: stealing Bud's key to the elevator and coordinating the escape with her boyfriend, Spider, who would meet Zoe in the underground parking lot and take her to a safe place.

Zoe was a little nervous about the last part. She knew why the boys were helping her. They were her friends, but Mary was not. Aside from the overly indulgent monologue she'd given after their fight, the girl hadn't strung together more than two sentences at a time, and said nothing of the life she'd led on the outside. She spoke of her current boyfriend, Spider, but only in relation to his part in Zoe's departure. After three days of looking up just to see Mary look away, Zoe decided it was time to ask the question that had been on the tip of her tongue from day one.

"Alright, Mary, I know why the three stooges are helping, but what's your story? Why are *you* doing this? For fun? Is this some sort of penance, or are you just bored?"

"Because," Mary replied with a dead pan stare, plucking at the words on her black tee shirt. It read: Mean people suck.

"Oh," Zoe said, more or less satisfied. "Thank you for your candor."

22

DOLL PARTS

Most people didn't like Monday, but Bud thought it was the best day of the week. Monday was easy crossword day: a day when even the simplest of men could finish the puzzle and bask in a glow of accomplishment. Of course, Monday's puzzle was the only one *he* ever did. The rest were for those Jeopardy nerds and only made him feel dumb for not watching the Discovery channel twenty hours a fucking day. Tuesday through Sunday he read the comics. That Dilbert was such a goof.

If it had been any other day but Monday, like a smarty pants Friday, he would've been reading at the nurses' station, comics spread before him on the desk—instead of there in the hall, on a stool—and wouldn't have overheard two young men speaking in whispers about his current love interest. Yup, any other day, like rocket scientist Saturday, he wouldn't have heard Zoe's name then three sentences later, his own.

Puzzle forgotten, Bud's pencil hovered over a three letter word for gorilla for about five minutes as a plan unfolded right around the corner from his perch. He knew the speakers by their voices, but they were just apes. It was to her he thrust his mind, her and her broken promise. His ears burned and his bundled hands shook with rage. How could he have been duped by his girl and her sweet little honey cunt lies?

Bud felt his gorge rise. He was going to throw up all over the comics before he had a chance to see if Dilbert would get his promotion. Now that the little bitch's plot was uncovered, he wanted the two boys to shut up and go away. If they stayed he might pound their dicks through the floor tiles, or something else that would cause him to get a real suspension this time.

To cool himself off, he closed his eyes and counted; a trick he'd seen shrinks teach to the loons. *One: shut up, get up, and get fucking gone! Two: quick now, boys, before I stomp on you. Three: I can't think of anything badass for three, but, Four: I'll spill your guts right out on the floor...*

From beyond his rhyming count, Bud heard his name again, and then the words "key" and "Mary". He jerked so fast he nearly fell from his stool. *So,* he thought. *That's how that little black haired slut was skipping out.* His anger deflated from the slow leak his pursed mouth provided as he imagined the bright side. He'd be the hero for uncovering the means by which the girl managed to escape, and the pool...

Fuck! It's my key. How can I tell anyone about this?

Even as his shoulders slumped and a sullen look descended across his broad face, a dim bulb sparked to life and gained brilliance along with the shit eating grin which replaced his sour masque du norm.

Imagined dollar signs replaced pupils and irises as his thoughts shifted to his benefactor; the man who'd promised him five-thousand dollars just to watch Zoe Beaupre. In watching, he'd gotten too close, and she'd played him for a proper fool. *Who's the fool now, bitch? I know your game. They wasn't watching out for you,* he said to her mental image, *they was just plain watching you. Oh, you're so gonna get it.*

Bud's internal crossword dictionary didn't hold the word "cozened", but that was how he felt right then—cheated and pissed off. The latter he'd deal with silently; if there was one area in which Bud excelled, it was following orders. He sure as hell wasn't about to blow the chance of banking some extra green at the little liar's expense. Cash was the cure for a lot of shit. It may even cure a bad case of pissed off. Given the nature of the web site belonging to his benefactor, Bud imagined how the girl would be dealt with and assuaged his hurt feelings with those very promising, brutal images.

Hell, he thought. *They might even let me watch while they do her.*

A-P-E, he penciled into the provided blocks, and then looked at his watch. The rest of the night was going to pass like an ass rape, but at least he had his paper. Nothing kept Bud from the Monday puzzle.

~~oOo~~

Gideon swiveled away from his desk after hanging up with the idiot orderly. The man's information had been quite disturbing. *What could the girl possibly find so frightening within the walls of such an institute that it would call for escape? Is it you, Bud? Have you been a naughty boy?*

He could speculate all day, but didn't actually care enough to do that. The girl's reasoning didn't matter. She couldn't be allowed to leave. Zane would have to understand.

And this was how he justified his next phone call: Nothing more than a friendly intervention, an executive decision which would make things easier for all involved, even the girl. *What sort of future could a heroin addicted prostitute expect, anyway? None. And if by some remote possibility disease or drugs didn't kill her by thirty, she'd grow old and fat, living in squalor and sucking at the teat of Uncle Sam—and who would that benefit? Certainly not her.*

"Yeah?" queried the voice from the earpiece.

"Am I speaking with Spike?"

"Hang on a sec." Muffled sounds preceded a muted shout of, "Dad, pick up the phone," and then the faint response: "Ask who it is."

Gideon spoke before the man could relay the message. "Tell your father I'm an old friend with some work I think would be right up his alley."

Again, the receiver was covered and Gideon listened as the

young man translated, "Dad. Get the phone." ...unintelligible response... "I don't know. Some guy who says he used to bowl with you or something."

Seconds later an extension was picked up. "Who is it? Hang up, Adam. I got it."

Gideon waited until he heard a click, and then drawled, "Spike. How have you been? Still trying to keep those two boys of yours from killing the cat?"

"Your line secure?"

"Of course, what do you take me for?"

"Can't never be too careful. They're everywhere."

"Calm down, Spike. You're too high strung." Gideon imagined the other man clutching the phone in both hands, his gaze darting around the room like a cornered squirrel. "Or, should I say *careful?* Listen, Spike, I have a task that requires a certain amount of stealth...which is why I thought of you. Are you available, or shall I call someone else?"

"I'm listening."

Without offering up any back story (partly because he knew Spike wouldn't care to know the girl's particulars), Gideon gave him the girl's name and the contact number for the orderly. Then he asked Spike if he'd mind capturing the act on film for him.

This wasn't a normal request for a man like Spike. Spike Schrickt was strictly an eraser. But he *was* cheaper than an actor, and Gideon didn't feel he should waste any more money on the Canadian whore than necessary.

"Sure, I'll film it, but it'll cost you. And I'll need help. You'll pay for that extra like."

Excellent. "Would you like me to see if I can find someone?" he asked, knowing the little man would turn him down.

"No way," Spike said. "I want my boys with me if'n I'm gonna do it. That okay?"

The doctor smiled into the darkness of his study. "That would be splendid. It warms my heart to see a family work together."

"When?"

"As soon as possible. You see, the young woman is planning—"

"Don't care. The less I know the better."

"That's fine."

"One thing, though," said Spike. "I got my own tools, but ain't got no video camera. I ain't buying one just for this job, neither, so you're gonna have to bone up for one of those in advance."

In the dim glow provided by his computer screen, Gideon spied a stockpile of video equipment on the shelf below the D thru G section of his movie collection. "I'll leave everything you'll need in the regular spot. Do you remember the place?"

"I do."

"Fine. That's fine." Gideon replaced the receiver, relit his cigar, and relaxed back into his soft leather chair. To the computer screen, he said, "Finally." *This should have been done weeks ago. You'll see, Zane.*

Thinking of Zane made him wonder how his favorite actor was spending his forced vacation.

~~oOo~~

Two days later, Gideon found out just what his favorite Manimal had been up to.

Luckily for him, Zane called his cell instead of the office. Given his agitated state, he would have scared Erica half out of her mind; Zane's end of the conversation consisted of tortured wails and feral grunts, mingled with the word 'demon'. Gideon hoped Zane wasn't referring to him. That would be bad. It seemed a house call was in order.

~~oOo~~

Mouth wrapped around the wet end of a dead stogie, Gideon stood on the sidewalk in front of a two storey brownstone as a van backed into the driveway. Otto Gruber stepped down from the driver's side of the vehicle and approached him. The man wore coveralls with the same insignia as the side of the truck, complete with a phone number as false as the name on the door.

"Doktor," The big man grunted.

Gideon nodded in greeting and plucked the cigar from his mouth. "How was traffic?"

"Not bad for the lunch hour rush." Otto raised a hand to shade his eyes from the sun. Together, they stood facing the house; Gideon fidgeting with his cigar and the large German kneading his back muscles.

"Have you been inside?"

"No." Gideon chuckled nervously. "I was waiting for you."

Otto squinted sidelong at him. "Ah, I see. So today is the day, then?" He pulled a thumb, quick as lightning, across his throat.

Gideon raised his hands, palms out, as if to say *Whoa*. "I hope not. Not today, anyway. I don't really know what to expect when we get inside and it wouldn't hurt to have you here, if you know what I mean."

"Will there be a mess like the last time, Doktor?"

Standing next to Otto, Gideon, who was six-two himself, felt like a child in the shadow of a giant. "Your guess is as good as mine. All I could ascertain from his phone call was that he'd been 'a bad boy'. Take from that what you will, but it does us no good out here." The doctor gestured toward the house. "Shall we?"

Otto's scarred face widened into a grin. "After you."

"Very funny," Gideon said. "I'll wait on the porch."

"Ya, I suppose you will," the big German shot back, and entered the house.

The doctor waited.

And waited.

After five minutes he became acutely aware of his high visibility, and the late afternoon sun—which seemed to focus its heat right onto the back of his neck. When Otto reemerged, Gideon fought the urge to dive past him and slam the door.

"I hope, for the sake of your suit, you have non slip shoe

bottoms, Herr Doktor."

Gideon's heart skipped a beat as he elbowed past Otto. "Is it bad?"

Otto shrugged. "See for yourself. Your Zane is in the kitchen." His face split in a wide grin. "He was not kidding around about being a bad boy. Come. Come see."

They needed to trek no more than a few feet inside the door for a taste of the marvelous horrors that lay beyond the front hall. A blood splattered satchel lay overturned near Otto's feet. Its contents, mostly pamphlets, had spilled out and were strewn down the hall—some stuck in gobs or dried puddles of blood. Several distinct handprints of varying sizes ran sporadically along the walls and floor; pasted like a kindergarten art project in a pattern only the artist would understand. Gideon bent and picked up one of the booklets from the satchel. Its cover held the word Watchtower. He let it fall from his fingers and followed Otto down the hall and through the kitchen door.

The charnel smell was so overwhelming Gideon gagged and plugged his nose. So far, though, during their walk from the front hall, there'd been no bodies to account for the copious amount of blood covering almost every visible surface. Gideon would have to keep wondering; the only body in the kitchen still had a pulse.

Naked except for his socks, Zane Ellis sat in a metal kitchen chair, covered from head to toe in his medium, holding his head in his hands. An oblong puddle of drool had collected on the table beneath his chin, and his open eyes stared vacantly across the room. At his elbow sat a blood encrusted cordless telephone.

Otto took a step toward Zane, but the doctor called him back. "Hold on. I brought a tranquilizer gun," he said, and pulled a gun from his coat pocket and shot a dart into Zane's throat, just to the left of his Adam's apple. "Okay. Go ahead, but be careful."

Zane's response to the dart was a miniscule twitch of an eye as it struck him.

Otto retrieved the telephone, licked his thumb, and wiped blood from the screen. "It has been off the hook, Herr Doktor."

"Probably been like that since he called me. Hit redial, like a good lad, won't you?"

"It is your cellular number," said the German, and showed him. "Shall I wake him?" He held his hand poised behind Zane, ready to slap him in the back of the head.

"No, leave him for now. Let the sedative do its work while we see what mischief he's been up to behind my back."

Now that Zane had been sedated, Gideon relaxed. He strode to the dining room door and pushed. It moved about a foot before striking something soft yet unyielding. He put his shoulder to the door and pushed harder. It moved grudgingly at first, then easier as the sound of ripping Velcro signified whatever blocked the door was freed from its resting place.

He'd found the body—or *bodies*, if he was correct. Given the amount of pieces, the only way to tell would be to do a head count. Literally. The doctor whistled softly as he gingerly tiptoed through two lips and part of a nose that lay amid a coiled bundle of chewed intestines. To look at the carnage, Gideon couldn't imagine any two strong men, never mind one, being able to do what Zane had done to this/these person/people.

Mangled doll parts, thought Gideon. *This looks like a little girl's bloody, raging temper tantrum.* "Oh, Zane," he said and chuckled grimly. "You really *are* my favorite Manimal."

From over his shoulder, Otto said, "It is a very large mess, yes? Look there, in the light fixture. I believe those are fingers...and—*yes*—an eyeball." He slapped the Doctor jovially on the back. "I do so like him, this Zane of yours, but not so much the cleaning. Do not worry; I have called for my boys to join us for the tidying. I hope you do not mind, Herr Doktor?"

"Do you trust them?"

"Why else would I call them?" Otto seemed hurt. "Did you believe that I would, zip zip," he waved his arms, "and all of this would disappear? Do not worry." He thumped his broad chest. "Me and mine will fix this for you."

"Apologies, my large friend." Gideon soothed him. "I wasn't thinking...I'm sure you have everything well in hand."

"Ya, my little piggies will feed well tonight." He pointed to the opposite wall. "Did you see that yet? He is brilliant, yes?"

Gideon followed the other man's gaze to the indicated wall. When he realized what he was seeing, his mouth dropped open. A floor-to-ceiling mural covered the entire wall; the work carried a depth that belied the use of just one color, and the attention to detail was inherent in every shadow or eyelash, cloud or tree. Each movement of the eye carried one effortlessly, inexplicably, toward the figure at the center of the painting, as though the artist pushed you there physically: at the center stood no angel, although she was beautiful enough. The face which stared back at Gideon was none other than the whore, Zoe Beaupre. The hair was longer and the face too slender to be the sister. Yes, he was sure of it—it was the whore.

"May I keep it?"

"What?"

"Truly glorious, is it not? Herr Doktor?"

"That's fine," said Gideon. "Take whatever you like." He barely registered the question. This picture was a bad sign. What Gideon thought to be mere fixation on Zane's part was something more. The boy seemed to be obsessed.

"Danke." Otto moved closer to the mural.

Gideon reentered the kitchen and approached Zane. The cannibal still drooled, still stared at nothing. "Otto," Gideon called over his shoulder. "We need to move him somewhere safe until this is cleaned up."

"I will be back. I have the Pandora box out in the van."

The "Pandora box" was a large chest on wheels, big enough for a man, with false drawer fronts and tools hanging from hooks along the outside. Gideon had seen it used for similar operations many times. The chest was lined with epoxy, and was thick enough to muffle the most persistent wails from anyone unfortunate enough to be alive upon entry.

Otto rolled the cart up to the table and pried the lid away. The lingering odor of death, fear and bodily excretions rose in an almost tangible cloud. As Otto dumped Zane into the box, Gideon wondered if he'd wake before reaching their destination. Just to be sure, he fished the tranquilizer gun from his pocket and shot Zane once more...for luck.

23

THE KEY

Zoe sat reading the same page for ten minutes. She felt restless, wanted to move, to do something, but couldn't concentrate long enough to decide on any one activity, so there she sat.

She placed her thumb between the pages of her woodpecker book as her eyes strayed to the window. Something was coming...something bad. There was no way for her to know this, but the uneasiness she'd felt the day before as nothing more than a minor ache, had amplified overnight into a throbbing, festering pain. It was as though her little voice had found itself a megaphone.

And then there was the ever present Bud, who quietly followed her every movement. If she was in the common room, he was on the stool near the door; if she was in the shower room, he would just happen to walk by as she exited.

And his eyes...his eyes had darkened in a way that made Zoe sense that he, too, knew evil was on the way. He'd not spoken a word to her in days or given any indication her fears were justified, but in his nightly visits he remained as regular as a bran fed pigeon.

When the uneasiness first settled over her she'd wanted to lay the meat portion of the blame on the persistent monkey, who'd been alternately pacing and beating the stuffing out his threadbare chest. As the days wore on, she doubted he was responsible. Sure, there were times when the monkey wailed at her like a trailer park stepfather, but she'd fought back through diversion. Whether it was the confusing woodpecker book or any one of her newfound friends, she'd been victorious...*so far.*

Besides, the monkey, in all of his many incarnations, had been so close for so long that he was as familiar to her as her own face in the mirror. No. Whatever this new sensation was, it was something *different*, and she did *not* want to be there when it arrived.

She needed to find Mary.

Each day since the first ad hoc "Retribution Club" meeting, Zoe questioned Mary regarding her progress in acquiring Bud's key, but each query was met with a frustrated gaze and a magic eight ball style answer: not today, or, the time may not be right, etcetera and so on, until the girl stopped answering all together.

Mary was playing chess with an old woman when Zoe found her. Before she could ask about the key, Mary cut her off with a narrowed gaze that said: *Don't say a fucking word. Not one.* Aloud, she said something that nearly stopped Zoe's heart.

"I think he knows."

"What do you mean?" Dread tugged her belly into a squirming, hot knot. In a panic, she thought, *How could you get the key any god damned time you want a Pepsi from the store, but when it's a matter of life or death you come up empty?*

"I mean," snarled the Goth girl, "that his hand hasn't strayed further than an inch from his fucking keys in a week. God, you'd think the ring was his dick he's been fondling it so much. And he's had this smug fuc—"

"Mary."

"-king look on his face. Like: *I'm the fucking man. Look at—*"

"Mary!"

"What?"

Zoe pointed to the old woman at her left, holding a finger to her lips. "Should you be saying shit like this in front of grandma?"

"Her? She's a vegetable, see?" Mary clapped her hands in

front of the old woman's nose. "A regular head of lettuce."

"So why are you playing chess with her?"

"I'm not. I don't even know how to play," Mary said, then double jumped her black bishop over the white queen and a pawn.

Zoe tilted her head and grimaced. "So what are you doing, then?"

"It's almost shift change," Mary said with a look of determination. "He should be here any minute."

Zoe toyed with a plastic button on her pj's as her gaze shifted to the double paned, steel reinforced bay window. From where she stood, she could see the late afternoon sun as it fell behind the trees. Time was short: Zoe's tiny voice had taken on the pleading bleat of a condemned lamb. Tonight was the night she escaped, or not at all.

She placed her hand over Mary's. "Whether you get it or not, thanks for trying." Satisfied she'd conveyed all she needed, Zoe removed her hand.

"Holy melodrama, Batman. Take a chill pill, bitch. I'll get it. Don't worry your little blonde, bimbo head." She pocketed a few chess pieces, flicked Zoe a reassuring grin, then her gaze returned to the staff change room. "What's so special about tonight, anyway?"

"You wouldn't believe me if I told you."

"Try me. I've seen all kinds of shit you could never imagine."

"Um, don't think I'm nuts, but—"

"Nuts? Look around, chick."

"You know what I mean." Zoe slid into the chair beside her and told her of every incident—including the time with the hooker who took her place at a party—that the little voice had saved her ass. At the end of the story she looked at Mary, who was still watching the staff entrance with the tenacity of a pit bull waiting for the mailman. "Well, do you think I'm bonkers?"

"Who am I to say?" Mary shot her a fast smile. "Strange shit happens all over the world every day. My boyfriend

Spider's the one you should ask about that stuff. He's a regular walking, talking encyclopedia of shit nobody cares about."

"Thanks," Zoe said as she stood to leave, "for everything."

"Don't worry. He's gotta look away sometime, right? I got another hour left of phone time, so I'll call Spider in a few minutes and let him know you want to skip out tonight. I think he's got everything you need—clothes, too. Ain't he the sweetest?"

"Can't wait to meet him."

Zoe headed for her room in the same fashion she had on her first day: head down and counting floor tiles. Once in her room she turned out the light and crossed to the window to wait. She scouted each passing car, every pedestrian, ever searching. For *what* she didn't know, but thought she'd know when she saw it.

Six-thirty: Two and a half hours until lights out.

The monkey was nowhere to be found. That was too bad; she could've used some of his kind of distraction right about then. Maybe he knew she was a goner and didn't want to stick with a sinking ship?

Prick.

~~oOo~~

One hour to lights out and still no key. Mary came to Zoe's door, shrugged, then disappeared back into the hall. Soon, a nurse would stop by with the night time meds. If Mary hadn't returned by then, it would seem that all bets would be more than off, they'd be lost. So sure of Mary's abilities, Zoe never put any thought into a plan B scenario.

Exhausted and giddy, she turned her thoughts to Bud. Between his clockwork visits and her preternatural fear of whoever was coming for her, she hadn't slept more than an hour in the past two nights. Helpless and alone, she buried her face in her pillow and cried.

The unmistakable scuff of slippered feet outside the room roused her from misery, and she sat up. Her disappointment at seeing it was Meat, and not Mary, must have shown, because he halted mid step when their eyes met.

"Want me to come back later?"

"No, come in. I was just hoping you were Mary."

Eyes wide, he asked, "Still nothing? Don't you plan on leaving, like, tonight? Cutting it kind of close, aren't you?"

"You think?"

They both looked up at the sound of a cart rolling down the hall.

"She might still get it, you know," Meat whispered. "I better go. Everything's gonna be golden. You'll see." On the way out, he nearly fell over the cart at the sight of its pusher.

"Shouldn't you be in your room, Mr. Berry?" Bud asked, as he wheeled the cart into Zoe's room.

"Yeah, I was just leaving. Say, are you allowed to be serving our cocktails, Bud?"

Over his shoulder, Bud said, "Goodbye, Mr. Berry," then waited a few seconds before turning back to Zoe. His smile was so wide Zoe swore she could see his back teeth.

"Hello, darlin'. Miss me?"

Zoe backed up until her leg bumped the bed. "Where's the nurse?"

"Thought I'd help out tonight," he said, scratching one bandaged hand with the other. "A little good will goes a long way, as they say. You seem upset, Miss Beaupre...something wrong?"

"Nope, nothing wrong here, but there's something I'd like to ask if you don't mind."

He backed up, dipped his head out the door, and then returned to the center of the room. "Sure. What's on your mind?"

"Well, you've seemed...I dunno...a little distant this week. Did I do something to change your mind about after I get out?" She stifled a burp as bile forced its way past her throat. "Sorry. Spaghetti does that to me."

"Why don't we talk about that some other time? Here," he said, and held out a plastic cup with her room number scrawled on the side. "Take your pills. I still have sixteen patients to go before lights out, so get 'em in ya."

After she'd made no move to take the cup, he shook it. "Come on, Miss Beaupre," he said. "Look. If you're worried about me dosing you, spit 'em out after I leave, but the nurse says I can't leave 'til you take these. Just take 'em."

His assurances did nothing to ease her fears. There was something going on but Zoe couldn't figure out his game, or if there even *was* one. She wanted to take the cup just so he'd go away, but her legs rebelled.

"Come on," he snapped. "Pretty please, with sugar and strawberries on it. Take the fucking cup."

The change in his tone liberated her legs, and she stood to reach for the cup. With a murmured apology on her lips, she closed her fingers on it, and then jerked as pain shot up her arm.

When she'd put her hand out to take the cup, Bud cut her exposed wrist with a shard of glass, then dropped it on the floor.

She gaped at the gash, then at the sliver of glass. Blood welled along the length of the cut and ran freely to the floor. Her mouth opened, working on words that wouldn't come. For reasons that probably dated back to her childhood in Canada—under the iron fist of Martha Stewart's evil twin, Natalie Beaupre—she cupped her hand and attempted to catch the blood before it hit the floor.

Bud shoved her by the face back onto her bed, and she made no move to defend herself. "Betcha didn't see that coming, did you?" he hissed down at her. "Whatcha gonna do now, you lying cunt? You thought you were so fucking smart, but I guess you're not smarter than ol' Buddy Hawkins. No sir. You really shoulda been nicer to me, you know." He nodded smugly as he reached for his radio.

"Yeah," chhhhhh. "I'm in room 719." chhhhhh. "I think the girl is trying to kill herself." Cchhhhhh. "No. She cut her wrist! Oh God..." chhhhhh. "Get someone down here with a gurney, fast..."

Zoe only registered pieces of what Bud said. She was held rapt by the flood of blood leaving her body. The flow was so captivating, she couldn't peel her eyes away; it was both mesmerizing and terrifying at the same time. The initial pain of the cut dulled, leaving her numb, and the panic that previously held her static poured out along with the blood, heightening her drowsiness, but also lending relief.

Am I dying?

If this is it...it isn't so bad.

Her mind tuned in, then out, as a second blurry form hustled into the room. Fragments of conversation swirled through her mind in incoherent chunks.

"...'s wrong with h..."

"...just the way I found..."

"...not much blood. She should be fine..."

"...infirmary..."

Fine.

That word stuttered throughout her as hands closed on her, turning her, lifting, up, up, and over.

Fine.

Fine is good, right?

So why does it scare the shit out of me?

"...k god you found her, Bud..."

Futilely, she fought the invisible weight of unconsciousness as it wrapped her in its demanding embrace. *Wake up, goddammit! You're fine. You heard the nurse; not much blood... Open your eyes.*

you...

can't...

let...

them...

...

win

~~oOo~~

"I think she's awake," said a fuzzy ball hovering before her face. Zoe strained to see the figure clearly as it bobbed and spoke. "Here, hold her arm while I clean it. Now, Bud! Get over here."

Although still a blur, Zoe recognized the voice of Gert, the night nurse, and relaxed as the woman went on in a clipped, professional tone. "Bud. Get a hold of yourself and take her arm. I need to get it covered before we move her."

Gert's face slipped back to a holding pattern over Zoe's head. "Miss?" she said, prying Zoe's eyelids back, then turned toward a blur across the room, "What's her name? Do you know?"

"Zoe."

"Fine, now get over here and help me with *Zoe*."

Nurse Gert bent down. "Zoe? Can you hear me, honey?"

A slight nod took most of her strength, then gravity turned her head toward the figure holding her arm. Somewhere between a silent scream and a whisper, she mouthed, "Bud...cut...my...wrist."

"She's delusional," Bud said. "It could be the blood loss, but she was spouting paranoid shit like that before she cut herself."

"Hold her," Gert snapped, then turned to Zoe. "We're going to get you to the infirmary. You'll be fine. We're going to take care of you."

She must have felt Zoe tense up, because she amended her statement. "*I'll* take care of you." She shined a motherly smile down at her. "I promise."

Zoe trusted her. She had to. The sand man would have her and nothing would loosen his hold, so she clothed herself in the nurse's last words and allowed sleep's master to carry her away...to the infirmary, to dreamland, with a guardian named Gert.

~~oOo~~

Zoe awoke to a hand closing over her mouth. Her eyes shot open and a scream stood poised to shatter past the clammy fingers. Strapped to the bed as she was, she had but one defense against the silhouetted figure: her teeth. She bit into the hand with enough force to pop her jaw.

The hand was yanked back. Then a backlit head emerged from behind the curtain to her left. "Zoe! God dammit, it's me, Mary. Shh."

"Oh God, Mary," Zoe sizzed back. "I think I pissed myself. What the fuck?"

"Shh. Shut up, stupid." Mary ducked behind the curtain again. "What the fuck me? What the fuck you, Zoe! You bit me!"

"But—"

"Quiet. The nurse is right down the hall. We don't have time, so shut up and listen: I got the key and I'm gonna—"

"Wait a minute. How'd you get out? The doors are electronically locked."

"No time," replied Mary. She bent close, but kept an eye on the door. "Let's just say it was a challenge and leave it at that, 'kay? You're getting out of here tonight if I gotta chew through that elevator door myself." She held Zoe's gaze long enough to give her hand a firm squeeze. "I'll be back when nurse Gert goes for her nap. That'll be in about an hour."

"Wait—nap?" Zoe whispered. "Hey, at least loosen the straps for me."

"Sure," said Mary, obliging her. "Now shut up and relax, you're in good hands." Then she slipped out the door.

Relax, she thought, rolling her eyes. *Relax* wouldn't happen until she was miles away from this place. Whether it was Bud, Simply Bob, that cannibal dude, or a pink bunny with solid gold fangs and a chainsaw for a cock, something wicked was this way coming and she wanted to be long gone before it came.

She sat up and opened the leg restraints. Her eyes fell to the tray beside the bed. On the tray were a curved sewing needle, an opened roll of gauze, and a small pair of surgical scissors. At hearing footsteps in the hall, she snatched up the scissors and managed to lie down and tug the sheet over her arms before

Gert rounded the corner.

Bustling quietly into the darkened infirmary, Nurse Gert walked over to the bed, smoothed the sheet and pulled it up to her chin. She ran a hand across Zoe's forehead, "tsk"-ed twice, then left the room.

Zoe fingered the cool metal of the blunt scissors. Things were looking up, but she had a long way to go. Scissors in hand, she eased herself from the bed and then held onto the rail until the room stopped spinning. Once it had, she headed for the locked glass cabinets that ringed the room.

It was time to do a little shopping.

24

GOING THE DISTANCE

Bud's entire body tingled with anticipation. Part of that might have been the pain pills he'd been liberally munching on all day, but he suspected it had more to do with the fact that the little bitch was gonna get what was coming to her. *"Tonight's the night"* had been his silent phrase for the day.

His benefactor hadn't gone into detail, but Zoe Beaupre was gonna die screaming at roughly twelve o'clock, and he was gonna to be there to see it. Live! He wanted to pinch himself to see if he was dreaming, but didn't for fear he might be. His instructions had been simple but explicit: 1) Get the girl to the infirmary by whatever means necessary, and 2) leave his spare elevator key on the front tire of his car in the underground parking lot. The rest would be taken care of by the pros. He'd guaranteed his benefactor that he'd be alone at the nurses' station when the men came, but that would all depend on whether Nurse Gert took her nightly nap on time.

Simple shit: Even an ape couldn't fuck it up.

Soon, Gert would be going for her nap. She hadn't missed a single nap in the three years they'd shared the night shift, so there was no reason to expect her to change her habits now.

Nurse Gert reamed him out for ten full minutes after she tucked the bitch in at the infirmary. She'd defended the girl and berated *him* for not showing more compassion in the face of an obvious cry for help, yada yada, and etcete-fucking-ra.

Unbelievable!

He'd held his tongue, even though he wanted to tell her to fuck off and mind her own garden. *Goody goody bitch,* he thought, then wondered if he could throw those guys an extra couple a bucks to do the cunt nurse while they were there.

Bud swiveled in his chair and watched Gert as she worked. He studied her, fantasizing about how *he'd* kill her if he were one of the characters from his benefactor's web site. Bitterly, he reminded himself she was the first person to insult him, to make him feel stupid or less than a man. *She thinks she's too good for her shoes, she does! And what about two years ago at Christmas, at the secret Santa gift exchange?* Someone wrapped a stick of deodorant and gifted it to him. No need to guess who it was.

Suddenly the fantasy question of how he'd kill her became "Why haven't I killed the old bitch *yet?*"

Bud narrowed his eyes at the back of the woman's head, but spoke casually: "You going first tonight or me?" Sometimes she let him take a nap first, but not often.

"I don't think I'll go tonight, Bud. The girl may wake up and it would be better for all involved if I were the one to see to her. You understand, don't you?" Without waiting, she answered for him. "Sure you do. Feel free to go now, if you like." She put down her pen and turned, staring down her nose at him. "As long as all your work is done, that is."

Ooh, I'd love to leave a fist sized dent in that smarmy fucking mug.

"Of course." His eyes wandered to the clock. "Doors are all secured, and there's not a soul awake 'cept you and me." He dropped his pen and kicked it under his desk. As he bent to pick it up, he pulled the phone cord from its wall jack.

He yawned. "Yeah, I might do that. Just need to finish up with old Garfield here." Instead of reading the comics, he drew an axe cleaving the air just above the fat cat's head, complete with a penciled in caption above the picture that read "WHOOSH – SPLAT!!"

Why did you pull the phone cord? It's not like you're gonna go through with it, he chided himself. *You're no killer, just some pussy with an Internet connection and a love for reality TV.*

He'd never answered himself before, but this was special. *Man up, boy. Whose fault is it she's too stupid to go for a nap? You gave her a chance, yes indeedy-dee. Kill the cunt. Why should them fellas coming for the little liar have all the fun?*

~~oOo~~

Zoe was no car burglar, but the small locks on the cabinets kept no secrets from the sturdy little pair of scissors. Each cabinet held a better weapon than the one before. She'd traded up three times, finally settling for a straight edged knife and two capped needles filled with liquid procaine, a fast-acting local anesthetic.

She'd hoped this would end up nothing more than needless diversion, an activity to occupy her until Mary returned, but paranoia and instinct warned otherwise. The panic that filled her earlier had simmered away, leaving a caramelized form of resolution; fear remained, but inaction was no longer an option.

More than once, she caught herself grinding her teeth as her mind's eye flicked back to a particular locker: The dispensary. Her mouth watered but, with no small amount of self control, she'd closed the drawer.

Weapons secured, she crept back to her bed to wait. Mary said she'd be back in an hour. Zoe guessed it'd been forty-five minutes, so that left roughly fifteen minutes—sixteen minutes too long, as far as she was concerned. And she *was.*

She laid the long knife just below her left hand and grasped a syringe in each fist, a thumb on each cap, ready to flick them off in a blink. This act in itself calmed her somewhat, and pacified the monkey enough to shut him up. Somewhere in the darkness, an unseen clock patiently stammered along, supplying a one to four base line compliment to the staccato snare drum caged in her ribs.

Tat tat tat tick, tat tat tat tock.

~~oOo~~

Each time Bud tensed to stand he lost his nerve and slumped back into the chair. He couldn't even focus on Garfield. He'd read the same dialogue balloon at least twenty times.

When the time finally came, Gert made up his mind for him.

"I've decided to go on record with the administrator regarding the accusations the girl made against you. You might want to start thinking about how you're going to answer for your actions."

On the shelf beside the radio was an old paint chipped bowling pin. None of the staff knew the exact story of how it came to be there. Maybe a patient had brought it in, or perhaps it was a former worker's souvenir from a perfectly bowled game. Bud didn't really give a shit, but couldn't help but wonder, as he wrapped his hand around its neck, if it had been left for him, for that very moment.

He hefted it with one hand; it was heavier than it looked and hardened by years of pounding. It was beautiful. In his fist the bowling pin wasn't a weapon, it was an extension of his hate. After two practice swings he addressed the stout nurse from just over her shoulder. "Guess what, Gert?"

"What?"

She didn't even respect him enough to look at him. *Good.*

"I know you were the one who gave me a deoderant that year for Christmas."

That got her attention. As she turned, her irritation flexed into jaw dropping shock a split second before the bowling pin connected with the left side of her head.

Bud jumped and rolled with her onto the floor, and straddled her rodeo style. He pummeled her with furious home run swings and didn't stop until the bowling pin was slick with gore. It slipped from his cramping fingers like a wet bar of soap and clattered to the floor. He reached to retrieve it, but slipped in the ever expanding pool of blood and fell across her body. Drunk with adrenaline, he lay there panting, unable to catch his breath.

Outside the room, silence reigned. His breath came in ragged gasps. Every nerve was aflame and he felt invincible. *What a fucking rush!*

"Whoa," he said, after slipping and falling backward again. "Oh Gert," he chuckled, prodding the dead woman with the toe of his blood drenched shoe. "Why you old alley cat. That was almost as good as sex."

"Man oh man," He wiped blood from his eyes, "I'm so stoked, I could..."

Really go for a good fuck right now. He stood and walked to the door.

With one last look at Gert, Bud set out down the hall. His wet sneakers squished and squeaked, echoing the story of his passing upon the checked tiles like a thousand screaming mice.

Bud be nimble,
Better be quick.
You ain't got long,
So dip that wick.

He stepped through the doorway of the infirmary and flipped on all the lights. "Hey, Zoe, got a few minutes?"

~~oOo~~

Zoe envisioned many scenarios in the minutes leading up to Bud's entrance. In each, she'd been as cool handed as Luke, as quick as Bruce Lee, and almost as witty with one-liners as Arnold Schwarzenegger—and since they were *her* daydreams, victory had been hers. But then the lights came on and he came for her with a voice as serene as a midnight lake.

Bud hunched toward her like a freshly bathed demon. When he reached the foot of the bed, he straightened and ran both hands through his hair, sending flakes and globs of some dark liquid to the floor in chunky splats and a slower shower of rust colored dandruff.

He smeared his blood soaked hands on his equally bloody trousers. "There. Did I get it all?"

"You missed a little on your ear," she said, her voice shaking. "If you loosen my straps, I can get it for you."

"No problem." He reached for the blanket.

Her grip on the syringes was so tight she feared she might crack the plastic casings. *That's right, a little closer, pull the blanket down. Come on, stud...come on.*

"Gotcha." He balled both hands into fists, brought them together, and hammer-punched her in the stomach. Then he stood back and smiled as she gasped for air.

"No." He waggled a finger in her face. "I don't think we'll do that, my little liar. As a matter of fact, I don't think I want to look at your lying, little liar face." Then he shrugged off his sweater and tossed it over her head.

The coppery tang of blood filled her mouth and nose, and she shook the sweater from her face. While he fumbled with the buckle on his pants, she alternately squeezed her eyes shut and opened them wide in an effort to clear them of the clotting blood left by the sweater.

"Okay. You wanna watch? Fine. Just keep your fucking mouth shut, hear?" He faltered, and then let out a breath. "Okay. Here's the thing: In about five minutes you're gonna be dead. I know, I know. It sucks." He dropped his pants. "But why not have a little fun before you die?" He shuffled closer, his pants bunched in a soggy brown ring around his tennis shoes. "Right? So? Have some fun?"

He didn't expect an answer, and Zoe didn't think she could say anything anyway.

As he touched the sheet, she took a breath and held it.

As he pulled the sheet away from her neck, she popped the plastic caps.

As he freed the sheet past her elbows, she tensed.

As he released the sheet, Zoe lashed out.

Her arms swung in a double haymaker and met at his stomach. One needle buried itself to the hilt and she jammed her thumb down on the plunger, dumping its payload in less than a second. The other stabbed through the bandage on his hand and pinned that hand to his thigh. The second syringe, still full, flew from her grasp as he yanked his hand back, breaking the needle off in his leg.

"What was that? What the fuck was that!" He raised his hand to his face. "Aw, fuck. You stabbed me in my hole…right in the…" He staggered forward and lunged drunkenly as the contents of the first syringe coursed through his already hopped up system. "…hand," he slurred. "You cund. Ah wul kill ooo."

"I didn't catch that." She put her hand to her ear. "Did you say 'step on my balls and pull my hair'? Sure, Bud. Sounds like fun." Adrenaline had taken her and it was empowering. "Anything you say." Zoe deflected a clumsy punch and launched a kick into his frozen groin. "Whoops. I bet that hurt. Did that hurt, Bud? Are we having *fun* yet?"

Bud crumpled like a paper doll, and she rolled out of the bed and stepped past him. Standing over him, she said, "You know what, Bud?"

Bud couldn't seem to form words. He blinked.

"You were right. That *was* fun. Thanks."

25

THE WAITING ROOM

From outside the infirmary, a soul piercing wail shocked Zoe back from triumph. The scream lasted long enough to become annoying, and then died. In its wake came the confused, abruptly roused, answering moans from behind many locked doors.

Spurred into action by the scream, she grabbed the knife from the bed. Bud's eyes followed her as she moved about the room. She hit him with a sour glare. "You look at me one more time, I'm gonna cut your eyes out of your fucking head. You got that, freak?"

Acutely aware of his situation, he squeezed his eyes shut.

Aside from the questioning wails of scattered patients awakened by the scream, the hall was silent—spooky silent. *Where's the nurse?* There should have been *something*...a struggle, footsteps...anything but silence. Zoe crept toward the door while images of characters far worse than the pathetic man-sized paperweight at her back came unbidden to her mind, characters like Simply Bob, or any of a thousand nightmares she'd injected into the blank warning left by her gut.

It's definitely time to get the fuck out of Dodge.

She stopped mid step. *The key! Oh God.* Then it occurred to her she hadn't seen Mary since before Bud came. Her eyes dropped to Bud's belt. No key.

But, the blood…

She needed to find Mary.

Two long strides put her in front of the open door. She slid silently down the wall and used the blade of the knife as a mirror to see around the corner. She was so engrossed in the act of moving the knife back and forth to pan the width of the hall she didn't see the person standing next to her until they spoke.

"Zoe?"

The shock of hearing her name propelled her backward into the doorknob. With the doorstop free, the door slowly closed and Zoe landed hard against the corner of a metal cabinet. Fear put a face at the end of a muscular arm that stopped the door from closing, and she slashed blindly at the air before her.

The arm disappeared around the corner, and the owner let out a curse. "Holy shit! She tried to cut my arm off."

"Frye?" she croaked, not slashing anymore, but still brandishing the knife. "Is that you?"

"I don't know," he said from around the corner. "Are you gonna stab me if I say yes?"

She dropped the knife and jumped into his arms.

After a short embrace, Frye untangled himself. "I'm sorry, Zoe. I thought you were full of shit or something, but now? Wow."

Looking past him, she saw Danny, standing as rigid as a post, eyes darting around as though following a fly.

Frye shrugged at the unspoken question. "He wanted to come too."

"Oh," she said, still confused. "I gotta get out of here, like ten minutes ago." She brushed past him.

"I know." Frye fell in beside her. "That's why I'm here."

"Me too," added Danny, still chasing his invisible whatever.

"Where's Mary? Is she…?"

"Down the hall at the nurses' station. What the hell happened? What's with the blood?" Frye grabbed her elbow.

She shook off his arm. "I'm fine."

Taking in the smeared blood on her clothes, Frye's expression turned to one of horror. "Were you there when it happened?"

"When what happened?"

"Somebody killed that night nurse. It's a real mess."

That explains the blood. "I think it was Bud." She felt guilty for not immediately feeling sorrow for the nurse who'd been so nice to her.

"Bud did it? Bud, the orderly?"

"Yeah, he's back there."

Frye turned with evil intent toward the infirmary door, but she placed a hand on his chest. "No, leave him. He's not going anywhere. We can talk about this later, though. Like after I'm ten kilometers down the road."

"Kilometers?"

"Miles, I mean. Whatever. Does it matter? Let's just get the hell out of here." She turned and sprinted away, and they followed.

At the nurses' station, Meat was crouched near a bathrobe clad form sprawled on the floor. He turned when he heard Zoe coming.

"She fainted when we saw *that*." He pointed into the nurses' station. "But believe me, you *don't* want to see it."

"You're right, I don't." Zoe crouched beside him. "Get up, Mary," she yelled into the girl's face and slapped her, loud enough to create an echo that chased itself down the length of the corridor.

Mary sputtered and sat up, rubbing her cheek. "What the fuck? What'd you hit me for?"

"Where's the key," she screamed into Mary's face. "I gotta go!"

"I think you've made that abundantly clear, bitch." Mary patted the pocket of her robe, and gazed blankly past Zoe at nurse Gert. "It's right here. Let's go."

During the walk to the elevator, Danny said, "Hey, Meat?"

"What, Danny?"

"With Lady Gert dead and that night orderly guy lying back there, does that mean the lunatics are running the asylum?"

"Yeah," Meat giggled. "I guess so."

"Just like that Batman movie."

"Yup, just like that, buddy."

The observation was a little dark but Zoe couldn't help but find their exchange oddly calming.

Zoe turned to Mary when they reached the elevator. "Okay, I can take it from here. You guys get back to your rooms before anyone comes."

As Mary fished for the key, Meat tapped her on the shoulder. "Mary?

"What?"

"Um, didn't you say the elevator only comes to this floor?"

"Yeah, they have it rigged up so no one can come here by mistake, and we can't wander off. So?" She handed the key to Zoe, who took it but was looking up, mouth open, at the numbers above the door.

"Because it's going down. Is that bad?"

"Fuuuck me," said Mary, as her face blanched. "Uh...hide!"

Each of them darted in different directions.

Zoe scanned around, searching for a place to hide, and then abruptly stopped. "I got it! Follow me."

She herded them to the room one across and one down from the elevator; the room in which she'd awoken on her first day in the hospital, the stinky white waiting room. She pushed through the door and held it as everyone filed in. After all five had crammed into the closet sized room, she closed the door enough to allow a sliver of light to pass through the opening. "Okay, shh. We wait here 'til they're gone, then we can go." The statement almost convinced *her* that she knew what she was doing.

"Go where?" asked Frye. "And how did you know someone was coming?"

Zoe ignored the questions and put her eye to the crack. The elevator had stopped at P-2.

"Do you think you could get back to your rooms before the

elevator gets here?"

"Not a chance," Mary piped in from behind her. "Well, we *could* get there, but to get into them I'd need Bud's cardkey, and you're gonna need it for the elevator."

"It stinks in here," observed Danny.

"Quiet, Danny," Meat warned.

"Kay. Sorry." And he remained quiet for all of five seconds. "Meat?"

"Shh. What, Danny?"

"Why are you shushing him?" Frye asked. "We're the only ones around."

"I see your point," countered Meat. "And I'll raise you another. I'm scared shitless and I want some quiet so I can think. Is that hunky dory with you, big guy?"

"Whatever, I'm just *saying*, that's all."

"Meat?"

"What?"

"I gotta pee."

"Pinch it off, dude. We're gonna be here a few minutes."

"Can't."

"Jesus Christ, you two," hissed Mary. "You sound like an old married couple. Go piss in the corner, but shut the fuck up."

"I'm already in the corner," Danny said, from right beside her.

"Then be careful while you do it," she snapped. "But I swear to God, if you pee on my slippers I'll make you eat them."

"Okay, but don't look."

"Are you shitting me?"

"She's right, Danny," Meat said. "Nobody will see anything. I promise. Go ahead."

"Okay," said Danny. "But I just want to warn you all in advance that, uh, sometimes I fart when I pee."

Three bodies pressed against Zoe simultaneously, and, in a strange way, it calmed her. Not just because of their proximity, but also by the levity they'd brought to an imminently dangerous situation. With a tiny smile turning up the corners of her mouth, she returned her attention to a "P" of a different nature. The elevator remained at the bottom of its span, boarding its cargo.

From the back of the small room, Danny chased a fart with a whispered, "Sorry."

~~oOo~~

Parking garage: Level 2

Spike Schrickt watched the lighted numbers drop to P-2. He'd already checked and double checked their supplies, gone over routes, what-if routes if the job went south, *and* he'd insisted the doctor give him a second battery pack for the video gear. Nothing had been left to chance. For the third time since pushing the call button, he reached crisscross and lightly brushed each of the shoulder holstered pistols. With a finger and thumb, he freed them and then let them fall back into their cradles.

The 9mm Glock in the holster under his right arm, he'd named *Justice*. She was his A-number 1 bang stick. Spike spent many a late night stripping Justice down, oiling her up, and lovingly polishing her butt, often falling asleep with her cradled in his arms. The other gun, a plain jane .22, he'd named One-Eyed Gary, for the previous owner of the gun. Spike had taken Gary right out of the man's belt and shot him through the eye.

One-Eyed Gary was only there because he came with a silencer (something Justice, like most women, didn't come with—she was only along for luck and weight distribution). For this special night, Spike had evicted his second best girl, Karen—a flat black pearl handled Beretta—in favor of Gary's quiet aplomb.

The added weight of the silenced barrel caused Spike to list ever so slightly to the left. He'd known this before leaving his house, but hoped to grow accustomed to the foot long gun during the drive. He had *not*, and could think of little else.

Gary's bulk was *so* distracting, in fact, that Spike moved his keys and coins to his right pocket in an attempt to offset the gun.

Then all he could think about was that his keys were in the wrong pocket. That wouldn't do, either.

"Adam," he said, squinting up at his son. "Give me your keys."

"Sure, Pop." Adam passed over his car keys without as much as a blink.

Spike dropped them into his left pocket. "That's better. Thanks."

"New gun still buggin' you?"

"Not anymore," said a contented Spike. He'd known Adam would relinquish his keys without protest. Adam was a good boy. He was everything Spike could ask for in an apprentice, and he worked for chump change.

"I want you to know something, son," Spike said. "And this is serious, so get it right."

"Sure, Pop. Shoot."

"This thing..." Spike pointed up with his thumb. "It's not what we do, understand? This is a onetime gig. It ain't *like* what we do; you know...two taps and disappear."

Adam looked at him in amazement. "You never did this before?"

"No, and I'll never do it again. Neither will you if you're smart."

"Well, why are we doin' it now?"

Spike shrugged and checked his guns again. "Because I owe someone a favor."

As the elevator doors opened, a car door being shut caused both men to turn. A teen with jet black hair and a graveyard tan stepped out from behind a pillar and headed toward them.

~~oOo~~

Zoe's eyes were glued to the digital display above the elevator door. The car had been stopped at P-2 for more than a minute and the tension level, along with a mixture of new odors, was steadily rising in the cramped former janitor's closet.

"Anything?" Mary asked, then pushed past Zoe to see for herself. After moving back from the crack, she said, hopefully, "Maybe there's nobody down there."

"Maybe." Zoe knew someone was down there, but saw no reason to scare the rest of them.

"Why doesn't somebody go push the button?" Mary asked.

Zoe let out an audible sigh. "By *somebody*, do you mean me?"

"Well, it *is* your escape."

Zoe worked up her courage. "You're right. You're absolutely right. I'll go."

"No you won't," Frye said. "I'll go."

"Thanks," she murmured as he squeezed his big frame past her.

"No thanks necessary. It's getting pretty ripe in here."

He strode over to the door, thumbed the button, and looked up. After about ten seconds, he turned and shrugged. "Must still be open on P-2," he said, then walked back.

~~oOo~~

"Come on, dad," complained the ghost faced newcomer. "You're not seriously gonna make me wait in the car, are you?"

Before Spike could answer, Adam preempted. "Get back in the fucking car, pintsized."

Spike reached up and backhanded Adam. "Language," he said, and then pointed at Lou, "We already talked about this. Stay."

"But I could—"

"Stay."

Lou shot his older brother a dark look, then climbed back into the rear seat of the rented Lincoln and slammed the door.

Inside the elevator, Spike squinted at the buttons on the wall. "You see where the key goes to make this thing move?"

Adam fed the card key into its slot. "What floor?"

"It only goes to one floor, push 'em all."

~~oOo~~

Everyone shifted for Frye as he dove back into the small room. After Zoe closed the door, Meat spoke up. "Um, I'm no elevator engineer or anything, but if the car started moving, wouldn't Frye have had time to sing the Star Spangled Banner before it got here?"

No one answered so Meat continued. "What I mean is: we're safe here, right?" The others murmured their agreement. "So then why don't we calm down and talk about what we're all thinking?"

Zoe afforded Meat's outline a glance in the near black room, and then panned the rest of the shadowed figures. "What?" she asked. "You mean that you all have to come with me?"

"We could wait for—" Danny started, and was cut off by Mary.

"No, we can't. She's right. We gotta go too. Besides, I wouldn't mind spending a little time with Spider."

The light behind P-2 went out, and then lit up 3. "Ready or not," Zoe said, "here it comes."

Mary stuck her head in front of Zoe's to see for herself, then squeaked, yanked the door open, and dove through. She immediately flopped onto her stomach, chanting like a hen with Tourette's. "Fuck-fuck-fuck," she yelped and floor-swam toward the elevator.

At first Zoe thought the girl must have lost her mind—or more of it—but then saw the trail of size twelve pee prints on the checked floor, standing out like, well, like pee prints on a checked floor. The prints would lead whoever was coming up the elevator right back to the room. She darted a quick look at the numbers over the door as she yanked her robe off and ran to the elevator.

Both girls mopped the floor, swinging their arms wildly as

they watched the numbers change. Ignorant of each other's proximity, they met in the middle of the floor, butting heads.

Three...four

"Hurry up!" Frye beckoned wildly with one arm.

Zoe latched onto Mary's moist robe and hauled her to her feet. "Get going," she wheezed, and propelled the girl ahead of her through the door.

Frye patted Mary on the shoulder as she passed. "Good eyes."

"Yeah," Zoe said, catching her breath. "You may have just saved our asses."

Five...six

Ding.

26

GO TIME

"He was pretty p.o.'ed, huh?" Adam faced the mirrored doors of the elevator, admiring his new leather jacket and nursing his recently slapped cheek.

Spike huffed. "He'll get over it."

"Why couldn't he come?" Adam checked his hair. "You think he's too young?"

"Yes...no. Not really," answered Spike. "I guess it's because he seems to like this weirdo stuff a little too much. You ever see the kind of things he downloads off the Internet?"

"He's a teenager. You ever take a look under *my* bed?"

"No, Adam. It's more than that. You remember that dog I brought home for you when you was ten?"

Adam smiled. "Boots. Yeah, I loved that dog."

"And remember how I said it ran away?"

"Uh huh," Adam slowly replied.

"Well, it didn't. I caught your brother eating him on the kitchen floor while you was out playing football."

Adam growled, but Spike cut him off with a chop of his hand, "Leave it. I just wanted you to know that he may not be right in the head, if you know what I mean."

Ding.

"We're here. Get ready." Spike stepped back from the door

and cleared Gary from his holster.

"Ready for what?" Adam asked, sullenly. "A retard swinging a bedpan?" Nonetheless, he drew his gun and stepped to the opposite side of the car.

The doors opened. Spike listened for movement outside the elevator, then stepped out and motioned for his son to follow. Gideon said their contact would be alone at the nurses' station, and that they may hear some of the patients if they were awake, but not to worry. They'd all be locked in their rooms with the exception of one. The orderly would take them to the girl.

"It will be the easiest money you ever make, old friend," he remembered Gideon saying. Spike could tell the old man was holding something back and probably should have pursued it, because now that he was there the job seemed too easy. He didn't like easy. It made him jumpy. Bad things happened when he was jumpy.

As they neared the nurses' station, he saw that things were about to get interesting. A trail of dark brown footprints led out of the room and down the darkened hallway. It seemed his hunch had been right. Hesitation and indecision wormed their way into his gut as he flattened himself to the wall and held his arm out to his son, stopping him. The words "forget this" surfaced, but he'd never quit anything yet, and wasn't about to start then.

A quick look around the corner revealed a body on the floor and a gore splattered bowling pin lying in a large puddle of blood. He rolled his eyes at his son, then motioned for him to follow.

He rounded on the open door with Gary at the ready, and swung in a circle before bending to study the dead woman. She was a mess. He dipped his finger in the pool of blood near her head and guessed it had been about a half-hour since she'd been beaten into a pulpy mush. The body wore a nurse's uniform. *Did the orderly do this?*

Adam stared down at the body. "Whoa, you see that head? *Somebody* got themselves a good workout."

Spike ignored the flippant remark and waved commando style down the dimly lit hall. "Move out. Let's do this thing and get out. But stay on your toes. We have an unknown, here, and—"

"Do you think somebody already called the cops?"

"Probably not. The phone's been unplugged. Just the same, we should hurry."

"Should I film any of this?" Adam nodded toward the corpse.

"No."

"Alright. You know, dad, all that moaning and scratching is really freaking me out. It's like the night of the frickin' dead in this place. Are you sure they can't get out?"

Spike shrugged and followed the trail off into the dark.

~~oOo~~

Zoe felt Mary shiver. She squeezed her shoulder and said, "We're almost there, Jeannie. Hang on."

Mary stopped shivering and pulled away. "Jeannie?"

"Oh," Zoe murmured. "Sorry."

Frye slid an arm around her, embracing her from behind— an act that, a month ago, would have garnered a hot 'n' spicy boot to the balls. He leaned in close to her ear. "Like you said, we're almost there. Everything's gonna be alright."

"Thanks." She placed her hand over his.

"Where are they?" asked Meat. "Can we go yet?"

"I think they're still at the nurses' station," Zoe said. "Feel free to see for yourself."

"No," Meat replied. "This shit's just making me jumpy."

"Hey, Meat?"

"Yeah, Danny."

"I think my hands are on fire."

"No they're not, Danny. Look again." Meat leaned forward to whisper into Zoe's ear. "See? I'm not the only one. We gotta go before something happens."

"You're right," she whispered back, then, louder, "We

ready?"

Zoe took their silence for acquiescence, and exhaled a calming breath before opening the door. She peeked out, then ran to the elevator and pushed the call button. The normally unassuming "ding" of the elevator shot through her nerves like a bobsled, freezing every limb as it passed. Mary shoved her through the opening, then she was pushed to the back as the rest of the group packed in.

"Close the door," Meat hissed. "Hit the fucking button!"

"Where's the key?" Mary spun toward Zoe. "You got it. I gave it to you. Give it to me."

Zoe slipped her hand into her pocket and pulled out the key. Mary snatched it from her and slid it home. Zoe let out a lungful of air and leaned back against the mirrored wall. After two punched buttons, the doors closed and the elevator began its descent.

"Alright," Mary said. "When we get to the parking garage, we go right." She grabbed Danny's right hand and patted it. "This one, Danny. We go right. Okay?"

Danny raised his eyes to meet hers. "I'm not stupid, Mary. Sometimes I just see stuff."

"I'm sorry," she snapped, "but we gotta act together. Everybody's gotta know, so buck up. Now," she went on, "There's an emergency exit about thirty feet from the elevator—to the *right*—and just outside, waiting like the angel he is, is my baby."

Ding.

"Let's go." To Meat, Mary whispered, "Keep an eye on Danny."

Danny stood in the center of the elevator, straining to hear the piped in music. "Is that Zeppelin?"

Meat grabbed his hand and yanked him out the door. "No, dude, I think it's Haydn."

"Huh, sounds like Kashmir."

The trail led the pair of killers past rooms alive with everything from soft sobs, to wails and frantic tantrums. It would be a lie to say Spike didn't find it extremely unsettling, and made it nearly impossible to concentrate. He was, after all, a borderline paranoid schizophrenic himself. He blinked the thought away. *Used to be paranoid; not anymore.*

He called it something different now: cautious.

And so, with caution—not paranoia—he approached the door under which the bloody trail disappeared. The sign over the door said they'd found the infirmary and the girl. Light filtered under the door. He prostrated himself to peer through the gap. There was a body on the floor—a bloody body.

Spike stood and signed to his son: "*You go left.*"

He pushed the door open and ducked in, rolling right, and Adam mirrored, rolling left. With a glance at the form on the floor, they swept the room, cleared it, and then circled back to the body. At a glance, Spike thought the man was dead, but upon closer inspection he was breathing.

"Where's the girl?"

The eyes remained closed, but twitched at the question.

"I know you can hear me." Spike kneeled and poked the man in the chest with One-Eyed Gary.

Under the lids, the man's eyes danced, but stayed hidden.

"Looks like somebody caught you with your pants down, slick."

At the mention of his pants, the prone man's eyes popped open and darted between Spike and Adam. His mouth struggled to form words, but his teeth clacked like a possessed typewriter.

"What's wrong with him?" asked Adam, standing over his father's shoulder.

"Let's find out—and get out from behind me. You know I hate having somebody looming over me."

"Sorry."

Spike waited for Adam to move, then searched the body for wounds. Under the man, he found a syringe and placed it on the man's chest. "Check for empty vials near the bed," he said to Adam, and resumed his search. He ran his hand down the left leg and something scratched his hand. He plucked out a broken length of needle and deposited it beside the empty syringe. To the body, he said, "The girl do this?"

The second the question was out, the teeth stopped chattering and the man blinked once.

"Oh," Spike said, and then stood. Adam handed him two empty vials of Procaine. Spike had never used it himself, but knew what it did; a bullet was how *he* numbed his marks.

Spike walked to the door, looked out, then turned to the body. His mind was a feuding mixture of rage and confusion. *How could something so easy go so wrong? Easy money, my sweet patootie.*

Adam stared at him, likely awaiting his next command. *Don't let the kid see you like this. You're cool. Calm and cool. This ain't nothing you can't handle.*

Leaning against the door frame, Spike extended his gun arm and peered down Gary's long nose. "I'm gonna make a wild guess here. You must be Bud?"

One blink.

Ding.

"You just couldn't handle one simp—" he started, then thought, *Ding? Oh, no!* "Adam," he snapped. "The elevator. Go! Go!"

Adam shot by, and Spike called after him: "Tell your brother. Make sure he keeps his eyes open down there."

Spike turned back to Bud and let out a heavy breath as he ran his fingers down Gary's barrel, tracing the silencer with a two fingered caress. "My friend, you're about to have a very bad day."

~~oOo~~

Lou Schrickt sat with his head propped out the window, staring at the elevator. Under his breath, he mumbled words of hate, and several specific things he'd like to do to his asshole father and prick of a brother. He knew why his dad didn't let him join them on this job. *Well fuck you, spawn. I don't need you. I got friends you don't even know about.*

Before he could say, "That was quick," five people bolted from the elevator and ran to the nearest exit. One of them looked like the girl in the picture on the front seat.

Keeping low, he lunged for the glove box to grab his father's spare gun. He found nothing more dangerous than a bottle of scotch. "Fuck!" he screamed in frustration, throwing the bottle out the open window to smash against the side of the car next to theirs. The girl was getting away.

"Stay." He snidely mimicked his father's last remark. "Sure," he said, reaching for his cell phone. "I'll just stay here while you go up there and fuck this whole thing up like the pros you are—fucking idiots!" He stabbed each digit of his brother's number, anticipating his chance to mock Adam and enlighten him as to just how dumb he was. The phone picked up after one ring and a recorded message informed him that "the customer you are calling is currently out of range..."

Lou stuffed the phone into his pocket and headed for the elevator, mumbling ever more descriptive invectives the closer he came. After fingering the call button, the doors opened and he stepped inside. *What floor was that?* He smiled as a number came to him, and he pushed seven. Nothing happened. He stabbed it again and nothing happened. Frustrated, he ran his finger up the bank of numbers, lighting them all up. The doors slid closed, and he said aloud, "Alright. That's more like it," but still, the elevator remained dormant. "Fuck," he spat, kicking the door. *Fucking dummies!* He pushed the "door open" button, half expecting it to not work either, but it did, and he stepped out.

He tried his brother's cell again, received the same message, and pushed END. As he was about to put the phone back in his pocket, he thought of a way to get his asshole father and prick brother into some mighty deep shit. He knew his father was doing this job for a man named Gideon, but what his father didn't know was that Lou knew who it was ultimately for.

The man had dropped the mark's name during

conversation a couple of times over the last month or so, so when Lou saw the file that had been Fed Ex-ed to his father, and noticed her name, he knew right away who really called the shots: his hero, Zane Ellis.

Oh, you guys are so boned when Zane hears how you screwed this up, he thought, practically rubbing his hands together with glee. *Who knows,* he mused, as he punched numbers into his phone. *Maybe he'll take me on as a partner.*

Three rings later he was speaking to his hero.

"Hey, my man," came the wary voice of Zane Ellis. "If it ain't Lou 'the Chew' Schrickt."

"Please, sir. That's not funny," Lou said, carefully, like a good little submissive.

"I thought you wanted a nickname, kid. What? Not terrifying enough for you?"

"I do," he whined. *Don't whine.* "But that one makes me sound like a dog."

"Fair enough. So, what can I do for a fellow conveyor of chaos?"

"You know that chick my dad was supposed to whack for you, the cute blonde?"

"Which 'chick' would that be? His tone turned icy, dangerous. "Her name wouldn't happen to be Zoe, would it?"

"Yeah, yeah, that's the one."

"Nobody hurt her, did they?"

"I thought you wanted her dead. Dad said—"

"You go find your father and tell him something for me. If he so much as hurts her feelings, I'll eat him so slowly he'll beg me to take bigger bites. You got that? Go. Go tell him before I decide to throw you in for dessert."

Lou gulped. "Well, see. That's just it. The girl escaped, and my dad's still upstairs."

"Upstairs where? Your house?"

"No, some nut ward in Saint Louis."

"No kidding? Huh...She truly is amazing, don't you think?"

"Yeah, Zane," Lou agreed, motivated by fear more than any kind of personal opinion. "She's great, sir."

"Now, if you'll excuse me, there's a certain doctor I need to reach out and touch. Don't forget to pass my message along to your father."

~~oOo~~

Spike poked his head out the door at the sound of feet slapping against the tile.

Adam stopped in the doorway, panting and holding his knees. "Gone. Hiding...elevator...piss."

Spike rolled his eyes and ran a hand through his jet black hair. He owed Adam a slap for cussing, but let it go. "Did you call your brother? Did he see anything?"

"No reception," wheezed Adam. "Tried elevator...you got key."

Spike nodded. "Get the camera."

"Well, somebody's starring in this movie," he said, as he rounded on Bud, "And since you let the subject escape, it's only fair you took her place. What do you say, Adam?"

Adam nodded, took off his new leather coat and threw it over a chair.

Adam closed on Bud, camera raised and already rolling, but Spike held up a hand. "Wait. Cut. Cut. Not here, son. Get that gurney and we'll make this a takeout order. This fella's made me awful sore and I don't think there's enough time for what I have in mind for him."

Bud's eyes widened.

Adam grinned. "Cool. We can try out some of them gizmos that dude you bowl with gave you."

~~oOo~~

Mary passed Zoe on the stairs leading to the outer second level parking area and burst through the door. "Come on, he's just out here," she called before the door closed between them.

Paranoia reared its familiar face as Zoe reached for the door's push bar. *What if she's in on it? What if they wanted me out of*

252

the hospital so they could kill me quietly?

"You could be right, bitch. Why don't you head back upstairs and let Bud finish you off?" chimed Monkey, after appearing on her shoulder like a big purple turd.

"Sarcasm duly noted; fuck you. But good point. I have to start trusting people if I'm gonna get out of this . . . Hey! Where the hell were you when I was attacked?"

The monkey ignored what the monkey wanted to ignore, and he ignored her question with his regular aplomb.

"What's the hold up?" Meat asked from the rear.

"Nothing," she replied, then trusted a friend and pushed the crash bar.

Just like Mary said, the car was there. And, just like she also said, her man muffin, Spider, stood beside it. Zoe took one look at him and laughed. In every conversation involving Mary's boyfriend, Zoe pictured him to be some tall, lanky, ghost faced black-on-black-wearing, living, breathing John Keats poem. The pimply teen presently hunched over the hood of the Beetle was none of these things. He was a class-A geek.

"What?" Spider stepped away from his old Beetle. "Don't laugh. It's paid for."

"No, it's not that. You're...not what I expected."

Mary glared at her and opened the passenger door for everyone to pile in. "Don't worry about her, baby," she said to Spider. "She's been under a lot of strain lately." Then she narrowed her eyes at Zoe, and mouthed, *Shut up, bitch.*

"Well," said Meat, as he climbed into the back seat. "I think I'll fit, but you may have to ride on the roof, Frye."

"Fuck that," Frye grumbled. "Scooch over."

"Why don't we wait here for the police?" Danny stood with his head cocked to one side, gazing into the confines of the back seat.

Mary pushed him toward the car. "Who do you think the cops are gonna believe, that orderly laying up there on the floor, or us?"

"She's right, Danny. Get in," Meat said.

And so, with Spider driving, Mary riding shotgun, Meat, Frye, and Danny in the back, Zoe was left to straddle the stick shift. The irony wasn't lost on her. The old yellow Beetle slouched out of the parking lot, muffler dragging noisily under the weight of her cargo, while Celine Dion blared from blown speakers.

Under a starless night sky, their path revealed itself in the flickering glow of the car's ancient headlights; the escape had fused them together in this struggle. Zoe felt it, and greeted whatever future awaited with new hope.

Part III

"Just 'cause you got the monkey off your back doesn't mean the circus has left town."

—George Carlin

27

TRUST ISSUES

Although she was sitting almost on top of him, Zoe needed to yell over the music for Spider to hear. "Where are you taking us?"

His eyes shifted in her direction for a fraction of a second, then back to the road. "I got it covered."

To look at him, Zoe didn't believe he could successfully *cover* tying his shoes without breaking a finger, but she left him to the driving. Her nerves didn't start popping until the third time they passed the same street. The music didn't help either.

Through most of Kermit the frog's rendition of *Rainbow Connection*, Zoe stared uneasily out the corner of her eye at the skinny boy/man behind the wheel of the old Volkswagen as he lip-synced along. Apparently, she was the only one in the group this act bothered. At one point she thought she heard Frye singing along, but might have been Meat—maybe both.

After five minutes of lame music and left hand turns, Spider snapped his fingers and nodded to Mary, "The room?"

Mary bobbed her head enthusiastically. "Fuck, yeah. That's a great idea, baby."

Zoe hadn't a clue what he meant by *room*, but Mary seemed

to think it was a good idea. For now, it was good enough for her too.

"So, Spider," Zoe said, for no other reason than to break the tension that had descended over everyone. "How'd you get a name like that?" She bent to gaze at St. Louis' famed arch as they passed it at an ear flattening twenty miles per hour.

"Spiedewski," he replied, white knuckled hands at ten-and-two, eyes continuously flicking from mirror to mirror, mirror to mirror. "It's Polish."

Zoe twisted the rearview mirror to check her face for any blood left over from her scrape with Bud. "Oh." She didn't add that she thought he was too lame for such a cool nickname.

"Seth," he said, yanking back control of the mirror. "Seth Spiedewski."

"Ah," she replied, bored with him already, and then ducked to see the exit he was taking. "Uh, where are you going? Are we going to East St. Louis?" Zoe gazed around in disgust. "At night?"

Seth bobbed his head. "My cousin works nights at the Ivory Pillars Hotel. When it was just going to be you, I was going to hide you in my tree house, but—"

"Tree house?" Zoe deadpanned. "Are you joking?" She turned to Mary. "Is he joking?"

"From when I was a kid," he fired back. "Where the hell did you think you were going, a safe house? I live with my parents."

"Uh huh."

"Trust him, Zoe." Mary leaned forward and smiled at her man.

"Yeah," echoed Spider, grinning through pimples and dimples. "Trust me."

~~oOo~~

Gideon sat basking in the blue-green glow of the computer screen, staring at the blinking cursor. He read the last paragraph, then relit his cold cigar and returned his eyes to the cursor. From near his left elbow, the muted telephone blinked candy apple red. *Who the hell could that be?*

At 1:32 in the morning.

He groaned at seeing the call display, but picked up anyway. After a fake yawn, he said, "Why Zane, my boy, what's on your mind that can't wait 'til daylight?"

"Did I wake you?" Zane asked, passively. "Or were you planning *my* murder now?"

"I haven't the faintest idea what you're talking about." Gideon gulped as icy shivers bled through him. "Is everything alright? ...Zane? ...Are you there?"

Dead. The phone line was dead.

He knows about the girl.

Gideon started to cradle the phone when a hand clamped over his and an arm shot around his neck. He was lifted, chair and phone, and tossed into the nearest bookcase, which collapsed, video cassettes and DVDs showering over him. He had no time to crawl, roll, or register anything more than pain before new pain was added; a kick in the stomach drove what little wind he'd managed to suck in, back out with a *whoosh*.

"Zane?" Gideon's barely audible issue was no more than a stretch of vocal chords, like cat gut pulled taut on a violin.

Backlit by a rheumy yellow, low slung sliver moon, the shadowy form paused; seemingly drinking in Gideon's terror, then he pounced. Gideon raised his arms to shield his face but a gloved hand slid between his slight defenses and gathered a wad of shirt.

My book! It's not finished, flashed through Gideon's mind as he was hauled from the floor and slammed repeatedly into the wall. Between white hot stars swirling through his vision, Zane's face, blackened by paint and shadow, loomed close. He stiffened as it came to hover inches from his own, and they breathed each other's stale air, passing the distinct coppery aroma of blood for Scotch and tobacco, until the mingled intimacy bore only the stench of fear and death.

Set deep within a mask of what the doctor first believed to

be a thick layering of lamp black, but now knew to be far worse, the cold, hungry gaze examined him with the intensity of a hawk.

Zane snuffed deeply from the nape of Gideon's neck to his forehead, and returned to his ear. In a hoarse whisper, he said, "What's up, Doc?" Then he removed his hands and stepped away.

Without Zane's strength to hold him, Gideon slumped and landed on a pile of DVD cases, which snapped like brittle plastic bones beneath him.

Zane bent and picked up a bulging, blood drenched pillowcase and dropped it onto Gideon's desk.

When the cannibal's back was turned, the psychiatrist stole a glance at the humidor on the closest corner of the desk. Inside the case, under a layer of cigars, was a snub-nosed .38. Three feet stood between his shaking hand and salvation, but the gun might as well have been three miles away, given his chance of reaching it before Zane could tear out his throat. On the heels of that last image, he turned up the collar of his shirt.

Zane lifted an hourglass from the pillowcase and—just as he'd witnessed so many victims do before him—the doctor could only watch. *Say something! Work this out,* he screamed at himself. *You know this man better than he knows himself.* But Gideon's mind was currently as blank as the space under the latest chapter heading of his book.

Zane wiped gore from the hourglass, flipped it, and placed it on the humidor. Before it landed, the white sand began its immediate evacuation from the chamber above to the chamber below. Then he shoved the still bulging sack to the floor, leaned on the edge of the desk and folded his hands in his lap.

To the rolling bag, Zane said, "I'll get back to you in a minute, darlin'." Then he faced the doctor; the mask of dried blood cracked along his laugh lines as he smiled. "I think we can safely assume this has gone far beyond blame. Would you say that's a fair assumption, doctor?"

A tic from the corner of Gideon's mouth was his only answer.

"I thought I'd made myself clear when I said...*what?* Can you tell me what I said?"

Gideon knew there was no escape through lying, but remained baffled as to how Zane could have learned so quickly of the girl's execution. From a million miles away, he heard himself respond. "You said if the girl—"

"Zoe," Zane corrected. "She has a name. Use it."

Gideon snaked his tongue along his lips, then started over. "You said if Zoe died that I would be dead too."

"By dawn. I said you'd be dead by dawn."

Gideon swallowed a gasp. "So she's dead?"

Zane shook his head. "We wouldn't be having this conversation if she was dead."

Thank God. Gideon praised the ineptitude of Spike Schrickt. After a glance at the hourglass, he asked, "So, what's that for?"

"Good question." Zane's smile widened, causing more fissures to erupt in his mask. "That's how long you have to convince me not to kill you." Each word slammed into the next like shunting box cars.

The doctor mentally sped through every reason in his arsenal, stammered several times, and came up with nothing. But in that realization he eventually found not comfort, but something akin to it: acceptance...acceptance with one exception; his book. His life, his knowledge, his years of field work, would be swept away in the wake of sensationalism. Any news reports of a ghoul's death, a snuff director's death, would outshine the relevance of his book...his legacy. Doctor Bartholomew D. Gideon would not be *remembered* by colleagues, so much as reviled by the multitudes.

The last of the sand found the bottom bowl.

"Well? Thrill me." Zane leaned forward, eyes glistening, mouth half open in anticipation.

"Nothing," Gideon rasped, then cleared his throat. "I have no reason you might find redeeming. My book," he shrugged, and winced at the pain in his shoulder, "but that's all."

"Huh. I've gotta say, Bartholomew, I didn't expect *that*. I took you for the 'beg for your life' type." Zane bent and grabbed the discarded sack from the floor, then tossed it into the doctor's lap. "Lucky for you I like being wrong." He tweaked Gideon's nose, leaving a smear of blood.

Gideon knew Zane well enough to guess what the sack held, but had to ask. "What's in the bag?"

"Another good question." Zane turned his back and walked across the room to a set of shelves piled high with tapes, discs, and reel-to-reels, and fingered through the Ta to Z section. Without turning, he said, "To me? What's in that bag is a three course meal. To you," he turned back to the doctor, "it means a chance for salvation."

"That's it?"

"Yeah. That's it. Just one thing, though," he said, pulling a digital camera from his hip pocket. "Open the bag and hold it up."

"Hold the bag up?"

"No, Doc, the head."

Gideon stared longingly at the humidor. This could all have ended right then and there. Surely he could reach the gun before Zane reached him, but the coward in him asked: *is it even loaded? Is the safety on?*

The gun was loaded, and the safety was broken, but so was he. He reached into the bag. Almost immediately, the coppery tang of blood overwhelmed him.

Two fingers dipped into an open mouth and found the yielding sponginess of a tongue. He gagged, then pulled his fingers back and probed north, finding the nose, then the hair.

"Come on, old boy," Zane said from behind the camera. "Tick tock."

Gideon held his breath as he slid his hand through the cold, slimy hair. He knew what Zane wanted, and also that he'd be satisfied with nothing less. Zane wanted what every weasel pounding porn devotee wanted; what Gideon himself demanded of all his actors: Zane wanted a money shot.

For the sake of his own salvation, Gideon would give him one.

With a stiff dignity born of loathing and spite, he yanked

the head free and held it aloft, face toward the camera. "Take it," he grated. "Take your blackmail picture and leave. I won't harm you or the girl. You have my word. Just leave."

"What's the rush?" Zane chuckled as he snapped pictures. "Give her a kiss. But don't worry," he said, kneeling a few feet away. "That one will be for my personal scrapbook."

Gideon's heart stuttered and, for a brief instant, he welcomed the idea of a heart attack—even steeled himself for one—but the damn thing kept beating. *Oh well,* he sighed, and, for the first time, gazed down at the head swaying in his hand. It was Erica, his secretary. Her face was thinner, her lips puffy.

Funny, he'd often wondered what it would be like to kiss those lips.

~~oOo~~

Long after Zane had gone, Gideon sat at his desk. Once his hands stopped shaking, he opened the top drawer of the desk and retrieved a bottle of scotch. Two gargled swallows sanitized his tongue, but to soothe the memory of the night's events would require the remainder of the bottle. He pushed the hourglass off the desk, pulled a cigar from the humidor, and lit it with a wooden match. For a moment he sat perfectly still, alternately drawing on the fat cigar and staring at the cursor, and then he began to type.

It seemed fear was the inspiration needed to spur him on. Gideon's fingers flew over the keys, tapping out a tale which wouldn't see print until long after he was safely six feet below the ground. He would have his legacy.

~~oOo~~

Zoe was pleasantly surprised by the cleanliness of the motel room. It was plain, but nothing like the cockroach infested dive she'd imagined it would be. The bathroom proved to be as well maintained as the rest of the unit. Gloriously hot water pelted her skin, stripping away tension along with the thin film of fear she'd worn like a body suit for the past week.

Fully refreshed, she was towel drying her hair when a screech erupted from the next room, followed by raised voices. Seconds later the bathroom door burst inward as Frye ran toward the tub clutching the flaming remnants of a blanket. Zoe shrank back as he threw the whole works into the tub and cranked on the water.

The room immediately filled with the stench of melted poly-fibers and scorched hair. Amid the steam and smoke, standing with his mouth half open, Frye stared at her.

Zoe covered herself with the towel and stared right back. "What. The. Fuck. Was. That?" She measured each word with a stomp of her foot. It didn't bother her that Frye had seen her naked—skin was only skin. What bothered her was that she hadn't seen a razor for well over a month and her once pretty, blonde landing strip looked more like a corn field gone to weed.

Meat popped his head around the corner. "Everything okay in there? Do you need any help?" His eyebrows wiggled in tandem with his words.

Zoe guessed he'd seen too many porn videos. Those lines always seemed to work for a guy with hung, or any synonym for *huge* in his name, but didn't sit too well coming from a skinny guy wearing a bathrobe and one slipper.

"Not that kind of help, smut boy. Out." She swept both him and Frye out the door.

The tattered remains of the blanket, still sizzling in the tub, was a wakeup call. With the exception of herself and Seth, there wasn't one of them who didn't suffer *some* sort of malfunction...though Seth's taste in music left her mildly curious of his mental state. They would need to watch out for each other from then on, until...*Until when, Zoe? How many people do you think will be looking for you by morning? Or after all this shit hits the television? What about them? They saved you and you repaid them by turning them into fugitives. Nice going, stupid.*

When she entered the room, Danny was standing in the corner with his nose pressed to the wall. Zoe mouthed at Mary,

What the hell?

Mary shrugged. "Meat put him in a time out."

"A time out?"

"The label said strike here," Danny mumbled. "So I did."

"We need to talk," Zoe said. "All of us."

She voiced her concerns regarding their varied imperfections, and emphasized the fact that they *all* needed to take care of each other, which was possible if they all stayed vigilant.

Afterwards, she filled them all in on what they didn't already know regarding Bud's last visit. Then Mary, in turn, told her of the electronic locks, her wonderful collection of earth magnets, and all that led up to their meeting at the nurses' station.

"By the way, dickhead," Mary shot at Danny. "You ruined my slippers. *And* my fucking robe. There's piss all over them." Squinting, she said, "Betcha thought I was gonna forget that, didn'tcha?"

Danny shuffled back to the wall and took up his former penance.

"Oh," Spider snapped his fingers. "I almost forgot. I have clothes in the trunk for Zoe. I didn't expect the rest of you, but there's a thrift shop around the corner."

"That's all cool and all, Seth," Zoe said. "But we don't have any money. Shit, I don't even know how we're gonna fucking eat. I have credit cards, but they were all in my purse back at the hospital."

An object the size of a small pillow hit her in the chest and landed in her lap. It was her purse. "How...?"

"You're welcome." Mary beamed at her, and then sneered at the back of Danny's head. "Sorry it's wet."

Zoe retrieved two credit cards along with her bank card, and handed them to Spider. She told him to take five hundred from each account.

As Seth opened the door, Zoe called him back. "Seth?"

"Yeah?"

"Throw the cards away when you're done."

"Sure."

"Seth?"

"Yeah?"

"Don't take the money out anywhere around here."

With a forced smile, he said, "Do I look stupid?"

Zoe bit her tongue.

28

ALL IN FAVOR

Mary grew increasingly more agitated the longer Seth was gone.

"What's taking him so long?" Mary dropped the curtain, then yanked it back, thinking she'd spied a car. Seeing it wasn't, she returned to pacing the length of the room.

"Not to seem rude, Mary," said Meat, "but I wish you'd quit with the fucking pacing. You're really ruining my calm. And look what you've done to poor Danny."

Danny sat in the corner of the room, fast asleep.

Mary opened the curtain, then dropped it. "What? Danny's sleeping. He doesn't even know what the hell's going on."

Meat tsk-ed. "It's worse than I thought. His brain has completely shut down."

"Is that your diagnosis, doctor?" Mary picked up then slammed down the clock/radio. "It's three-thirty in the fucking morning. He's tired. We're *all* tired."

Three minutes later, for no apparent reason, Mary threw her hands in the air, grumbled, "Fuck this," and left the room.

When the door opened minutes later, Zoe thought it might be Seth coming back, Mary in tow, but it was only Mary. She seemed to have calmed though.

Zoe looked her up and down. "Are you good now?"

"Yeah, sorry."

Instead of commenting on the winter/summer mood swing, Zoe patted the bed beside her. "Sit down. We should talk."

"What about Spider?"

"We'll catch him up later."

Zoe rolled onto her stomach and pulled a pillow under her elbows. "What do you all think we should do? Are you guys going back in the morning? I can't—that's my problem—but you can."

From across the room, sitting in a tipped back wooden chair, feet on the dresser, Frye smiled at the ceiling and bobbed his Adam's apple twice before speaking. "We're with you, Zoe. What are *you* planning to do?"

"Me?"

"Uh huh," Meat said. "You really think whoever it was that came to the hospital is gonna stop looking for you just 'cause you escaped?"

Mary's head bobbed in agreement. "Yeah, from what I saw that night at that party with Clive, these people are way beyond *hardcore*. Way, way, way worse than Clive and his two ghoul friends. Those fuckers aren't done with you by a long shot."

Zoe exchanged glances with each of them in turn, with the exception of Danny, who was awake now, but appeared to be meditating.

She blew a stray lock of hair from her face, and grimaced. "What the hell can I do against *them*?" She pointed at the door, to an imagined *They*. "I…"

"No, Zoe," Frye said, dropping his legs from the dresser, "not you, *we*. Whatever you decide, we're with you.

"Yeah," Meat cut in. "You've got everything you need to start with right there in your purse, plus Mary knows where to find that Clive guy. He's gotta know something, right?"

No, Zoe thought. *That's crazy, right?* Her hand closed on the old cloth purse and she pulled it into her lap as she sat up. She reached in and plucked out the first item her hand touched. It was the picture she'd taken from Jeanne's apartment, the one of them together, smiling. Her heart skipped a beat as she recalled the promise she'd made.

For the briefest second, say, enough time for an impulsive whim to pop into existence somewhere deep within the center of a brain, scale down through the nervous system, take a right at the left lung, and give the heart a how's-she-going—in that shimmering golden nanosecond, alive with possibilities of vengeance and adventure—that idle promise to 'do what she could to make it right' didn't seem so farfetched. As a matter of fact, it seemed downright doable.

But courage fled before Zoe could give over to it. Instead of saying, "Yeah, let's get 'em," or something as equally harebrained, she buried her face into the pillow and groaned. "What could we hope to accomplish? I mean…look at us."

From her station at the window, Mary dropped the curtain after another scan of the parking lot. To her own shoulder, she said, "Whatever we accomplish, it's a fuckload better than waiting here for those two dudes with the guns, wouldn't you say?"

"I don't know." Zoe thought the group was nuts, even by their own standards.

Mary strolled over, pulled the purse from Zoe's lap and dumped the contents on the bed. As she pushed papers and news clippings back and forth, she said, "We should really wait for Spider. I had him follow Clive around last week."

Zoe was skeptical, but everyone crowded in close to the bed to plot their course, to hatch a plan. Of what, no one knew, but at least they all of a mind that they would eventually be doing *something*. Even Danny joined in, staying well clear of Mary, and seemed to take an interest in the hypothesized takedown of Zoe's tattooed mister X.

"Hey, Meat?" Danny cut Frye off in the middle of an "If I caught up to that motherfucker, I'd fuck him up" rant.

"Yeah, Danny?"

"Does this mean we can be the Retribution Club again? You know, since we're gonna fix this mess up for Zoe?"

"Sure does, buddy."

There was a single knock at the door followed by a short

burst of lighter taps.

Zoe tensed.

Mary smiled. "It's about time, lover," she called. "Get in here."

Mary latched onto Seth and planted a long sloppy kiss on him. When she pulled away, she said, "Guess what?"

Spider looked down. "I poked you in the stomach with my boner?"

"Well, yeah, you did, but that's not it. We're gonna help Zoe."

"Isn't that what we're doing?" he asked, in a *no duh* kind of way.

"No. We're gonna get the assholes who are trying to kill her." She kissed him on the nose. "I voted for you."

"Yeah? How'd I vote?"

"The same way I would've told you to vote if you were here." She winked.

"Cool."

~~oOo~~

The next morning, after the thrift store clothes and bags from the drug store had all been dumped on the bed, they separated the outfits Seth had picked out for everyone. In one box, Zoe found a set of barber's shears; in a bag, Mary found makeup and boxes of hair dye. Seth was a thorough shopper. He reminded Zoe of her mother in that way. Like him, she was also an anally retentive bitch.

Zoe watched Seth watching Mary from his perch on a footstool in the corner of the room. "Are you sure you're not a closet gay?" she asked him.

Seth frowned and turned on the television, grumbling something about finding a football game.

By the time hair dye was in the soak stage atop five heads, the chemical smell had become stifling, and breathing remained difficult even after opening the windows. Eventually, they all took turns stepping outside for air.

Frye was first to reach the rinse cycle. When asked by Zoe, the self elected barber of the group, how he wanted his hair, he bobbed his head, and said, "a jock mohawk." Zoe complied, and made a few mistakes, but none he'd notice without a second mirror.

Danny and Meat were easier. They'd used the platinum blonde dye and both wanted number four clippers. Once finished with them, Zoe pinched their cheeks. "Oh, you guys are so cute. You look like Slim Shady bookends." They shrugged at each other, and in stereo, said, "Cool."

"Hey," Zoe said, cheerily, "I'm really getting the hang of this haircutting." She brushed the recently vacated chair with her hand, and pointed at now blonde Mary. "Next! Get that towel off your head, Biatch, and come on down."

Mary's swami-swirled head shook side to side as she waggled her index finger, "You ain't going anywhere near this head with those fucking clippers. I'm not even gonna cut my hair. I'll look different enough, trust me. But, gimme," she said, holding out her hand. "Let me do you."

Meat popped his head in the door, porn brow wiggling. "Need a hand?"

"As if, horn dog," Mary said. "Go back outside and keep an eye on your retarded twin." To Zoe, she said, "Sit, if you dare, and I'll cut yours."

"Okay," Zoe said, drawling it out like a fifteen letter word. "Vogue me," she said, then flinched when Mary flipped on the clippers. "Just an inch or two, though."

"Uh huh."

Hum zing zwong. "Oopsie."

"I said two inches!" Zoe gaped at a six inch lock that fell onto her lap.

"Sit still and let me create or I'll cut off one of your ears," Mary warned her, and then said, excitedly, "Oh, I know how it'll look good. Hold still."

And Zoe did. Not one more comment, not one more question. She let the towel headed, recently escaped mental patient alone and closed her eyes. *Oh, well,* she thought. *The worst that can happen is that it's ugly, and ugly ain't so bad.* But then she thought ugly and bright red might not be so *good*, either.

During the ten minute trim, there were enough "oopsies" uttered by Mary to cause Zoe's sphincter to shrink, but she never flinched an inch.

From his vantage point, hanging from the ceiling fan by one foot and one hand, Zoe's monkey swung in lazy circles, catching her eye on each turn. He dug deep into one nostril and pulled out a long strand of stuffing. After licking it, he grimaced and flicked the fluff booger into the air and it immediately winked out of sight. Zoe rolled her eyes and looked away from him, hoping he'd follow the booger and vanish, too.

Long ago, she'd ceased wondering whether anyone *else* could see the little purple bastard, so it didn't register when she noticed Danny, his head tilted slightly to the right, following the fan's orbit with his eyes.

"Okay," Mary said, stepping around to face her, teasing Zoe's hair with her fingers, "all done." To Spider, she said, "What do you think, babe?"

Seth walked over to stand beside his girl, then slowly curled his lip. "Well, on the bright side, it'll grow back."

Mary punched him in the shoulder. "Don't be an ass. Tell her it looks good."

Seth smiled down at Zoe. "It does, I was kidding. You look awesome. Tell her she looks good, Meat."

"Dawlink," Meat said, with an overextended bow. "You look mawvelous."

"Why thank you, kind sir," Zoe answered, with a queenly nod followed by a prima donna curtsy.

Zoe hurried into the bathroom to look in the mirror. After expecting the worst, she was happily surprised with the cut Mary had been able to pull off with an old set of barber's shears. "Mary," she called through the door. "You have the hands of a fucking genius."

Zoe smiled as she listened to Mary's reply: "Tell me something I don't know."

~~oOo~~

After a short detour to White Castle for a sack of takeout burgers, Spike and Adam arrived at their rented cabin just west of St. Louis at one forty-five a.m. Spike hadn't bothered to buy burgers for the man in the trunk. He wouldn't need food where he was going.

They tied the orderly to the top of a chipped formica dinette table in the cabin's kitchen and taped the headphones from Adam's mp3 player to his ears. After a ball gag and blindfold were in place, father and son retired to the living room to eat their food.

Gideon wanted screams and horror. If they did the orderly before the freezing wore off, they, as well as their benefactor, might be sorely disappointed with the victim's participation level in his own death scene. Spike decided to wait.

At five minute intervals, Adam left the room to poke the captive with a sewing needle. The first time he flinched they could do their job and get the heck back to Chicago...with or without Lou, who'd been gone when they'd returned to the car with the orderly. Lou also hadn't answered his cell phone. Spike wasn't alarmed. Lou had run away before. He knew his way home.

"Adam," Spike called from his perch in front of the television.

"Just a sec."

"It won't be long now. Go get the two cases out of the trunk." Spike tuned to the local channel, looking for anything on the news about their hospital visit. After a few minutes of nothing special on the news, he joined his son in the other room.

Adam had emptied the cases and placed Gideon's equipment on a makeshift table beside the victim's head. At the moment his son was hunkered down over the orderly, intently working away at...something. *Oh no. Not you, too.*

"Did you start without me?"

"Nope, I'm doodling." Adam said without lifting his head. "Hang on a sec, I'm almost done. So is he. He felt those last few scratches. One of his chest muscles fluttered."

Spike hadn't finished high school, and there were a few words he'd never gotten around to using. He thought he knew what it should mean, but asked anyway.

"Fluttered?"

Adam looked up, then dropped his father's gaze. "Sorry, Dad. Fluttered means when something moves quick like, back and forth like a bird's wings."

"Scratching?" Spike asked, backing the conversation up. "I just told you to poke him every once in a while." *Well, at least you weren't eating him.*

"See, Dad?" Adam stated proudly, as he wiped smears and dots of blood from Bud's chest with a dish towel. "I made a picture. Guess what it is?"

Spike leveled a look of disdain at his eldest son. "Cut it out. This isn't the time for fun and games." His stern view didn't stop him from looking at the picture. He nodded grudgingly after taking it in. "Good artwork, though, especially with the…those." He wasn't lying. He really did think it was good. But then, Spike didn't draw—except with his gun. He didn't know any big time artist's names, but he was with a gun what one of them was with a brush: a master.

"Yeah," Adam agreed, as he pulled the blindfold from his live canvas. "Those are my favorite parts too. I even signed it with a little A at the bottom."

"That's covering your tracks, boy," Spike said, sarcastically. "Maybe you could cut that piece out and keep it for a memento." *Good lord, boy, you're as dumb as a dog sometimes.*

The scene he *thought* he'd walked in on sparked thoughts of his *other* son. Spike was little more than put out by the disappearance of his younger son, and didn't like to dwell on *what*, exactly, Lou did while away on one of his adventures. There were times when the boy would come home much the same as he had left, petulant and miserable. But there were the other times; times when he would come home after a long absence muddy, bloody, jovial to the point of lunacy, and sleep for days.

Killing was killing, but what that boy did was unnatural. Spike couldn't help feeling that he was partially to blame for the way the Lou turned out, what with his own vocation and all. Being a contract killer kept him away from home more often than not, and that left the boy to find his own way.

Spike was never one for heart to heart conversations, nor did he deal well with some of the boy's darker passions, like, for example, eating a dog—sitting cross-legged on the kitchen floor, going through the poor thing like there was a stash of candy in the middle. The memory still gave Spike the willies, but what was he to do? Have a sit down with him? He couldn't. He never knew what to say to his boys, especially Lou. His wife had always done the child rearing and he'd brought home the money. He liked it like that and wished to God she was still alive to mother the boys like they needed.

Spike waited beside the table, holding his neoprene gloves in one hand like a ten fingered bouquet, until Adam had peeled the headphones and blindfold from the orderly's head. The ball gag, Spike had decided to leave in place. The orderly looked like a screamer and Spike's nerves were already frazzled.

"Mr. Hawkins," he said, nodding politely at the wide eyed orderly. "You'll be happy to know I'm not nearly as put out with you as I was up there at the hospital. I think we can all agree it was just a case of bad timing and leave it at that. However, I want you to know what was—and I say *was*—behind door number *one* for you." He pulled Gary from his holster and expended a bullet into the palm of his hand.

He re-holstered the gun, and then held the small bullet up between two fingers. "Tiny, isn't it?" He placed it on Bud's chest. "That, Mr. Hawkins, was your door number one. So quick, so painless." He chuckled when Bud's eyes widened. "You didn't actually think you were getting out of this alive, did you?"

Bud emitted a keening sound, and raised his eyebrows, as if to say: *Yeah. I was kinda hoping.*

"Well, you're not, and you're certainly not getting another chance at door number one. Which is a darned shame, too, 'cause I'm good at that one. This," he said, and picked up a wicked looking tool from the side table, "well, I don't even know what *this* is, but you can for darn sure bet it'll hurt." *Just as soon as I figure out how to use it,* he thought.

Spike turned the tool in his hands, unsure which was the business end, then noticed a small trigger at the base of what looked like a long handle. He twisted the trigger and four spikes emerged from the other end. Impressive, but its function eluded him.

"You make anything out of this, Adam?"

He passed the item to his son, who stared at it, baffled, then snapped his fingers. "We went on a school trip to this pioneer village. You know, like where the people there are all dressed up like in the olden days and talking funny and shhh—stuff."

"So?"

"Well," Adam continued. "There was this old lady sitting at a wheel, spinning wool on something that looked like this. Hang on," he said, as he inspected the small handle.

"There," he said, triumphantly, and turned the object for his father to see what he'd found. "See that little trigger above the handle? Watch." He pulled the trigger, and the four spikes took off in a circular motion.

Spike took the tool, tried it for himself, and then dropped it onto the table. He understood the tool but still didn't know what he was supposed to do with it. *Oh, Justice. I wish you could just pop this fella so we could get the heck out of here. This just ain't natural.* He almost pitied Bud, lying there on the table with a mouthful of rubber ball. This wasn't going to be pretty, especially when Spike didn't know how to run all the weird gizmos. Mistakes would be made.

Spike turned to Bud, "I want you to know that this is in no way enjoyable for me." He raised a black hood and settled it over his head to conceal his face from the camera, and picked up a knife. Or at least he thought it was a knife; it was nearly long enough to be considered a sword. The handle was bone and the blade itself was fat with a boomerang shaped body that widened into a broad, barbed tip.

"To be perfectly honest with you," he said, mesmerized by the exotic blade, "and I don't see why it matters—you'll be dead in a few minutes—but I'm going to let you in on a little secret. I've never done this before, so it may not be pleasant. For that, I'm sorry, but remember this: you *did* bring this on yourself. Without that little adlib of yours up at the hospital, things might have gone very differently."

As the blade loomed just below the picture Adam had etched into the Bud's chest, Spike let out a shallow breath. "Welcome to door number two, Mr. Hawkins. You will not be missed."

The first incision began smoothly enough, but was caught and held by the man's hip bone, causing Bud's keening to take on the looped and fevered shriek of a junkyard gull. In an attempt to dislodge the barbed end from the joint, Spike yanked too hard, lost his balance, and dragged the razor sharp blade across the man's abdomen. The smell that poured forth was immediate and vile. Dark blood and the linked sausage of intestines, lacking their former muscular restraint, took the path of the least resistance and spilled over the mouth of the wound, and then to the table.

Behind him, Adam vomited onto the floor. "I'm okay. Keep going, Dad."

Spike was having troubles of his own. The slimy links of intestines weren't cooperating. He'd picked up the spool thing and attempted to seem as though he knew what he was doing. But the guts wouldn't stay on the spool long enough to work the winding mechanism, and Bud's screaming and flopping around didn't make any of it any easier. Spike found it altogether extremely distracting, and thought more than once about cutting the man's throat deep enough to sever his vocal cords. But since he didn't know where in the throat they were located, and a deep thrust might kill the orderly too soon, he decided against it. Besides, if he did cut the wailing man's throat, the doctor wouldn't like that at all.

Between the gurgled screams that bubbled past Bud's ball gag, and Adam's throaty, ever rising crescendo of cheers and grunts from behind the camera, not one of the three of them heard the police sirens as they neared the cabin.

One second there was a fully intact front door and three men in the cabin, the next the door lay in two pieces on the floor and a black clad army swarmed through the opening, like ants after a dropped ice cream cone. Most screamed, "Freeze! Freeze! Drop your weapons," but some of those in the front, the ones who could see what kind of party they'd crashed, were just plain screaming.

Spike may not have been the most book smart man but he saw the situation for what it was, calculated the odds of escape—of shooting their way out—and came up with his answer in less time than a bird would take to flutter one wing, one time. He let the stainless steel spool clatter to the floor and raised his hands.

Adam may have known the definition of fluttered, but obviously couldn't count worth a diddly: he dropped the camera and drew down on the wall of uniforms. He was shot dead before his gun cleared his waist band.

Spike's cry for Adam to "Leave it" was lost among gunfire and hoarse screams of "Hands! Hands! Let-me-see-your-hands!" Before Adam's bullet riddled body struck the wall and slid down, Spike was slammed to the gore slicked floor and immediately covered by the bodies of those who had intentionally jumped on him, as well as those who'd either tripped on, or slipped in the ropy guts.

As Spike was led out the door to a waiting cruiser, no less than ten red laser scope dots danced along his chest. He felt no fear or loss, nor anger or remorse. His only feeling was embarrassment. He would be thought of as something less than he really was, as a savage, a beast. Before rough hands pushed him head first into the back seat of the squad car, his gaze swept the small crowd of cops. Tears streamed down his face as he began to shake. "It's not me, you understand. This isn't what I do."

Spike was told by his court appointed public defender the next morning how they'd been found: Adam had left his new leather coat in the mental facility's infirmary. In the front pocket of the coat, the police found a receipt, paid by visa and signed by Adam Schrickt, for one cabin by the lake.

29

FRESH MEAT

Mud Vein, the sign read. Even the name of the bar scared the shit out of her.

Zoe couldn't recall at which point during the previous day hypothetical had turned to action, but as she reread the sign over the door of the roadhouse, she thought, *Maybe I should try the police again.*

To look at Frye, Zoe would have believed him if he'd said he was a navy seal or a green beret, or even a professional cannibal wrangler—which was what he'd need to be for them to pull this off. On the surface he was calm, but his clenched jaw revealed the truth: that he was wound tighter than a golf ball and eager to crack some skulls. Right then, Zoe realized how little she knew about him and his so called anger issues.

She gently slid her smaller hand into his and looked up. "Tone it down a notch, big fella. I already don't want to do this as it is. And that scowl's creeping me out, so if you keep it up I'm not going in."

Frye gave her hand a gentle squeeze and relaxed his jaw. "Don't worry about me, Zoe," he said, smiling his 'ain't I cute' smile, which had, Zoe guessed, aided in the removal of more than one pair of panties during his college football career.

"This isn't anything more than a two pronged blitz. I'm

going in. See you in five." He strutted across the half full parking lot and threw open the door.

Before the darkness of the bar took him and the door slowly muffled the trip hammer pound of the music from within, he whooped at the top of his lungs, then shouted, "Oh Yeah! What are you lookin' at, fuckwad?" Then the door closed, cutting him off from them.

Real subtle, she thought, staring after him, at the heavily painted black door. With a glance at her watch, she ducked down to the passenger window of the Seth's beetle. "Did you guys see that? He's gonna get his ass beat acting like that in there."

From the back seat, Meat said, "Don't worry about him. Worry about yourself. Frye's doing his thing. Just stick to the plan and—"

"Be careful," Mary said. "You all don't know Clive like I do. He's dangerous."

Zoe had been so wrapped up in her own fears she hadn't stopped to think how all this was affecting Mary. "We're okay. Just look at it like a two-for-one whammy. I get my information, and you can hoof him in the balls until he pukes one of them up."

She laid her hand on Mary's arm and felt her shiver. *This is really happening,* she realized in that touch. Lacking anything cool to say in parting, Zoe took a breath and said, "Oh, fuck."

With her heart pounding in her ears, she turned and followed Frye's five minute old footsteps.

The plan was simple enough; like fishing, or quail hunting...according to Frye. Zoe had never cast a line nor held a gun in her life, unless you count the kind that shoots pearl jam, but she did agree with one thing: she *should* be the lure. Zoe at least knew what *that* task entailed.

Sixty seven steps brought her across the parking lot.

It would be up to her and Frye to go into the bar, but not together.

Three deep stairs and four strides placed her at the big, black door.

Zoe would make contact with Mary's ex, Clive, and seduce

him. And once outside, bada boom bada bing—according to Frye—they'd wrestle him into the trunk and make a tire-spinning escape into the foggy night.

The door was heavier than it looked, and vibrated sympathetically with the base line blasting from within.

From there, they'd take the captive to a remote location and extract the required information.

Upon opening the door, the full gust of the thrash metal hit her like a punch in the chest. She let go of the door and counted paces all the way to the little girl's room.

Simple. Simple plan.

Just like fishing...for Jonah's whale.

Just like quail hunting—if quail had teeth.

And she didn't believe Spider's Bug could put together enough horsepower to spin the radio dial, let alone the tires.

At least it was foggy. That much was one for the plus column.

~~oOo~~

Any worries Zoe had about Frye were put to bed as she passed him on the way to the bathroom. He hadn't wasted one second of his five minute head start. He stood at the bar, passing a beer to a giggling broad faced woman with pink hair and wearing a plastic jumpsuit.

Although the girl fit in fine with the class of patrons and general theme of the bar, with her thick makeup and Billy Idol sneer, Zoe thought the woman looked more like a parody of herself—overdone, like an eighties brat pack girl, or what a Park Avenue prom queen might consider "dressing down" to go slumming with Andy Warhol.

Zoe looked down, as any girl would, and took in the woman's shoes. *Huh. Pink, like her hair. Pink and...huge?* Then Zoe went back over her once over for the *second* time. Hands: manly. Hips: There...but probably padded. Adam's apple: check.

Zoe shot a quick glance at Frye, who'd now pulled his new

friend into his lap and wrapped an arm around his/her waist.

Frye nodded slowly in Zoe's direction. He winked, and mouthed, *"I'm the man. Oh yeah."*

You sure are, she thought, *but so is she.* She smiled to herself and moved on.

There was a handwritten out-of-order sign taped to the women's washroom, which didn't matter; Zoe didn't have to pee. She only needed a destination after entering the bar. Either way, mission accomplished.

Zoe searched the faces in the crowd and found Mary's ex on the first pass. Thanks to Clive's lack of imagination and apparently good genes, he hadn't changed a bit. He even wore the same two-year-old hair style from the picture. Zoe peeked over to see if Frye was paying attention. A nod said he'd also spotted him. It was time to introduce Clive to Candace.

She'd given a lot of thought as to how to gain Clive's interest, and after tossing out a few bad ideas, circled back to some sage advice received from an old hooker: "If you wanna get some Jones' attention, get everybody's attention, then keep it 'til he sees how much the next motherfucker wants you. He'll want you, want you more'n air. Then you got him."

And that's how Zoe got him: just how she'd planned.

The bar was full but the dance floor was virtually empty— perfect for what she had in mind. Zoe poured Candace drunkenly onto the dance floor. Stumbling at first, she walked in a bee's lazy course to within ten feet of the band, a thrash metal quintet whose apparent specialty was old show tunes done jackrabbit fast.

Heedless of the beat, Zoe moved through all she could remember of *Swan Lake*, and threw in the odd pirouette or twirl to offset forgotten steps. The spins also helped her keep an eye on the target. The target, she noted, also kept an eye on her.

Soon, she lost herself in the dance, and as *Green Acres* turned to *I Dream of Jeanie*, she sensually ground and spun her way toward Mary's fledgling cannibal, Clive Purdy.

He's looking...looking and liking.

Within arm's reach of Clive's table, she stopped, sweat soaked and out of breath, and swayed, eyes closed, to some imagined beat that defied the race car rage of the band's current rip off of the *Mission Impossible* theme.

She'd gotten his attention, along with just about every other person in the bar—including the band, which broke from theme music and freight trained their way into Elton John's *Tiny Dancer,* just for her.

Hook, line, and sinker. It seemed Frye had been right about it being like fishing. But then she wondered about the bait's fate after said successful catch. *Better not to think about that right now.*

With a calculated stumble, she caught herself before falling into Clive. With her eyes half lidded, she proffered a slow building smile in the general direction of his table and yelled over the music, "Sorry, guys," then resumed her slow grind.

After a few seconds, she turned toward Clive and waited until he looked up, then she widened her stage grin. "You're yummy."

"And you're drunk," he called back.

"Or something," she yelled, and then frowned at the band. "Loud," she said, and plopped onto his lap, knocking bottles off the table as she bumped it on the way down. While the last of the bottles found their way to the floor, with death splats and pops that died under the gale force hurricane of *Mack the Knife,* Candace tossed a hook into Clive's mouth, a hook that looked suspiciously like a tongue.

She lingered on his mouth, then smiled her way out, retracting her tongue, but stayed well within his halo of yesterday's deodorant and Budweiser.

"Hi," she said. "I'm Candace. What's your name?"

He didn't answer right away, but if she didn't already know and had to go by body language, she would've guessed his name to be Boner, or maybe Rod.

"Clive."

"Hi, Clyde," she said, kissing his nose, then his forehead, then leaned back and peered upside down at his two leering friends. "Hi," she waved, then pulled herself back to Clive. "Can I tell you a secret, Clyde?"

"Clive," he said, grinning. "But you can call me whatever the fuck you want."

"Sorry. Guess what, Clive?"

"What?"

She put a finger to her lips, leaned in close to his ear, and said, "I snuck out of the house."

"Did you?"

"Uh huh. My daddy doesn't even know I'm gone."

"Oh, you naughty girl," he said. "Do you live around here?"

"Yeah, and I better get back soon, too, or my old man's gonna flip." Over Clive's shoulder, she locked eyes with Frye, still at the bar, still holding tight to his *gal*. Frye raised an eyebrow and she answered with a wink: *It's on. Get ready.*

"That's too bad you gotta go," Clive said, looking from her to his two friends. "Here I am just getting to know you."

"I have a few minutes if you want to walk me out."

The offer hung in the air for a whole nanosecond before Clive's hand shot out to his nearest friend. "Gimme your keys, Digger."

She stood and waited while Clive snatched the keys from Digger and whispered something to him. Digger laughed and glanced up at her. It was a laugh that would have normally sounded like any other belly laugh, but right there, right then, it made the small hairs on Zoe's arms stand up and dance. To that end, it was probably a good thing Candace was in charge, not Zoe. And Candace showed her teeth. *Bring it on, motherfucker.*

Clive swung the keys on his finger. "Why don't I drive you?"

"Yeah, why don't you," she said. "Bye Dagget, bye other guy."

As they wound through the crowd, Zoe slid her arm under Clive's jacket and around his waist. In the small of his back, something hard bumped her elbow with each step they took toward the door. With her fingers tucked into his front pocket, she lowered her elbow over the hard object. *Yup.* Her heart sank.

She placed her head on Clive's shoulder and dropped her other hand behind her own back and prayed for two things: 1) For Frye to have seen her leave and be right behind her, preferably without the she-man. And, 2) That the sign she made with her hand—Index finger out/thumb wiggling—was a close enough approximation of what Frye would understand to mean *gun.*

Clive straight-armed the door and they walked out, Siamese twins joined at the hip, into a night milkier than a bathtub full of cloud shit. Across the parking lot, the side by side shapes of Spider's Bug and Digger's black Chevy pickup were barely visible. Halfway there, as Clive whispered whatever in her ear, the door flew open and hit the wall with the resounding thunderclap of a shotgun, followed by the unmistakable patter of hurried feet.

This caused two things to happen: When the door hit the wall Clive whipped in a circle, separating himself from Zoe; and when he spun, Zoe's hand popped out of his front pocket. As she fell away from him, her hand reflexively closed on the pistol tucked into the back of his jeans and pulled it free.

During her attempt to point the gun, Zoe tripped and fell on her butt, and accidentally squeezed the trigger. In shock, Zoe sat at Clive's feet, mouth open, staring up at the tattered remains of Clive's left ear.

Wide eyed and furious, he slapped his hand over the wound. "You bitch! You—"

Clive's next words were ripped from him as a body hit him, sending both him and his assailant rolling in the direction of the car.

From the shrouded mass of the two bodies, Frye hissed, "Get to the car. His buddies were following you out." Then one shadow swung a roundhouse punch, sending the other to the ground.

Zoe scrambled to her feet and ran. Not far from the car she collided with Meat.

"Go," he said. "I'll help Frye."

Two strides toward the car, the black metal door slammed against the wall again. Clive's friends had come out for some action.

Zoe shot a look over her shoulder before ducking into the back seat of the Bug. Meat and Frye dragged Clive's unconscious body toward the front of the Beetle, and Clive's lackeys were still no more than barely recognizable shades across the lot.

Fog was a funny thing. Not funny 'ha ha', but funny 'scary'. It threw the book on spatial values right out the window. Clive's goons *felt* closer. Perception carried the smallest audition and amplified the effects, lending a hollow yet distinctly singular eeriness to even the most mundane sound channeled along the sleeve of fog between them. Zoe would've swore she heard them breathing, scuffing shoe leather, swallowing spit—hell, she even thought she heard them blink.

She gleaned all of this from the back seat of the car. Add imagination to fear and it becomes a conduit, hardwired into every nerve.

She jerked forward in the seat when Danny tapped her on the shoulder. "Is Meat coming back soon? He never finished his joke."

Danny received a daisy chain of "shushes" for his trouble, and kept further questions to himself.

Through the open window, carried along her imagined conduit, one of the thugs said, "I hope he don't cum in her. I didn't bring no rubbers."

And then, the reply: "Yeah, me neither. I don't want whatever disease you assholes got."

Chuckles, then...

From halfway across the parking lot—from right beside her—Zoe heard, "Hey, look. Ain't that Clive?"

Oh, shit! "Hey you guys," Zoe hissed. "Hurry up!"

POP-POP—POP

Zoe joined the rest of the group and screamed as a bullet smashed the passenger side mirror. There was angry yelling, more shots were fired, then Frye's familiar bulk appeared at the open bonnet of the Beetle, but no Meat. *Where's Meat?* Zoe couldn't move, couldn't formulate anything akin to a coherent sentence.

The car dipped as Clive's body was dumped into the Bug's cargo space. When the hood came down, revealing Frye through the windshield, his face twisted by pain and rage, Zoe saw the blood. The left side of his face and upper body were covered with smears and splatters.

Frye fumbled at the passenger side door handle, and yelled, "Come on Mary, unlock the fucking door!"

Mary popped the lock, then recoiled from him and covered her head with her arms. From across the parking lot, shouts followed a volley of gunfire.

With a scream of rage, Frye shoved the front seat forward, pasting Mary against the dash. "Zoe, the gun, gimme the fucking gun!" His eyes were wide and filled with murderous intent. "Now," he wailed, hand grasping, fingers flexing.

Startled by the total stranger wearing Frye's face, Zoe shrank back, but handed him the gun. She found her voice as he yanked it from her fingers. "What about Meat? He…"

…*was just there.*

Frye growled at Seth, "Start the fucking car." Then he was gone again, running straight at the two barely visible lumps. Firing wildly, he charged through the fog like a modern day kamikaze samurai; spent shells tinkled to the ground in his wake like tossed dimes. "Murdering motherfuckers! I'll fucking kill you!"

Seth ground the car into first gear and stomped the accelerator. The little car lurched forward as he tugged the headlights on and angled the car toward the two men. He caught up and pulled the car between Clive's posse and Frye. Above the carload's mantra-like question of, "Where's Meat?" Spider yelled across Mary, "Get in!"

Frye slid through the window as Mary flopped into the back seat.

"Oh, shit. They're coming, but one of them is limping."

Seth slammed his foot down and the Bug sputtered before it kicked into gear, and then they sped out of the parking lot. Soon, they drifted into obscurity as the fog swallowed the car's taillights.

Zoe pounded at the back of Seth's seat. "Wait! Stop," she shrieked. "Where's Meat? We have to go back! He's…he's—"

"Gone." Frye coughed as he fought to catch his breath.

"What do mean, gone?"

"Just gone," Frye croaked, his voice raw from screaming. "Those two friends of that fucking guy," he said, between clenched teeth. "One of them shot him…shot him right in the face. One second we were hogtying that prick—he was joking, you know the way he is when he's nervous—then poof."

"Poof? Poof, what?" Zoe screamed, pounding the back of his seat, "What the hell happened?"

What happened to simple?

He didn't need to elaborate. Zoe knew what happened. She happened. Meat was dead and it was all her fault. Zoe turned inward—much the same as they all did—and lost herself within a mirrored maze of shame and blame. Every injurious remark she'd ever suffered, whether true or false, gathered together and flaunted before her.

I could have said no. I should have said no. They didn't know. How could they? She was a pariah, a scourge to any unlucky enough to know her. *All Meat ever wanted to do was help… That should be me back there.*

Zoe missed him already.

She tried to recall his real name. He'd told her once, but she never used it. *Was it Mike? Mark? Mickey? Yes, Mickey. Mickey Berry.*

Dumb, heroic jerk!

Beside her, Mary quietly wept, wide eyed and shell-shocked. Danny remained silent, shedding neither tears nor comment, seemingly oblivious to the fact that Meat hadn't returned. From beneath the boy's hand, his head resting against Danny's chest, Purple Monkey glared at Zoe, then snuggled deeper into Danny's side.

Seth snorted and punched the steering wheel. "We sure fucked that up. Where did those two yahoos come from? Were they with him?"

No one answered.

"Am I talking to myself? Zoe, was one of them named Digger?"

Startled by his urgent tone, Zoe snapped back to reality. "Yeah, Digger...he was one of them."

Frye doubled over in a coughing fit, and then wiped his mouth. "When they got up to follow Zoe I was gonna cut them off, but then I saw Zoe pointing at the creep's back, pointing like he had a gun. I saw that and took off out the door."

After sitting back in her seat, Zoe felt a tap tap tap on her boot. She looked down and saw blood on the leather. The blood dripped from beneath the front seat. She leaned forward and touched Frye's shoulder. "Uh...is that yours?"

Over her quiet question, Seth exclaimed, "The pickup!" and slammed his palms against the steering wheel. "I should have sliced the tires while I was sitting there doing nothing. Man, I'm stupid."

He pushed the Bug further toward the red, causing it to shimmy and knock. Once he'd eyed each of his two remaining mirrors in turn, he punched the radio on then immediately jabbed it off again. "Digger's gonna come for us, man. He's gonna get us."

"Frye?" Zoe shook his shoulder.

"No," Frye ignored Zoe and rolled his head drunkenly toward Spider. "I got the keys. That clown in the trunk had...'em," he trailed off sleepily, and his head fell forward onto his chest.

"Frye," Seth squeaked, leaning across the front seat. "Are you okay?"

Frye stirred, and moaned when Seth pushed him back in the seat.

"Oh my God," Zoe said, after pulling up his shirt. "We've got to stop or he's gonna bleed to death." She pulled her mini-tee over her head and pressed it against the bubbling wound as her eyes searched forward, desperately seeking out a dark alley, a parking lot, anywhere they could stop without being spotted. *Oh Jesus, not him too.*

Suddenly, she jerked up as an image streaked through her mind. The image could have been wishful thinking, but she threw doubt out the window and pointed left. "There," she exclaimed, as blood dripped from her index finger onto the steering column. "Take that side street."

"Why?" Spider nervously checked his mirrors. "What's down there?"

"I don't know, just fucking do it."

But she *did* know. The little voice told her. There was a good place down that dark street; a quiet place; a remote place. She took the street's name as a good omen, too: Haven Court.

They passed another sign shortly after turning. This one read: Dead End.

Um....

After several rows of squat, three and four-storey tenements, the street did what it said and ended at a derelict train switching yard. Long weeds and piles of rotted rail ties dotted the pitted tarmac leading up an open domelike hangar which stretched back into the fog, hiding its true vastness.

At the conclusion of a short argument regarding their lack of an escape route, Seth sullenly drove into the building. The little car bumped and rocked as it passed over a series of crisscrossed tracks, and after coasting past dozens of dented rail cars and stacked pallets of rust-brown drums, they came to a stop near the last car.

Seth pulled the emergency brake and killed the lights, but left the car idling.

"What now?" Mary asked. "I mean, is Frye gonna die?"

Zoe had already dealt with the blame aspect of Meat's death. She could cry later. He was gone and nothing she or anybody did would bring him back, but Frye was alive and that was something they *could* do something about. *Take charge, Zoe, you fucking pussy. He's gonna die.*

Bathed in the greenish glow of the dashboard lights, Seth turned in his seat, shook his head like Old Yeller's vet, and said, "Yeah, he doesn't look so good. He needs a hospital, not this," he waved out the window into the darkness. "He could die."

"No," Zoe snapped. "No one else dies. Let me out."

She crouched beside Frye at the passenger door and dropped the seat back. With Seth's help, she turned him on his side. The bullet had gone all the way through; about four inches to the left of the spine was a dark oozing circle. She didn't watch enough television to know whether it was good or bad that it had gone through, but guessed, *better out than in.* She stuck her already blood-soaked shirt over the exit wound while Seth searched for bandages.

"This do?" he had asked, holding up a wad of maxi pads and a roll of duct tape.

Zoe took the pads and tape and fashioned a thick bandage, while Mary reluctantly mopped the blood from around the wounds.

"I don't think he's breathing," Mary whispered.

Annoyed, Zoe said, "Yes, he is. Now, shut up." She pushed a stray lock of hair away from her eyes with her forearm, and asked Seth, "Hey. You wouldn't happen to have first aid kit, would you?"

"No," he replied, like it was the dumbest thing he'd ever heard. "Why would I keep...wait a minute. I have some wet wipes from a restaurant."

"So get them," Zoe shot, irritably.

Shortly after she began swabbing the wounds with the wipes, Frye's eyes flew open. "Stings," he whispered and rolled his head to face her. "You trying to kill me? That shit burns."

Relieved to see him awake, she beamed at him. "Don't be a baby. They're only wet wipes."

A cough, then: "You know those are just lemon juice, Right?"

Zoe dropped the towelette. "Now I know that. But on a brighter note, we *do* have bandages. Can you sit up?"

Zoe used most of the roll of duct tape to secure the thickly wadded sanitary napkins. Upon examination of her handiwork, she thought she remembered seeing it done like that on ER or some other show, but he *was* going to need a hospital. Soon.

The next time Frye roused, Zoe took his hand. She needed him to stay awake, to fight.

"That was some gal you picked up for yourself back there, big guy."

In answer, Frye's forehead wrinkled in question.

"That chick had a dick, Frye."

"Yeah, so?"

Zoe raised an eyebrow. "Oh. That's cool. You know...whatever."

"I'm sorry," he said, lifting his hand to her face.

She covered his hand with hers. "Who am I to judge?"

"I mean Meat. If I hadn't stopped to tie up that guy..."

"Don't you dare try to take the blame for this. It's all me, all me." She held his face. "If I'd have said no, none of this shit would've happened. But I'll tell you one thing: now that we have that asshole," she nodded toward the front cargo space, "we're gonna get what we came for. Meat can't be dead for nothing. I owe him that, my sister too. I made her a promise and I'm gonna do something totally out of character and *keep* it. But first we need to get you to a hospital. Then," she said, her voice trembling on the edge of rage, "I'll deal with that cannibal wannabe. He'll talk. Believe you me, Frye, he'll fucking talk."

"No," Frye said. "Now. I want to be here for it. Please."

Zoe shook her head. "You've already lost too much blood, and I can't have you ending up like Meat."

"Mickey," Frye said, his eyes brimming with tears. "His name was Mickey."

"I knew that. I'm sorry."

"No, I'm sorry. We all called him that. And as far as I'm concerned, I'm a tough guy. Take a lot more than a bullet to stop me, especially when I got a doctor like you around."

"Playing doctor is one of my specialties. Are you sure you'll be okay?"

"I am." Then his smile faded. "But there's something you gotta know."

"Like what?"

"I couldn't leave him back there in the parking lot. I couldn't. Not when I know what I do about them." Frye gulped and looked away. "Do you really think that dude's a cannibal?"

Zoe's eyes widened. "You mean Meat's in the trunk?"

He nodded.

~~oOo~~

EWN 24 hour News
Channel 12
St. Louis, Mo

"...one eyewitness states that the abducted male, a Clive Purdy, 22, last seen inside the bar known as 'The Mud Vein', had exited the building with an unidentified female patron. According to the only eyewitness to the event, a local street person, Purdy was swept away along with the woman, by a cigar shaped saucer that, as the bystander states, "beamed them the (bleep) up, man." The witness went on to describe how it zipped away like a big yellow insect.

His statement was corroborated by several revelers who'd left the establishment to investigate "strange sounds" emanating from the vicinity of the parking lot.

Fact, or one too many drinks? Is E.T. dating your sister? You be the judge. This is Kelly Blonde, Eye Witness News, everywhere you are. John?"

"Thanks, Kelly. Up next, we'll be checking in with Anita Cox, who's been following the shocking story surrounding the brutal deaths of two local hospital workers at the Paradise Valley Psychiatric Facility. We join Anita Cox live on the steps of city hall. Anita?"

"Good evening, John. Even at this late hour, the tension in the air surrounding those inside city hall, as well as out here, on the steps of the building, remains palpable. I'm being told that the suspect, Spike Schrickt, of Chicago, Illinois, whose son was slain during the early morning raid of a rented cabin just south of Three-piece Lake, has denied allegations that he and his deceased son, Adam Schrickt, had any part in the murder of the first of the two victims.

Schrickt states and I quote: "I did that second one—I can't deny that—but what happened to that lady, well, it was just unnatural. It ain't what I do".

Sources inside City Hall refuse to comment regarding allegations of these murders being of a Manson style nature, and have stated that all avenues are currently being pursued. A spokesperson close to the investigation states that they are near to resolving the case, with or without the confession of Schrickt.

St. Louis: City under siege? Are the police working hard, or hardly working? Live from city hall, and keeping you updated hourly, this is Anita Cox, Eye Witness News: Your eye on the street. John?"

"Thanks, Anita. That's all we have time for today, but Anita Cox will keep us up to date, up to the minute, as this disturbing tale unfolds. Is there a cult presence in St. Louis? Will these recent Manson style slayings stir up the ten year debate regarding relocation or closure of the sorely outdated Paradise Valley Mental Facility? You be the judge. Join us online to vote or leave your opinions."

30

RECYCLED

Shoulder to shoulder, Zoe and Seth stood in silent anticipation. She could only speak for herself, but guessed Seth shared her dread at opening the trunk. Clive's arms and legs were bound, and, according to Frye, bound well, but escape wasn't the issue. It was his teeth. No one blamed Frye for what he did, putting Me—Mickey's body in the trunk with the cannibal. Any one of them would have done the same, but that didn't change the fact that it might not have been the smartest thing to do.

Frye had passed out, breathing fitfully, and shivered under a cold sheen of sweat. Mary volunteered to stay with him to keep an eye on the bandages, but remained hunched over in the back seat, staring at her hands and rocking. Zoe couldn't fault the girl for being afraid. Zoe was scared shitless and she didn't even know Clive that well.

Danny remained blessedly oblivious; sitting in the back seat, hands folded across his lap, he stared out the window at nothing, mumbling to himself. Zoe envied him his ignorance, his detachment, his unbridgeable disparity. Insanity sometimes had its advantages.

The ear-shot cannibal was awake; not talking or yelling for help, oddly enough, but Zoe could both hear and see the evidence that he *was*. The muffled grunts, accompanied by a slight shift of the small car with each struggled movement, spoke volumes to her imagination.

At her side, Spider attempted to seem larger than his bony frame and braver than his knocking knees. He looked *so* young.

"We have to get Mickey out first. He's on top of Clive," she stated.

"Who?"

"Meat." Zoe swallowed a lump. "His name is Mickey. We can't leave him like that."

"No. I guess we can't." Spider made no move to open the trunk.

Zoe elbowed him. "So pop the trunk."

"Shh. Listen," whispered Spider. "Can you hear that?"

"Yeah, but I'm trying not to."

"No, not that," he said, turning toward the closest rail car. "Rats, lots of them."

"So? It's an old building," said Zoe. "You afraid of a few rats after what we just did?"

"Whatever. Let's just hurry, that's all I'm saying."

After a short tableau—a mental rock, paper, scissors—Seth sighed. "How about this: You pop the trunk, I pull him out."

Zoe pulled the trunk release and stared at Seth until he went to work. As he leaned into the trunk, she heard him whispering to himself: "Nothing to it. Just like a big old carpet...a bag of dog food."

Struggling with Meat's body, he grunted, "He's stuck. I need help."

Zoe moved closer, fighting the urge to purge—knowing if she puked, she'd most probably lose her nerve. She averted her eyes, and said, "Put my hands on his legs...but find me a dry part."

"I don't think there *are* any."

Just then, the arm that was previously "caught" on something suspiciously dropped free, and Meat's body slipped past the lip of the trunk, carried Zoe to the ground and pinned her there, face to face. She stared in shock at the mouth that had once told her about a king and a woodpecker—a mouth that, just an hour before, had been smiling, joking. Now his mouth was a slackened slit and there was a saucer sized divot in the top his head. He'd never smile again.

From the blackness of the fore lit trunk, Clive chuckled.

Zoe shoved Mickey off and rolled away. She pushed herself into a sitting position, hands in the dirt behind her, and closed her eyes. *Don't listen to him. Don't look at Mickey. Don't think about Mickey. Get up.*

She couldn't move. When she opened her eyes and looked to Seth for some sort of support, he was staring, open mouthed, into the trunk. *What...? No! Don't think about it. Don't look directly at him. Get what you came for and lea—*

She froze as something tickled the back of her hand. "Fuck me!" she screamed and jumped up, rubbing frantically at her body in an attempt to dislodge whatever had touched her.

The giggles from the trunk continued.

Startled at the outburst, Spider let out a short scream of his own. "What? What?"

"Rats," she yelled, angry at herself for being such a girl. "I fucking hate rats!"

From the darkness of the trunk, Clive teased, "Rats? Not afraid of a few little rats, are you...Candace?"

"Shut up! Just shut the fuck up," Zoe hissed. She sobbed, and to Seth, said, "I can't do this, any of it. Meat wasn't supposed to die—"

Clive's laughter abruptly ceased. "Meat? Seriously? That was this asshole's name?" He erupted in a bray of laughter. "That's rich. That's sooo fucking rich...Oh-my-stomach."

That's it! Zoe strode past Seth, reached into the trunk and grabbed two handfuls of Clive's hair. She placed her foot on the bumper and pulled until his head was over the lip of the trunk. "Think that's funny, motherfucker? How's this for funny?" she screamed, and slammed the hood into his face. In the grip of rage, both fear and reason bled away. All she wanted was to hurt him, to end the taunts, the laughing. "How funny is it now?" *Slam!*

"Zoe!"

"How 'bout now?" *Slam!* Her mouth twisted into a snarl, she lowered herself close to his face, a face that showed not fear but wild eyed hatred and hunger, and she spit in his eye. As she raised the hood again, her breath coming in ragged gulps, and her arm shaking from the exertion of holding his thrashing head still, a hand closed over hers and pulled it away from the hood.

Spider drew her from the trunk by the waist. "Stop, Zoe. That's enough. You got him, calm down now."

Clive spit out a mouthful of blood and pieces of his front teeth. Through a freshly broken smile, he lisped, "Seth? Seth Speedo? Is that you?"

"Shut up, Clive," Spider said, gritting his teeth.

"Is that what this is about? That cunt you stole from me? Hell, I thought this was part of my initiation into the club."

"What club?" Seth asked.

"The kind of club that sends you some skank so you can baste 'em with sperm and then eat 'em." He winked at Zoe as he licked his broken lips. "Mary was gonna be my first, you know," he went on, smirking. "She was gonna be my number one...right after I fucked her."

Without warning, Seth kicked Clive in the face, lifting the savage's head away from the bumper, sending him back into the cargo space. "You keep her out of this, you fucking freak!"

"Oh shit," Zoe squeaked, shocked at Seth's sudden attack. "Whoa." She pushed herself between Seth and the open trunk. "He's just baiting you. It's what he wants."

Seth rounded on her. "What difference does it make? He's not gonna tell us anything anyway."

"But we haven't even *asked* him anything yet. I know I freaked, too. That was the rats...and, well, him, but I'm okay now. Let me ask."

"Ask me what?" Clive said.

"See?" she said, motioning toward the trunk. To Clive, Zoe said, "We need some information."

"Really? If I tell you what you want to know, can I keep the meat? I only had a taste on the way here and I could go for a little more. He was finger licking good."

His remark spurred Zoe to glance down at the body. *Oh god.* One of Meat's hands resembled a half chewed chicken wing, and was missing two fingers. Zoe gulped a breath that hitched in her throat, then tore her eyes away from the body. She left Clive's dig unanswered. Instead, she said, "Mary told me about the party you brought her to, the one with televisions with stuff on them. Do you remember that night?"

"Stuff?"

"Killings," she said.

"Don't you mean *snuff* stuff?" he asked, amused by her discomfort.

"Okay, right." she said, slowly. "So you know the night I'm talking about?"

"How could I forget?" He moaned. "It was the night I took that slut's cherry."

Seth tensed and Zoe put a hand on his arm. "Don't." To Clive, she said, "Do you remember any of the actors from the movies…maybe one that was at the party that night?"

Clive fell silent for a moment. Zoe thought he might not answer, out of some cannibal comradeship, or fear, but then he let out a whistled breath, and asked a question of his own. "Oh, you're looking for Cannibalangelo? Is that all? If you untie my hands, I'll just get his address for you. It's in my back pocket." Then he spat a mouthful of blood and said, "Fuck you, slut. Even if I knew, I wouldn't tell you shit."

Spider moved closer. "You're really not helping your own cause, you know. You might want to answer her. She wants you dead."

"Fuck you, pussy."

"Suit yourself." Seth shrugged.

Clive's slightly amused gaze jogged back and forth from Zoe to Spider, like a squirrel on a fence, then he said, "I really can't help you, bitches. You don't find a man like Cannibalangelo, he finds you."

"Hi Clive," Mary said from behind Zoe.

"Jesus, Mary. You scared the shit out of me," Zoe said,

then saw the gun in Mary's hand. Frye had emptied it at the men in the parking lot, but Zoe thought she'd add a little theatre to the act. It certainly wouldn't hurt. *They* weren't getting anywhere with him. What Zoe didn't know, though, was whether or not *Mary* knew the gun was empty.

When Clive saw the gun, his eyes widened. "Mary," he breathed. "I didn't know you were here. I didn't mean what I said before about you. I was just having fun with your friends."

Mary thumbed the hammer, said, "Goodbye Clive," and closed her eyes.

"Wait! No, baby. Hold on. Doesn't what we had mean anything to you?"

Unmoved, Mary opened her eyes and glared at him for a beat before she stuck the gun down the front of his pants and turned her head. "You got five seconds. Answer the fucking question. If I don't like your answers, you lose your peashooter. Go."

"Come on, baby, I—"

"I'm not your fucking baby and I'm not fucking around! Two seconds."

He talked. Zoe leaned in to hear him, but he babbled nonsense: "Something, something, internet," and "yada, yada web site," and then he said a name.

"One," Mary said.

Clive was terrified. Whether it was the gun or the girl was unknown. Zoe suspected Mary didn't know the gun was out of bullets. "Wait, Mary," she said, and turned to Clive. "You said a name. Chan? Chan Chow?"

Clive sobbed, tearing his eyes away from Mary. "Chin Choi? Yeah," he said, beaming, eager to keep his jewels. "Harry Funshine, he knows everybody." To Mary, he said, "I don't know anything else, baby. Truth. Find Chin Choi. He works for Harry Funshine. He can help. Honest to God, that's all I know. Please don't shoot."

Zoe stepped between Mary and the fledgling cannibal. "Where? Hurry now. I don't think I could stop her from blowing your balls all over the carpet if you don't tell me."

"Michigan," he said, spraying her face with a fine mist of spittle and blood. "I went there once for a get-together."

After they'd extracted the address, Zoe and Seth hauled him over the lip of the trunk and allowed gravity to carry him to the dirt.

Blood dribbled down his chin as he pleaded, "I did what you said. Untie me. My ear's bleeding and I can't feel my arms; I got no circulation. Come on, Mary. Please, for old time's sake? What do you say?"

Mary gave him a smoldering look. "I *say*...stay here and die." She aimed the gun at his face and closed her eyes.

Clive flinched.

Click.

"Huh," Mary said. "Imagine that." She dropped the gun beside his head, then walked around the car and threw up.

Zoe looked pointedly at Seth. "She didn't know the gun was empty, did she?"

"I thought it was loaded too."

"Huh," said Zoe.

"Yup." Spider shifted his feet uncomfortably. "What about him?"

"You wanna untie him?"

"Not particularly. You?"

"Not a chance."

"So?"

"So fuck him. He's a ghoul." Zoe spat toward the cannibal.

Clive tried to roll over, but settled for raising his head. "Still here, people. I can hear you—and I'm not a ghoul, thank you very much. I'm an interspecies recycler."

Zoe kicked him. "Shut up." To Seth, she said, "Help me with Mickey. We're taking him with us."

After placing Meat back in the trunk, Seth jabbed a thumb toward Clive. "So, we're just gonna leave him tied up?"

"He'll be fine."

"What about the rats?" Spider asked, loud enough for Clive to hear.

"Rats?" echoed Clive. "You can't do that. They'll eat me!"

"Not afraid of a few rats, are you?" teased Spider.

"You don't have to look at it like that, Clive," added Zoe. "Just think of it as *them* recycling *you*."

Back in the car, Zoe checked on Frye. He was still breathing, but cold to the touch. "We gotta get him to a hospital."

"Didn't I say that a half an hour ago?" Spider replied.

"Save it," Zoe shot back. "Just drive."

Seth navigated the car around Clive. Zoe stuck her arm out the window as they passed and dropped a nail file near his foot. As Clive disappeared from the taillights, above his shouted curses, she called, "Don't ever say I didn't give you a fighting chance. Good luck and fuck you."

~~oOo~~

Danny remained in the car while they moved the bodies, but was aware enough of their situation to say goodbye to a semiconscious Frye and tell him to take care of Meat.

After leaving them on a park bench near the hospital, Zoe called 911 from a payphone: it was the best she could offer. Parked in the shadows of a dumpster half a block away, they waited until the ambulance came, and then Seth pulled away before the police arrived.

A few blocks away, Seth turned to Zoe. "Where to? Michigan? 'Cause if that's the case we're gonna need some gas."

"Clothes first," said Zoe, sitting in a blood splattered bra and skirt. "And we're gonna need to wash this car inside and out, 'cause if we get pulled over, we're screwed. *Then* we can go after Clive's pen pal."

After bypassing two car washes for being too visible, they were able to find an out of the way all night coin-op car wash. First they washed themselves, taking turns scrubbing one another with the fat, soap spewing brush and rinsing off with the sprayer, then they tackled the car.

Zoe had to coax Danny out of the back seat with the

promise of chocolate, so that Seth could wash the interior of the car.

"Not bad," Zoe said, after she rushed through a final wipe of the crevasses in the vinyl seats. "I think we got the worst of it."

Danny stood shivering in the early morning cold. When Zoe told him to get back in, he did a double take. "Hey, how come you guys are so wet? And where's Zoe's shirt?"

God, I envy him, Zoe thought. "Get in, Danny. We gotta go."

Danny pulled off his shirt and handed it to Zoe. "Here, take this. Your boobies are hanging out." He wrapped his arms across the worst of the burn scars on his chest and shot her with a tightlipped smile, then looked away.

She pulled the shirt over her wet bra and then touched his hand. "Thanks, Danny. You're a true gentleman: my knight."

In answer, he turned his back to her and resumed his window watch.

He knows, she thought. *He just can't filter it.* She'd hoped none of what happened had broken through the cocoon he'd woven around himself, but it had. He just didn't *want* to know. An overwhelming pity surged through her. Danny didn't deserve this, any of this, but they couldn't leave him with Frye and Meat. With Mickey dead and Frye unconscious, he'd be all alone, and Zoe didn't think she could bear that.

She pulled one of his hands away from his chest and held it, tears blurring her vision. He allowed the intrusion into his personal space, but stared out the window at the world—a world out there, but also in his head. One in which Meat might still be alive, still right there beside him, telling a joke.

She wanted to say 'everything's gonna be alright', but couldn't find the courage to lie. Instead, she let go of his hand. It was time to finish what they'd started.

"Seth?"

"Zoe."

She pulled a scrap of paper from her purse. On it was written the name and address of Clive's online buddy, an old Chinese man named Chin Choi. "Let's go."

31

AND THEN THERE WERE FOUR

They stopped at a roadside diner in Illinois and ate breakfast in silence. From there, Zoe took over driving while Seth took a nap.

Danny asked if they were there *yet* forty-three times before reaching their destination. The last time was just as Zoe pulled the car up to a barely visible mail box, the name all but obscured by the wild grass that covered the entire area. To the left of the mailbox, twin ruts trailed off and disappeared behind a thick stand of trees.

The name on the box said they were there.

"Yeah, Danny, I think we're there."

At least Clive hadn't lied to them.

Zoe rolled up her window and locked the door before turning into the laneway.

Clive's "pen pal" lived in what could only be described as a shack with tumors. At one point it must have started as a trailer, but had sprouted double-wide fiberboard blisters from each side, and a broad wraparound porch.

Barely visible from the dirt road they'd traversed to get there, the property had all but given up its struggle with the local vegetation. Ancient oaks crossed limbs above the sprawling homestead, creating a natural umbrella of flora, while climbing ivy and wild grass carpeted nearly all of the outside walls and windows. Even the stairs sported a veined, greedy, green toupee. A derelict checkered sofa with puffy wounds of exposed ribs and springs sat to the side of the only visible door, a dust caked glass slider with an interior curtain consisting of taped together pages of newspaper.

Zoe couldn't imagine *anyone* having lived in this place for a long, long time. Then again, she'd never won a game of clue before either. This was the right place, she was sure of it.

"Nice, wholesome friends Clive has," Seth said.

On the other side of the grimy sliding door, the newspaper moved. "Hey, did you guys see that?"

"Yeah," Mary said. "At least we know he's home."

Zoe opened her door. "Clive *did* say this guy wasn't dangerous, right?"

"No," Seth piped in, "he said he was old."

Mary moved to stand beside Zoe. "Which one do you think it was? That Harry guy or the Chinese dude?"

Spider circled the car. "I don't think it was either of them. Look."

A small face appeared at the bottom of the sliding door, and then vanished.

"Holy shit," Mary said. "Is that a cat or a rat?"

"If it's a cat," whispered Zoe, "it's the ugliest one I've ever seen. See the size of those ears?"

Seth walked around to the side of the trailer. He waded through the thigh high grass, arms raised, waving away a cloud of bugs, but stayed far enough away from the dwelling that it couldn't flick out a demonic clapboard tongue and gobble him up. He stopped at a six foot privacy fence, covered in much the same way as the rest of the trailer, with creeping weeds, and boosted himself up to see the other side.

"Hey guys, get a load of the backyard. There's all kinds of stuff back here."

Mary left to see what Seth had found, and Zoe ducked her head into the car. "Danny, you wanna come?"

Danny didn't reply. Aside from 'are we there yet', he hadn't said a word during the nine hour drive from St. Louis. *Kid, therapy's gonna be the least of what you're gonna need by the time this is done.* "I'll be back in a minute," she told him.

Nothing. Not even a blink. He was still out for that Sunday drive, and, oddly enough, Purple Monkey had stayed behind with Danny, perched on the boy's lap like he was giving his Christmas wish list.

She normally didn't speak to the monkey, or at least *speak first*, especially if someone else was present: she'd learned from experience to not engage the foul mouthed little bastard in any type of discourse. It always ended badly. But this time Zoe felt she had to.

"*What the hell are you doing, monkey?*" He should be gone, disappeared along with her addiction—well, he shouldn't exist in the *first* place—nevertheless, there he sat; like a demented Muppet with a hair lipped sneer and a tongue that bit like barbed wire. At the moment he glared up at her, accusation filling every silent beat of his cloth covered heart.

"*Go away,*" she told him. "*I don't need you anymore.*"

"*Don't you? Without me, you'd be dead a hundred times over, bitch.*"

"*You know that isn't true. I'm done with it. Candace is gone and so is that life. I'm different now. I have friends now…people who care. And you're not real, so go away.*"

"*I'm not real, huh? If that's so, then who the fuck are you talking to?*"

"*Myself…?*"

Really? So you're crazy, then?

"*That's not true. The doctor said it was perfectly healthy to have—*"

"*An imaginary friend like me? Besides, that was twelve fucking years ago.*"

"*Then go away.*"

"*I can't.*"

"*Why not?*"

"*Because I found somebody who needs me more than you do, so piss off.*"

"*What?*"

"*Go, bitch. You're friiieeends are calling you.*"

Mary called to her, "C'mere. Leave him there for a minute. You gotta see this."

"Go ahead, Zoe," Danny said quietly, still gazing out the window. "We'll be fine."

"Alright." She turned to leave, then stopped. The small hairs on the back of her neck and arms began to tingle. "What did you say, Danny?"

"Go ahead. I'll wait here."

"No, that's not what you said. You said *we*, as in more than one."

He didn't respond. He was gone again.

The purple monkey settled back and dismissed her with a shooing gesture, but said nothing. Then, like a miss-delivered pizza at a Weight Watchers convention, he disappeared.

Hanging halfway over the fence, Seth called over his shoulder, "There's a whole fucking circus show set up back here—a pretty cool one. It's probably where he does his killing."

"Coming," Zoe said, sparing one last look at the boy huddled in the back seat of the Bug.

As she rounded the car, Zoe spied movement out of the corner of her eye. Startled, she shrieked and fell backward into the waist high waves of grass, causing both Seth and Mary to scream in turn and swish back to see what happened.

"What?" Seth yelled, tromping toward her. He halted when he saw what had spooked her: a short Asian man stood on the other side of the car. Seth placed a protective arm in front of Mary, who'd bumped into him when he stopped, and said, "Who're you?"

The little man glared at them each in turn, shaking his fist. "What you kid do here? This no camping prace. You go now."

Spider gave the man a wide berth as he walked Mary over to Zoe. "Did he hurt you? Are you okay?"

Behind Seth, Mary smirked at the old man. Zoe stood and turned to see why Mary was grinning. The old man looked like a tiny, rumpled old elf.

Zoe brushed dirt from her clothes, and gazed at the curious

little man who was attempting to articulate, with great animation and gesticulation—amid short broken sentences—that he wanted them to leave.

Other than naked irritation, there was nothing menacing in his words or actions. The scariest thing about him was the tiny hairless animal cradled in his arms. It resembled nothing she'd ever seen and was just about the worst skin-and-bone jigsaw puzzle God had ever created, and she'd seen a platypus. She thought it might be some kind of rat.

"Chin Choi?" Zoe asked.

The man tucked the animal into his heavily stained voluminous yellow satin robe, and squinted down his finger at her. "I not want buy nutting. Go now." He clapped his hands in dismissal. "You keep you rerigion. I buy nutting. Go."

Suddenly, Zoe wondered where the other man was, the old cannibal, Harry Funshine. She swept her gaze around the clearing and saw no one, but that didn't mean there wasn't someone out there, waiting to pounce, needing only a nod from the straw haired oriental.

"Ask him about Clive," Seth whispered.

"You just did, moron. He's right in front of you." To Chin Choi, Zoe smiled, ignoring his pleas for them to go, and said, slow and loud, like any ignorant explorer in the darkest depths of Africa would: "Do you," She mimed along—badly. "Know a man"—she puffed out her chest and tried to look dumb— "named Clive Purdy?" She finished by pretending to eat her arm, then licked her fingers and rubbed her stomach. She shrugged. "Well?"

"Crime party?" the old man wrinkled his nose in confusion.

"No. C-l-i-v-e P-u-r-d-y," she spelled. "Do you know him?"

It wasn't until the little man turned and started to walk toward the trailer, shaking his head, that Zoe saw his footwear. Now she understood the unquenchable smirk on Mary's face. He wore clown shoes—big red ones. "Well, if you don't know him, how about Harry Funshine?"

He halted his retreat and visibly stiffened. Still facing away, he asked, "What you know 'bout Harry crazyman? He stone cold kirrah. He eat you and you friend and burp for more. You no want him. You go before he come."

At seeing his bare, chopstick thin legs and enough thigh to suggest he wore no pants, Zoe fought a mental image that he might be free-balling. *Gross.*

She attempted to put together how she could approach the reason they were there, and Jeanne's face came to her mind, causing her breath to catch in her chest. Thinking of her still hurt so much. "Well, you see, Sir, we're looking for Mr. Funshine because I believe he could help me find the man who killed my sister." *There. That wasn't so hard,* she thought.

"Please don't say you can't tell us where he is. We need to talk to Mr. Funshine. If you tell us how to find him, we'll go, promise. Please, Mr. Choi. I need your help."

Zoe watched as the little man slumped slightly, bowing his head, then he turned, shaking his head, "No. Maybe you stone cold kirrer, too. Maybe you sent by coo coo doctor to snuff Harry, or raugh rike he dumb tiger in cage. Maybe you just as crazy rike you Crive was. That right, I know who Crive is." The old man sniffed and shook his head, stroking the bundled animal under his robe. "That man—that Crive Puddy—he got the crazy rike wild badger."

"Yeah, no shit," said Mary. "I used to date him 'til I found out what a freak he was."

Zoe put up a hand to quiet Mary. She felt like she was getting somewhere with him, and had a feeling he was going to tell them something important. And, for reasons known only to God and her gut, she knew they needed him. For *what*, she had no idea, but trusted her intuition explicitly. The sensation was subtle, but insistent. It was nothing as dramatic as the alarms that warned her away from dangerous people, like it had been with Buddy and the two killers, but *something* told her he was no murderer—now or ever.

She said: "Clive Purdy and two of his friends killed my friend Mickey. We're nothing like *him*." she said, hotter than she'd planned, tears welling in her eyes. "But he won't ever hurt anyone again, the fucker. We made sure of that." At least she thought she did.

Zoe halted long enough to calm down and let her anger pass. "Listen," she said "We're not going to hurt you or Harry Funshine. We just want to know how to find a man named Cannibalangelo so—"

"Are you out of your god damned mind, child!? That man will—"

Zoe's jaw dropped as he spouted perfect English during the rest of his journey to his front door.

"Cut you into tiny pieces—all of you!—and mix it into a big fucking stew. You don't want to find him. I'm sorry about your sister and that other friend of yours, but I can't help you." Chin Choi snorted at his own words. "Help you? I mean *get you killed*. I won't have it on my conscience. You have no idea how big this is, girly."

A cold finger of fear traced its way up Zoe's spine. *That's almost exactly what Simply Bob told me.*

"Wait a minute. You know about these people and they let you live?"

He shrank back as she advanced.

Emboldened by his meek posture—and the clown shoes didn't hurt either—Zoe stalked toward him. "You *can't* be hiding out here, because if that idiot Clive Purdy knew where to find you, so would *they*. So what are you, some kind of pet for this Harry guy? Or maybe his boyfriend? Feel free to stop me if I get it right, but just cut the shit like you did with your stupid accent and help me."

During her rant, his look of fear had been replaced by a smile, then the smile stretched into a grin, smoothing out the creases in his cheeks. "My dear," he said, "You have no idea what that man is capable of. If I told you how to find him, I might as well have killed you with my own hands. Can't you see I'm trying to save your lives?" Chin Choi pulled the sequestered animal from his robe, sat down on the top step, and stroked the creature's bald back. Now that Zoe was closer, she could see it was, in fact, a dog.

She also caught a "Basic Instinct" style look up the old

man's robe as he crossed his legs, and wasn't able to turn away fast enough. The image was there forever and she'd never look at a scrotum in quite the same way again.

"Rats." Zoe said, looming over Chin Choi. She had no intention of frightening him, but by standing above him, she couldn't see his balls anymore.

"I don't follow."

"Rats," she repeated. "That's how we left that motherfucker, Clive, to die. We left him, tied up and bloody, surrounded by hundreds of rats." The uncertainty of Clive's death, and the cowardly way they'd left him there, made her angry all over again. "That's what I'm capable of you old bastard, so start talking!"

"Zoe! I don't think you should talk like that to him." Mary warned from the safety of Seth's arms.

Addressing Mary, Chin said, "It's alright, Miss. I know she doesn't mean anything by it. So does Poco." He flipped the dog onto its back to rub its bony chest. "Isn't that right, Poco?" he baby-cooed, "She's not a meanie at all, is she?"

"Look," Zoe said, "maybe we should just wait for Harry Funshine. Can we wait here for him?"

He ignored her as he stroked the dog's saggy skin. Each push of his hand caused the dog's enormous scrotum to jiggle like a balloon full of loose Jell-O.

Zoe averted her eyes. *Great. Another image to take to the grave.* "Mr Choi? Is it alright if I call you that?"

"You could," he said, as he pulled the dog to his chest. "Or you could call me Harry."

Harry? Zoe took a few guarded steps back from the porch and stole a look over her shoulder. Then she thought: *Wait a minute. He can't weight more than a bag of buttered popcorn. Why are you scared?* She squared her shoulders and faced him. "Cannibalangelo," she said. "I need to find him."

"And what, pray tell, would *he* have to do with me?"

Isn't that the million-dollar question? "Well, Harry, if you *are* who you say you *are*, then you must know how to find him. And if you're full of shit, then you're full of shit and we'll wait for the real Harry."

"Was your sister in a video?"

Zoe's heart sank. "I'm not sure, but probably."

"Can't say as I've seen it—I don't watch those sorts of things—but I do know him; blonde haired, handsome fellow? He should be about thirty years old by now. Does that sound close?"

"Good guess," she said. "But do you remember anything specific about him? Buck teeth, bad acne?"

"No," he said, shaking his head, "no buck teeth, but..."

"Thanks for nothing, *Chan*," Zoe said, frustrated, thinking, *So much for my little voice.* "We'll wait for Harry in the car."

"It's Chin, Zoe," offered Spider.

"...he did have this rather large tattoo."

Zoe stiffened.

"Oh my god, Zoe," Mary stated, excitedly. "That old fart *does* know him."

"I also know the name he uses. Gideon stole it from a head stone: Zane—Zane Ellis. But knowing that name does you no good. You'd have to go a different route..." he drifted off, as though contemplating his next statement.

Harry held three fingers in the air and whistled, and the little dog did three consecutive backward somersaults. The old man beamed down at the dog, then tossed the dog a treat. "I'm not like him, you know, like Zane. Or even the good Doctor Gideon, for that matter."

"Nice try," said Seth. "We were told all about Harry Funshine, mister, so you can drop the act. We don't give a shit about you or your diet. Just tell us where to find this Gideon. We'll make *him* tell us what we want to know."

"My good man, the doctor does what he wishes and nothing you could ever do would change that. Why don't you try the police or a private eye, like that Magnum fellow. I hear he hasn't worked in years."

"Won't work," Seth said. "The police can't help."

"And," Zoe said, "They'd arrest us on sight. Some things happened back in St. Louis..."

Mary punched Zoe in the shoulder. "Hey!"

"What? I already told him about Clive. What's he gonna do, call the cops? He's not gonna say shit." She turned to Harry. "Are you, mister?"

Harry's eyes twinkled as their predicament became clear to him. "Oh my, how exciting," he said. "You're on the lam, eluding the long arm of the law. How sinfully gauche."

Zoe toyed with a fingernail. "I mean, a man like you, with your own secrets and all. Wouldn't it just suck for you if we were caught?" She raised her eyes to his. "Especially when the police ask us about all the interesting people we met along the way. People like you."

Undaunted by her naked threat of exposing him, he smiled a big crooked smile. "There's no need for blackmail, dear. I've decided to help you. For a price, that is." Still smiling, he said, "Let's go negotiate. We can go out back. I always think better in the back yard."

Stepping out the back door was like stepping into another world. Seth was right about the back yard being strange—and not only in comparison with the rest of the property. The lawn was a meticulously neat carpet of green, and large beautiful flowers flourished in lush gardens. Along the back fence, a barn board shed sheltered three identical kennels. In each of the two occupied cages a bald dog stared silently at the group, tail wagging.

Nothing strange about any of that, but in the center of the yard was a full circus setup, complete with two-tiered bleacher seating off to one side. Near the outer edge of the circle a rack held balls of varying sizes and colors, hula hoops, and three unicycles. Propped against the side of the rack was a tiny two wheeled bicycle. Center stage, there was a small trampoline and four old mattresses; Harry Funshine had a one ring circus right there in his back yard.

Apparently, Zoe thought, *the old fella has a little too much time on his hands.* None of what he showed them seemed to have anything to do with a price, though. "What's your price, Harry?" From the corner of her eye, she spied Danny reaching for one of the striped wooden balls. "Hands in your pockets, mister," she growled.

Danny ducked his head and moved away from the shelf.

Harry ignored Zoe's question of price as he nodded toward the kennels. "That beautiful pair over there is George and Gracie. George is the black one. They're Poco's parents. Aren't they adorable?"

Seth stepped in front of Harry and snapped his fingers. "What's your price, Chan?"

"Chin," corrected Mary.

"Or Harry," said Harry, executing a cartwheel followed by a comical curtsey. "The real Harry Funshine."

Zoe wanted to scream. He was as annoying to talk to as the fucking monkey. "Yeah, we get it, mister. Your name's Harry. That's super awesome, but what's your fucking price?"

"Let's make it a surprise, shall we? Come with me, miss. I'll show you. Your friends can wait out here for us. The price itself is inconsequential."

"Oh, yeah? Like what? You can see we don't have any money. Look at our car."

"Fine, I'll tell you here, but we may spoil the surprise."

"I'll risk it."

"My price is this," said Harry. "You, young lady, must do something for me. Something I haven't been able to do by myself in quite some time."

"That, I understand," she said under her breath. *Awe, man. Do I have whore written on my forehead?* "Seth, Mary," she said, woodenly. "Take Danny back to the car. I'll just be a minute."

"That's alright," said Harry, waddling like Chaplin toward the trailer. "They can wait here and watch. Come on. It'll be fun."

"We're not leaving her alone with you," Seth said defiantly. "What do you need? I'll do it."

Zoe couldn't help but smile. "It's okay, Seth. What's he gonna do, gum me to death? Stay here, and if I need you—*trust me*—you'll hear me."

"But—"

"No, Seth. Get Danny off that trampoline before he kills himself, and sit down. It's cool. This is something I can take care of all by myself." With a sidelong look toward Harry, she wrinkled her nose. *I've probably done worse…can't imagine when, but probably.*

~~oOo~~

Zoe left the slider open. "Okay, let's do this, but not in front of them. Please."

Harry Funshine ignored her comment, and led her *not* to a bedroom, but to what served as a study or a den. This was a guess, of course, because there might well have *been* a bed under the thousands of yellowed newspapers and hard cover books, but she didn't see one.

"Okay, what are you waiting for? Let's do this." She tugged her shirt over her head and tossed it into his lap. "But I'm telling you, if you so much as flash those green teeth in my direction, you'll be picking them out of the wall. Do you get me?"

"I enjoy your enthusiasm, but I believe you misunderstand my intentions."

"Huh?"

He walked over to an ornately carved wooden chest, pulled back the lid, and tossed her a rhinestone studded body suit. "Put that on. I believe it should fit. Size six, right?"

She made no move to catch the thrown tights. They hit her chest and fell to the floor. Zoe stared at him in confusion for a few seconds, then picked the clothing up by its bedazzled shoulders. "What the…rhinestones?"

"Indeed. You wear it. Can't do the show naked, can you?" A lopsided grin formed under bobbing eyebrows. "Well, I guess you *could*, but then who'd pay any attention to the dogs?"

Dogs? Whoa. "Okay, back the truck up, there, sicko."

"Zoe? That is your name, is it not?"

"Yeah."

"Well then, Zoe, I think there's something I need to show

you before we join your friends in the yard. Isn't that right, Poco?"

Harry sat down at his large cluttered desk, cleared away a few old magazines, and pulled a fat, dog eared, file from a drawer. He opened it and carefully flipped through a few oversized pictures, smiled at some frozen memory or other, then moved on to the next. After separating three photos from the bundle, he beckoned her over to see. Zoe balked at first, remembering the last time someone asked to look at some photos, but reluctantly complied.

The closest picture was of a clown riding a unicycle. On his shoulder, perched like a species confused parrot, rode an ugly little dog. She didn't understand what the long toothed devil was attempting to show her. In the second snap shot, there was the same clown, same unicycle, balancing on the back of an elephant. The third photo was of the clown again, caught mid air by the photographer, jumping through fired hoops, as a little dog trailed in his wake.

Harry pointed at the dog. "That little monster was Book. He was the brains of the outfit. Without him I would have been just another clown."

There were several more photos, all similar, all circus shots, which only served to compound Zoe's growing confusion. "What? So these are supposed to be you? What does this have to do with you being a killer?"

The old clown smiled and slapped a hand down on the scattered pictures. Dust rose, and then resettled on the desk. He raised a finger in the air. "Exactly. These photos have nothing to do with my life as the so-called Killer Klown, because I never was one. I've never killed anyone. I am an actor...or at least I used to be."

To this, Zoe tilted her head and raised an eyebrow.

"It's true," he went on, "Once upon a time, I was twenty years old."

"Yeah, so?"

"Those were the best days of my life, the summers I spent with the circus."

"Is that when you started killing people?"

Harry slapped the desk again, another change of address for the dust bunnies. "No! You're not getting any of what I'm telling you. I didn't kill anyone *then*, and I probably never will...unless I ever meet Simon Cowell. Him, I'd consider killing. He's really hard on those kids..."

"The circus," Zoe said, and snapped her fingers before of his face. "You were saying how you're not a killer clown—just a clown."

"Sorry. You'll have to excuse me. I don't get many visitors these days. Let's see. Oh, yes. I was approached by my best friend and college classmate, Bartholomew Gideon, to do some camera work for him; at the time, I was head of the student A/V club. You see, for his thesis, he'd been doing a field study of the culture of cannibalism in the 20th century, and was supposed to have taped interviews to show the board for his presentation. To his dismay—and you may or may not find this amusing—my dog, Book, ate the only interview he'd been able to tape with an actual killer. Yes, the dog ate his homework. Ha ha. Aside from his initial outburst, he didn't blame me for his situation, although I knew he thought it was my fault."

"That is kind of funny."

"Yes, it is, but could you try to stay quiet until I'm finished. It's very disruptive."

"Sure."

"Let's see. Oh yes. He came to me three weeks before he was to meet with the board, several psychiatrists, and a handful of medical practitioners from various hospitals and universities, and told me that he was, in no uncertain terms, fucked—fucked by Fate's fat forefinger.

"To this, I asked, 'How is that, my friend?' So he told me. He said that he'd exhausted every source and was unable to rebook another interview with the same killer as the unlucky gentleman had been executed the week before. Apparently, cannibals are harder to come by than a matching pair of socks in the clean laundry. Dumb luck, huh? I told him that it sounded like he needed to get drunk. So he did. More to the point, *we* did.

"That night, numbed by alcohol—and God bless my stupidity—we fudged a phony interview together. I played the part of a crazed lunatic, bent on devouring the human race, while Bartholomew asked the questions he asked the original killer. Between snarls and grunts, I confessed to every murder I could think of all the way back to Abel. At the time it seemed innocent, all in fun. The movie would be something for us to laugh over the next day, or next year. I thought nothing of it at the time. Hell, the next morning I couldn't recall *most* of what we did. I would have forgotten the deed entirely if not for his phone call the week after his dissertation. Do you know what that slippery bugger did?"

Zoe shrugged.

"I'll tell you what he did," he went on, angrily. "He had spliced me—ME—in as an actual killer—his best friend—then he added my drunken bawling together with the crime scene photos from his original interviewee. It was quite ingenious, actually...but still wrong. What if someone recognized me?

"Further, he mentioned a proposition. A proposition, he said, that would change our lives forever. I was upset—as you might well imagine I should be—but I was also intrigued. Keep in mind I was still very young at the time, and my brain hadn't yet caught up to my sense of adventure. So decided to hear him out.

"Gideon asked if I'd like to be rich. And I responded, as anyone would, 'Who doesn't? But, whom would I need to kill?' Gideon had smiled at me then, and said, 'Absolutely no one, my good man.'

"I didn't say yes right away. It wasn't until I was fired from my part time job with the circus that I returned to him and agreed listen to his proposal again. It seemed that, among one or more of the doctors present for his dissertation, Gideon had inadvertently found fans with a taste for, well, the darker side of humanity. Fans who could be a great aid or the worst enemy of a student with a B- average, such as he was. I'm ashamed to say that when Gideon slid that first envelope across the table to me, I took it without as much as a blink. We were now in the movie business. So, for the next ten years, Bartholomew and I, with nothing more than red dye and corn syrup, built our fortune indulging fat sophomoric socialites with fake snuff movies."

"Sounds a little hokey to me," said Zoe.

"In today's world of high resolution movie magic it probably would. But please, let me finish."

"Oh. Sorry. I thought you were done."

"No, where was I?"

"You said yes to Gideon and made fake blood movies," Zoe prompted.

"Ah, yes. Thank you. Put your costume on, please."

"Oh. Right," Zoe said, and unzipped her skirt. *Kinky,* she thought, as she doffed her boots.

"That hoax and all that followed paid for my student loans, a new car, and—I'm embarrassed to say—sex. It was wonderful to be the center of attention again. It was like I was back in the circus. That is, until Gideon decided to branch out and add new talent...*real* talent. I knew nothing of this sideline venture at first, but when I discovered it, I confronted him with my concerns and informed him, quite firmly, that I would leave if things didn't change. I believed at the time that he'd listen to me. After all, I was Harry Funshine. I *was* the show."

"So what was he *doing?*"

"Why, creating snuff. What did you think, child?"

"At this point, I can honestly say that I don't know what to think."

"Now it's my turn to be sorry. I'm sorry, Zoe. You'll have to excuse me. I'm not the people person I once was. I have to tell you, at first I was angered by your presence here today, but now I see that you coming here—just one of the many victims of Gideon's monsters—was going to happen someday. I'm glad it was you." He cleared his throat and plunged back into his story.

"Gideon had taken an act that began as a lark, a well paying prank, and perverted it into the filming of *real* criminals committing *real* crimes. God knows I'm sorry. I'll be paying for my part in it for the rest of my life and answer for it in the next, but I couldn't involve the authorities. He had me, you see. Harry Funshine: Cannibal Clown.

"I was stuck. After a while, as the popularity of my movies waned, Gideon lost interest in doing my kind of movie. He asked if I would consider doing a real "scene". I realized then that my closest friend, now tenured doctor of psychiatry, Gideon Bartholomew, was as crazy as a syphilitic monkey. I took his loss of interest in me as my cue to leave before I did anything more stupid than I already had."

Zoe was spellbound by the sheer insanity of the tale. "Did he try to stop you?"

"I left my home during the night and never looked back. Call me a coward if you must, but you have no idea what he's capable of. I believe if I had remained, I would have found myself the lead in one of his other vehicles, and *not* as the killer."

"Was he that dangerous?"

"Him? No, but he'd begun surrounding himself with very unsavory individuals. Dogs, he called them. Any one of them would have killed me for my pocket change."

"Oh."

"Yes, 'oh.' And after I left town, I saw nothing of him for ten years...until last year, to be precise. I don't know how he found me *here*, two wipes north of the asshole of the world, but he did. He walked right up to my door, shadowed by the ugliest man I've ever seen; a huge, barrel-chested brute; German, if I placed his accent correctly. The big bastard scared my poor dogs half out of their minds."

Zoe remained doubtful. "So why didn't he kill you then?"

"The very same question I asked him," said Harry. "Well, believe it or not, the doctor said he was glad I'd found a place for myself, a quiet place. I took his words for *exactly* how he meant them: *Good. You've kept your mouth shut.* He said I'd left in such a hurry that I must have forgotten to inform him I was leaving. I don't think I need to tell you that I was afraid for my life, a fact Gideon had no problem picking up on. He assured me I was in no danger and that Otto was just his driver, but I had my doubts.

"I remember searching for a camera, and even went so far as to ask him where it was. He laughed the accusation off and went on to tell me that he had work for me, easy work. All I would need to do is answer email and advertise his movies within certain forums online. The way he worded the offer told me refusal was not an option. What was I to do? I could hardly relocate. Again, I found myself stuck. Harry Funshine, Killer Clown went online that very night. That's how *you* found me through that hoodlum, Clive Purdy."

"And how did Gideon find you after all that time?" asked Zoe.

"Well, first of all, he wasn't searching for me. He'd found me through my dogs. Two years ago, I put George up for stud. I never imagined Gideon would be able to find me that way, but he did. It seems his secretary was looking to breed her dog. Dumb luck, for sure, but at the time I thought it might be karma."

"*You* are a fucking actor?" she snorted.

He ducked his head; sort of a submissive shrug. "I'm more like an old whore than an actor these days. Not really much of a difference if you ask me."

"You're right. There isn't. I've been accused of being a little of both myself."

"Do tell," the old man said, and slid his tongue comically along his upper lip.

"I do tell, and don't do that again. It's gross. We all make our own decisions in life, and some just aren't as smart as others. But here's one decision you may find interesting: I've decided you aren't a real killer. How do you like that?"

He smeared cake makeup over his face, and said, "You're not so bad for a whore."

"Yeah?" Then, she mimicked his earlier accent, "And you A-number one pretty good Joe, for an old gook."

He donned a red nose and shook his head. "No, honey, gooks are Vietnamese, I'm Chinese. That would make me a Chink. By the way, are you afraid of fire?"

"Why?"

So he told her.

"…and then you light the ring of fire. We're going to finish the show with it and you need to hold the flaming hoop for George, Gracie and I. Poco can watch with your friends. Sadly, he's never learned this trick." He covered the little dog's ears with his hands, and whispered, "He may singe his privates, if you know what I mean." After removing his hands, he gave Poco a treat.

Zoe tugged at the itchy material bunched firmly at her crotch in the shape of an inverted heart. "Fire? Say, why don't you forget about this roasted weenie show and just fuck me like any sane man would? This pussy's accepted everywhere visa is, and some places it's not."

"No offence, my dear, but you're not exactly my type."

And with that he pulled the pompom zipper of his purple and yellow suit up to his chin and tucked it under an oversized bowtie. "Knock 'em dead," he said, as he exited the trailer.

Zoe turned up her lip and followed him out, muttering to herself, "I think I liked it better when you were a killer."

32

ATTONEMENT

Zoe was pissed. She wanted to scream and smack every goddamned one of them, especially Danny.

Seth pushed the dog from his view of the road for the third time since they'd all piled into the beetle. "Mister, keep your dog off the dash. I can't drive like this."

"Poco's sorry, young man, but he's never been in a car before."

Seth regarded Harry with open disdain. "Stop answering *for* it. It's a dog. Will somebody tell me one more time why we brought these fucking dogs with us?"

Mary lifted her head from the bandage she was applying to Zoe's wrist. "Because Zoe says we need him, baby. And what were we gonna do? Leave them there?" She playfully rubbed Gracie's chin. "Besides, they're kind of cute in a freak of nature kind of way."

"Fine, just keep them off my steering wheel."

Mary ran her fingers through the back of his hair. "Come on, Spider. Loosen up."

As though he was revealing something new and startling, Seth said, "Mary. There are dogs in my car."

Harry patted Seth's gear shifting hand. "Get over it, son. Life's full of little challenges. Drive."

"Stop touching me, mister. You may have Zoe snowed over by your little clown act, but you're still on my shit list, so back off."

Mary tried to look concerned, but couldn't stop smiling or repeating, "Jesus, I wish I had a camera for that. That was awesome."

"Yeah, awesome," Zoe bit off. "That motherfucker almost burned my hand off. And, Danny," she turned her gaze accusingly toward the youngest member of the group, "What the hell were you thinking?"

Still interested enough in their situation to *not* be staring out the window, Danny ducked his head in shame, and murmured, "I'm sorry, Zoe. I couldn't help myself."

"Really?" Zoe retorted.

"Yeah, it looked like fun. You know, with the fire and all. It was dancing, the old man was bouncing around—and the dogs did it too! Why shouldn't I get a turn? I made it through the hoop, didn't I?"

"You burned my arm, you little shit."

"I said I was sorry."

Zoe bit her tongue. She ran a hand over her scalp, searching for bald patches. To Mary, she said, "I thought I asked you two to watch him."

"Yes," interrupted Harry. "I believe it may have been wise to inform me that one among you was a pyromaniac. My poor George is still shivering."

Mary stifled a giggle. "Come on, Zoe, admit it. It was a little funny."

"You weren't the one rolling around on fire with three dogs trying to hump you, were you?"

"It was only two of them. Gracie's a girl."

Zoe sighed. She obviously wouldn't receive any sympathy from Mary, at least in this matter. "Okay, enough. Can we just drop it? Harry, where are we going?"

"Weren't you listening when I told you about Gideon?"

"Excuse me all to hell for not taking notes. I repeat: Where to?"

"Why, the windy city, of course. Chicago."

~~oOo~~

It seemed that the closer they came to Chicago, to Harry's old friend—and maybe some answers—the more the atmosphere inside the tiny car took on the brooding solemnity of a wake in progress, or a long walk to Old Sparky. But the lack of conversation gave Zoe much needed time to think, and not about Cannibalangelo or some crazy old doctor or bald dogs.

Zoe studied Danny's scarred face for a moment, and then pondered the mystery that is/was Purple Monkey. Was he real, or was something in her head broken? *No, I heard Danny. He said 'we', I'm sure of it. And how the hell is it that the little shit gets to keep my monkey? Let him find his own imaginary friend, like Puff the Magic Dragon or Wheezy the Cigar Smoking Bear, and leave Purple the fuck alone.*

~~oOo~~

Four hours after striking a deal with Harry, they were parked just north of the doctor's residence in a sleepy suburb of Chicago.

Zoe pushed a dog—couldn't tell which one: they were all fugly—out of the way of the window. "You're sure he still lives there?"

"Positive…I think."

"Doesn't look like anyone's home," offered Spider.

"Yeah," said Zoe. "Do you think he'll be back soon?"

From somewhere lost in his own memories, Harry gave her a one-shoulder shrug. "How should I know? I'm a clown, not a psychic."

"Well, where do you suppose he is?"

Perturbed, Harry turned in his seat. "Gee wiz, Zoe, I don't know…*work*, maybe? He *is* a psychiatrist, you know." Squaring around to face them, he opened his mouth, then stopped.

Instead, he pulled Poco into his lap and flipped him onto his back. He stroked the tiny dog's chest, rubbing its loose skin back and forth along a xylophone of ribs, and phrased his question: "Are you kids sure you want to do this?"

The slow rise and fall of the dog's testicles fascinated Zoe. Having seen more than an average squirrel's share of nuts, she guessed that, of its total weight of ten pounds, two of those pounds swung between the dog's legs. If his father, George, was any indication, Poco's meatballs were a singular oddity or a trait passed down maternally through Gracie. Zoe spared a thought for her former imaginary friend and supposed he would have also been suitably impressed with the pooch's grapes, and would have, rather descriptively, told her so.

Jiggle, jiggle, flop. Jiggle, jiggle, flop.

"...Well?" Harry's face loomed before her.

"Well what?" Zoe looked from Mary to Seth to Danny, then back to Harry.

Exasperated, Harry slumped into his seat and rubbed his temples. "Young man, take me home."

Seth jumped on the opportunity to be rid of the clown. "You got it. No problem, Dick."

"Wait," Zoe said. "I'm sorry, Harry. I'm tired. I zoned out there for a minute, but I'm cool, really."

"And?"

"And, *yes*, I want to do this." Again, her eyes fell to the dog's apples. *Will you please flip that dog over or something?*

Harry stopped rubbing the dog. "Do you all understand how dangerous this may be? Think hard before you answer; once the wheels are in motion, things could get hairy."

Like that dog's big, bouncing...

"Mister?" Danny said, holding his hand in the air as though he were back in school.

"Yes, Daniel?"

"Your dog has really big balls. Meat would have gotten a real kick out of him."

Zoe let out a burst of air, "Thank-you-Danny! They're huge, right? I mean, I couldn't take my—"

"Enough! I'm getting a headache." Harry covered the dog's body with the tail of his shirt. "Young man, let's go."

"...so big Guinness should be called. That's not natural." Zoe had no control over her mouth. With the exception of the faux cannibal, none of them had slept more than four hours out of the last thirty and it was beginning to show.

Seth poked Harry. "Your place?" he asked, hopefully.

"No, damn me for a fool. Find us a motel."

"Whatever."

Harry hugged Poco to his chest. "Sleep first. Let clearer heads prevail. Then I'll ask you all again if you think it's wise to poke a slumbering lion."

~~oOo~~

Twenty minutes later, shortly after four o'clock, Zoe forked out forty-five of their last sixty dollars to Seth for a motel room. It wasn't until they'd parked the car in front of their unit that Seth told Harry the hotel had a "no pets" policy.

"Gee, that's too bad, Harry," Seth said, smirking. "Guess they can't come in."

The old clown lingered at the car, picking gum from one of his oversized shoes. "They'll be all alone."

Mary stepped in front of her boyfriend. "Oh come on, Spider. Who's gonna know? They don't bark."

"No, Mary. I asked the guy at the desk. So *he's* gonna know."

Zoe didn't care either way whether the dogs stayed in the car or in the room, but one thing she hated was when one person lorded over another. That dogma was something she'd been able to relate to on more than one occasion, growing up under the roof of the original frost queen, so she thought she'd speak up in favor of the downtrodden. "Who elected you keeper of the keys, Seth? I don't like the dogs either, but who put you in charge?"

"You did when you asked me to get the room. That clerk took a copy of my credit card as a damage deposit, and that includes the cleaning of dog hair and dog shit—so, yeah, you did. Fair enough?"

Zoe squeezed Harry's arm. "Sorry, I tried."

Seth handed the room key to Mary and she went inside.

"Nothing personal, Harry," Seth said, after the door closed, "but rules are rules." He sighed and then chuckled. "Who am I kidding? Yes it is personal. I don't like you or trust you. He turned to walk away, then stopped and snapped his fingers. "Hey, I just thought of something. Why don't you stay out here with your dogs? That way, I won't have to look at you either."

Zoe pushed Seth toward the door to the room. "He's not staying out here. Get inside and go to sleep." To Harry, she said, "Don't let him bother you. If you haven't noticed by now, he can be a little neurotic."

After waiting for Seth to slam the door, Harry hoisted his small travel bag over his shoulder. "Don't blame him, Zoe. He cares, that's all. He thinks he's protecting all of you from a big, bad meanie. It's actually very sweet."

"Sure is. Try to get some sleep. I'm gonna do the same."

Harry fished a bottle of sleeping pills from his pocket and shook it. "Want some? They work wonders."

Zoe thought about it, but not for long. "No thanks, you go ahead. I'm gonna hit the rack."

He nodded. "I'll be along after I tuck in the kids."

~~oOo~~

The Sandman: that patient tracker who'd chased them from St. Louis, to Harry's trailer in southwestern Michigan, through a ring of fire, and on to Chicago, had finally caught them. No food, no chit chat, just sleep.

Sleep for most of them, anyway. Zoe's sleep was fitful at best.

"...ooo—"

"Zoe!"

"Seth..? What..?"

Dropcloth Angels

"You had a nightmare. Wake up and go back to sleep."

What the..? Past Seth's outline in the darkened room, she saw the clock radio. 7:04 pm. She'd slept for about two and a half hours. "Where is everybody?"

Seth flopped back into the bed he shared with Mary, rolled away from her voice, and mumbled, "Still asleep. Stop bugging me."

Sleep was out of the question. She couldn't recall the dream, but sure didn't want to see the sequel. "I'm gonna go get some smokes. Want anything?"

"A little peace and quiet would be nice."

"All right then." *And fuck you too.* "Where are your keys?"

"In one of my shoes...on your way out the door. Go."

Zoe grabbed the keys and let herself out of the room. When she popped the car door lock, a head lifted from the passenger seat and she jumped back. *George, you little motherfucker.* She could tell it was him by the seared tuft of fuzz on his head, singed when Danny leapt through the burning hoop Zoe held for Harry and his dogs. She recalled her own pain and rubbed her bandaged wrist.

"Go back to sleep, George. We're going for a little drive. If you're good, I'll get you some nice tasty Draino."

George circled five times, dropped back onto the seat, and curled into a tight ball of impending snores and twitching paws.

A 7-11, two all night grocery stores, and a Food Express: Zoe passed all of these in search of a pack of cigarettes she didn't need; there was a half pack of camels in her purse. What she *needed* was alone time, time to think, to find some answers.

She hadn't originally set out to go there, but fifteen minutes after leaving the motel, she coasted to a stop two doors down from the house they'd visited a few hours earlier; the residence of Dr. Bartholomew Gideon, snuff magnate and handler of maniacs.

There was a late model Lincoln in the driveway now, and light seeped between the tightly drawn curtains of the main floor. He was there. Oddly, she wasn't afraid of being so close

329

to the man who was ultimately—or at the very least, laterally—responsible for the death of her sister. She'd been beaten to her knees by fear's big stick so many times over the past weeks that it had become something of a norm in her life, like blinking or breathing. It was just *there*. She knew coming here alone was dumb, but she wasn't planning to walk up to the door and knock. *Reconnaissance,* she thought. *But that's it.*

She finished her third cigarette since she'd pulled up to the curb, and glanced toward the house. The light no longer shined behind the curtains. Zoe held her breath and waited for another light to come on elsewhere in the house. Two minutes, three minutes, no light. *Could be at the back of the house somewhere...*

Five minutes, and another smoke later, there were still no lights.

Just as she reached out to start the car, the taillights on the Lincoln flashed, and it fired to life. *Oh shit.* She threw herself across the seat, pushing George to the floor with Poco. She peered over the dash and watched as a tall thin man in a trench coat emerged from the house, locked the door, and walked to the car.

To George, she whispered, "What do think? Should we follow him or go back to the motel?"

George perked up at hearing his name, licked his nose and his butt, respectively, and then closed his eyes.

What do you think you're doing? Go back to the room. You got your look. Zoe palmed the bug into first and crept forward as the Lincoln backed down the driveway. *I'm just gonna see where he's going, then I'm gone.*

The Lincoln turned left at the second street. Zoe pulled away from the curb, flipped on the headlights, and turned left at the second street.

~~oOo~~

She tailed cautiously, never closing to within one block of the black Lincoln—just like she'd seen detectives do on television. Ten minutes later, she was still with him.

Ahead, the doctor had slowed to a crawl, riding his brake. *Is he looking for something? Did he spot me?* Zoe pulled to the side of the narrow street and killed the lights. Without warning, the Lincoln darted into an adjacent alley and was gone.

"Fuck." She ground the transmission into second gear. It belched and fumed in protest of her heavy foot. She reached the alley in time to see the car turn right at the other end.

Still creeping forward, at a bark from Poco, Zoe returned her gaze to the windshield. She jammed her foot down on the brake a split second before hitting a man who'd stepped off the curb to cross the street.

Fuck me! Furious at the man for not paying attention, she angrily cranked down the window. "Watch where you're going, you fucking moron!" *Good thing I was going slow. I could have killed him.*

The man passed by the front of the car without so much as a return insult, and she glimpsed his profile in the white glow of the headlights. The pedestrian had a handsome face, an amiable face.

A cannibal's face.

Him! It was Cannibalangelo. Here. Walking right in front of her car. And she could do no more than follow him with her eyes. *Get him. Run him down,* she urged her body, but her body rebelled. Opportunity passed like a scream on a rollercoaster as he continued crossing the street, oblivious to her, the car, or anything that didn't involve moving his feet.

He entered the well lit doorway of an old building and disappeared around a corner. A cardboard sign had been taped to the steel door he'd passed through. The print was large enough Zoe could read it from across the street. It read: MIXED SUBSTANCE ADDICTION MEETING—8PM

Poco had joined his father on the passenger seat and stared intently across the street, growling. Apparently, the little pooch was deserving of his generously proportioned ball sack. Zoe checked her watch. 7:55.

For the first time in a long while, she thought about getting high. Both immediate and unrelenting, the need settled in like a well oiled car salesman or a carnival barker, saying all the things she wanted to hear with equal parts condescension and allure.

And here she was, thinking she was cured.

She'd been a fool to believe she could outrun addiction; a fool to believe there was anything she, a dumb whore, could do to make things right with the memory of her sister; a fool to believe she could be anything more than she *was*. A fool.

She lit a cigarette and pulled a half-inch cherry with her first draw.

7:59 pm. Zoe figured if she left right then, she could be back at the motel in fifteen minutes, collect the gang, and be back by 8:45, 8:50, tops. Without knowing for sure how long a meeting like this lasted—if indeed that's where that Zane guy went—he might be gone before they returned. Did she dare tempt the Fates any further than she already had? *No*, she thought. *Mama may have been a bitch, and I may be a fool, but she sure as shit didn't raise a* stupid *fool.*

She started the engine and checked the side view mirror. A car coasted slowly toward her. Zoe had no time to evaluate a proper response to this new development, so she closed her eyes and played the "you can't see me" game.

With her mind's eye, she saw the car creeping forward, ever closer. Then, above the irregular heartbeat of the bug, she heard the distinct sound of its larger engine. As if waking from a trance, she opened her eyes and turned her head. It wasn't a Lincoln and it wasn't the doctor. It was a Grand Marquis—a black and white Grand Marquis—with a scary word printed on its flank.

The door read, "POLICE," and the man above it said, "Ma'am?"

Zoe killed the engine and rolled down the window. "Yes?"

"Everything alright, Ma'am?"

Thinking fast, she smiled and pulled the keys. "Yeah, it's my first time, that's all." She pointed past him at the sign across the street.

The officer took in the sign, then he nodded knowingly.

"Piece of cake, Ma'am. First time's the hardest. I'm five years in myself."

Boldly, Zoe stepped into the street and skirted the police car. "I better get in there, it's about to start."

"Sure thing, Ma'am. You have yourself a good night."

Zoe had just stepped up onto the opposite curb when the policeman spoke again: "Ma'am?"

She turned, anticipating cold bracelets around her wrists, ink under her fingernails, and the flash of the camera as she turned, then turned. "Yes, officer?"

"Unless you want to lose that dog, you should really roll your window up."

Stupid-Stupid-Stupid. "Thanks," she said, lightly, as she crossed back to roll up the window.

"Say, is that a Chinese Hairless?"

Zoe couldn't recall if Harry had said, but it made sense, what with the dog being bald and Harry being Chinese. "Yup, sure is. It's my boyfriend's dog. I'm watching it while he's out of town."

"No kidding?"

"Why? It's just a dog, right?"

"No ma'am. I have a mutt named Gringo I picked up at the pound for my kids. That's a dog." He pointed to Poco, who defiantly stared him down. "That little bugger there is about fifteen hundred bucks."

"You don't say? Maybe I should take him home and come back another time." *Jesus, Poco, don't wake up mom and dad. I don't think I could explain away forty-five hundred dollars worth of dog meat locked in a five-hundred dollar car.*

"I wouldn't hear of it, ma'am. You get your butt in there. I'll drive by and check on him a little later."

"Would you?" she gushed. "That would be just swell." *Fuck a rubber duck.*

Moving quickly, so as to not garner further conversation, she waved over her shoulder and strode through the door she'd seen the cannibal enter. She stopped at a set of glass doors as she caught her reflection. *Shit, chick. You look rough.*

With her disheveled hair, metal pelted ears, and heavily penciled eyeliner smeared into black circles surrounding her eyes, she thought she looked like a junkie.

Suddenly self-conscious, she took in her slept-in clothing. The baby-tee wasn't bad, it was too tight to wrinkle, but the short plaid skirt looked like it had been wrestled from a pack of hungry weasels. No bra, a rip almost to the waistband of the skirt, and scuffed calf high army boots. She morosely thought: *Who's gonna notice you?*

Through the second set of doors, she was given the option of turning left and following a sign that read: English as a second language, 9pm—*nope, too early*—or right, and go to the advertized substance abuse meeting. She opted for twelve steps to the right.

She entered through a pair of propped open steel doors into a small gymnasium. There were roughly sixty chairs boxed away into two sections, creating an aisle up the center. At the end of the aisle was a small portable stage with a podium set up at its center.

Her boots squeaked as she walked up the aisle, causing all occupants, with the exception of the man headed toward the podium, to turn and stare. She procured herself a chair near the back of the room and slumped as low into the seat as possible without falling to the floor.

"Hello," the cannibal began, as he adjusted the microphone to his height. Feedback caused him to step back from the podium and offer a sheepish grin to the audience. Once the feedback ceased, he leaned forward and tapped the mike. "Hello, my name is Thomas."

33

PLACATE & TRANQUILIZE

"I'm…I'm an alcoholic," Zane said. Though spoken softly, his words easily reached every ear in the assembled crowd of twenty-three. Twenty-four, he amended as he watched a young woman slide into a chair near the back of the room.

Hot. It's so goddamn warm in here.

Zane psyched himself up. *Placate and tranquilize. Don't find your sheep; let your sheep find you.*

He remembered Gideon's words: "Take it easy. Get a tan, get laid."

Zane had a one word answer to that: *"Go fuck yourself."* Things had changed since he'd taken those pictures of Gideon. The doctor had almost become friendly, like a puppy.

Today had been a bad day. Earlier in the afternoon the demon had come for him, tore at him, at his mind. But Zane had been stronger. Of course, the victory hadn't come without its scars. He'd been left with a limp as a result of the struggle, and, since late in the afternoon, he'd lost all sensation in his face. A small price, but next time he might not be as lucky. Next time the angel may not be there to save him with soft words and uplifting praises.

And that was why he'd decided to dedicate the evening— The Hunt—to the memory of the angel's words, a great and ancient saying: Yabba dabba doo. Zane had forgotten exactly who the quote was first attributed to, but thought it might have been Genghis Khan or Nietzsche.

Who it was or what the words meant didn't really matter. Zane focused more on the inspirational tone of the words themselves: both battle cry and wail of gleeful exultation, the angel's chant had healed him like no medicine ever could.

Zane recalled, with perfect clarity, the exact circumstances surrounding the angel's arrival. She'd come to him as a shimmering wave... No, that's not quite right. Maybe the angel had called him on the telephone. Yes, that's it! Or was it the drain in the kitchen sink? Hard to say, now; it was all becoming fuzzy. The only certainty is this: *it was real.* An angel-angel—for *real*—and she'd come to him from the garden of Chaos. She'd said so.

Gideon had told him things were too hot for them right now, that he should lay low, but what was Zane to do? Deny an angel her due? Besides, he'd made new brushes and wanted to use them. Not to mention the hours he'd spent preparing the speech he was about to deliver...and if he ate one more bowl of Froot Loops he was going to start shitting rainbows.

As he stared out over the restless group, his day suddenly rewound. *The television,* he remembered. *The angel came out of the television. I'm sure of it.* Then, he began to doubt it was indeed a female angel. Not that it mattered—it was still an angel, and she or he had healed him! *Trifles, trifles. Let the games begin!*

And on that command, his left eye went dark.

It's possible the angel hadn't cured him after all.

~~oOo~~

From the personal notes of Dr. Bartholomew D. Gideon, Psychiatrist
Re: Case subject #11901 Ellis, Zane
STATUS-ACTIVE

"Throughout history syphilis has been largely undiagnosed

for the simple reason that it mirrors a wide variety of other afflictions: Thus known as the Great Imitator. How then, is syphilis, to be diagnosed? What is *undoubted syphilis*? What are the characteristic symptoms of a disease that imitates every disease in the nosology? If anything from cold sores to cancer, from pimples to heart disease; from a skin rash to insanity can be diagnosed as syphilis, what are its characteristic symptoms?"

~~oOo~~

"Hello, Thomas," intoned the group, sounding air through their tired bellows. A disembodied, "good for you!" drifted from somewhere near the middle of the room.

Without so much a burped warning or a quivering of his bowel, a wave of nausea sailed through Zane, and threatened to expel the aforementioned rainbow from at least one orifice. *Uh oh. Please, not now.*

He planted his palms firmly on the cool surface of the podium and attempted to hold back the demon with sheer will alone. In the reflection of the podium's glossy finish, black shapes circled like dark angels just above his head. He didn't bother to check the crowd's reaction. They couldn't see them. They were unenlightened swine.

~~oOo~~

From the personal notes of Dr. Bartholomew D. Gideon, Psychiatrist
Regarding Patient #11901
STATUS-ACTIVE

"Oscar Wilde (1854-1900), Vincent Van Gogh (1853-1890), Al Capone (1899-1947), Ivan IV "The Terrible" (1530-1584), Adolf Hitler (1889-1945), Henri de Toulouse-Lautrec (1864-1901), Friedrich Wilhelm Nietzsche (1844-1900) Just a few of many prominent figures in history who died (or showed many symptoms) of syphilis."

~~oOo~~

In spite of the white hot pain, Zane smiled and waved in reply to the volley of hellos. He daubed his forehead with a paper napkin and took a long slow sip of coffee. He was going to have to watch what he said. When the demon came to party crash, Zane could only remain calm and ride it out. Bad timing as far as that goes, but the show must go on—cautiously. During delicate times like these he could say or do *anything*. For example: If he meant to say, "What a lovely shade of blue your eyes are." He might say, "I want to pluck out your eyes with a soup spoon and eat them because they're blue." When his devil reigned, it lorded supreme.

"It's been six long weeks, but I...I'm going beat this." Unseen by the audience, the demon plunged through his mindscape, raping thoughts, killing at will. Each episode ate away a little more of his soul and shat its corruption into the void left behind. *They* wouldn't see his demon, of course. Most would be too busy wrestling their own.

A sudden shiver passed along the nape of his neck, signaling the demon's evident boredom. In a blink, the beast fled back to wherever demons hung their hat.

Inwardly petrified, Zane gazed out over the crowd, believing the worst was yet to come. He thought that the minor slip up with the demon might have been a result of his recent inability to control his emotions.

Also, as often as he'd plied his routine before an audience, he'd never succeeded in quelling his bowel quaking fear of public speaking. A few years back he'd enlisted the aid of a professional public speaker to help throw a collar on his fear. "The pro", in the cannibal's opinion, had done nothing to exorcise his glossophobia, and further, had only served to cause Zane to feel inadequate. So Zane beat the tutor to death with a dictionary.

He'd resisted the urge to keep a small souvenir, and had fostered no intentions whatsoever of eating him. The man was simply too fat, too hairy, and smelled funny; like tacos and ice cream served in a bear skin jock strap. Instead, he'd given the meat to an old acquaintance by the name of Vulture, a spindly-legged, twitchy man with more warts than skin. Vulture, by the very virtue of his name, wasted nothing, not even the fat. Good for him.

He pulled his mental mask a little tighter and launched into his stolen spiel. "I used to think I could find peace at the bottom of a bottle, but I'm here to say..." Almost en masse the fidgety herd of alkies and pill poppers drifted into a coma of naked indifference. Some stared around the room or at the ceiling or the floor under their feet, but not at him. To most of them, he was background; another wasted ten minutes of a miserable existence, and that suited him fine. A scattered few stayed with him, maybe in hopes of gleaning something from his lies that might make sense if applied to their own frayed reality.

These stragglers confounded him. He'd made every effort to craft the most *average*, cliché filled, sob story he possibly could. He wasn't here to *change* anyone's life, just end one or two.

He painted a mental picture for those still listening of an adulterous wife who'd berated his every shortcoming and flaunted her lover in his face. As he spoke of nonexistent children and their nonexistent non-knowledge of their non-mother he'd never spit seed into, he noticed the few who'd stuck with him were now crossing the state line into Noddingham. *Good.*

"...and that's when my neighbor, Tony—I mentioned him earlier—handed me this book." He raised a copy of the alcoholic's bible. "So here I am."

Scattered claps from a few listeners brought the rest of the room back from their happy places, and soon everyone joined in. Well, everyone except the red head near the exit. He thanked them and walked back to his seat as the group leader stepped up to the podium.

The speaker made his closing remarks for the night and

gave details of upcoming events: Transvestite fashion show and casino night, co-sponsored by the Gamblers Anonymous Group.

Zane's gaze moved from face to face, seeking out that special someone. As he searched, a nursery rhyme came to him. He whispered:

"Eeny, meeny, miny moe
Catch a fella by the toe
If he hollers let him go
Eeny, meeny, miny more
A Blackbird came down
from heaven and said
you are the one
who will be dead."

~~oOo~~

Are you shitting me? This is the nightmare that's been haunting my dreams? Zoe didn't know whether to hate him or give him a tissue to wipe his chin. He was pathetic. He'd drooled through an entire litany of garbled, incoherent sentences, then he grinned like he'd given the Gettysburg address. *This can't be the guy.*

That was what she thought *before* he'd placed his palms on the pedestal, exposing the edge of a tattoo that had etched itself into her mind like a...well, like a tattoo.

"Motherfucker," she whispered. "It's *so* on."

~~oOo~~

The cannibal's gaze finally came to a stop at a thin twenty-something man in a huge jogging suit. Zane doubted whether there would be enough meat on him to even bother. Further, he wondered if the man had Aids or some other debilitating communicable disease. Zane had to be careful. He wasn't an immortal—not yet, anyway. It hadn't always been so, having to be so cautious, but over the years he'd become more and more choosy with his victims, squeezing the fruit, checking the best before date. It wasn't easy being him.

From the twenty or so feet that separated them, Zane tried to make out the name on the skinny young man's "Hello" sticker, but could see only that there were two letters. He closed his eyes and began to prepare a conversation, but soon, his thoughts drifted inevitably toward the past, to a woman he'd only met briefly but whose image lingered in his heart. He could almost, if he tried hard enough, still smell her…

~~oOo~~

He was just standing there chatting with some bean pole in a knockoff designer track suit. *When do the fangs come out, prick?*

"Miss?" said a melodically androgynous voice from Zoe's left.

Zoe looked up at the man standing beside her. *Speaking of prick,* she thought. The honcho, grandmaster, or whatever the fuck they called the guy who ran the show at one of these cryfests, stood above her with a clipboard and a fat, felt tipped marker.

"You're too close, Pops." He'd insinuated himself too far inside her personal bubble. "Back up a bit, you're dripping *needy* all over me."

Gazing down a nose so sharp that it threatened to cut his round beatnik glasses in half, the space invader clucked twice, and said, "You didn't sign in."

"I never learned to read and write, mister. I'm *awful* sorry." Across the room, the cannibal was openly staring at the skinny guy, like a daft monkey held rapt by a dancing banana. *What the hell kind of game are you playing?*

The balding hippie shifted his weight to one leg and plucked a stray hair from his oversized, over fleeced, and, quite probably, overpriced, turtleneck sweater. He dropped the hair—a hair that likely came from the back of his own balding head—and scribbled on his clipboard, then handed it to her. "Nice try. Write your first name and your addiction there, where the x is."

"And what if my name *is* x? Do you still want me to write it again?"

He poked the clipboard with a long, slender, nicotine stained finger. "Write whatever you like, young lady, but write something."

With the provided pen, she scratched a larger X beside his smaller one, and then handed the clipboard back.

"Not so fast, Missy. Before you binge yourself on our free goodies," he waved toward the small table of cookies and cake. "What's your addiction? You didn't fill that part in. For all I know, you could be some street person, here for the free food."

Zoe pulled her skirt up and pointed just below her underwear. The puncture marks there had faded, but remained as scars. "Good enough for you, jerk off?" She dropped the skirt and glared at him.

His mouth tightened, pulling wrinkles and his ears inward as though they were caught in a tempest. In answer, he pushed the fat marker into her hand and held out a business card sized sticker. "Write your name on this and wear it so we know what to call you."

Zoe thought for a second, tapping the marker against her chin, then smiled. (*Squiggle squiggle squiggle.*) She peeled the backing off the sticker, and slapped it onto her baby-tee, just above the glittering bubble letters that indicated the wearer of the shirt to be a "Party Pussy."

Mouthing the word out as he read it, the bespectacled speaker snatched the marker from her as though she planned to pawn it for drugs. "I'm sure your parents are proud," he bristled.

"I shirked my slave name when I left home, dad. Deal with it." *Jesus, how rude do I have to be to you to get you to just fucking go?*

"I get it," the hippie shot back. "Power to the people, fuck the Man. You don't have to write your own name, but next time something more appropriate would be nice." Then he sniffed disdainfully, raised his nose like a bitch poodle, and floated over to place his arm around a wraithlike black man.

After Adolf Von sticker Nazi had gone, Zoe blew hair from her cheek and glanced at Cannibalangelo. He was working it harder than a bar shark at closing time, and not doing a very good job of hiding it. *This is the guy who made me pee my pants?*

~~oOo~~

"Who's Zoe? She your woman?"

It took Zane a few seconds to understand what had happened or who'd just spoken, but he recovered instantly. He stood before the skinny tracksuit guy, the one with initials for a name. The last thing he remembered was sitting in his chair, thinking about…her.

"Dude?" Skinny guy was snapping his fingers rapidly in front of his eyes. "I said, is she your woman?"

"Zoe?" Zane repeated, then dropped his voice to a whisper, "How do you know Zoe?"

"I *don't*, man. You was just talking to me about hockey and, *shwing*, you switched channels on me, that's all." Initials paused, looked sideways at Zane, and then swept his head around the room. "Said Zoe or Zola something. And anyway, I was just tryin' to help you 'member what it was, is all. Dig?"

Zane's fear crept back to its perch, satisfied with the man's response. "No. Ah…yeah, I was thinking out loud." He pretended to knock on his head. "Sometimes my mind has a mind of its own."

Initials screwed up his face, then shrugged. "Sure, I getcha. What'd you have, a stroke, or what?"

A stroke? "Huh?"

"Your chin, man, wipe your chin."

Zane scrubbed his sleeve across his face. "Oh." *What's happening to me?*

Initials sucked for a painfully long time at the last few drops of Folgers choice, upended the cup, then let it fall to the floor. "Let the cleaners get it, right?"

Zane nodded. He was afraid to do more. Suddenly, even

the tiniest movement shot bolts of pain down his spine.

"Damn skippy, I'm right." Initials bent at the waist and studied Zane's eyes. "Dude, you're fucked right now, aren't you?"

Zane opened his mouth, and then closed it. He wiped his chin with an already soaked napkin, and shrugged.

"I mean, I ain't here to judge or nothing, but dude, you're at an A.A. meeting. Chill out. If Willem sees that, he'll get churned up into a bitch hissy fit. You don't want that."

"Good advice. Thank you." *What the hell else can I say? Abort! Abort!* Will Robinson's robot danced along his vision, waving his arms as he intoned: *Danger, Will Robinson. Danger!*

Initials poured another coffee, and dropped six sugar cubes into the small Styrofoam cup. Noticing Zane watching, he said, "What? Helps me cope, dude."

Whatever floats your boat, Dude, Zane thought. "Whatever floats your..." *What's that word?*

"Boat? Is that what you was looking for? Duuude, you *are* fucked." Then the young man quickly put his hand on Zane's arm. "But that don't mean we can't work somethin' out."

"Work something out?"

Initials' lips pursed around the stir stick. "Yeah, man." *Slurp, slurp.* "I saw you checkin' me out."

"Do tell?" Zane wiped his chin. *Go on. You have my complete and undivided attention.*

"Yeah, and like I said: I ain't here to judge. I mean, you got your problems and shit, but who don't?"

"That's true." Zane swayed slightly, but recovered by continuing forward to drop the soaked napkin into the garbage can. "I don't normally do this sort of thing, but—"

"Save it, dude. You want this ass it'll cost you a hundred bucks. Hope you brought your wallet."

So Initials was a man whore. *Fuck,* he thought. *They should have to wear a sign.* As invincible as Zane believed himself to be, this new development confounded him. *Should I stay or should I go. If I stay, there may be trouble, (aids) and if I go, my stomach rumbles...*

Slurp, slurp. "But, like the home shoppin' network, dude, this offer won't last long. I'll hang tight for a bit and you can think on it."

But I worked so long on this speech. I deserve this!

"Tick tock, dude."

Tick tock? Tick tock? Zane narrowed his good eye at Initials, who sipped and scanned the crowd, sipped and peeked at Zane. *That's my line, punk. Get your own.*

Initials sipped. "You know that chick?" he pointed with his eyes, "'cause, brother, she's been starin' a hole right through the back of your head."

Alarms started buzzing in the killer's head like Vegas on a Friday night. "Me?" Zane asked, calmly. "Maybe she's looking to better your price." He chuckled and turned, cleverly pretending to look at the clock. Saliva hung between his chin and chest like a single stringed, one-pluck banjo, mingling and adding to the spread of splatters and stains on his chest.

~~oOo~~

From the personal notes of Dr. Bartholomew D. Gideon, Psychiatrist

Re: Patient #11901 Ellis, Zane

STATUS-ACTIVE---AWOL

"This wild proliferation of theories showed that nobody really knew where the pox had come from; it also showed people were deeply troubled by it, and thought something had gone gravely amiss in the world to provoke such a strange and awful evil. Their confusion and anxiety were also revealed by the names people gave the new arrival. The name most commonly used today, syphilis, came from an Italian poem, written in 1530, which traced the disease to a punishment inflict by the God Jupiter on a fictional character named Syphilus, an impious shepherd."

~~oOo~~

You know what thought did?

It did nothing, but thought it did and really enjoyed the results.

~~oOo~~

It took a few seconds for his eyes to focus on the girl near the rear of the hall. She looked like an experiment done by a six-year-old using crayons and scissors on a Barbie doll after freebasing children's Nyquil. She may have been pretty, but it was hard to see past the gaudy black eyeliner and jack boots. And there was enough fishing tackle stuck in her ears to field a salmon derby! He guessed she'd look away when he continued to stare, but she didn't. Her gaze stayed with him for a few long seconds, and then she stood. Zane couldn't escape the feeling that he should know her.

The woman peeled the "Hello" sticker from her shirt and held it up for him to see, then slapped the sticker onto the seat of the chair she'd vacated, shot her middle fingers at him, and walked out the double doors of the hall.

"Probably some junkie, here for the free food and shit," said Initials. "I 'member this one time, I think it was last—"

"Hold that thought, friend," Zane said. "I'll be right back."

Initials shrugged and called after him, "Sure, dude, your loss. But watch out for your pecker. She looked hungry."

Zane strode over to the doors in an attempt to get another glimpse of the girl, but she'd vanished. A familiar scent hung in the air around him, and he inhaled deeply. He could almost, but not quite, drape it on a memory.

Half in half out of the doorway, he was searching the street for her when an old VW Beetle unhurriedly pulled away from the opposite curb and crept past. He bent at the waist to better his chances of catching a glimpse of the driver, but tinted windows gave him nothing more than a vague outline of a head that could very well have been the girl—or the Pope, or his dear dead mother, come to wish him a happy birthday.

Then the car was gone. After sparing another glance in either direction, he shrugged and walked back inside. As he passed the seat the girl had been seated, he remembered the show she'd made of the sticker, and he stopped to look.

Not a name.

Nor was it a phone number with a cutesy little "call me" scratched beneath.

One word, all block capitals: VENGEANCE

What the hell? he thought, then said, "What..?" *Who the fuck was that?* Zane knew he wasn't going to find the answers on the chair, and the girl had long since gone, so he turned to head back to Initials.

Initials was gone. So were the rest of his twenty-two fellow addicts. The only person left in the hall was the speaker who'd introduced himself as Willem. He was busily stacking chairs onto a trolley as Zane approached. "Hey, Willem?"

Willem's flushed scalp glared like an irritated hemorrhoid. Without the need to look at Zane's sticker, he said, "Thomas."

If Zane would have been himself, his normal *alert* self, he would have translated that one word to mean, "What the hell do you want?" But since he was sorely incapacitated, he took the word for just a word.

"Where did everybody go?"

Willem snorted and returned to stacking chairs.

"No, really. Where did everybody go? I was just talking to a guy right over there," he said, and pointed to the now empty refreshments table. Three used stir sticks (chewed) and several dark brown coffee rings were the only evidence left of his earlier conversation with Initials.

Willem folded a chair and stacked it. "You really don't know, do you?"

"No."

"Are you drunk?"

"No. I—"

"High?"

"No, why?"

"Because I don't believe you, Thomas. What little I can

understand of what you say reeks of lies. Go home. Go home and take a good, long look at yourself in the mirror. Then ask the guy in the mirror if he's worth saving."

How do you know about the mirror? "I can't."

"You can't? What the hell's that supposed to mean? *I can't.*"

"Because I can't see myself anymore."

~~oOo~~

From the personal notes of Dr. B. D. Gideon, Psychiatrist, & Hobbyist Voyeur:
Re: Case subject #11901
Status: FOUND

"General paresis, otherwise known as general paresis of the insane, is a severe manifestation of neurosyphilis. It is a chronic dementia which ultimately results in death in as little as two to three years. Patients generally have progressive personality changes, memory loss, and poor judgment. More rarely, they can have psychosis, depression, or mania. Imaging of the brain usually shows atrophy."

~~oOo~~

10:07pm.

Zoe circled the block, then tucked the Beetle behind a parked van and waited.

The alarm back in the motel had been set for ten o'clock. While she waited for the cannibal to exit the building, she imagined what must be playing out at the motel at that very moment. *Right about now,* she thought, *Seth is whining about his car to Mary. Mary is wondering if I'm okay and telling Spider to calm down.* Then Zoe wondered why Mary always calls Seth *Spider.* Does she think it'll make him seem less lame than he is? She pictured Harry and giggled. *There's Harry, running around in his clown shoes, screaming, "My dogs, oh my! George, Gracie, Poco! My babies, where are my babies?* She couldn't fathom what Danny might be doing right then so she mentally placed him facing the wall, counting cracks in the drywall.

10:23pm.

Okay, where the hell is this guy? Everybody else came out that door—including the skinny wigger wannabe the cannibal was chatting up by the coffee urn. God, it stinks in here. Dog farts. They're like a three piece wind section—and why does it always smell like cabbage? Patience, Zoe. He's in there. She looked down and noticed she'd been rubbing Poco's belly. "Gross," she whispered, and put him down beside his sleeping dad. *Wait a minute. Where the hell is Gracie?* Zoe hadn't seen the dog since she'd entered the motel. *Oh, shit! don't tell me I lost one of them. Fifteen-hundred bucks. That's what the cop said.*

"Gracie?" Zoe strained against her seatbelt, but couldn't turn far enough to look over her shoulder.

From the back seat, she heard a faint, whistling snore. *Whew, good enough. Wish I could sleep like that. Bitch.*

10:37pm.

Alright, that's it. He's not here. She started the car and it immediately rocked forward, coughed, then stalled. *Clutch, dummy. You had it in gear. Remember? Seth said the emergency brake doesn't work.* Irritated by the fact she'd let the killer slip past her *and* that she let a silly thing like the car jumping forward cause her to pee a little, she stomped her foot down on the clutch and fired the engine again. As she reached to switch on the headlights, her quarry stumbled out the door, two steps ahead of the felt marker Nazi.

She ducked down and watched as the men went their separate ways. Marker Nazi turned left, walked toward Zoe on the opposite side of the street, got into a rusty, powder blue Honda and sped away. The killer crossed the street and entered the alley, where she'd first seen him, and disappeared into the darkness.

Poco had made his way over to her lap again, and his growl ticked along like the smallest chainsaw. With his paws on the armrest, breath fogging a pup sized patch on the window, he seemed to really want a piece of that guy. Zoe was touched.

Oh, you sweet little big-balled bugger. You just got cuter. "It's not too late, little fella," she said, and scratched his head. "Your call, Poco. Should we follow him or go back and get the gang?"

Poco stopped barking and licked her face.

"Yeah, me too. Buckle up." Zoe swung out into the street and passed the alley.

Zoe turned right at the first intersection and right again at the next corner. She pulled to the curb and cut the lights as the cannibal emerged from the alley. *Okay, buddy. Where's your car? Parking garage...or do you live around here?*

Zoe settled for none of the above as she watched him walk to a bus shelter and sit down.

A bus? Nah, couldn't be. Zoe took in his face, rendered little more than highlights by the streetlamps overhead. He swiveled his head, left and right, left and right. An image of Ray Charles danced momentarily through her mind. *No, really. This is where your driver is picking you up, right?*

After a few minutes, a bus rocketed past the car. The Beetle rocked gently in the wake of the bulkier vehicle. Even as the man stood and walked to the slowing bus, she denied her eyes, *Really?*

"How fucked is that, Poco?"

Ruff.

"I know, right? A bus."

~~oOo~~

Gideon squinted through his windshield.

"A bus stop? Really, my boy, I had no idea you were this far gone."

He touched the screen of his cell phone and it lit up, bathing him with light: Blue Man, with a beard. Without a glance at the number pad, he pushed an oft used speed dial button and then held the phone near his throat as he waited for a connection.

With a sadness he was ill equipped to foster, Gideon slumped in his seat. After the insults, the goading, and even the incriminating photos Zane had taken of him only a few nights before, the doctor felt sorry for him. His favorite manimal looked more pathetic than a soaked cat. This didn't change the fact that Gideon was going to have him put down the second he found the pictures. All the same, he'd give the order to terminate with a tear in his eye.

Fifty yards past the yellow hippie car, Zane sat at the bus stop. *How simply and utterly wretched,* he thought. An emotion he rarely cavorted with was guilt, but right then, it straddled his chest like a twenty-dollar strip show. He really should have taken care of Zane's *other* problem; the syphilis. Maybe if he had, none of this would've happened. Finding inspiration in his guilt, he whispered out his window into the night.

"I stand alone among millions, casting along the shores of this once great city; now Gomorrah; now ashes. There's murder mingling with the night air. Slipping silently among the denizens like an unseen mist, swaying seductively as it savors the unworthy. Suffocating, intoxicating; I taste its bounty and shudder."

Hey, not bad. I should use that for my book, he thought, and patted his pockets in search of his micro recorder. *Where the devil?*

"Yeah, boss?"

He'd almost forgotten about the phone. "Perry?" Gideon held the phone away from his head as ear splitting Techno music pounded from the phone's tiny speaker. "Is that you, Perry?" *Boom boom boom ba ba boom boom boom...* "Turn down that infernal noise! This is important!"

Ba ba boom "Can't boss, I'm at a club."

A club, he says! Back in my day, a club was something you joined. Membership was earned. Today's youth have corrupted or squandered every legacy left them. Idiot! Gideon didn't voice these thoughts. He knew their truths would be lost on the young cameraman. Besides, the dolt was a Satanist, and, as such, reveled in the torture of any and all he saw as an authority figure. "I need you, Perry. Find somewhere quiet so we can talk."

"Sure, boss. No problemo."

After a moment, the music abruptly muffled; still there, but Gideon could speak without the need to yell. "Perry, get to your house and set up a feed for me."

"But, boss, It's my night off. Plus I met this really rad death punk chick that says she can fu—"

"*Now*, Perry, or you'll not have a job to pay for her ... services."

"Come on, Doc, have a heart. The fuck fu is strong with this one. My dick told me so."

"Now, Perry. This is important."

"More important than getting laid?"

"I'm afraid so, my boy. Now hurry along and say good night to your little friend." *What the hell is wrong with today's youth? They have no work ethic at all.* Gideon cringed at the thought of paying extra, but said, "I'll pay you double. How does that suit you?" *You worthless pile of dog snot.*

"I don't know..."

Alright, you little bastard, try this on for size: "What do you say I have Otto come round the club and pick you up?"

"Fuuuuck, dude. That was harsh. Okay, okay, I'll go. Where and when?"

"Location forty-seven."

"You say forty-seven—as in four seven? Cannibalangelo's pad?"

"That is correct."

"I thought you said he was off the grid."

"Not tonight, he's not."

"Um, you doing him, or is he doing his thing?"

What is this, twenty questions, you little whelp? "Just get home and record it, for Christ sake!"

"Harsh."

"Be that as it may, I still need that feed."

"Okay, but—"

"Right now, Perry"

"Oppressor."

Idiot. Gideon rang off and dropped the phone between his legs. He felt the onset of a tension headache, and rubbed his temples. *What were you thinking, Zane? You just couldn't stop for a little while, could you?* He watched as a bus pulled up to the stop and Zane drunkenly ambled up the steps. Before the doors closed, the bus sped away down the street. Then, the girl in the Beetle swung out and followed in the bus's wake like a fat, yellow, bumper-jumping street skier. Gideon had no need to tail them. He already knew their destination. With the feed in place, there was no need for him to even be present, but—by God—he would be. *There's nothing in the world like live theatre.*

All the world truly is a stage.

34

YOU

This is the man who caused a cross border manhunt involving not only the FBI, but also the RCMP and every local law enforcement agency between? From all Zoe had seen, she couldn't imagine the man she'd followed home—*via the cross-town #9!*—to be able to organize enough wits to hit the floor with spit, let alone confound the above mentioned law professionals. *Master mind, master criminal, master painter. More like masturbator.*

She pulled Poco down from the dash and set him next to his pa. "Well, little man? Wanna go for a walk?" A woman standing on the street in the middle of the night might raise the suspicion of nosy neighbors or a passing security patrol; her every glance, every step, would scream *stalker* to any octogenarian with a set of binoculars within a two mile radius, but not a girl out for a stroll with a dog. *Wouldn't hurt to walk by, you know, just to get the address from the mailbox.*

Poco sneezed, then licked his eyebrows: *Hell, yes I wanna go for a walk.* Wag wag, wag wag.

"You got a leash? Go get it Poco. Go get that leash. Get it, boy."

Poco either didn't care for the notion of being shackled like a convict, or had no idea what the woof she was talking about, because he yawned and sat back on his bountiful twin pillows.

Zoe checked his neck. No collar. *Oh well. There's gotta be something around here we could use for a leash...a belt, some string...*

Ah ha. Zoe pulled the tape holding the bandage in place around her wrist. She unwound what she deemed to be about three feet of gauze, and bit it off. *There,* she thought, and tugged the length taut to check its strength. The gauze rope wouldn't hold a pit bull, but was good enough for a ten pound rat. After three tries, she managed to navigate the mystical art of the slipknot. *Excuse me very much for never doing bondage tricks!*

Poco wagged his tail and pranced back and forth along the dash. *Whatcha got there, lady, huh? Huh? What's that? What's that?*

She slid the knotted end over his head and closed the slack. "There you go, Ug ug, a leash. What do you think?"

Indignantly, Poco dug his paws into the vinyl of the dash and latched onto the gauze restraint. His look said: *Not woofing much, lady. I thought you wanted to go for a walk, woof you very much.*

Zoe picked him up and cradled him to her chest. Once outside the car, she set him down. "Go, dog. Do your thing." He stood still, shivering on the pavement. She didn't need to speak Chinese or even dog-ese to realize he was not amused.

"Deal with it, Ug ug. Make like a frying pan and wok."

Zoe had been so proud of herself for solving the "no leash" problem that she'd forgotten to tie the other end into a usable handle. Instead, she held that end between her fingers, like a doobie or a pair of unknown soiled underwear.

Right. See ya. Poco bolted forward, gauze trailing like a mummy's dinner tie, and crossed the lawn, all the while barking like a broken laugh track. He darted up the steps and plunged through the door left ajar by the man-eating mush head.

"Oh, shit." Zoe covered her mouth. She circled around to the driver's side, dropped into the seat, and fired the engine. *Ohfuck-ohshit-ohno, Harry's gonna kill me.* The barking grew louder and she looked up. Poco had reemerged, yapped at her, then darted back into the house. She killed the engine, pushed George away, and hopped out. She was at the bottom of the driveway before realizing how stupid she was being. From where she stood, she whisper-yelled, "Poco, come here boy. Leave that nice man alone and let's go."

Yap, yap, yap.

Zoe weighed her options: *Fifteen hundred dollars. That's five straight lays, an over/under, and two, maybe three hand jobs.*

Well, Harry did have two more. Given the right atmosphere—Barry White, a Benji video, and a bottle of wine—they could make another Poco.

One heartbroken old clown: how could she ever go to another circus and not cry like a baby?

Um, when exactly was the last time you darkened the doorway of a big top? And, duh, he's a killer.

Oh, hell!

Zoe stepped onto the porch. *Hey, mister,* she practiced. *Sorry about my dog.* She rapped on the open door. *I'll just get him out of your hair. Jeez, I'm really sorry about this.* "Hello..?"

Yap yap yap.

She stepped into the front hall, knocking on the wall as she went, and was assaulted by the unmistakable aroma of fresh paint, and the foam rubber scent of recently laid carpet. She'd expected vomit and the charnel smell of rotted corpses. *Jesus, dog. I'm so gonna kick you in your balls when we get out of here. I swear to god I will.*

From the next room the canned laughter of a sitcom filtered out beneath Poco's seizure-like battle cry. *Okay, run in, scoop up the dog, and then run like hell.*

Zoe went in low, expecting the dog to be on the ground. She stopped and slowly straightened. Cannibalangelo held the gauze leash above his head, face to snout with a snarling bundle of teeth and balls. Poco swung in a slow arc, choking and snapping at the man with each pass.

The cannibal didn't flinched from the dog, nor did he raise his head when Zoe entered the room. Oblivious, he held the struggling dog in one hand, and balanced a bowl of cereal in the other. Just as Zoe filled her lungs to scream, he bobbed his head toward her, dropped the dog, and proffered a slack jawed grin.

He closed one eye and squinted through the other, and said, "This is awkward. I wasn't expecting company."

Startled, Zoe backed away and bumped a solid object with the heel of her boot. A stolen glance showed it to be a vase. Wasting no time, she grabbed the vase with both hands, and spun around, swinging it in a swooping arc. The bulky jar struck the cannibal on the cheek, pulverizing bones and teeth alike, and lifted him off his feet.

Still holding the vase in a fear induced death grip, momentum pulled Zoe in a complete circle and she landed on the ground beside the man. Winded, she let the urn fall from her chest and then rolled to her feet.

Zoe forced herself to take in her handiwork. She wasn't a doctor, but she'd had sex with one in front of a TV. So, with that smidgen of expertise, she was able give a fairly accurate prognosis for the cereal pasted cannibal at her feet: "You're so boned, buddy."

She let out a calming breath and clasped her hands to stop them from shaking. This was nothing like she'd imagined it would be. But then, she'd based this scenario on the works of actors like Clint Eastwood, Bruce Willis, and Will Smith. This wasn't like it was in the movies at *all*. For the past two months, she'd been running on nothing but cold Pop Tarts and fear, getting shot at, fucked at gun point, spit on, poked, prodded, and—to add salt to the wound—dumped by an imaginary purple monkey.

Just a thud; like the sound you'd get by whacking a bag of flour with a leather mallet...kind of disappointing, really. She'd been hoping for movie magic, like thunderous crashes and tormented maniacal screams. She hugged her arms across her chest. *It's done. Isn't that good enough?*

Her disappointment with the sound department's handling of her vengeance scene aside, he *was* bleeding pretty badly. That fact *alone* should have raised her spirits, but it didn't.

She thought when the time came she'd feel something other than dirty and drained of emotion. *Righteous glee,* she thought. *Vindication...even giddiness, but this? This sucks.* Zoe wasn't proud of how she'd done it, but, in her defense, he *was* bigger *and* he was a killer. She, on the other hand, couldn't say the same. All she could add to her credit was that her ballet was fair and that for four days a month she could be a real bitch.

Cannibalangelo rolled his remaining *working* eye around to settle on her and stared for a few seconds before he was able to place her face. His eye went round and what was left of his mouth smiled. "You," he said, and then his eye wandered past her, to the doorway.

Zoe had no time to formulate a proper Samuel L. Jackson-type comeback before she heard a floorboard creak, followed by a short, muffled cough.

In that instant, the dog bounded past, serving up a fresh batch of barks—and pain erupted in her shoulder, rocking her forward and spinning her around. Unable to breathe, she staggered, gaping impotently into the eyes of the man who'd just shot her.

Zoe sucked in a partial breath, and traded a look between the gun in the newcomer's gloved hand and, through a halo of cigar smoke, his face. "You," she wheezed. Then the room swirled around her in a vortex, ever faster, stealing first her vision, then sound. Zoe fell backward over the convulsing form of the cannibal as fire blossomed and spread in rolling waves through her chest and down each limb.

In seconds, she could no longer feel the awkward lump of the body beneath her. The pain bled away, replaced by pins and needles, then, to a solitary arctic finger that became thousands, numbing her to the basement of her soul.

Zoe's last thought—in the brief seconds before memory failed along with her brain—was of Jeanne. Proudly, she spoke to her sister's memory: *I did it, Jeannie. I did it. I got...* And then she was still.

35

SLEEPER

Gideon stepped forward to meet the rushing dog and shot it in its exposed chest. The dog yelped and slid backward, coming to a stop at the whore's foot. With effort, the little dog raised its snout and nuzzled the toe of her boot, then, he too, fell still.

"Good boy. Stay. At least one of you went down without saying, 'You.' How droll." Gideon used his foot to slide the dog away from the other bodies, then kneeled and pushed the redheaded girl from atop Zane.

The old doctor lowered his ear to the Zane's chest. The cannibal's heart pumped at the speed of erosion, but he was alive. With the nurturing hands of a slighted schoolmarm, he turned Zane's head to better see the dent that ran in a circular crease from his chin to his ear. The damage was heavy, but not the worst he'd seen. He dropped Zane's head with an unceremonious *thunk*, and then wiped his hand on the man's jacket.

"I hate to say I told you so, but I will. Women are nothing but trouble. See what your dalliance has wrought for you? A broken head. But don't fret, my boy. We'll fix you up and have you back to the dance in no time."

It would have been easy to just let him fade away, *then* call Otto for a cleanup, but there was a certain matter of some less than appropriate pictures involving Gideon and his former receptionist Zane held in his possession. Like a marriage of convenience, it seemed he was stuck with Zane until he was healthy enough to be tortured into divulging the whereabouts of the photos.

Just for the tactile experience of it, Gideon stood and kicked Zane in the ribs. "Do you realize how lame that entire footage is?" He sneered and mimicked Zane, lending a girlish whine that wasn't originally there, "*This* is awkward. This is awkward? Garbage," he fumed. "Fodder not fit for a gag reel."

He huffed in frustration, then walked into the kitchen and straight to the pantry. In seconds, he was back in the living room with a coil of nylon rope and two rolls of duct tape. After a loud sigh, he went to work trussing the bodies.

Once finished, the doctor put his hand on an overturned chair to boost himself up. The cartilage in his old knees audibly creaked as he stood and stretched his back. As he hobbled over to the window, he fished his cell phone from his jacket pocket and thumbed a few numbers. While the call connected, he pulled the curtain back to look outside. The young woman's car sat just down the street, but nothing else stirred.

"Pick up, Otto. Pickup-pickup-pickup," he said, as he licked his lips. Finally, just as he was about to hang up and try again, Otto answered.

At first there was nothing except the serene backdrop of Mozart's *Lullaby*. After what seemed like minutes to the doctor, the pig farmer answered. "Yes?"

"Do you know who this is?" the doctor whispered.

"Of course." Otto's distinct European accent clipped the words off like toenails. "Is there urgency?"

"You might say that." Gideon let his eyes drift toward the two bodies on the floor. "How soon can you be in the city?"

"Do I need tools?"

Gideon shuddered involuntarily, and grinned. "It might not be a bad idea for you to bring a few tools."

There were artists who worked for the doctor, and there were brutes. This man, Otto Gruber, was the latter. He nonetheless had his skills.

"Where?" asked the gruff voice, expelling the word like a bowel movement.

"Do you remember the gentleman you planted flowers for this month?" He couldn't just come out and say where he was. There could be *anyone* listening. He wasn't paranoid, but a little caution wouldn't hurt. "You remember…when he was sick?"

In the background, *Fur Elise* had replaced *Lullaby*. "Yes, I recall the place. But, Herr Doktor, I thought Zane was off the grid, as you say."

Gideon's blood pressure rose like morning wood on a teen, and he counted to ten. "Was there a memo sent I didn't know about?"

"Doktor?"

"Nothing, just hurry."

"Forty minutes," he grunted.

"Oh, and Otto?"

"Ya?"

"The house needs to be thoroughly searched, so you'll need a few extra bodies to help. Is that a problem?"

Gideon could almost hear the big man's indifferent shrug. "As you wish, doktor."

Say what you want about Germans, but they were an industrious bunch. Gideon ended the call and bent to scoop the dog from the floor. Through his glove, he felt a steady heartbeat. *I haven't the foggiest idea what I'm going to do with you, you little devil,* he thought, recalling the last time he'd seen the dog.

What the hell is Harry doing in Chicago?

~~oOo~~

Harry awoke to a hair-of-the-dog situation; a plumed puff of tail lay like a blindfold across his eyes. Without needing to see which canine perpetrated the hairy onslaught, he rolled away to face the seat back. Gracie hopped to the floor, then jumped immediately onto the seat again and curled into the back of Harry's knees. Autopilot brought his hand to his face to extinguish an itch on his nose then mine a nugget from within. "Good morning, Gracie. Where's that lounge about man of yours?" He didn't expect a response—from Gracie, anyway. She wasn't much of a barker.

Woof woof.

Eyes closed, still half asleep, chin resting on the cold steel of a seatbelt buckle, Harry mumbled, "Top of the morning, George. I'll be along presently. Get your dish."

Each morning, for more years than Harry could remember, George—like his father, Putter, and Putter's sire, Book—met Harry in the kitchen with a yip and a wink, food dish clamped firmly between their pearly whites. Always and ever, it was a tradition. Harry, for his part, never failed George in meeting him for their Purina moment. And he'd be damned if he was going to let a simple thing like a road trip mess with the yang to their yin. "Ten more minutes, George."

Woof woof woof.

Still with his eyes closed: "You know, George, back in China they eat your kind for breakfast. Keep it down or I'll slap a stamp on your bottom and send you there." The residue left from dry swallowing the sleeping pills left Harry's mouth feeling like he'd been gargling gravel all night.

He resisted the urge to snuggle in and go back to sleep, and tried to straighten his legs, but couldn't. Then the seatbelt buckle poked him in the throat.

Oh yes: the car, the odd group of companions, and the motel. *I hope they slept better than I did,* he thought, as he recalled the young driver's invitation for him to sleep in the car. Harry had intended to only stay with the dogs until they settled and the rude driver fell asleep, but he must have succumbed to the sleeping pills.

Woof woof.

Harry sat up and pried his salted lids apart. "Oh, do shut up, George. I..." He trailed off as he regarded the scenery surrounding the car.

The motel was gone.

He was no Charlie Chan, but neither was he stupid. A four

fingered roll call came up one short. And, Zoe's cigarette's and purse—both items he'd last seen being trucked by her into the motel—were presently wedged between the front seats.

He slapped his forehead. It was becoming all so clear to him. He was amazed he hadn't seen the warning signs sooner. Poco, after stewing over being shunned from joining the troop for Harry's famed "Ring of Fire" leap, must have fashioned a lock pick, crept into the motel, stolen Zoe's purse and the keys to the car. Thus beginning a life of crime the likes of which the world will crumble before.

But, like the great detective Charlie Chan, he instantly tore a gaping hole in this theory: Poco didn't smoke.

The only other alternative was this: Zoe hadn't been able to sleep, took the car out for a drive, needed company for a walk, and took young Poco as an escort. Sure it was a stretch, but he really didn't want to believe Poco had been smoking behind his back.

From the darkness of the back seat, Harry's gaze moved from one lamp lit pool of light to the next. No girl, no dog. Upon his second visual voyage up the street, he noticed a Lincoln parked two driveways over. One look at the car and he knew it belonged to Gideon. He was almost sure of it.

The vanity plate read: GIDEON 1

He placed his palms over his eyes and sunk back to the safety of the darkened rear seat. "That won't do. That won't do at all." Just when he thought it couldn't get any worse, he took his hands away in time to see a dingy, grey van ease in behind the Lincoln. The crooked magnetic sign on the side of the van read:

Final Solution Pest-Popper Squad
We kill what you can't!

Harry suddenly found that he couldn't breathe. *Don't be him. Don't be him.*

It *was* him: The gorilla shouldered mass of scar tissue, Arian nightmare walking—the one, the only—Otto Gruber. George agreed. The dog had begun to evoke his ancestral right as alpha male with a low slung growl and bared teeth. The effect was ruined when began to shake so badly that he slipped from the seat and fell under the dash.

With a voice as palsied as the old dog's flesh, Harry ducked his head in shame and told George something that the dog's flared nostrils said he already knew: "Please don't think ill of me, old friend, but I seem to have peed a little."

~~oOo~~

The big German squeezed past Gideon to survey the situation. He lingered on each body for a few seconds, then spun to regard the doctor. With a belly lifting "Humph"— which could have passed for anything from indigestion to professional indignation—he waggled his meaty hand toward the girl trussed up in a floral rug cocoon.

"Were you planning to kill her or smoke her like one of your cigars, Herr Doktor?"

Gideon shifted his weight from one leg to another. "It seemed like a good idea at the time."

"But you knew I would have my cart, ya?"

"I don't answer to you, Otto. Remember that."

Otto's grin vanished. "And the animal?" He jabbed a thumb over his shoulder. "Did you really need to tape it to the wall? That is cruel, Herr Doktor."

You think that was cruel? After all the things I've seen you do, you think taping a dog to a wall is wrong? Gideon's cheeks reddened. "Again, I don't answer to you. But if you must know, he wouldn't stop squirming—even after tying him twice. Then I tripped over him."

"What is it? A weasel?"

"A dog. And if memory serves me, you've met before. Do you recall the trip we took last year to Michigan, to pay a visit to my old friend, Chin Choi?"

"Oh yes." The big man's grin was back. "I remember…the wonderful little dancing dogs. I loved the dogs."

"Otto, the bodies. We must hurry."

"Why? They are dead, no?"

"No. We need to get Zane to a doctor before his condition worsens."

For some reason, this revelation irked Otto. "I thought you wanted him dead, ya?"

"Ya. *Yes*, I did. I do. But it's complicated. You wouldn't understand. There have been recent developments which require further contemplation on my part." Gideon had rarely seen the bullnecked European lose his temper, especially at him. It was frightening to watch the transformation from Igor to Evil. *Maybe I shouldn't have said that he wouldn't understand?*

"Ya, stupid Otto. I would not understand at all." Otto glared across the space between them, flexing his fingers. Finally, he grunted and pointed to the girl. "And the floral cigar, they are not dead as well?"

"Not quite, but—"

"So now I am nothing more than a porter? An ambulance service?"

"Would you allow me to finish a fucking sentence, Otto?"

Otto folded twin tree trunk arms across his chest. "Please do, Herr Doktor." He was not amused.

"Zane has something I need, but the girl is yours to keep."

All was forgiven. The grin returned like a reopened knife wound. "You are too kind."

"But there's just one thing."

"Yes?"

"You have to kill her."

"Yes. And? What is the catch?"

Gideon produced a small video recorder from his trench coat. "I'd like a memento of the occasion."

Close to tears, Otto bobbed his enormous head. "I will not let you down."

"I'm sure you won't, but we really should hurry. Remember? Zane?"

Otto hesitated. "May I also have the animal? He is wonderful."

"Why not, but watch yourself. The little bastard almost took my finger, even *after* I tranquilized him."

36

HEROES

As he fought the urge to give in and sink into despair, Harry held George under one arm and Gracie under the other, like a pair of flotation devices. Although he'd yet to see a body, it was only a matter of time. He'd never felt so helpless in his life! Gideon and his monsters had killed that poor girl and there was nothing he could do for her except pray. Tears were out of the question. He'd exhausted that well years ago, and most days he could barely muster enough liquid to blink.

And, pray? Pray to whom? I don't believe Buddha would listen, but God might, he thought, ruefully. *He always enjoys a good joke.*

Or, instead of sitting on your ass, you could do something, you worthless old coot, he berated himself. *Save her. You could run over, hit him with one of the tools from the cart, and snatch the girl away. She might still be alive. You were once a world class athlete and Otto's a big slow lummox. It's not too late to care. Do something good for once in your useless life!*

But no; Harry's concept of the disparity between what was good and what was evil had been ground down to rotted nerves from years of masticating his own dark deeds.

He'd lost the race with one shoe still planted firmly on the block. He was no hero. *She's brought this upon herself. I warned her. What more could I do? And why—why bring my poor little Poco with you?* Thoughts of Poco caused him to hate the girl, even if only a little. Then he hated himself for hating her.

And as far as being a world class athlete goes...you were a clown, a tumbler, nothing more than a joke between real performances. He sank deeper into the seat, into an impotent self loathing, and watched. If nothing else, he could at least witness the girl's passing and mourn her.

If Otto Gruber was attempting to conceal the fact that he was removing a body from the house, he was sure doing a union job of it. Gideon's lackey carted his rolling "tool chest" out, stopped beside the Lincoln and, without even a cursory glance toward the street, clean jerked a body from the chest and chucked it into the back seat of the car. *Oh my dear child, I'm so sorry.*

Harry relaxed in stages, believing the worst to be over. All that was left to do was wait for the men to leave. That's when Harry would slip out of the car and leave with his remaining two dogs. As part of the 'clean up', Otto would be back for the Beetle later. Harry hoped to be sitting in the nearest bus station by then. He'd call the kids from a pay phone to tell them about Zoe.

Seconds later, Otto's scarred cranium appeared in the house's doorway. He looked directly at the Volkswagen, and then slipped back into the house. Harry stared down the barrel of his own mortality, and found he wasn't as afraid as he thought he'd be. Running for it was out of the question. Although he was bulky, Otto was at least ten years his junior, and Harry's floppy footwear didn't allow for mad dashes. *Dignity, old clown,* he thought, and shook hands with his destiny as he waited for Otto to come for him.

Harry flirted with the idea of opening the door for the dogs to flee but knew they'd go nowhere. With the courage of lions, they'd each expel their last breath defending him from the killer. Their bravery would be their undoing, but he could no more stop them from championing him than he could keep the sun from rising. *At least we'll be together to the end, friends.*

Harry's bravery, nonetheless, couldn't cease the

overwhelming need he had at that moment to urinate.

Otto must have seen his silhouette in the car. *Why didn't he come running over? Oh yes, tinted windows. Bless you Seth.* Harry held his cramping stomach as he searched the floor of the car for a cup, a water bottle, anything that might hold what felt like a gallon.

In spite of the tinted windows, Harry ducked when Gideon and Otto reemerged from the house. Gideon allowed his "cleaner" to pass him with the wheeled tool chest as he stopped and locked the door. *Why would he lock the door? And why would Sergeant Shultz have brought the meat wagon back into the house? A second body? Was Zoe alone? Or was Zane Ellis dead too?* His own imminent demise suddenly rode shotgun to this new batch of questions. *Where's my boy? Where's Poco?*

The doctor climbed behind the wheel of the Lincoln and waited for his henchman to load his meat wagon and leave. Or so Harry thought.

Otto stopped at the rear of the van, lifted the lid of the tool box and threw it into the back. Then he hoisted a rolled carpet and dumped it into the rear. *Two bodies?* Speculation died as the man reach into the box for a third, much smaller package. What he pulled out was a limp, ten pound pup named Poco.

As Poco hit the floor of the van, he lifted his head slightly. Then the door closed before Harry could see more. But that was enough.

I knew it! I knew you were alive. His heart had been jostled and shoved over so many rapids in the short time he'd been awake, he was exhausted from the strain of keeping afloat. But now he coasted. *Crystal clear waters now,* he thought. Poco was alive.

Suddenly, Niagara Falls loomed large before him. Poco was alive but he was in a van with a ghoul.

Another Chan whom he vaguely resembled, but was nothing like, was Jackie Chan. If he would have had *that* Chan's skill in martial arts, his youthful lust for adventure, Harry would have tracked the van to the villain's hide out and rescued his dog—the girl, too (if time allowed). But alas, he was no Jackie Chan. He wasn't even much of clown anymore.

Right then, something happened that Harry thought would never happen again. He cried. The well he thought would never see another drop of water filled and spilled from him with body racking sobs; it was a bitter harvest that drowned all else, even fear.

I'm coming, Poco. Daddy's coming! Determination settled over him like a red and blue suit with a big S emblazoned upon the chest. He would be God's hairy arm of justice. *Taking a girl I've known less than a day is one thing, but never fuck with a man's dog.* One-hundred and five pounds of pissed off clown waited until the Lincoln left the driveway, and then he climbed into the driver's seat to follow the van.

There was one small detail standing in his way. Like a child taking a tour of a cock pit at twenty thousand feet, he had no idea what all the switches and knobs were for. As many times as he'd emerged cart wheeling or falling comically from a clown car, he'd never learned to drive one. Hope faded along with the taillights of the grey van as he twisted, kicked, and jabbed every button, knob and switch in view.

Then he remembered: *Keys. Turn it and push the pedals.* He turned the key. It lurched forward and died. Again...same result. He pushed his feet to the floor over two out of three of the pedals and tried again. *Bingo.* It only took him seconds to figure out he'd need to find a higher gear if he had any hope of keeping up, but the process eluded him. Since it had worked to start the car rolling, he plunged his feet to the floor again, and tugged on the stick near his elbow like he'd seen Seth do. The car lurched again and sputtered, then it slowly gained speed. *Ah ha.*

He continued to use this same method until he'd caught up to and matched the van's speed. Just as he became complacent with driving, the van turned, so he slowed to turn as well. As he released his foot from the accelerator, his shoe lodged under the brake pedal, spurring him to yank until the shoe came off his foot. He feathered the brake with his bare foot then released it and caught up to the van. With his unshod heel resting on the threadbare carpet below the gas pedal, he wondered how many diseases, at that very moment, crawled up his leg. *It serves you right, you old coot, for taking your first driving lesson with clown shoes on.*

George hopped up onto the dash, obscuring his line of vision, and Harry pushed him aside.

"George! Get out of the way. Can't you see daddy's on a mission?"

The dog jumped down, then immediately back, stepping on the radio's volume knob in the process. Scrabbling for purchase, George slid the knob to its apex, and then the dial snapped off and rolled under the passenger seat.

The instantaneous blast of distorted guitars caused Harry to swerve. The car jumped the curb and struck a mismatched pair of garbage cans, and their contents spewed across the windshield. Harry fumbled for the wipers, found them, but not before he side swiped a parked car and slammed a mail box into a second car.

Back out on the road once more, he caught the van's distant lights as it turned two streets ahead. With the fast tracking skills of an idiot savant, Harry slammed the car into second and left an inch of smoking rubber in his wake.

To lessen the throbbing beat of the unstoppable onslaught, courtesy of the busted radio, he rolled down the window and stuck his head into the night air. *Oh that dreadful racket!* He waggled his finger at George as he loudly rebuked him, "Why can't you be more like Gracie? You don't see her crawling all over the dash trying to kill us."

Upon hearing her name, Gracie let out a woof and jumped up to join her husband. Unable to match her mate's ardor in their quest, she instead became hypnotized by a banana peel stuck under one wiper, and she licked the window as it swished back and forth.

Unnecessarily screaming to hear his own voice, ropy veins stood ready to pop along Harry's neck. "Oh-for-the-love-of-God, that racket! Damn you, Seth!"

I'm coming, Poco! Daddy's coming.

~~oOo~~

Gideon glanced in the rearview at the shape of the unconscious man in the back seat. "You know, if not for those pictures, I would have let her beat your skull in, don't you?" Response not required, response not given. He merely needed to vent. Like an abacus, his brain had racked up quite a tidy sum for the day already, and he hadn't even spoken to the plastic surgeon yet. The feed: ching ching. Overtime for that rude little bastard, Perry: ching ching. Otto: ching (He was actually pretty cheap, so only deserved one ching). Otto's crew: ching ching. The approximate cost of the surgery: too many chings to count. Going to jail for murder if Zane dies and the pictures were discovered: Priceless.

He shucked his cell phone from his pocket and thumbed the screen. Dead. *Oh my.* As he steered toward the plastic surgeon's home, he reached blindly into the back seat and felt along Zane's body for his cell phone. After a minute, and a nearly struck street sign, he was rewarded with a rectangular bulge in the front pocket. He turned it on, then wiped an unexplainable dampness from the screen. From memory, he punched in a number he hoped was right, and waited, holding the phone away from his head as though it were a loaded diaper.

One buzz put him through to the surgeon. He smiled as though the other man could see him.

"Robert," he purred. "How's my favorite doctor?"

"Not technically a doctor anymore, Gideon, but what about you? How's my favorite bible?"

"Who reads the bible? Listen, I need a face."

"You sure do."

"No one likes a smartass, doctor."

"They do if they don't know another doctor who does what I do."

"Touché. Where to? Your place?"

"Yes." Robert paused, and then asked, "Just for giggles, Gideon, who is it? Do I know him?"

"I don't think it would be wise to say over the phone, Robert."

"I see. I guess it doesn't matter. Just come around back of the house. My girlfriend will let you in."

"I should probably tell you he has syphilis."

"No shit?"

"No shit."

"Why has no one taken care of it? There's a fix for that if caught soon enough, you know."

"Can you do it? I mean…from your home?"

"Of course. Not tonight, but I can get everything I need in the morning. Do you know his blood type?"

"AB. So you're in luck there. Also, you might want to keep him in restraints…and gag him. He's a cannibal."

The surgeon whistled, causing Gideon to wince. "No shit?"

"No shit." *Thanks. Now I'm deaf.*

"I guess it just goes to show that you should always watch what you put in your mouth, eh Gideon? …Gideon? I said, I guess it—"

"I heard what you said, Robert. I just didn't think it merited a response."

"Okay then. Guess I better kennel my cat. See you in about half an hour?"

"Five minutes. I was already on my way over."

"That's fine, just fine."

But Gideon had a sneaking suspicion it wasn't.

~~oOo~~

"Aw, fuck." After he hung up the phone with Gideon, Robert scrubbed his face with both hands. Dr. Robert Hawthorne, specialist in the art of all things rhinoplasty, winner of the Surgeon General's award of excellence two years in a row, was so stoned he thought his shoe was staring at him. "Trudy!" He ran to the bottom of the staircase. "Trudy! We got company coming, honey. Put some clothes on."

He shook his head and slapped himself repeatedly in the

face. This caused his face to sting, but did nothing for the rude shoe. *Fuck.* Back at the bottom of the stairs again, he said, patiently, "Trudy, honey. Guy's gonna be here in less than—"

Tap tap tap tap.

Well, it wasn't his shoe—he'd been looking right at it when the knocking started.

He was halfway to the door before realizing he was naked. *Bummer.* "Coming," he called to the door.

From the corner of his eye, he spotted Trudy's bath robe pooled on the kitchen floor. *Good deal.* "Tru? Come on, sweetie, we gotta roll!" And just to get her in the right frame of mind he dropped his voice an octave and boomed, "Stat, nurse."

Upon opening the door, he ducked his head past Gideon, and then pulled him in. "Good to see you, doctor."

Gideon eyed him, taking in his bare legs and the short flowered robe. "And you as well, Robert. Did I catch you at a bad time?" he gestured to the robe, then the path of clothing that led to the open refrigerator.

"Whoops. Sorry about that." Robert smirked. "It's theme night. Trudy wanted to do *Nine and a half weeks.* You know, the one with Mickey Rourke and that chick—"

Gideon cut him off. "Robert. You seem to be suffering from a severe case of coitus interruptus." Then, angrily, added, "I have a man dying in my back seat. Do you mind?"

Robert turned and yelled, "Trudy! Come on, hon..."

And she was standing right next to him, tying her damp hair into a bun. She was naked except for a pair of flower topped flip flops.

"'Kay," she said. "You don't have to yell, Rob. I'm right here. Let's go save a life." Then she bustled past the men and out into the backyard.

Gideon turned to watch the naked woman, and then he raised an eyebrow. "Is there something I should know?"

Hands in the air, Robert chuckled. "It's nothing, really. I did her boobs two months ago and tonight was the first time she's been able to have any fun with them. It's fine. But when she comes back in, be a sport and tell her they look nice?"

As they walked into the yard, Gideon whispered, "Have you and Florence Nightingale over there been smoking the marijuana cigarettes? Really! You reek like you just had relations with a skunk."

Mustering as much indignation as a man wearing a ball grazing kimono could, Robert huffed. "What do you take me for, doctor?"

Gideon grunted as he threw an arm under Zane's shoulders and lifted. "Right now you look like a tranny porn star."

Robert opened his mouth, stopped, then shrugged. "I can deal with that."

Gideon and Robert followed Trudy; man handling Zane through the kitchen door, they dropped him, collected him, and bounced him down the stairs into the basement. His head only missed two steps on the way down but they made up for it by dropping him again before reaching the table.

Once they'd lifted him to the makeshift operating table, Gideon stretched his back and turned to the nurse. "Your breasts are quite impressive, young lady. I'm sure your mother is proud." Then he walked a short distance away and beckoned Robert to follow. In hushed tones, he said, "This is important Robert...very. Would you like me to stay and assist. She doesn't seem very bright."

"But you're a shrink and she's a qualified nurse."

Robert watched proudly as Gideon drank Trudy's beauty in.

Gideon sighed. "She's a qualified something, but I don't believe it's a nurse."

Robert draped a silken sleeve over the taller man's shoulder. "Trust me, it's all good." He snapped his fingers. "Oh yeah, I almost forgot. Do you have a face in mind? You want I should prettify him?"

With the look of a man who just invested all his money in freeze dried farts, Gideon slouched and handed the surgeon Zane's passports and travel case. "Surprise me," he said, and then left.

37

HANNIBAL'S FOLLY

"Fuck, Trudy. You were such a slut back there. You might as well have started sucking the guy off right in the backyard."

"Uh, are you kidding? He was like eighty fricken years old. As if. I was just being nice to the geezer. He *is* paying you a lot of money to fix that guy."

"Speaking of 'that guy', maybe you should keep all swinging appendages and fingers away from his mouth."

"Why?" She pouted. "Do you think I'm gonna fuck him, too?"

"Awe, c'mon Tru. It isn't that, honest. It's just that he's got a disease." *And he may snatch off ten grand in one shot if you don't get your tits away from his fucking mouth!* "What do you say, Tru? Put a shirt on? For me?"

She hugged her arms beneath her ample bosom and turned away to watch *Scrubs* on the television. "You think I'm ugly, don't you?"

Beeeeeeeeeeeeeeeeeeeeeeeeeeeeeeeeeeeeeeeeeeeeeeeeeeeeeeee—

"Shit, Trudy, he's crashing. Check his pulse. Trudy! Turn that fucking television off and help me. He's dying."

—eeeeeeeeeeeeeeeeeeeeeeeeeeeeeeeeeeeeeeeeeeeeeeeeeeeeeep.

"Forget it," he said. "He's gone."

"Fine," she snapped. "Whoopdi fuck for him."

Wow, that's cold. Note to self: never piss Trudy off. Out of habit more than anything resembling professionalism, he asked her the time of death. Arms folded, she didn't budge. *But what an ass!*

The patient was gone. And so was the money Gideon was going to pay him. *Oh well. Not the first, won't be the last,* "What time is it, Nurse Goodbody?" He tried to get her to smile. "Tru? Trudy?"

"What! Oh," she said, narrowing her eyes. "03:14, Doctor Dickhead."

"Okay, for the record, we'll note the time of death as 03:14. Would you write that down?" Nothing. "Holy fuck, Trudy. Are you listening? I'm trying to do this like a fucking professional, for fucksake."

Trudy switched off the television and spit her gum onto the sterile tray of instruments. "You think just because you make me cum so hard I speak in tongues that you can talk to me like that? I am a fucking lady, you asshole, and I would appreciate a little goddamn respect, capiche?" She scribbled the time onto a match book and stuffed it down the patient's pants. "There. Happy?"

Feeling a little guilty for taking his frustrations out on Trudy, Robert looked at his shoe. The shoe stared back. He was over that already, but beside the shoe was an unplugged power cord. He bent, told the shoe to fuck off, and plugged the cord back in. Instantly, the machine blinked to life and chirped like Sinbad's owl. Beep beep beep

"Never mind, Trudy, he's not dead after all."

"You're still an asshole."

"Yes," he held out a blood smeared glove, "and you're still beautiful. Now, would you be so kind as to hand me that scalpel, my moist, mountainous playground."

Trudy slapped the scalpel into his gloved hand, looked at him sternly for a second, then smiled, and said, "Scalpel, my throbbing hunk of burning love."

Robert flicked a clump of chewed gum from the scalpel. "Suction, my pink split peach of passion," he said. As she dropped to her knees, he quickly clarified his request. "No sweetie, I meant suction for his eye socket."

~~oOo~~

While he coasted slowly past Zane's house, Gideon noticed two things: The yellow shit box was gone; Otto must have returned for it after killing the whore. But if that was the case, what does that say for the quality of the video he'd turn in?

The second thing he noticed was that there was no one presently *in* the house. That was bad. Otto's nephews should have been there. It had been almost two hours since he'd left the house with Zane to have him pieced back together. Otto's crew should have either been in there tearing the house apart looking for those damnable photos, or standing on the lawn having a weenie roast in the ashes of the fire they were to set upon finding nothing. No lights in the house, no weenie roast on the lawn. That was bad.

When he reached the front door and unlocked it, Gideon found no one had been there at all. "This is bad."

He courted the idea of tossing the house himself, then recalled the manicure he'd had that morning. He'd wait. Otto's boys would be there soon and take care of everything. *Good old Otto.* The leather faced kraut had never once let him down in all the years he'd known him.

To occupy his time, Gideon let his mind wander back to Dr. Hawthorne. Well, not Robert, really—*her*, more specifically. During his time in the black market surgeon's home Gideon had remained what he hoped they would conceive as stoic, detached, and professional. *But that woman! Oh, that woman. What was her name? Trudy? Yes. That's it.*

If a brain could letch, if a mind could leer, his Ego would have been stroking his medulla oblongata and dribbling Id *everywhere*. Like a young Bettie Page, walking straight out of sticky dog-eared fifties rag and right into the room, she was perfection personified. Adorable vixen, coy temptress; she was the cure for her own venom. Trudy. Gideon could honestly say he hadn't felt so smitten in years. More potent than any pill or pump, even in her absence she'd made his little Freud sit up and beg.

Caught in a brain cramp, his mind held fast to the image of her descending the stairs and walking toward him—play, rewind, play, rewind. *Full-bodied hair tied back with two stray locks framing the oval, almond-eyed face of a goddess; her lips, a sailor's tale, full and pink, down-turned in a permanent pout. Glistening beads of water here and there, remnants of a shower or sweat from love making— or not water at all—clinging like tiny gems of morning dew to a thin strip of tightly wound pubic hair.* Gideon's mind was adrift in the ocean of possibilities an encounter with her might yield.

A car's headlights swept past the window, jerking him back to the present. Believing it to be the cleaners he walked over to check, but even as he drew the curtain the car rolled past.

He dropped the curtain and sat on the edge of the couch. *They should have been here by now,* he thought, reaching for his phone—a phone that lay on the seat of his car, charging. It wasn't until he'd left the Surgeon's home that he'd remembered leaving a charger in the dash. Using the house phone was out of the question, and leaving didn't seem prudent either. *What if they don't come? What then? The girl may have friends who will come looking for her. This is bad,* he thought, recycling his first impression upon reaching the house.

Left with no other course of action, Gideon slapped his knee and shouted, "Fuck!" which lessened his tension by a fraction but still left the house un-tossed and incriminating photos unfound.

Gideon did only two things for himself on a daily basis (well, three, if expelling body waste counted). One: he gave orders he expected to be followed. And, two: He lit his own cigars.

This was bad.

But today *was* a day for revelations and new adventure. The problem with that Canadian whore had come to fruition, and tonight he'd had his first erection in two years. Yes, today was a day for firsts, so why shouldn't he get his hands dirty for the cause? Why not indeed?

He placed a bookmark in his reverie and stood, his knees popping like bubble gum, and took matters into his own hands. Gideon immediately found he was short of breath and felt slightly dizzy. He suspected the culprit was *not* the act of standing, or a failing heart, but a certain Junoesque, howitzer breasted babe.

After firmly reinserting the mental bookmark, he entered the garage, hoisted a pair of gasoline cans and slugged them back in. He trekked the entire width and breadth of the house, pausing in each room, dribbling twin trails of fuel in his wake, until each can was empty.

As he was paranoid by nature, Gideon long ago had each of the houses he owned retrofitted in such a way that in the event necessity called for one of them to be destroyed, destroyed it would be.

Each of his nine holdings, including his parents chalet in Canada, had been made fire friendly by a former patient of his; a man whose rare talent had been utilized by certain men of Sicilian ancestry who, from time to time, desired certain items or people to go away.

His name had been Flannery Kuntz, born an Irish-German mutt with a ready smile and a penchant for flame. But sadly, he also carried a passion for food. It seemed one night while four-hundred pound Flannery was moonlighting and torching a townhome, he suffered a massive coronary and took a Vikings exit—which was too bad, because his services would have come in handy right then. Gideon had ordered many houses burnt to the floor drains, but he'd never been present for the show, nor had he ever fired anything larger than a cigar. How could he have been expected to know how extravagant, how *grand*, the late Flannery Kuntz's pyrotechnical genius actually was?

Acutely aware of the bitterness he felt toward his soon to be unemployed employees and their sloughed responsibility, he stalked through the benzene-heavy cloud of gasoline, entered the kitchen and blew out the pilots on the stove top, then opened each valve.

With one last task left, he walked to the front door and pulled a book of matches from his pocket. He lit the entire pack and tossed it onto a puddle of gasoline. The bluish flame snaked along the f.oor and spread its wings, coursing up the walls, the staircase, and then he turned to leave.

As he stepped off the porch, he had time enough to think, *well, that wasn't so hard. If the pictures were there, they wouldn't be for long. And why am I paying all those deadbeats so much money when I could simply do—*

The rest of the thought, together with his body, was caught up in the first explosion and belted like a line drive most of the way to the sidewalk.

He picked himself up twenty feet from where he'd left the ground, let his broken cigar fall from his lips, and reverently said, "Very effective, young Flannery. You will be sorely missed."

He brushed cinders from his suit and hopped into his car just in time to answer his cell phone. A glance at the screen told him nothing; the number was unfamiliar. He unplugged the phone from the cigarette lighter and accepted the call. Upon answering, he heard the voice of the last person he expected to ever call him.

Searching for something to say as he drove away, he finally gave up, and said, "You're the last person I expected to ever call me." After a short but rewarding conversation with the last person he expected to call, he dropped the phone onto the passenger seat and reached for a cigar. Things might fall into place after all.

Three blocks away, as he coasted onto the turnpike, the soaring inferno winked in his rearview like Lucifer's hot tub. He flicked an ash out the window and made a mental note to send Flannery Kuntz's parents a bunt cake and a bottle of wine.

He'd been scorched by fire, nearly deafened by the resulting explosion, and thoroughly shaken by both, but had never felt so alive in his life. He thumbed back to the suspended bookmark, to Trudy, and toyed with the idea of a little alone time…just him, his imagination, and little Freud. Alas, there was still much more to do before he could rest.

"This isn't so *bad.* Not so bad at all.

~~oOo~~

Zoe awoke to the mixed sound of a dog's confused whimper and the mechanical whine of rusted calipers as they gripped rustier brake pads. They were stopping. Just *who* the driver was and *where* that someone had brought her was a complete mystery. She was still alive—there was at least that much. *And Poco, too;* she felt his shivering warmth against her leg. Zoe understood. She was scared too.

She smelled and felt rather than saw the scratchy covering over her face and body. It smelled like an old wool sweater, fresh from the bottom of a garbage can. And no matter how hard she strained, she failed to free her mouth from the tape that held her lips together. With waning hope, Zoe realized she was at the mercy of the unknown driver, who, by the sound of a door creaking open then slamming shut, was about to clear up a few of her questions.

Sunday school aside—or the many times her mother cornered Zoe and forced her—she rarely *ever* prayed, but was becoming more religious by the minute. She began with the only words that came to mind:

Now I lay me down to sleep…How could this have happened? Why couldn't I sense it coming?

A door opened near her feet and she was hauled out and dropped. Zoe felt herself rolling, and then the covering was gone. Lying on her side, she blinked away dirt and hair as she strained to see her captor. Backlit by an overhead security lamp, he was enormous, but his features were lost in shadows.

I pray the lord my soul to keep,

She didn't have to wait long to see more. Although in retrospect, it was a face she could have lived the rest of her life without seeing. He reached down with one huge paw, pulled her up by her jacket, and held her aloft as he cut the bonds holding her hands. Then he pulled her close and loudly filled his nostrils with her. She recoiled, but his grip was like iron. If anything, her thrashing caused him to pull her closer. Still bouncing like a prize fish, she found she couldn't take her eyes off him. He was a hideous mass of scar tissue with a few boils mixed in for contrast. *And big! This guy could probably kick Cherry's ass, easy.*

May angels watch me through the night,

Zoe was scared, but not terrified. Through it all, she was able to hold onto a certain truth, a perspective that kept her sane. *Whatever you do to me, whatever happens, I won.* The big man studied her face for a moment, then struck her, and its resounding peal echoed in the darkness. Her vision swam, and she began to slip away. Whatever the purpose for the blow, she stopped thrashing, and he smiled a wide, crooked, tightlipped smile.

"So, mein liebling, you are the one." He tore the tape from her mouth and she fell backward. Again, he hauled her up, this time by her hair. Smiling impossibly wide, his teeth were a polar opposite of the rest of him. Each tooth gleamed, and had been filed to a brilliant white spike. Okay, now she was terrified.

And keep me in their blessed sight.

Music. Zoe could hear music from…his open mouth? Yes, each time he opened his mouth the music became slightly louder. Then she saw the buds trailing umbilical cords down from his ears. *Classical,* she thought. Tinny yet transcendent, Chopin bled from his ears like his own personal soundtrack of death. His overconfidence shattered the illusion of bravery she'd polished for his viewing pleasure, and his grip sucked the very life force from her—draining her from the inside before starting on her skin. He set her on her feet and stepped back.

The second she felt the ground under her toes, Zoe began to hop away, screaming at the top of her lungs. She managed three tight bunny hops before falling on her face. Even then, she screamed. Until her lungs burned with the need to be filled, she screamed, cutting through the night like an air horn.

With the slow deliberate step of one holding all five aces, the foreigner strode over and kicked her in the stomach.

"Scream if you like, liebling, but I assure you, we are alone." To punctuate this, he rose up, like a shorn headed, bullnecked god of old, and bellowed.

"You see?" he stated, wiping spittle from his patchwork chin. "Alone. So, as I said before this, scream if you wish, but I would rather you saved your energy."

"You don't have to do this, mister. I don't know you."

He watched her as he set a camera on the hood of the van. Seeing her lips move, he plucked a plug from one swollen ear. "Find your God while you still can, liebling. The show is about to begin." Then he pushed a button on the camera and angled it above her and to the right. He returned the plug to his ear and swayed to the music as he worked. His lack of interest seemed like a thrown glove, daring her to run, to do anything *but* be a victim. His playful nonchalance sent another crack cascading through her armor.

She followed the camera's course with her eyes and saw she was lying in front of an old swing set. Its pride, along with its paint, had long since been eaten by whatever creature it is that dines on lead paint and children's laughter. Bubbles of brown rust and Swiss cheese framing were the swing set's only support. It wouldn't be long for the playground cemetery.

Before Zoe could react, she was lifted again and held tight to his chest. He laughingly waltzed her over to the end of the swing set and propped her up with his body. Then her mind switched over to a test pattern of "Oh God", and the world slowed around her. Every movement, no matter how infinitesimal, took on the grave import of an oracular vision.

As he jabbed a grimy, fat finger into her forehead, the brute affected a stern look. "Stay." Reaching down, he retrieved a rope and effortlessly lifted a struggling arm to tie it to one side of the "A" bracket on the swings.

After reciting the same prayer thirteen times—probably the most important tally she'd file into her personal accounts payable folder—her body sagged against his. His face neared hers as he lifted her other arm. His cracked, leathery lips blew an admirer's challenge. *Kiss me*, his lips taunted.

Zoe closed her eyes. With a grace born of humility, she finished the prayer one last time and awaited the stroke that would set her free from pain. *Amen.*

When she opened her eyes again, a chariot was sweeping in to take her away. She couldn't help but feel a little disappointed. She always thought—hoped—it would be a wondrous winged horse, not a bright yellow carriage.

Her end danced along the edge of a raised blade, and she faced that end without fear. She mustered what saliva she could, then parted her gummy lips and spat in death's eye.

Onward rolled her celestial deliverance…its lights loomed closer by the second.

Otto Gruber's blade arm tensed to rend her and she thought of Heaven.

For some unknown reason, she suddenly envisioned Heaven to be a lot like Vegas.

Then all Herbie broke loose.

~~oOo~~

"Where the devil..?" The grey van had turned up ahead, but a few seconds later, as Harry rounded the corner—poof—the van disappeared. In his defense, Harry had a few things to contend with that may have distracted him. The dogs were a constant nuisance, skittering and yelping, barking and sliding along the dashboard—and he'd had no luck at all with that damnable radio.

He'd pulled most of the wires under the steering column and *still* it rocked and still it rolled. He stopped yanking wires when he lost the interior lights. Also, although he was doing a smashingly good job of staying between the curbs, he was scared witless. It was a good thing he had George and Gracie for back up.

If not for George and his uncharacteristically large honker,

Harry would have soared past the wooden construction wall and wound up downtown somewhere. That would not have been good. But, because of George's gorgeously bulbous proboscis, pepperoni pizza sniffer-outer, and faithful finder of the flatulent and most foul, fates would change. Next to a nose like that, any true clown or bloodhound would have been absolutely green with envy.

Harry slowed when George leapt from the dash, bounced into the back, then up into the space at the rear window. In a very Timmy-esque 'where is he, Lassie?' way, Harry yelled, "Where is he, boy? Where'd he go?"

Ruff ruff woof.

"Is he back there, boy? Speak, boy. Speak." *This is silly. He probably needs to pee.*

Woof.

Harry backed the car up and watched George as though he were a compass. As they passed a construction site—Harry thought it was an old school—the dog found his way over to the side window and continued to bark. Harry's gaze swept the face of the tall wooden safety wall that surrounded the lot, searching for some sort of opening, but found nothing. He backed up a little further for a better look, and a headlight between two of the construction walls caught his eye. "Gotcha!"

Upon closer inspection, the two panels were a gate. Through the gate he saw the van and Otto, but nothing else. Otto faced someone or something that was blocked by the panel van.

And then he saw his young dog through the open rear doors of the van. *Poco!* The young Chinese Hairless was tied, but very alive. He flopped around the open space in the rear like a bass in a bucket.

Up until then Harry had been flying by the seat of his baggy brown trousers, but if he was going to rescue his pooch, a plan would be needed. So, like all great minds to have ever hatched a plot and nursed it to fruition, Harry scratched his chin. It wasn't itchy; he just did so because in every picture he'd ever seen of a great mind, they'd always been posed thusly: Scratch scratch.

In seconds, he'd stitched together a pretty straight forward A-Team assault. With him playing the part of Hannibal, he left George and Gracie to fight over who got to be B.A. and wear the bling. His plan was this:

He would creep slowly through the gate, gently picking up speed as he went, circle around the van, spin out, causing dust and debris to fly up into the ugly German's ugly head, thus momentarily incapacitating him. This would give Harry two, maybe three seconds to jump out of the car, run over to the van, grab Poco, run back to Otto and spit in his ugly eye and kick him in his ugly balls, then jump back into the car and lay rubber all the way out the gate. The big, dumb bastard wouldn't know what hit him.

Well, that was the plan—with the exception of the spitting and the kicking in the balls. That part seemed much crazier than the rest.

The only similarity between his plan and how it actually went down are as follows:

1) He nosed the car through the gate.

That's it.

The rest of what came next was plain *ugly*.

Once past the gate, he stomped down on the accelerator with so much force he put his foot through the deceptively sturdy seeming layer of rust that had, until that very moment, kept the rotted carpet from falling through onto the road. This was a setback to be sure, but nothing special. He could always pull the emergency brake.

Upon pulling the lever, he found it had more play than a double-jointed gymnast. With a scream rising in crescendo along with the current song, he ground not one, but both feet into the brake pedal. The pedal passed only half of the full stroke it would need to stop the racing car and would go no further.

He tore his eyes away from the scene unfolding on the other side of the banana peel and soupy waste that covered the windshield, and stole a look between his legs to see why he couldn't stop. *The shoe! The goddamned shoe!* Try as he might he couldn't seem to make his hands relinquish their fear induced cramp on the steering wheel.

With his eyes bulging over the ten digit mutiny of fingers, and dogs bounding protectively along the border of their glass fence, his mind kept pace with the tires. He thought of Hannibal and B.A., Face Man and Murdoch. More specifically, of Hannibal's "standard pincer attack"—the one he himself employed at that very moment—and the fact that it never worked for them either. *Fucking Hannibal.*

Onward sped the heroes.

Above his scream, the howl of the dogs and five-thousand rpm's of roaring Volkswagen, Tom Jones told him at one hundred and sixty decibels that It's not unusual to be loved by anyone.

What happened next happened so fast it took Harry and Zoe about an hour to piece it all together—and even then they weren't sure of their facts...but it sure sounded good.

38

DEAD ENDS

Zoe poked her head up over the passenger side mirror of the grey van, where she'd been busy searching out and extracting pebble sized nuggets of windshield from her scalp. She smiled at Harry, and said, "It was the bravest, most daring thing I ever saw."

Perched on the bumper of the van in the parking lot of the motel, Harry held Poco to his chest like a winning lottery ticket. "So that's when I made my decision. Sure the dogs were terrified, but I attempted to bolster their spirits with a quote from the St. Crispin's Day speech from Henry the V—alas, to no avail. The poor pups were simply beside themselves. Of course, there was no other option. I knew in my heart I had to save Zoe from the clutches of that evil madman, whatever the cost. Don't get me wrong, I was scared, but did what any man of valor would have done."

"Is that when you broke my fucking car, you maniac?" Seth sat on the stoop, leaning against the door to the motel room, seething over the theft and destruction of his vehicle.

Harry nodded gravely. "I'm sorry, son. It had to be done."

"*Son?* Fuck *son*, you old bastard! You broke my ride!"

Zoe rounded the mirror and stood at Harry's shoulder, fists on her hips. "Is that all you're worried about—your precious car? He saved my life, you little jerk. I'd be tonight's burp and tomorrow's shit right now if Harry hadn't *bruised* your piece of shit car, so go fuck yourself."

"Bruised it? From what you've said, he totaled it. All this does is reinforce the old saying about you people, chink." He put a finger to each side of his eyes and pulled while affecting the worst Chinese accent since Mr. Moto. "Looka me, I dliving leally ok. No use blinkie blinkie, but that okay USA."

Everyone pretended to not hear the slur. Mary slid down to sit next to Seth and rubbed his leg. "Come on, baby. Don't you think you're losing sight of the big picture? Isn't it more important that Zoe's okay?"

Seth shrugged a grudging *I'm sorry* at Zoe then let his head bounce against the door, eliciting twin barks from the other side—George and Gracie had huffed in Harry's direction and retired into the motel soon after they'd been branded cowards.

"Yeah, I guess," Seth said, slowly. "But you don't understand. I bought that car with my own money—*my money*—not my mom and dad's. Mine. Worked all summer last year inseminating turkeys to pay for it."

Zoe halted in the process of flicking a sliver of glass onto the growing pile at her feet and turned her lip up at Seth. "Inseminating turkeys? Really? We're definitely gonna circle back to *that* later, but for now, would you like to hear how your bug died a hero?"

Just then, Danny poked his bleached head out the window of the van. "Guys, you should get a load of all this cool shit back here."

Everyone turned in his direction, and each face registered the same glaze of patient indulgence. Only Zoe spoke. "If it sparks, lights, has a blade, bleeds, or goes bang, don't fucking touch it. 'Kay?"

He shot her a *whatever* grin and said, "What? I wasn't gonna touch nothing."

Mary rolled her hands like she was about to call travelling. "Get on with it, guys. Is this when you ran that dude, what's-his-name, over?"

Harry cleared his throat and tried to stand a little taller. "Quite right, my dear. I——"

"Why don't you let me handle this, Harry. I think I got a better bead on this part."

Harry bowed. "Lay on, McZoe. And damned be——"

"Right. Thanks." They didn't need him yakking all night to finish the story. She felt sore in places she didn't even know had muscles, and wanted nothing more than to have a shower.

"Okay," she said. "So there I was, praying, thinking, 'This is it, I'm toast.' Shit—I actually thought Harry was an angel, coming to take me to heaven. Can you believe that?"

Still sullen, Seth tossed rocks at his shoe. "And God shuffled his feet," he muttered.

Mary pushed the pebbles out of his fingers like a stern mother and slid her hand into his. "Shut up, baby. I think her question was rhetorical. Go on, Zoe," she urged.

"Thanks. So there I was, like I said, praying, and all the sudden the Bug came barreling around the corner of the van, headed right for me and that Übermensch motherfucker, with Harry screaming out the window at the top of his lungs. Sounded like some kind of war cry or something. The big guy didn't even see it coming! Had an mp3 player plugged into his pumpkin listening to Mozart or some shit—just smiling and taking his Texas time with me—when all the sudden, *whack*! He went down faster than a fat guy on a dropped jelly roll. The car jumped—yeah, *jumped*, with him still stuck to the hood—and swiped one of the poles right out from under me. The force of the car hitting the pole spun me around and threw me, screaming and peeing—yeah, I said it—pole and all, about ten feet away. It may not sound like it, but it hurt like hell. I don't know what happened right after that, but when my head stopped spinning, Seth's car had plowed through the side of the school, radio still blaring some show tune, and that big German fella was about three feet shorter. It was pretty fucking gory. You want to take it from there, Harry?"

With the smug look of a chef bearing crème brûlée, Harry inclined his head. "Why certainly. Now, as I've said, the dogs were extremely agitated, but I needed to stay focused on my plan, which, I might add, went off without a hitch—although my calculations might have been off a bit off in regards to the pole. I had no intention of coming that close to Zoe." He inclined his head again. "I'm sorry, my dear, but necessity called for a hasty decision. Oh, yes. After the collision with Otto—his name, incidentally: Otto Gruber—the car sailed forward with him stuck to the bumper, like some unfortunate bear struck on a country road. I'm sorry, I wax needlessly. I hit the wall and kept going. Incredibly enough, Otto was still there, plastered like a three-hundred pound bug on the—again, sorry. It wasn't until after I'd climbed out the missing windscreen that I discovered, much to my disgust, what I thought was *all* of Otto, but was merely the *top half* of Otto. The rest of him was under the car somewhere. I shudder at the thought.

I crawled to the van first...um, to find something with which to cut Zoe's bonds, and there was my little Poco. Imagine my surprise. Naturally, since I was already there, and poor George was in hysterics, I freed my pup and *then* went for Zoe. She was shaken, and rightly so, but no worse for wear. We retrieved the keys from the, uh, bottom half of Otto, and borrowed his van. Now here we are, all safe and sound."

He studied their faces as he smoothed Poco's tuft of hair, quite possibly checking to see if there were any bull-shit-o-meters going off, then he asked, "Any questions?"

Mary raised her hand. There was a doubting frown tugging at the corners of her mouth. "Yeah, I got one. So let me get this straight: You were sleeping in the back of the car while most of this shit was playing out? And you, Zoe, you didn't even know he was there?"

Harboring more than a few doubts of her own as to the validity of most of her cohort's story, Zoe raised an eyebrow. "You think *that's* the most incredible part of that story? Really?"

Unable to let the issue over the destruction of his car drop, Seth pointed accusingly at Harry. "You're Chinese. Why didn't you leave my Beetle out of it and sneak in there with your ninja skills and throw some chop suey on that guy's ass."

Zoe glared at Seth. "Jesus Christ! Cut that shit out, Seth! What are you...Five? Grow up."

"It's quite alright, Zoe," Harry soothed, holding his hand out to her dramatically, always the gracious victim. "Well, first of all, allow me to say this: Ninja's are Japanese, chop suey is a food and not a dark art of killing, and, believe it or not, is as American as apple-pie—also, contrary to popular belief, not every person of my culture can fight like Bruce Lee. That said, remember your car for the true hero it was and move on."

And with that collection of busted hick myths still bouncing around Seth's cranium, Harry tucked Poco into his coat, stepped over Seth, and entered the motel room.

Before he closed the door, Harry said, "By the way, my brooding young bigot, your gas pedal sticks. Or, I guess *stuck* would be the more accurate tense. Just FYI."

The door bumped Seth's head when it was slammed, and he yelled loud enough to be heard in the room. "I'm sorry to have inconvenienced you. Next time I have to send a car into a kamikaze-type situation I'll make sure to have it tuned up first, asshole!"

Mary shot Zoe a *'hands off girls, this one's all mine'* look, and stood, brushing dust from her dress. She regarded Zoe thoughtfully for a few seconds, and then unloaded *the* question. "So that's it, though? You got him?"

Zoe shrugged a yeah. "I think so...well, I'm almost positive that cannibal guy is dead. He was pretty fucked up to start with, you know, like something was already shutting him down." Zoe shook her head in disbelief at her own words. Despite doing everything wrong, she'd still won. She nodded her head slowly, recalling the sturdy vase. "I hit him real hard. Yup, he's dining with Hitler and Nixon tonight."

Mary nodded along with her, but seemed like she wanted to shake her head. Neither spoke, nor did Seth add anything to fill the uncomfortable silence. Finally, Mary scrunched her face up in a way that said she didn't want to say it but just had to, "Are you thinking what I'm thinking?"

"What?" replied Zoe, "That your *Spider* over there used to fuck turkeys? I'm really glad you brought that up, Mar, 'cause I would have felt a little uncomfortable asking for further clarification as to how exactly he got them to hold still for the hot mayo injection. Give 'em a donkey punch? Choke 'em? What? Come on, Seth. You can tell us. We won't tell a soul." She crossed her heart. "Honest."

Caught off guard, Mary let a bark of laughter sneak past her lips before she could cover her mouth with her hand.

Instead of standing and stalking off, which was the reaction Zoe was hoping to elicit with her remarks, Seth snorted and rolled his eyes.

"Ha ha, very funny, Zoe. What I think Mary's getting at is: should we go see if the cannibal guy is dead? It just seems to me we came an awful long way to find the guy and, you know, take him out, so we might as well make sure he's really gone, that's all. But this time I'll drive, okay?"

Zoe wanted to agree with him but she was still a tad bit pissed off at him and how he seemed more concerned about his precious car than he was about *her*. "I don't know. If it'll make you feel better, sure." *But you're still a jerk.*

Right then, Zoe remembered how and when the night had gone sideways on her. She entered the motel room with the memory of a promised kick in the balls topping her things to do list. Harry wasn't in the room, so she called, sweetly, "Poco, honey bunny, come to Zoe."

~~oOo~~

She'd had her chance but let it slip through her fingers. The little troublemaker trotted over and jumped trustingly from the bed to her chest. She barely had time to cradle her arms before he would have bounced off her glittered baby-tee and fallen to the floor. Then he was in her arms, licking her chin. She couldn't hurt him. He was just too damn cute. His oysters would remain unkicked…for now.

Shortly after four in the morning, Harry, who said he needed to pick up something for the headache incurred during the crash, offered to turn the key in to the desk clerk and check them out while the group piled into the van.

Zoe slid onto the dirty floor behind the passenger seat and sat on a blanket covered foot. She nearly swallowed her tongue before recognizing Danny's shoe. Curled up under a soiled moving blanket, he hugged a fire extinguisher in one arm and a blow torch in the other. The cylindrical teddy-canisters lay against his chest like his own personal yin and yang angel and demon. He looked happy so she let him sleep; it was safer that way... for them *and* him.

As though the conversation from the parking lot had never stopped, Spider turned to Zoe and said, "And for your information, I didn't fuck the turkeys, I used a turkey baster."

"You fucked a turkey with a turkey baster? Spider, you should get your own web site. You could call it *Mastur-basters.* You'd be a hit!"

"I give up."

"You never stood a chance, little man. I am woman."

"Hear, hear," agreed Mary.

"You've got to be shitting me. Et tu, Mary?"

"Lighten the fuck up, would you? I love you baby, but someday your head's gonna pop from the strain of holding in all that misdirected blame and angst. And trust me, I should know." She tugged up her sleeves to validate her point. Some of the cuts looked fresh.

Zoe, who had been grinning and listening in, lost her smile and turned away when Mary exposed the grid work of crooked gashes that ran the length of each forearm. The scars reminded her of another of the myriad reasons the girl had been locked up: self flagellation.

And then, as though connected by an unseen strand, she thought of her own scars, both visible and remembered alike. It seemed each of them had their burdens to bear in one way or another, but with a little help and a lot of understanding, they might end up making it through this—except for Danny.

He was kinda fucked.

~~oOo~~

Seth pulled the van to the side of the street about a block from where the cross-town #9 had dropped the cannibal. There was no need to go closer to the killer's house to see that any information they *thought* they might find within the home had gone up in smoke along with half the neighborhood.

Past two fire trucks, they could see the house had been completely obliterated. The entire area looked like a living relief of Milton's fabled Tartarus. Not just the cannibal's home, but both neighboring houses as well as many tall oaks still smoldered amid smaller fires which dotted a three yard radius.

Zoe poked Seth in the shoulder, and whispered, "Get us out of here. If Danny wakes up I don't want him to see that. He might lose his shit and try to go swimming in it."

Harry pulled Poco closer. "Sound advice, my dear. I believe, as the saying goes, your quest is over."

"Wait a minute," said Mary. "Was the place on fire when you left?"

"Mary, I don't even remember leaving. Maybe that old guy started the fire so he didn't have to get rid of Cannibalangelo's body. I dunno."

Zoe turned to Harry, "You never really said much about the house. Did you see who started the fire?"

"No," Harry said without pause. "The house was still intact when I left to save you."

Seth dropped the van into drive and did a u-turn that didn't quite stay on the road, and jostled the group like a bunch of empty bottles in a bike's basket. George bounced off the window and slid from the dash to the floor. "Oops, sorry." Seth smiled. "So, where to now? Is that it? Do we just go home now, or what?"

"Or what," Zoe said guiltily. "I've been thinking…"

Seth fixed the mirror to better see her on the floor. With a barely veiled smirk, he said, "Isn't that kind of dangerous?"

"What?" Zoe asked. "You don't even know what I was going to say."

"No, I meant the thinking part. Aren't you blonde under that red dye?"

"Listen, this is no joke. Now, there isn't one of us in this van that doesn't know this is a lot bigger than what we first thought, right? And when this shit started, we all thought when that Zane creep was gone it would all be over and we'd be able to just go home. Maybe it's just me, but this doesn't *feel* finished."

Zoe received raised eyebrows all around and one agreeable snore.

She looked on as faces found their bellybuttons—no one more so than Harry. He said: "If I may, Zoe. I believe tha—" Or tried, at least.

Seth fixed him with a sneer. "Why don't you shut the fuck up and hear her out?" Then he tipped an invisible hat to Zoe as if to say, *Glad to be of service, ma'am. Carry on.*

"Tone it down, Rambo. He's got a point. And he *is* old and frail."

"I am not." Harry snatched at the thrown crumb. "What I *am*, it seems, is the only rational mind in this vehicle. You want us to go back to Bartho—Gideon's home and do what, exactly? Confront him? Burgle his premises? I say no, and I implore you all to do the same. This is madness and I won't stand for it. I say we leave and let the police handle this."

Zoe let out an exasperated sigh. She wasn't thinking about going to the doctor's house, but, now he'd said it, it seemed like a good idea. "You know something, Harry? For being a fucking clown, you haven't made me laugh once—until now, anyway. The police? Are you serious? When they find those old videos of yours, what do you think will happen to you? Besides, they haven't done shit since this whole mess started, so hardy fucking har har. You finally made me laugh."

She regrouped and took a needed breath. "And another thing: You're *so-called* white knights couldn't even catch a carload of escaped mental patients in a crappy bright yellow

1977 Beetle!"

"I—" Harry managed before he was overridden by Seth.

Seth said: "Must you speak ill of the dead, Zoe?"

"I'm sorry, Seth. Your car was a true cape wearing hero, a big yellow swinging dick of vengeance—now shut up."

She rounded on Harry. "I don't give a shit what you do, Harry Funshine, but I'm going. And I think I can speak for my friends when I say we don't care if you come or not. This isn't just about Jeanne and Mickey anymore. What about the next Jeanne, the next Mickey. No, this is it. This snuff thing—this unchecked madness—all of it stops now. Here. With us."

"Yeah," Mary said, possibly because any other response would have seemed like leaving someone hanging on a high-five.

Seth bobbed his head. "Damn straight," he said, most likely for the simple fact that he hated the clown's polka dotted guts.

Harry pointed a finger at the dozing Danny. "And him? Will you also speak for him?"

Zoe smiled defiantly at the old man. "Don't worry about him, Harry. He's with me. He's the only knight I have left."

All eyes turned to Harry. He seemed to be in the grips of an inner battle, one that he was apparently losing. "Fine. If you'll not listen to reason, I won't try to stop you. But when the time comes and this backfires in your face, don't forget that I did warn you."

Something just didn't feel right. Zoe was unsure if whatever the voice had said about Harry had happened yet or not, so she plied another tactic. "You know, Harry, I'd think you'd be the first one to jump all over this thing considering your past with this guy, Gideon. Isn't he the one who caused you to miss out on the best years of your life? And on top of all that, didn't he threaten you—pimp you out on the internet like a fucking freak in a travelling circus?"

The old clown bowed his head.

Zoe patted Harry on the shoulder with a confidence she didn't feel. "I was only kidding about not caring whether you came or not, Harry. I'm glad you changed your mind."

"Me too," said Seth. "I'm *ecstatic.*"

When Zoe sat back against Otto's rolling tool chest, Mary leaned over and whispered in her ear, "That was friggin' awesome. You worked him like a boardwalk grifter. You could be a politician for sure. One thing though, why do you care if he comes? He's all, well, old and stuff. What the fuck is he gonna do?"

Zoe searched Mary's face and saw something that she, herself, lacked: Courage. *I'm glad you're here with me* is what she wanted to say, but instead said, "I don't know why we need him, Mary, but I kinda feel like we do, you know?"

Mary leaned back and put her head on Zoe's shoulder. As she stared at the roof vent, she said, "Not really, but if you say so."

"Last chance, everyone," Harry said, apparently still holding out hope that some sort of mutiny might spontaneously break out. "You don't have to do this."

As the van slowed, Zoe nodded to herself and followed Seth's finger out the window. They were there, one house over from the psychiatrist's. She could see the empty driveway, the shadowed house, and the front door she'd seen the doctor open about a million years before, when he'd led her to Zane Ellis. The only thing missing was *him*. No lights, no car, and it was four-forty in the morning. A thrill of anticipation snaked through her midsection. Every nerve had surfaced and coursed like aching vines along the landscape of her skin. In her head, silence reined.

Right then, she really missed the voice.

39

THE PERFECT NIGHT FOR A CRIME

Nothing stirred on the sleepy street; no early morning paper boy, no octogenarian insomniac strollers—nor was there the telltale glow of the late late show behind drawn curtains. It was the perfect night for a crime. Mother Nature had even chipped her weathered hand into the pot in the form of an impending sky scorching storm. Ponderous and sooty, cotton candy clouds black-washed the sky, painting shadows into every corner with broad ebony strokes. Nothing but the tight cone shaped beacons of scattered streetlights remained to lend witness of the group's passing.

Zoe was glad of the added cover, but it did little to alleviate the nagging feeling she'd missed something. If that wasn't bad enough, her ass had clamped down around her underwear and threatened to swallow it. After this was over, she thought she might need the Jaws of Life to pry them free.

Harry rolled down the passenger window as the rest of the crew filed out the sliding door. "I should probably stay with the dogs and keep an eye out."

"Uh uh, you're coming with us," Zoe said.

"But I'm not cut out for this type of activity. I'm old—remember?"

A shiver ran up Zoe's spine. The night had cooled down

and a breeze picked up, replacing warm and stale with cold and eerie. "Take a look around, Harry. None of us are cut out for this shit. You're coming. Let's go." She opened the door and waited for him to get out, then shut the door behind him. The sound of the slammed door reverberated through the night like a robot taking a dump in a sheet metal shithouse. Needless to say everyone jumped.

Like twin flat tires, Seth and Mary whipped around with fingers to their lips. "Shhhhhhh."

Zoe pointed at Harry. "It was him." She shot Harry a half smile, and said, "Say, who wants to find us a way in?"

"I'll go," said Seth.

Mary put a hand on his chest. "No, you won't. You suck at stealth. I'll go." Then she turned to walk away.

Seth grabbed her arm. "No way, Mar. I should go. I'm—"

"You're what?" Her eyes narrowed. "You're the *man*? Ever break into a house before—even your own? Shit, baby, you can't even open a Slim Jim by yourself."

Seth bowed his head. "But Mary," he whined, like *not in front of them, please*, "I don't want you getting hurt. I could figure it out."

Mary smiled and patted his chest. "You're cute, Spider, but this isn't a computer, and there are no elves or orcs with dark magic. Besides, unlike you, I *have* done this before."

"Oh," he said, letting go of her arm. "Is there anything else you haven't told me?"

"Tons, but it'll have to wait." She spied along the shadowed driveway, and then pointed to a bush lined garden. "You guys wait over there and I'll circle around and meet you."

Zoe watched in admiration as Mary sprinted across the lawn. She'd come so far in such a short amount of time. The once dark, death loving suicide-waiting-to-happen, was now a plucky, down to earth daredevil with a quick smile.

It seemed escape had been the best therapy for the girl. Scampering into the dark, she was the ghost of yester Sears; a blonde wraith in a flowered baby blue summer shroud, trailing pink ribbons and the light staccato *thwack* of her sandals as they slapped the bottoms of her feet. Then she was gone.

The very second Zoe turned and began to move through the shadows toward the driveway, the sky opened and poured its liquid argument against their plan. She was soaked through to her dental floss panties in seconds. *Great,* she fumed, and turned to wait for the boys.

Danny splashed down into a rapidly widening puddle beside Seth and tugged his hood up over his head. "I don't like the rain," he mumbled. "It makes everything all wet and stuff."

Surveying his sodden shoes (thanks to Danny), Seth said, "So why don't you wait in the van? Nice and dry in there, Danny. Besides, things might get dangerous inside."

"Can't stay here." Danny's sour dough face flickered in the remnants of a far off burst of lightning. "I'm the last knight." He zipped the jacket up to his chin and plunged his hands into his pockets, making him look more like a petulant child than a misunderstood teen. His eyes darted around rapidly for a second, as though uploading from a hard drive, then, he said, "Zoe said so." He brushed past Seth and fell into step beside his damsel.

With the hem of her dress bunched in one fist, Mary ran back from inspecting the only viable entry point, a window on the main floor that hadn't been barred like all the rest. She waited until she reached them before hissing, "Well, *that* sure is fucked up."

Gathered in a tight semi circle in the shade of a great elm, five would-be burglars scratched their heads as they regarded the window. They might as well have been Neanderthals seeing fire for the first time. *Why just one window,* Zoe wondered. "There's got to be a catch here somewhere," she said. "Why the hell would this guy have bars on all the windows except this one?"

Seth kicked a fist-sized stone free from the garden and brushed loose dirt from its underside. Hefting the stone, he said, "Step back, ladies. Let a man sort this out."

Zoe stepped out of the way. "Knock yourself out champ, but hang on a sec. Mary, are you sure you didn't see any alarm pads or wires?"

"Nada. 'Course, I could be wrong."

Seth ran toward the house, let out a grunt, and pitched the rock at the window. Instead of smashing through the window, the stone bounced with a muffled *"bonk"* and clattered to the pavement below.

Seth was backing away, staring at the window, when a light came on in the room. "Shit! Everybody down," he squeaked, and then rolled toward the house just as a hand pushed the curtain aside.

Zoe dove behind the closest bush, pulling Harry with her, and bumped heads with Mary, who'd chosen the same bush. "Ah, fuck," Zoe hissed. "Mary, we really got to stop meeting like this. Are you okay?"

Mary sat up, rubbing the side of her head, and spat out a mouthful of mud. "Great. I'm just super. What happened?"

"The window," Zoe whispered, pointing. "Someone's in there. We've got to get the fuck out of here. Seth, we gotta go. Get to the van."

Harry wiped mud from his face and rubbed his arm where Zoe had grabbed him. "I couldn't agree more. Let us make haste before we are found." When he moved to stand, Zoe yanked him back down. The window was sliding open.

"Psst."

Mary looked questioningly at Zoe and mouthed *what the fuck?*

"Shut up, Spider," whispered Zoe. "You're gonna give us away."

"Um...That wasn't me," he moaned, and then he took off down the driveway, hissing over his shoulder, "Run! run!"

Zoe held tight to Harry's coat, and turned to Mary. "Come on," she said and hauled Harry out from behind the bush. Movement at the window caused her to turn her head, and then she stopped in her tracks after getting a better look. Harry bumped into her and knocked her forward, her teeth clicking together as his face connected with the back of her head.

"Hey!" she said, rubbing the newest knot. "Stop, stop." She

played traffic cop, and then let out a growled foot stomping sigh. "Danny, you little shit! Slow down Mary—and you better go get Seth before he shits himself."

"What? What?" Mary yelled, eyes wide as she ran past.

From the window, a voice asked, "Where you guys going? I thought you wanted to come in?" Danny pointed toward the open gate leading to the backyard. "Back door's open."

Zoe rolled her eyes and turned to Mary. "Can you believe that little shit?"

Mary's eyes shot wide. "Fuck!" And she took off for the backyard.

Zoe raised an eyebrow at Mary's dash, but said nothing. Harry started down the driveway. "I'll get Seth, Zoe. You should see to your friends."

Zoe caught up with the former Goth girl just inside the back door, as she stared intently at an alarm panel. Zoe peeked over Mary's shoulder at the unit. "Did it go off?"

Mary turned on her heel with a bewildered crinkling of her nose. "No," she said. "As a matter of fact, it wasn't even on."

"No shit?"

"No shit," she echoed and shrugged. "Guess he must have left the house in a real hurry or something."

It seemed to Zoe to be more of a question than a statement.

"Maybe." Zoe didn't want to freak Mary out by telling her she seriously doubted it, and that they should hurry the fuck up. Of course, that was fear talking; her inner oracle was still out to lunch. She woefully decided her spidey senses picked a fine fucking time to bail on her. "But let's not waste time anyway. You know, just in case he's coming back soon."

With that in mind, the girls didn't bother to wait for Seth and Harry. They huddled together, arm in arm, and opened doors until they found the room with the indestructible "Pope" window. Danny was gone. *Go figure,* mused Zoe. "Jesus Christ. I wasn't kidding when I said we should get a bell for that fucking kid."

"I know, right," replied Mary, as she stepped into the room.

"But you know, if it wasn't for him we'd still be scratching our asses and staring at the window. What is that thing anyway, bulletproof?"

"Dunno, but that would explain why Hercules couldn't throw that rock through it."

"Be nice, Zoe."

"Come on, Mary. You know I'm just messing with him." She grabbed a throw cushion and wiped water from her face. "I think he's great, really...for a geek." Then she began to randomly pluck videos from the overflowing shelves, and toss them into a pile on the couch.

"Yuck." She held an old VCR cassette up by the edge. "I think this is one of Harry's. Check out the title: *Big Top Chop*. Are you fucking kidding me?"

"Speaking of..."

"Yeah, they should be back by—"

They froze as a door closed at the rear of the house. From down the hall, Harry whispered, "It's only me, girls. Where are you?"

Mary stuck her head out the door. "Where's Seth?"

Harry followed her back into the room and removed his coat. After he'd squeegeed his face with his fingers, he said, "He'll be along in a minute. The poor lad must have startled one of the dogs when he ran back to van. He got himself munched on."

Mary sucked air through her teeth. "That sounds like my baby," she sang. "Is it bad?"

Harry smiled. His eyes twinkled with the knowledge of a joke that shouldn't be shared among women. "To him, I'm more than positive it *seems* bad—just a scratch, actually. Why don't we try to find what you are looking for instead of wasting valuable time waiting for Seth to lick his wounds? Have you found any of my tapes?"

"One, maybe," said Mary. "But there's gotta be more somewhere."

"All right," said Zoe. "Let's grab some more DVDs—as many as we can carry—and the hard drive off that computer, and get the hell out of here." She walked over to the desk and pushed papers back and forth, opened drawers—and a few other things she'd seen cops on television do—but found only an overflowing ashtray and a stack of pages that must have been a manuscript. She deduced it was a manuscript after reading the top page. It read: Manuscript. She rolled it up and tucked it into the inside pocket of her coat.

Next, she dumped the contents of a cigar box onto the desk, and a gun fell away from the cigars and bounced into the garbage can. "Two points," she muttered.

As she reached for the revolver, Harry spoke up. "Maybe you should let me take that, child. I wouldn't want you to shoot your foot off with the damned thing."

"Sure." Zoe stepped back. "Spoken like a true chauvinist. Let's just hope we don't need it for...you know." She affected a gun finger and mimicked what she believed to be an excellent replica of a series of gun shots, "Pew pew, pew pew."

Harry waved toward the door with the gun. "I should go keep an eye on the street if you don't need me."

As Zoe began to read a piece of paper she'd retrieved from the garbage pail, she absently waved him away, "'Kay. And can you see what's taking Seth so long?"

"Most assuredly," said Harry.

Mary crouched beneath the computer and yanked the tower from under the desk. "You gave *him* the gun?" she snorted. "Good fucking call, Zoe." She hoisted the unit onto one hip like a harried laundress, ans shook her head. "Spider doesn't trust him, you know?"

"Really?" Zoe faked astonishment. "I would've never guessed. And here I thought it was idle flirting."

"And I don't trust him either. He's been acting kinda creepy tonight. Ever since you guys came back to the motel in that rolling meat wagon, he's seemed...I dunno, *off*."

"Well, duh," said Zoe. "A near death experience will do that to a person. Cut him some slack." But she wasn't as convinced as she led Mary to believe. The voice had said they needed him, and she was betting their lives on that truth.

"Consider it cut," said Mary. "I'm just *saying*, that's all."

They looked up as the front door opened, then closed. "Just me, girls," called Harry. "Seth will be along in a minute."

"Cool," Zoe said to Mary, picking up their conversation where they'd left off. "Find something to bag those tapes."

"Harry," Zoe called. "You might as well tell Seth to forget it and keep the engine running, we're basically done."

40

KNIGHTS & DAMSELS

Danny gazed around the room, then back to the phoenix. "Well? What do you think, Fireball?"

The recently morphed two-foot phoenix ruffled its flames and hopped from one of Danny's shoulders to the other, sending embers to fall away and wink out like dead stars. *"I think, you little punk, that you should find me a more suitable name than Fireball. It sounds like some sort of drink you'd find in a gay bar."*

Danny gazed in wonder at his new friend, watching orange and red flames blend and stream down its wings to coalesce with the fluorescent blue white glow of the bird's slender body. "Sorry. Well, It's just that you're real pretty," he said, breathlessly. "Ooh, I got one. How about I call you Pretty Bird?"

The phoenix swatted him, sending sparks flying that winked out before travelling more than a few inches. *"Are you really that feeble minded, or are you just an asshole? Pretty Bird sounds three shades pinker than Fireball. Do I look like a parrot or a fucking toucan?"* With as much disgust as an imaginary two-foot tall mythical creature could muster, the phoenix huffed and flew a few feet down the hall, then turned and hovered. After seeing the downcast face of his new charge, he flew back and lifted Danny's face with his beak and pecked him playfully on the head. *"Just forget about it for now, kid. Come on, I wanna show you something."*

Danny glanced over his shoulder toward the room where his friends were talking and—by the sounds of it—making a fine mess without him, then he followed the bird. "'Kay," he said.

When Danny turned the corner, he saw the most beautiful thing he'd ever seen in his life. That is, of course, the most beautiful thing *after* the phoenix—but this was a whole new type of cool! It was like oil fires in a desert, a volcano in mid-vomit, or an unlocked cabinet full of lighters—which was exactly what the heavenly sight was. The cabinet shone with the inner brilliance of a holy artifact, of the promise of cleansing spires, of Armageddon! Upon its cushioned shelves, there was every imaginable tool used to produce flame.

The voices in the hall faded to a far off murmur, and then died all together. He reached forward, his hands shaking with delight, and the bird moved into his line of vision.

"No. Not that, kid. Not yet."

Danny puffed out his bottom lip. "But… why not? You're burning, why can't I?"

"You're warped, kid. Put your dick away and come with me. What I'm gonna show you is way cooler—trust me."

Danny squinted dubiously, and slowly shook his head. "Better than this? You're the one who's warped, Fireball."

"Shut up and c'mon. There's not much time."

Still skeptical, Danny hung his head, and followed the bird. As he shuffled past, he ran his fingers lovingly across the clear glass door of the case. "Stay warm, babies. I'll be back."

"WILL YOU COME ON!"

"Alright, alright, I'm coming; Spaz down, Fireball."

"One more time! I fucking dare you, kid. Call me that one more time."

Danny watched the bird disappear straight through the kitchen door, then he pushed the door open and followed. "You know, you're not as cool as I thought you were gonna be."

~~oOo~~

Seth awoke sputtering, choking on a mouthful of water. As he attempted to rise, he barked his head against something cold and greasy. A grainy substance fell away from the 'something greasy' and covered his face, filling his eyes and mouth like a shovelful of dirt. His eyes watered and stung but he managed to wipe away most of the grit with the sleeve of his jacket. As he blinked away the final remnants, he swung his head in search of answers—answers he didn't even know the questions to.

It was dark, but he could make out a tire to his left. *Where..? How did I..?* Then it came to him: There'd been a voice, footsteps, an apology, and then nothing. "Harry," he grated, then coughed and spat rust down his chin. He shimmied out from under the van and rolled onto his stomach. Once free, he finished with an impromptu expulsion of undigested french fries and, from the looks of it, a half pound of squid guts.

He fell on his face after a failed attempt to lift himself to his knees. Again, he pushed himself up, barely making it to his knees before his head began to throb like an abscess tooth packed in tin foil.

It felt to him as though his brain had broken loose from its stem and now wallowed in an overflowing pool of its own regurgitated juices—and judging from the reddish pink stream running freely from his ears and scalp, he didn't think he was too far from the truth.

He held his head between his hands and tried to stand and take a step, but fell against the van. *Mary, Zoe... Come on, Spider, man up, boy!* He really *wanted* to go, to get to them, but first the world would have to stop gyrating around him so damn fast.

Got to get to Mary, he thought, desperately, then took a sliding step forward and tripped over a fist-sized stone. He Peered drunkenly at the rock. It looked familiar. Then he saw blood on it, and, if he wasn't mistaken, hair. His hair.

"That dirty, double-crossing, clown motherfucker," he

grated, but you wouldn't know it by listening to him. His words resembled more a frustrated wail than anything coherent. He stooped, fighting back the pain as blood rushed to his head, and scooped the rock up. He cradled it to his chest, pushed away from the van, and lurched toward the house.

"Get some, bitch!" he slurred, and fell flat on his face. Watching gutter water sluice past his face, the curb seemed like Mount Everest.

He would have his vengeance—and it would be swift in coming, to be sure—just as soon as he remembered how to walk.

~~oOo~~

"You should have listened to me, Zoe." Harry shuffled dejectedly into the study with the gun raised in her direction, but apparently couldn't bear to look at her. Instead, he found a spot on the carpet between the girls and focused his eyes there. "Put the tapes up and put your hands down. Er. Just do it. Now, please."

Zoe glared at him. "I did listen to you, Harry. You said you were going to have a look out the *window*." Frustrated, she threw a handful of DVD's at him, and missed with every one. "You never said anything about selling us down the fucking river!"

Harry ducked the wild throw, and said, timidly, "No. I told you this was too much for you."

"Well, it was sure as hell too much for *one* of us."

From the hall came the unmistakable self important scuff of Italian leather. She didn't need the little voice to know who was coming.

The doctor stepped into the doorway behind the twin pipes of a double barreled shotgun and leaned casually against the frame, puffing on a freshly lit cigar.

Zoe felt sick. They'd played right into his hands. In a flash, things came together for her. Harry was the one who'd insisted he be the one to check them out of the motel—said he had a headache and was going to ask the clerk if they had any Tylenol. *Did he call Gideon while they were all busy packing up?* Bitterly, she guessed there was a good possibility he did just that.

And in the van, the whole time I thought I was working him, he was actually working me—the slick bastard. After what I'd said about it not feeling like it was over, he was the one who said they would be crazy to break into Gideon's house—way before anyone was even thinking about it! She wanted to tear her own hair out, she was so angry with herself.

With tears in her eyes, she screamed, "I trusted you, goddamn it! I believed in you...I wore *sequins* for you. Doesn't that count for something? How could you do this to me after last night? Why did you save me *then*, huh? Is it because you wanted to do it yourself, you sick fuck? Go ahead, shoot me. I don't care anymore."

With her hands in the air, but nowhere near as shocked by his treachery as Zoe, Mary smiled nervously and nodded toward the pair of men. Then she tilted her head toward Zoe and whispered out the side of her mouth, "Speak for yourself, bitch. I got plans."

Gideon watched the exchange from behind three feet of shotgun and six inches of Cuban brown leaf. He plucked the hoagie from his mouth and blew on the heater until it glowed bright red. He stepped out of a halo of smoke and gazed around the room in mock surprise. "It would seem I am a few minutes late for the party. No matter. What did I miss?"

"Not much," Zoe deadpanned. "The donkey and male strippers will be here soon. I ordered them with you in mind."

Gideon chuckled, and then he stab pointed at her three times. "Very good, miss Beaupre. I'm glad you still have your sense of humor. So many people are unable to bring laughter in their lives. Or *death*, such as it is in your case. But, bravo, you've made an old man smile. You know, at first I couldn't see what Zane thought was so special about you, but now that I've met you...well, I still can't. But you *are* original; I'll grant you that much. In short, you are nothing but a common street strumpet, and as such, unworthy of my attentions nor pardon."

Zoe bit back a retort. "Tell it to me straight, Doc; how do you really feel about me?"

Gideon glanced over at the old clown. "Harry?"

"Yes, Bartholomew?"

"Shoot her."

"I can't," Harry mumbled. "You said—"

"What? Speak up, man. Did you just say *no*?"

"No."

"No, you didn't say no, or no you won't shoot her? Which is it, man?"

Harry shuffled his feet and glanced nervously at Zoe, Mary, then the gun, and finally back to whatever portents the floor held for him. "No, Bartholomew. I won't do it. I can't. All you said I had to do is get them here and you'd leave me and the pups alone for good. I won't be party to murder."

Gideon tucked the shotgun under his arm, shrugged off his overcoat, and wiped his face with the sleeve of his shirt. Instead of responding to Harry's refusal, he turned to the girls. "Do you know that Harry called me earlier tonight?"

Harry turned to Gideon, still holding the gun toward Zoe. "Bartholomew, please."

"Hold your tongue. I'm just telling your new friends here about the accord you worked out with me from…where?—the Journey's End Motel, if my memory serves…and it always does." To Zoe, he said, "You see, Harry here wants his life back. He seemed to think I'd be upset with him for killing my favorite dog. Don't get me wrong, young lady, I am somewhat put out over the affair, and his belief that some sort of backlash—a retribution of sorts—would follow, was an astute observation on his part. Nothing, and I mean nothing, ever happens that doesn't eventually find its way into my hands. Somehow, I would have found him out, and when I caught up to him he would have been…taken care of in a proportionally satisfactory manner. But don't blame this unfortunate wretch, for he did what anyone in his position would have done."

Zoe glared first at Harry, then back to Gideon, and raised her chin defiantly. "I wouldn't."

Mary spoke up, her voice quivering and soft, "Me, too." She cleared her throat. "Is it okay if I put my arms down, mister? I can't feel my fingers."

"Well bully for you," Gideon said to Zoe. "A whore with a heart of gold; isn't that sweet? Later, as I am sipping sherry by that very fireplace you are about to spill your life blood into, I may enjoy a moment or two of regret." He cocked one barrel. "Regret that I will need to replace such an expensive rug." He breathed a sigh as his gaze dropped to the rug. "But as they say: You can't make an omelet without killing a few women. And unless my friend, Harry Funshine, wishes to be the cheese in that omelet, he will do as I say. Shoot her, Harry."

Harry whimpered, but raised the .38.

Zoe replayed Harry's words as she stared cross-eyed down the stubby barrel of his revolver: *"Here. Give me the gun, Zoe. I wouldn't want you to shoot your own foot off." Fuck, Zoe! Why didn't you just put the gun to your own head and pull the fucking trigger! Fuck!*

On each side of the open ended cylinders, Zoe saw the bullets, each with an x gouged deep into their tip. She wondered why the x was there, and why the cylinder was open ended like that. Wouldn't it get dirty? How did the bullets not fall out the end when the gun tipped forward? Was the x on the bullet there for the purpose of, in lieu of a priest, sending you to God in style? These questions and a plethora of other equally nonsensical queries flew at the speed of light through her Universe, and then her Universe offered its answer in the form of another question: *How did you think this was going to end, you stupid bitch?*

You forgot Zoe's number one rule, kid...

Back in the first grade, she'd been introduced to her first act of male treachery by a boy in whom she initially found both beauty and experience. Jacob had the dreamiest azure eyes and gorgeous blonde hair—and if that wasn't enough, he was in the *second grade*. Over lunch he'd confided to her, in a conspiratorial tone, that 1+1= window, and, if allowed to prove it, Zoe would have to give him the cupcakes in her lunch pail. Now, Zoe wasn't the best student, or the first to raise her hand in class, but she knew for a fact that one plus one equaled two. Duh. She could do that much using just her nose finger and the dirty word one beside it. She'd counted it out three times in her head before saying, "And what do I get if I win? Jell-o! Jell-o! I want your jell-o." Jacob stabbed a glue-and-dirt covered thumb in her face, winked, and told her, "You're on."

Jacob made quite a show out of rolling up the imagined sleeves of his short sleeved Darth Vader t-shirt, then took thirty seconds to sharpen his pencil, holding it up to his eye three times to gauge it's worthiness for the presented task of refuting two thousand years of mathematical truth, to shake the very foundation of the Einstein's known universe. And then, with the clumsy pomp of a child prodigy, first he placed a one, connecting it to a plus sign. Then he added the second one.

It was right about there that Zoe realized she'd been duped. And even as he penciled the equals sign above and below the plus sign, she was digging into her plastic Strawberry Shortcake lunch box, past a foil wrapped peanut butter sandwich, for her cupcakes. He was still pointing proudly at the obvious picture of the window when she dropped the cupcakes onto the drawing and silently stalked away.

She realized two things that day. Firstly: Things are not always as they appear. And the second, more important of the two: Never trust a boy. They lie.

This two pronged doctrine had worked for her in all the days following that one, and with a few exceptions, worked well. This man, this clown, was one of those few exceptions. *But how the hell could I let this happen?* The shitty thing about *this* time was that instead of cupcakes, the only thing at the bottom of her lunch box now was her next breath.

Harry's gun arm lowered slightly and bounced with the rise and fall of his chest as he sobbed. "I am so very sorry. I...I begged you...and you just wouldn't leave it alone. I tried to turn you from this, Zoe, but you..." He raised the gun to

Zoe's head and squeezed his eyes closed, forcing tears from the closed lids. "I'll make this quick." His voice broke. "You won't feel a thing. Forgive me."

"Forgive you?" she spat, lowering her arms. *What's he going to do, kill me twice?* She folded her arms below her breasts. "I don't think this counts as something somebody could be forgiven for, Harry. It's not like you stepped on my foot or farted during Grace. You're gonna fucking shoot me!"

"Oh, for Christ's sake," complained Gideon. "Enough." He shouldered the shotgun and fired a shot between Harry's arm and Zoe's face. Shards of brick and mortar exploded from the fire place and pelted them, driving them apart. "Just shoot her already and stop playing around."

Gideon took two steps forward through the ring of smoke left behind by the fired weapon and glared down the long nose of the shotgun. His eyes had taken on a wild shine in the wake of firing the boom stick—as though its sheer power and thunderous report had awoken some atavist from deep within his reptile brain. "Who's it going to be?" He bit off the words like they were beef jerky. "You?" He pointing the gun at Zoe's chest, and then skipped to Mary. "You? Last chance, Harry; live free or die with them."

Not that she was complaining, but Zoe was confounded by his apprehension at just shooting them himself. *Why make Harry do it, you asshole. What's-a-matter? No balls of your own?*

The reason came to her in a flash of red. Cherry red.

"You're a virgin," she whispered.

Gideon lowered his gun and turned his head slightly to favor her with an ear. "Pardon me?"

"A virgin," she said, and smiled as she did so. *Why not? Again, what's he gonna do?* "As in, never done the deed, 'offed' anybody, blew out someone's candle, busted one off in a bitch. You know, snuffed them."

Gideon blushed, flustered at first, but recovered immediately. "True. Yes, it's true I have never actually taken a life myself, but it seems, since Harry has turned out to be such an abysmal failure in his role as a lackey, that *that* is all about to change. It seems ironically fitting my first time will be with a prostitute."

Zoe had never been much of a poker player. She thought Gideon might fold before the pot became too big; she'd always been able to read people's faces so well, but as it turns out, not as well as she thought. "Why start now?" she said, backpedaling. "Be a shame to start now, right? And hey, what about that carpet? I bet it's expensive. It looks expensive." *God! Stop babbling.*

"I was going to remodel anyway."

Leftover whiffs of cordite snaked lazily from the doctor's gun and wafted toward Zoe, stinging her nostrils; water dripped in meandering rivulets from the rain slicker lying at Gideon's feet, soaking into the carpet; a bead of sweat ran down from Harry's temple and followed the contour of his jaw, leaving a map for the next drop to follow; Gideon's Adam's apple bobbed once, twice; and a shadow passed along the hallway and stopped short of entering the room, and swayed.

Zoe saw all these things in an instantaneous, yet seemingly hour long parade of images—all from the crystal clear perspective of a person staring at a future that didn't include them and needing to drink in as much of this world as possible before passing to the next, or to nothing.

"I've decided we shall start with you," he said, raising his chin so he was able to look down his nose at Zoe. "You filthy gutter slut—you just couldn't walk away, could you? Even after I *let* you have Zane Ellis." With one shaking hand, he pawed sweat and rainwater from his brow. "You, who brought this upon yourself," he spat. "You, who led these poor people to their deaths," he growled, lowering his eye to the shotgun's sight. "You—"

"And you've never been married, doctor? How *have* you stayed single? Smooth talker like you."

There it was again. Or, they, actually: The accusation that she was the cause of all this was one. But more importantly, the shadow Zoe *thought* she saw a few seconds before, well, it moved again.

~~oOo~~

Zoe was the first to see him enter, but after he tripped and fell at Gideon's feet, he had everyone's undivided attention. Seth Spiedewski—Spider to his friends—rolled over, fixed a one-eyed squint at Gideon and waggled a finger. "This is a really nice house, mister," he slurred, then gained his feet. With the straight legged blinders of a drunk on a mission, he bumbled toward Harry and Zoe.

No one lifted a finger, and, although four sets of eyebrows arched at his single-minded struggle to stay on his feet, no one said a word. Dumbfounding would best describe the general consensus of his viewed actions. Gideon swung his gun toward Seth, then lowered it and jammed the now dead cigar nub back in his mouth and began to chew the tip.

Harry registered a mixture of guilt and indecision at Seth's crooked approach, but left the gun trained on Zoe. He looked as though he was about to say something, to possibly plead his case, but the old clown never got the chance.

Seth pushed his hand down his sleeve, raised the rock he'd concealed there, and swung his arm so fast Harry's free arm was still dangling at his side when the stone connected with his temple. There was no pumpkin-like splash, no scream, and no blood. Harry fell sideways toward the open window, taking the curtains with him, and crumpled to the floor.

Seth let the rock fall from his fingers and he turned to Zoe, blood coursing freely from just above his right ear. "S-S-See," he stammered, swaying like a reed in a gentle gust, "I t-t-told you he-he was a d-d-dick." Then his eyes rolled back in his head. He dropped to his knees and toppled over sideways into the cold fireplace.

"Spider!" Mary screamed.

Zoe clutched Mary's arm as she moved toward Seth. Zoe wanted to let her run to him, but couldn't. "No, you can't help him."

Mary retreated from her touch. Instead of moving to Seth, she backed up until she found the wall.

"I'm sorry I got you into this Mary. You've been a good friend," Zoe said, never taking her eyes from Gideon.

Behind her, somewhere near the window, Mary sobbed softly.

The open window! Zoe turned to get Mary's attention and pointed meaningfully at the window with her eyes, but Mary gazed through her as though Zoe were already a ghost.

"You there, Blondie," Gideon said to Mary. "If you shut that window I *may* let you leave. You don't need to play anymore if you don't want to. What do you say?"

Movement behind Gideon caught Zoe's eye. For the second time in as many minutes, she couldn't believe what she was seeing. *Where the hell did you come from?*

Danny strolled into the room with a mystified grin stretched tight across his face, and a pail in his hands. Zoe couldn't have stopped her jaw from dropping if she'd used both hands, so, with her chin resting firmly on her chest, she watched as the teen doused the doctor with a runny, jelly-like substance. *I say again: Where the hell did you come from? And what is that, Smurf jizz?*

"Can I play, too?" Danny stood in the doorway, blinking like an owl under a floodlight.

The doctor lurched forward as the spray hit him, and turned quickly, catching the rest of the liquid in the face. Gideon clawed at his eyes, as he rounded on the newcomer and raised the gun. "Nice try, kid," he growled. "But not good...Hey," he sniffed his fingers. "What is this stuff? Is that gasoline?"

In answer, Danny pulled his shirt over his head and let it fall to the floor, exposing large masses of burn scars. "Your lighters are cool, mister. Can I keep one?"

"Tell me...tell me what this is," Gideon shrieked, as he pawed at his face and sniffed at the chemicals that, by then, filled every nostril in the room. "I'll shoot you in the gut. I'll do it. I will."

"I don't think you want to fire that gun right about now, mister." Danny said. He mouthed *Boom* and mimed an explosion as he pointed at the thick substance dripping in slow globs from the end of the gun. Then he produced a container of lighter fluid and squirted its contents on the Doctor's feet and along the carpet at his own feet. "Here," he said. "Some for you, some for me," He bled the last bit down his own chest and rubbed it in like baby oil.

"You're crazy," the snuff mogul sputtered. Cradling the gun, he wiped the gel from his face. "You'll kill us all."

"I'm not. I'm not crazy." Danny produced a lighter and flipped the lid back. "I'm misunderstood." Then he brought forth a flame with a flick of his thumb.

The guttering yellow of the flame danced in his eyes as he turned the lighter this way and that, seemingly losing himself in its flickering ballet. Just when it seemed he would never look away, he found Gideon's face again and, in one swift movement, let the pail fall to the carpet at his feet and stepped toward the shotgun leveled at his chest, grabbing the barrel with his free hand.

Danny leaned forward over the gun and blinked rapidly for a couple of seconds. Then, as inspiration found him, he held the doctor's gaze, and whispered, "Do you want to know what would be a really cool way to die?"

Since no response was forthcoming, Danny offered his answer: "To a really cool soundtrack. Mine's playing in my head right now. How about you?"

"Danny," Zoe ventured, softly, edging forward now that the doctor's focus was no longer on her. "Danny, listen to me. You got him. I knew you would, 'cause you're my knight, and that's what knights do: Rescuing damsels in distress. But you need to stop now, okay? We need him alive." *Need you alive.*

The reek of the jelly-like substance caused her eyes to water, and a feeling that she was just a helpless spectator began to worm up her spine. She didn't give a shit if the doctor died, but *not* Danny. She couldn't lose him. *Not another one. Please, God, make him stop,* she pleaded silently. She shook her head and stated firmly, "Step away from him, Danny. What do say?" Her voice broke. "Will you do it for me?"

Danny might as well have been on the moon or staring blankly out the back window of a rusty yellow Beetle. He only had eyes for the game and, of course, the flame.

At Zoe's remark about needing him, a tiny smile curved the corners of Gideon's gel-pasted mouth. "Sure you do," he purred past smoke yellowed teeth. "Without me there's—"

Danny cut him off, "Time to go, mister."

Gideon wiped goop from his chin. "You're not going anywhere, you little bastard."

"No," Danny said, but his eyes were now on Zoe. "Not me—you."

And where is it you think I'm going?"

Danny's eyes flicked back to the doctor and a smile spread across his face. "Hell," he said. Then he dropped the lighter.

"No!" Shocked into action, Zoe dove forward, but too late.

A split second after the lighter hit the carpet a blue wave of flame bled toward the doctor's feet and the shotgun barked in his hands, then sprouted a roman nose of fire that coursed up the barrel and along Gideon's arms. Danny had disappeared amid the resultant flash.

Switching course mid step, Zoe lunged backward and landed between the bodies of Harry and Seth. As she frantically searched for Harry's dropped gun, Gideon thrashed and screamed in agony. From a part of her mind not occupied by terror, Zoe registered the cloying aroma of burnt hair and pork chops.

As suddenly as the screaming began, so it trailed off. Zoe craned her neck to see if the doctor had died or passed out from the pain, but found him dancing in place, whipping at his flaming shoes with the tail of his trench coat. *You've got to be fucking kidding me. There's no way.*

Cocooned tightly around his body, steam rose from the collar of the trench coat and collected like a storm cloud above Gideon's head. Although obviously badly burnt—and would definitely be feeling the post roast effects of his fire dance the next day—he was still very much in the game.

The audible emissions from beneath the voluminous coat had been reduced to a continuous high-pitched keening of, "ho ho ho", like a helium dosed Santa or his mini-me elf, but pain or no pain, he still reached for his gun.

All her life, Zoe had passed time by counting—counting steps, breaths, at night she would sometimes drift off while counting stars or her own heartbeat, the imagined money she would need to retire, or the amount of times her mother had ever told her she loved her. That last number, by the way, was zero. Just like the number of shells left in Gideon's shotgun. She'd counted. 1+1 didn't equal window *this* time.

She redoubled her efforts, probing furiously beneath the limp clown.

~~oOo~~

"Oh, you little bitch. I'm gonna get you." Gideon grabbed the shotgun by the barrel, and shrieked as he snatched his hand to his mouth, sucking on his fingers. Then he knelt and, using the sleeve of his coat as an oven mitt, picked up the gun. He laid it across his arm and stabbed the breaching mechanism. Cradled across his body, the fire heated gun sizzled, sending steam to mingle with the smoky haze curling from his collar. After he plucked the two expended shells from the twin chambers, he reached into the pocket of the coat for fresh ones.

Zoe had searched under and everywhere around the body and couldn't find Harry's gun anywhere.

Gideon's gun snap closed and she turned in time to see the doctor's hard drive perform a task not built into its ROM. It flew through the air and struck the old man hard enough to knock him off his feet. Reflexively, Gideon's finger squeezed the trigger as he fell, blowing a grapefruit-sized hole in the wall just above Zoe's head—sending plaster, splinters of wood, and shredded hundred-dollar bills showering down around her. Through the cloud of gypsum and Franklin-faced confetti,

Mary flew over the couch like a screaming Valkyrie and dove at the doctor. The girl landed on top, and pummeled him with both fists.

Using the gun as a staff, Gideon pushed the girl back and smashed the butt of the gun into her cheek. Mary groaned and crumpled to the floor.

"Oh, you little vixen," He said to Mary, cocking the second barrel as he turned to face Zoe. "Wait there. I shan't be but a moment."

Just then, a suet shrouded ghost from the fire place coughed and said, "So how's e-e-verything w-working out for us?"

Zoe turned and—*tada*—Harry's gun lay half buried in ashes near Seth's face. As she reached out and snatched the gun, she blurted, "Ask me again in five seconds." She flipped and brought Harry's gun around just as Gideon's gun swept toward her.

With her arms still on an upward swing, she closed her eyes and fired. Not ready for the recoil, the gun flew backward and punched her in the jaw. Pain exploded from her chin, but she managed to keep the gun. When she shook her head and opened her eyes, the doctor's gun was lying on the floor and Gideon was rolling back and forth, cradling his hand.

Zoe ran over to him and, just like the cops she'd seen on television do, moved to kick his gun away. The thing was, she didn't realize how hard and heavy a shotgun was, so only managed to viciously stub her toe and trip over the gun. She fell over the doctor and landed in the doorway, hitting her head on the frame on the way down.

"Is it safe to come back in?" she heard from the hallway.

She opened her eyes but couldn't see much past the stars and little birds circling her head. "Danny?"

"Are you okay, Zoe? I mean, did he shoot you?" Danny stood above her, a halo of light surrounding his head, throwing his features into shadow. "And, um, can you stop pointing that gun at me."

Zoe gulped. "Danny?" she repeated weakly, attempting to

shake the ringing from her ears. "Are you an angel?"

"Nope," he said, kneeling down so that the ceiling light no longer crowned his head. "I'm your knight. I mean, right? You said so, right?"

Zoe rolled over onto her knees and found her feet. She held up her gun finger to mark their conversation. "Hold that thought. I'll be right back."

She took three long strides and booted the snuff producer in the face—another thing she'd seen done by cops on television. *What a wealth of information that black box was.* The kick didn't knock him out like it would have for Magnum or Dirty Harry, but at least he stopped squirming.

She kneeled and placed the gun to his head. He froze. "Good," she said. "You understand what's happening *now,* don't you, asshole?" He gave a slight tilt of his head. "Alright. Now, if you move while I pick up that shotgun, I'm gonna pop another asshole into that asshole head of yours. You got that, asshole?"

Mary sat up, rubbing a large oval welt on her face. "I think the *asshole's* got it, chick," she said, wincing and massaging her jaw as she spoke. Then her eyes went round and she jumped up. "Spider," she yelped, and scrambled to the fireplace.

She pulled Seth feet first out of the cold pit and rolled him over. Seth groaned as his head hit the tile surround. "Oh, baby, are you okay? That was the...the..."

"Stupidest, most unbelievably fucked up thing you ever saw?" Zoe finished for her.

"Hey," replied Seth and Mary in unison.

"C'mon," Zoe said, looking up from the doctor to face the couple, "Really? What were you thinking, waltzing through the door like that? Are you out of your fucking mind, Seth?"

Seth winced as Mary daubed at his face and scalp with her sleeve, then he sat up and shook his head. Suet and blood flew away, speckling the ground and Mary's flowered dress. He pointed a shaky finger at the body of the clown and said, "W-well it worked, d-d-didn't it?"

Zoe stepped on the doctor's chest as he attempted to rise.

"You don't remember doing it, do you?"

Seth sheepishly glanced at Mary. "Well, n-no. Not really." He bent forward and coughed a load of grey phlegm onto the carpet. He regarded Zoe for a few seconds and looked away. "It worked, didn't it?"

"You already said that."

He waggled a powdered finger at her. "I told you he was a dick."

"You already said that too," Zoe said, her eyes following the trail of shredded bills to the hole in the wall. She'd seen the bills when they'd initially fallen into her lap, but now that she had more time to think about it, a plan began to form.

She turned and leaned down to the doctor's ear. "Do you have any rope? Keep in mind I'm only going to ask once."

Gideon turned his head until the barrel was pointed directly at his right eye. "Go fuck yourself, whore. I don't give a damn wh—"

" 'Kay." Zoe pursed her lips, shrugged one shoulder, and shot him in the foot. She stepped away and watched as he thrashed and screamed on the floor. She could really sympathize with that kind of pain. She *did* just stub her toe on his shotgun.

"Whoa," breathed Mary. "Zoe, he's not the one that killed your sister—or even Meat, for that matter. Take a chill pill and calm down."

Zoe walked to the pile of DVD's and sorted through them. "Here," she said, tossing it to Mary. "Read that, and then tell me to calm down."

Mary gaped at the plastic case for a few seconds and gasped. "Jeanne," she mumbled. Her sorrow was immediately sniffed back and replaced by a cool resolve as she turned to glower at Gideon. "Blow this bitch's brains out, Zoe."

Zoe nodded soberly and placed the gun to his head, effectively silencing the worst of his moans. "Okay, doc, since you didn't seem to like that question very much, here's another: Do you have any throw rugs or drop sheets kicking around castle Frankenstein here. You know...something we could load a couple bodies into?"

She let the question settle in before...

"Before what, bitch? You're not gonna kill him."

"No. I'm not, but I really need that rope—Hey! Purple, is that you?"

"Ah, no, you dumb whore. This is your—your conscience speaking. Look over there. Is that an elephant?"

"Purple Monkey? Hello?" Huh.

Her eyes narrowed. She jabbed a finger at the doctor. "Don't you fucking move." She picked up the shotgun and handed it to Mary. "If he moves a finger, blow his balls off."

Mary grinned. "Hands up, creep," she said, as she thumbed the hammer back and closed one eye. Gideon didn't immediately comply, so she slapped him. "I said hands up, bitch!"

Gideon let go of his bleeding foot and raised his hands. There was a finger missing from his right hand and blood ran from the stub like a popsicle under a summer sun.

Mary snorted. "Look at that. You shot his finger off."

Zoe gazed evenly at the hand. "Well, I didn't want to *kill* him."

Seth coughed and jumped into the conversation. "Fucking bull shitter. I s-saw you. Y-you had your eyes closed the whole t-t-time."

Zoe shrugged. "Well, it worked, didn't it?"

She walked out into the hallway while Mary held the gun on the doctor. "Danny, can you tell me something?"

"Sure, anything you want."

"Did you steal my monkey?"

He flicked a glance sideways. "What do you mean? I don't know what you're talking about."

Zoe folded her arms and shifted her weight to one leg. "My monkey—could you see it?"

Danny licked his lips and looked away. "I don't—"

"Cut the shit, you little shit. I know you saw my monkey. I just want to hear it from you."

His bare chest rose, then he dumped the entire load of air before answering. "Yes. I saw it," he said, then turned his head.

"What?" A pause, then, "Oh, okay."

"Who were you talking to?"

He hesitated, and then said, "My friend." Then he smiled, and added, in a whisper, "He's a phoenix."

"I thought you said you saw my monkey?"

"Not since we were at Harry's trailer..." Danny spotted the lighter he'd dropped on the floor, and started past Zoe to pick it up.

"Whoa. Not so fast, there. You're not just gonna drop a bomb like that and walk away. You saw my monkey?"

He stood looking at her for a moment then blushed and turned away. "Yeah. It was when you were changing. I'm sorry. I didn't mean to peek, but you were all naked and I could, you know..." he pointed to her crotch, "see your monkey."

"*What?*" She didn't understand what the hell he was talking about until she looked down. "Oh... Oh!" she said, finally getting it. "That's okay, Danny," she mumbled, deflated, "It's no big thing."

"And not much hair, either," he said, and brushed past her.

She shook her head and walked back into the room. "Okay, where were we?"

Mary answered without moving her eyes from the cringing doctor. "You were asking creepo over here what he wanted on his tombstone." To Gideon, she said, "Right, creep?" Gideon let his head fall back on the carpet and said nothing.

Zoe knelt beside the doctor. "Right about now I bet you're wishing that you'd been smart enough to answer my first question, huh, doc?"

He nodded but said nothing.

"Well," she said, resting her forearms on her knees with her hand gun dangling between her legs, "I'll ask you again: do you have any—?"

"The desk! I have hand cuffs in my desk." After spewing the location of the cuffs, the energy seemed to drain from him and he closed his eyes. "May I put my hands down? I think I'm bleeding to death here."

He received a unanimous and resounding "No!" and left

them above his head.

Zoe crossed to the desk and pulled two drawers open before finding the cuffs.

"Now what?" asked Mary. "We gonna cuff him and call the police?"

From beside her, Seth spoke up. "Too bad about all this money, eh?"

Mary turned her head so fast it nearly spun in a circle. "What money?"

Zoe walked over and cuffed one of the doctor's wrists and flipped him over—just like she'd seen cops do on television. "It's in the walls."

Just then, Gideon started to thrash and convulsed as though he were possessed.

"You keep your filthy little paws off my money! You touch it and I'll...I'll..."

Zoe sat on his back and raised his arm until she heard a pop. "You'll what, doc?" Aside from resuming the keening she'd heard from him earlier, he fell silent. "Great," she said, snapping on the second manacle and squeezing until it pinched his skin. "Now that we've got your blessing, shut up."

Zoe turned to her friends as a slow smile worked away at one corner of her mouth. Then she told them about something *else* she'd seen cops do on television.

They were all ears.

With only an hour until the sleepy street would be alive with activity, they had a lot of money to move before Zoe called the police.

41

SWEEPING UP

"Say, Shaw?" the chubby detective called, leaning back in the sagging wooden desk chair. "You remember anything from that drop cloth thing from back in Ohio?"

Shaw thought his partner said drop cloth. "Did you say drop cloth? As in the 'heads and painting' drop cloth?"

Holding the phone to his chest, Shaw's partner rolled his eyes and waved for him to pick up the extension. "I think we might have some more pages for that file you been keeping, buddy. Get a load of this shit: Some chick—name's Zoe Beaupre—says she wants to talk to somebody who knows about 'that headhunter painter'."

Zoe Beaupre? Shaw knew that name. She was the sister of one of Cannibalangelo's victims. Said she saw him, just like Shaw did. "Why don't you let me take this one, Chris?" He held out his hand like a jealous toddler.

Shaw had been put through the ringer ever since his first encounter with the serial killer, Cannibalangelo. He'd been bumped down to detective, transferred three times, then he'd bounced to Chicago to wait out retirement.

Unable to shake his desire to make sense of his problem, he manifested the whole load in the painting he'd seen that fateful morning so long ago. Secretly at first, he'd collected any information, followed any lead no matter how small, questioned witnesses who'd already been rung out by the fed's, and still knew no more than he did that morning in Cleveland. That was where he'd met and chatted with the disguised Drop cloth maneater, Cannibalangelo himself.

"This is Detective Shaw. Could I have your name again please?"

The woman on the other end ignored his question. "And you know about that Cannibalangelo case?"

"Yes, Miss..?"

"I already told your buddy. What are you, daft or something, mister? It's Zoe. Zoe Beaupre. Do you know about him or not?"

"Who doesn't?" He remembered her clearly now. He'd read her witness statement so many times he could have recited it verbatim. Did you, ah, have something to add to the statement you gave to a Detective Jenks in Toronto?"

"Okay, smart ass. I guess you *do* know about this stuff."

"Alright, Miss Beaupre, now that I've told you something, why don't you tell *me* something? Something like, why are you calling?"

"I...well, it's kind of fucked up—really fucked up—but I know he's dead. Probably. And I also know who he worked for."

"Worked for? One second, please." He pulled a file from under a foot thick stack of folders in his bottom drawer. He dropped it on his desk and flipped it open, leafing through a pile of fax photos until he found her. She was pretty. After skimming the file he remembered more of its details. Then he recalled reading she'd been placed into a psychiatric facility, pending a twenty day evaluation. That was the last information he'd been able to find on her. "You, ah, still in the Paradise Valley Institute?"

There was few seconds of silence before she answered. "No."

"Released?"

Another pause. "No, not really—you don't know, do you?"

"Would you get to the point of the call, please?"

"I told you. I caught him, the guy responsible for all those murders."

"You did?"

"Uh huh. Singlehanded."

~~oOo~~

Lou Schrickt sat devouring the remainder of his happy meal in a cloud of smoldering rage. He'd specifically asked for no onions or pickles. Twice. As he sneered at the plump girl behind the counter, he wished her luck in hell. *Round one goes to you, pimpled servant of deception, but we shall see who laughs the last laugh and laughs—fuck it. Evil temptress!* In an attempt to put the slight behind him, he consoled himself with the fact that, if he squinted his eyes really tight, his fries looked kinda like worms. That was at least a little evil.

His search for a name to use in his struggle at the side of his master had, thus far, been fruitless; all the good names had already been spoken for. Finding an evil call sign wasn't as easy as he thought it was going to be. His dark lord had dubbed him "The Chew," but Lou suspected the master was having a little sport with him. *Seriously? Lou the Chew?* That label blew enormous demon dicks—even after capitalizing C in chew for effect. *Sounds more like a new character for Elmo's World.* The great and wise Zane Ellis seriously did work in mysterious ways.

And so the battle weary youth gazes into the unknown future with naught but bravery as companion. The young dread lord raises his great fists in defiance, ready to face heaven and hell alike, if destiny so chose. I will seek—say!

Seeker! That's it! It was both powerful and mysterious. He ran a chipped, black fingernail through a puddle of ketchup, drew a lopsided pentagram, and then called the four corners: French fry, salt packet, burger, soft drink. Finally, he scribbled his new name into the ketchup, tearing the grease soaked wrapper in the process. It wasn't pretty, but it was done. *All quail before the dreaded Seeker!* He held his breath, hoping for some sort of Highlander-type quickening, but settled instead for a burp.

Lou was staring menacingly at the remainder of his lunch when his phone rang. It was the P.I./minion he'd hired to find his master.

Lou preempted the caller: "Hail, dark oracle. You may speak to the Seeker."

"Uh, yeah. Right. Hail dark oracle to you, too, kid."

Caveman style, Lou said, "No. You dark oracle, me Seeker." *Oh, I am so gonna go Hannibal on your ass. Right after I wash it.*

"Right. For the grand you paid me, you can call me Betty. Say listen, kid. I—"

"Seeker," grated Lou. He was beginning to understand the saying about finding good help. "Say on, minion." He tore off a bite of the bun clad brain—with onion and pickle. *Bitch!*

"Right. Well, I found your boy. At least I think so, anyway. I got a hit off that cell number you gave me. Signal came through last night and I was able to triangulate—"

Lou stuck his tongue out at a staring child of about four and slid a ketchup smeared fry past his black lipstick. "Where?"

"Like I was saying, I have an address here for you." There was a pause, then, "Uh, Seeker."

Lou sensed his slave didn't really like him. That was okay. You don't need to like evil; you needed to fear it. "So where is he?"

"Well, the way I see it, you just paid me to *find* him. It'll cost you another thou for the location."

Oh, you gloriously evil man. I underestimated you. "That sounds fair." Fair or not, Lou only had fifty-two dollars and nineteen cents. "I will away to your lair ere the shadows reach noon."

"That means my office, right?"

"It does, slave. And I shall be there ere—"

"Yeah, yeah. I got that much. But don't be late. I got a lunch date."

You sure do, you fat, ugly sloth…you pathetic peon…maggot mouthed moron. "I shall endeavor to not be tardy."

"You do that. And don't forget the cash."

Lou pocketed the toy that came with his meal and left the restaurant. Upon stepping into the light, he cringed at the sun's baleful glare. The sun didn't actually burn him like a true creature of the night, but he thought it would sure be cool if it did. Against the floral splendor of Mickey D's front yard, he was a speck of printer's ink on a Matisse, a smudge on Walt Disney's technicolor chest x-ray.

His holy grail, his Master, was finally within reach. *Onward, Seeker. Your destiny awaits...*

But first, the Seeker needed to find a hardware store. One-thousand dollars he couldn't do, but he *could* afford a shiny new buck knife.

~~oOo~~

EWN 24 hour News
Channel 12
St. Louis, Mo

"This is Kelly Blonde, coming to you on location in Chicago, where the final gruesome chapter of the Paradise Valley Institute story played out mere hours ago, ending the week long search for at least one of the two remaining missing patients, gone since last Monday night. It seems the patient in question—who's identity has yet to be released—was kidnapped from the hospital by two men: A Chin Choi, address unknown, and a Dr. Bartholomew D. Gideon, a Chicago resident and psychiatrist. Little is known at this time, John, but it's rumored that, during young woman's struggle to free herself, one of the two men was killed. There doesn't seem to be much information filtering down to the media, John, but I'll be here when it does. John?"

"I'm sure you will, Kelly. Thanks. Kelly Blonde will keep us abreast of that situation as it unfolds, but for now, here's a look at the three day forecast for the tri-state

area…"

~~oOo~~

Zoe stayed as a *guest* of the great state of Illinois for three weeks while the city of Chicago's police department, under the leadership of one Detective James Shaw, hammered the pieces of Zoe's sketchy story into their proper holes.

Shaw succeeded in building an airtight case against the incarcerated Dr. Bartholomew D. Gideon. The corroborating testimony of Spike Schrickt claimed the doctor was the mastermind behind the abductions and murders at The Paradise Valley Institute. What the police didn't *have* was a money trail. Given the sheer amount of incriminating evidence and two eyewitnesses, they didn't actually need one, but recovered money was always good for morale.

On the morning of the 911 call, the first police officers arrived at the doctor's house shortly after eight a.m. and were met on the front lawn by an extremely agitated Zoe Beaupre. She'd escaped her bonds during an altercation between her captors that had started over one accusing the other of theft. The girl was able to wrestle the gun from the smaller man during the ensuing scuffle. She'd then shot the gun out of the other man's hands and cuffed him while she waited with her dog for the police to arrive.

That was her story.

But Detective Shaw knew a different truth. Aside from the fact the doctor's story was a complete polar opposite of hers, the doctor also said the girl and her accomplices had stolen more than four-hundred thousand dollars from him. Well, he didn't say, as much as scream and rant, but Shaw got the picture. He sure did—a lot of them, actually.

That's because, not only was he the lead detective on the case, but he was also the first officer on the scene. And, being the first officer on the scene, he'd also been the first one to find the video camera, blinking its dirty little secret from a vent above the desk in the study.

Why did he not submit this into an evidence bag along with the manuscript, reels, and discs? It's hard to say, really, but if you asked him, he'd probably pat his pocket and give you about seventy-five thousand reasons why not.

THE ONE AND ONLY...

DROPCLOTH ANGEL(S)

At a roadside diner in Tulsa, Oklahoma, a man wiped the remaining grease from his chin and pushed his half eaten steak aside in favor of dessert; a banana split with double chocolate sauce. He'd seen the report on the news about a girl, who, against all odds, had singlehandedly brought down an entire snuff film empire and captured the ring leader. Truly, it was pulp fiction at its finest. The news anchor said she was a former student, in the States on visa, but he knew the truth— sure did. That was okay, though. Good for her. She was a pretty good egg and deserved all the good things coming her way.

As he went to work on his double high dessert, the waitress came to remove his dinner plate and slap the bill face down on the table. "Anything else, doll?"

"Bob. Call me Bob," he said. Then read her name off her uniform shirt. "Betty."

Betty traded her work smile for an actual smile. "Bob. My father's name was Bob. Well Robert, really, but everybody called him Bobby."

Bob fought the urge to cringe. "Well, not me, Betty. It's Bob. Simply Bob."

After the woman had cleared his dishes, Bob dove back into his dessert while he thought about the girl whose face had become recognizable to anyone with eyes and a television. To no one in particular, he smiled and said, "I knew that girl was..."

~~oOo~~

Chicago, Ill.
The home of Dr. Robert Hawthorne

"...something special."

"What's so special about her, sir? She's just meat, right?"

"Aren't we all?"

Lou shrugged, "I guess."

"Say, kid. What do you say we blow this joint."

"I—I don't know anything about explosives, sir, but it would be an honor to do the research."

"I *mean* 'let's go'. God, kid, you've got your issues, don't you?"

"I knew what you meant."

Zane could see that he didn't.

"So what do we do with them?" Lou pointed toward the hogtied couple in the corner of the basement.

"That's my business, Lou." Zane tossed him a set of keys. "Go get my car out of storage. Have it washed and meet me out front in about..." he scrunched his bandaged face up as he guesstimated, "say, tomorrow."

Lou smiled wickedly, then nodded knowingly at the cringing couple. "I know exactly what you mean, sir. I—"

"Just go on."

Long after the teen exited, Zane stared at the surgeon and his nurse. He knew what he wanted to do, but wasn't sure if he was strong enough yet. *Guess there's only one way to find out,* he thought, as he rubbed the stiff muscles in his legs.

He sipped the last of his cola and stood, stretching his arms over his head as he gazed at Doctor Robert and Nurse Trudy. "You know, up 'til about five minutes ago, I didn't have the slightest idea how I was going to repay you for all the kindness you've shown me." He picked up his travel case and dropped it onto the bed. Then he pulled out the false top shelf, revealing an assortment of paint brushes. "I'm gonna do something for you—and I hope it turns out because I've never done two people on one canvas before. Before we start, Robert, do you mind if I use this sheet?"

~~oOo~~

By the next morning, when Lou pulled into the driveway to pick him up, Zane was a new man. He should have been tired, but instead felt as though he'd just woken from a long, restful slumber and had the energy to go ten rounds with God himself.

Lou started to move from the driver's seat, but Zane waved him back. "Why don't you drive, little buddy. Think I might relax and take in some of this beautiful day."

"Sure thing. Where to, sir?"

"Home, James."

"Uh, sir, by some dastardly act of evil or dark karma, your house is totally destroyed."

"No, Lou, my *other* home.

~~oOo~~

Inside the house of Doctor Robert Hawthorne, the painting was still wet. It was beautiful. A work worthy of tears and teeming with portent; mere words could barely scratch the surface. Two angels faced each other, fingers raised, imperceptibly touching, while light streamed gently through parted clouds frolicking in the ethereal embrace of a song or ballet from some far off unseen Eden. Each fold was a mystery, each stroke an epic poem. The dropcloth angels were truly the masterwork of a great artist. Stare at the wristwatch worn by the male angel long enough, and one would swear they'd heard it tick.

Flawless.

Priceless.

Robert Hawthorn raised a steaming cup to his mouth and paused before taking a sip. "Cool painting, but I would've rather had cash instead."

Trudy stepped up behind him and circled her arms around his chest, resting her head on his shoulder. "Do you think those wings make my ass look fat?"

"No baby, you're the hottest angel on the planet. Incidentally, why did you take your clothes off? You saw he was painting a robe on you, didn't you?"

"I just wanted to make sure he got the dimensions right, sweetie."

"Oh Trudy." Pronounced trewwdeeee. "You are such a fucking slut. You *so* wanted to do him. I can tell. That's so gross and so very wrong. It's just wrong."

She sniffed indignantly. "He *was* cute."

"Cute? He was a fucking cannibal." Robert sipped his coffee, cradling the mug jealously like a heart sized diamond or his favorite tie. After a few seconds, he took another sip, and said, "Kinda neat how he managed all that detail with one color, huh?"

"No kidding. To think, he did *that* with the paint you had left over from the bathroom. Beige never looked so good."

"Huh." Robert didn't know real art from a poster of two kittens playing with toilet paper, but he thought he'd try to say something deep to capture the moment. "Huh."

"Huh," Trudy agreed.

"Say, Trudy?"

"Yeah, Robby?"

"Wanna fuck?"

"Sure. Wanna tie me up and play cannibal and the unsuspecting bible thumping explorer?"

"You *did* want to do him, didn't you?"

"Is that a 'no' then?"

"No."

"Then go get the ropes, my evil maniac lover."

"Grr."

~~oOo~~

Following Zoe's release from custody, she endured a two week media hazing, giving interviews to everybody from The United Pentecostal Front, to Regis—and even the queen of daytime television, Oprah herself. Most of the interviewers left her feeling dirty and confused but, true to her title, Oprah had been both gracious and kind during their session. Afterward, they'd shared a hug.

The morning after the last scheduled interview, she met with Detective Shaw for the last time. She handed him an envelope containing seventy-five thousand dollars and he snapped a disc in half. Good trade, as far as Zoe was concerned. The next time she would see him would be at the doctor's trial, which, she told him, with a glint in her eye, "She wouldn't miss for the world."

~~oOo~~

One week later: Somewhere north of St. Louis
11:13 p.m

Zoe tossed the hand drawn map onto the passenger seat of the rented Mazda. The barn representing the X on the map was just up ahead, standing alone in a field of six-foot corn stalks. Poco did a double lap and plopped down onto the map, snoring almost immediately. Zoe didn't blame him. Playing navigator for the expedition must have tuckered the little fellow out.

She missed the double rut path the first time past, so she turned and crept along until she found it again. Upon pulling in, she lost sight of the barn under the wall of corn and hoped the path didn't fork. She'd seen *Children of the Corn* as a youngster, and the memory of Malachi and his brood stuck with her even still. Besides, there were worse things to be found in the dark—which was why she'd kept her doors locked.

After an uneventful but bumpy ride through the corn surrounded corridor, the path widened into a large circular clearing around the barn she'd seen from the road. There were no other cars, but, under the scant glow of the moon and sweeping orange of the rental's running lights, she noticed fresh tire tracks heading into the building. She pulled up next to the closed double doors and killed the engine.

Zoe took a deep breath and allowed it to deflate before opening the car door. As she stepped out, a shadow crossed the hood of the car then evaporated into the darkness.

From behind her, a hand clamped onto her arm and turned her. At arm's length, she could see nothing of the shape's features; aside from the arm, they were entirely encased in the deeper black of the barn's sprawling shadow.

"Zoe Beaupre," the shape said, deep and raspy, like a nail scraping a window pane.

Zoe answered first with her boot—having kept them as a memento of the weeks spent on the lam—and connected, expertly, with the unseen softness of the attacker's testicles. As the man fell, Poco streaked past her and launched himself, growling and snapping at the speed of a blender set for frappe. She was in the process of reaching for her second answer, mace, when the prostrated shape grunted her name again, then added, "It's me! I was just fucking with you. Call off the rat."

She squealed, recognizing the voice instantly. "Frye," she said, pushed Poco aside, and dove onto him. She proceeded to squeeze him tight enough to make him cry Uncle.

Poco saw that his mistress was doing fine without him and sat back on his twin pillows to watch.

Zoe helped Frye to his feet and hugged him again. "What are you doing here? I thought you'd still be in the hospital."

He winced as she squeezed. "Hey, watch the bandages.

You'll rip my stitches"

"Sorry." She backed off, but couldn't help grinning. "So what are you doing here? Not that it's a bad thing, but you were shot."

"Are you kidding? I told you it would take more than a bullet to keep me down."

"Apparently just a ten pound dog."

"With huge balls."

Arm in arm, they entered the barn to join the rest of the group. When Poco spotted Mary sitting on a bale of hay, he zipped over and jumped into her arms.

"Oh, you're even uglier than I remember. How ya doin' squirt?" Mary scratched his proffered belly.

Once past a large mound of hay, Zoe spotted Seth leaning against a bright yellow Volkswagen Beetle. "Hey, Seth, nice ride," she said.

Seth beamed a broad smile at her, causing hers to widen, then Frye, and Mary. Soon, they were all grinning like a pack of stoned Cheshire cats—and probably would have remained that way for another hour if not for the insistent barking from the front seat of the Bug. George and Gracie slobbered all over the driver's side window, taking turns jumping up and hitting the roof of the car with their heads—in the event no one had heard their barks.

Seth opened the door for the dogs, and together with Poco they tore off to explore the darker recesses of the old barn.

"Where's Danny? I was kinda thinking he'd be with you two," Zoe said to Mary.

Mary shared a look with Seth. "No. Sorry. After we got back to the hospital, he kind of went south on me."

"Like how? What'd he do, burn the place down?"

Mary looked away. "Yeah, kind of... I guess it just took him longer to process the fact that Meat wasn't coming back. Once we got back to the institute and Meat wasn't there, well...you know."

"Jeez, that's too bad," said Zoe. And it was, too. She was hoping he'd already hit his rough patch and could move on.

She forced a smile. "But you did alright, huh? They let you out."

"Yeah, they were actually pretty cool about that. Right after my old man's lawyer slapped a lawsuit on them."

Zoe turned to Frye. "What about you, big man? You didn't have to go back?"

Frye shook his head. "Uh uh. My parents were just paying to keep me there so I'd be out of the spotlight back home."

Seth cleared his throat. "I hate to break up this little gab session, but can we do this so we can get the hell out of here and go eat? I'm starving."

"That the money?" Zoe nodded toward a large duffel bag beside the car.

"Yup."

The wide smiles were back. "Alright," said Zoe, rubbing her hands together. "Let's do this."

The final meeting of The Retribution Club would now come to order.

GIDEON'S SWANSONG

The Big House

I know this man...Pete something. I'm sure of it. It'd been years since he'd seen the man, but Gideon never forgot a patient. What he couldn't recall was what Petey's affliction had been. *No matter,* he thought.

He tossed his prison issue towel, soap, and tooth brush onto the lower bunk and studied the man for a moment before speaking. "Ahem. Excuse me, but may I have your attention?" The sole indication the man had heard him was a slight stiffening of his shoulders. He was faced away from Gideon, seated at a metal desk, working at an unseen project.

"We'll be spending quite some time together, so I believe we should set a few friendly ground rules down, Mister...?"

No response.

"No matter." Gideon began to pace as he spoke.

His new cellmate sat quietly, humming occasionally, oblivious to Gideon and his friendly list. When Gideon finished, the man stood and turned, holding his project behind his back.

Believing it to be a peace offering, a gift from one new friend to another, Gideon nodded. All was as it should be. He

444

was in charge, and soon every dimwitted mother murdering soul in the prison would be eating out his hand.

"Petey, isn't it? I believe we've met before. You were a patient of mine, yes?"

Petey's eye twitched once, twice, then he smiled a heavy lidded knowing smile. "Oh, that's okay if you don't remember me, doctor. It's been a while."

"Sure has." *Well, Idiot? Are you going to enlighten me?*

"You got my name right, but I don't think you really remember me." Petey stepped forward and the smile vanished from his face.

"Sure I do. It was, ah…" Try as he might, Gideon drew a blank. The poor devil must not have made much of an impression the first time around. "Okay, you got me. But you were a patient, yes?"

Petey sighed morosely and nodded. "Oh yeah, I was one of yours."

This is absolutely splendid. He's already broken in! "And what, pray tell, was your affliction, son?"

"Maybe this'll jog your memory, doctor." Petey pulled his arm from behind his back. On his hand was a sock puppet, the eyes, mouth and goatee drawn using a bar of soap. Gideon thought the face on the puppet looked quite like him. Petey worked the puppet's mouth, and pulled off a fine impersonation of Gideon's own baritone.

The hand said, "How about now? Do you remember me now?"

The memories flooded back. Everything: the twelve murders, the seven court appointed evaluation sessions…and also Petey's modus operandi. He'd strangled each victim with a sock puppet made in their own image. The doctor swallowed his own tongue a split second before Petey's socked hand found his throat.

Gideon died on a Thursday. It was meatloaf day.

Here is an excerpt from

Shakespeare's Dead:

A Tragedy in III Acts

Due out in the summer of '13...if we don't all die in December.

1

Every story starts somewhere, but this isn't it. This one begins here so you could see how dead I was.

Ever stare down into a coffin and wonder, even for a brief second, what it's gonna be like when you die? How you're gonna look, or whether the mortician painted you up in a hurry because he or she had to make it home for dinner on time?

I could speak only for myself, but let me give you my answers to these questions:

1) It sucked.

2) I looked skinny in the face and boxy through the middle. Don't get me started on the suit! I didn't own anything that fugly. It was likely a parting joke by the gang. Fucking Dingo. He probably picked out that suit 'cause he was still sore with

me. I mean, aside from prick car salesmen, who wears plaid anymore? I couldn't see my legs...only the top lid of the coffin was open. For all I knew, there might not have been a lower half of me in the box. Why I wasn't going to be buried in full dress uniform remains a mystery to me. It's not like my dress blues were hidden. I kept them wrapped in plastic, hung up in the front hall closet, right under my Playboys and bong collection.

3) Yes. Strike that. FUCK, YES. I looked like I'd been painted up to look like that transvestite vampire from *The Rocky Horror Picture Show*. I was pretty sure the person responsible for my makeup was late for something—or hated their job...or me; you could plainly see the stitch marks from where the bullet exited my head two inches above my right eye. Even a novice golfer can replace a divot. Mr. Happy—that was his name—apparently didn't golf.

My name is Shakespeare Tiberius Poole and I'm on a mission from God. Or at least that's what Dave, the undead guy acting as my spirit guide, said. Apparently angels don't do wet work anymore, and there's something I need to do for Him. You know, the guy upstairs. I was on my way to complete that mission when I stopped by here.

Given the chance, who wouldn't visit their own funeral? Even if only to see who cared enough to come?

Aside from Sarah, who had no choice in the matter, a pimpled teen haunted the front door, handing out pamphlets, and the organist—a flatulent old woman so hunched over on the bench that her chin hung between her knees. Every once in a while she'd lift her head and mumble a few words of the tune she'd been playing for the last ten minutes. At the conclusion of each stanza she would lift a leg, fart, and then begin again. If I wasn't so stressed over the whole being dead thing, I might have found it humorous.

Sarah didn't think any of this was funny. But then, her thoughts collided with mine on more than one aspect of our current situation. Either she didn't believe Dave (the undead guy) when he said God specifically needed her help, or she was just pissed that I confiscated her body in order to complete my mission. Whichever it was, she fought me for control every step of the way. Have you ever slept on your arm and not had any control over it when you woke up? Try doing that with a whole body.

You'd think, by me possessing her body that she'd have to be gone while I was there. Well, there's one myth busted. Dave told me that I was a "free floater" and, as such, was able to coexist with a host spirit. My only question about that was, "If this mission was so fucking important, why the hell would I need to use a hostage—a pissed off gypsy one—to pull it off?

Sarah was still not talking to me—which was fine by me because she had no concept of just how loud she was in her own head. As for me, I figured I'd keep in the spirit of the funeral and stay quiet too.

While I waited to see if my friends were gonna show, I stared down at my own face through Sarah's eyes, tracing the lopsided stitches that ran back into the scalp and disappeared into my hairline. I wondered what Dingo would say when he saw that scar. Probably drop some lame ass Harry Potter battle scar remark, then go looking for the free donuts.

It was right then I started thinking...getting mad about how I died, all over again: murdered by some sneaky, asshole demon for being in the wrong place at the wrong time.

You know, my mother always told me I was gonna die young, but I thought it was gonna be on the job, or because some jealous husband with a shotgun caught me in the midst of a wild kingdom moment with his wife.

That shit would've totally better than this. But don't get me wrong, it's not like I had a death wish or anything. I just thought that IF I died young it would be because of one of those reasons. To be honest with you, I was kinda hoping for later on down the road, say, when I was fifty or something and had friends that were mature enough that they could fucking tell time.

The service started a half-hour before and not a soul had come to see me off. After much thought, I was pretty sure the gang was gonna be a no-show...what with how (and with whom) my body was found. Not to mention how me and that guy were, um, coupled. My friends were a pretty closed minded lot when it came to shit like that.

So, yeah, they weren't coming. The last thing they'd want to do is be seen at the funeral of a suspected homosexual.

First off, let me just make something perfectly clear. I'm not a homo. But I don't have any particular problem with them either, so don't go thinking I'm some kind of fag basher. Unlike my buddies, I'm more like a "you-be-you-and-more-pussy-for-me kind of guy." Live and let live, that's me.

Too bad the guy that turned my head into a fucking donut didn't share my lofty philosophy on tab A being the right fit for slot B. Not content to just kill us, the bastard then posed us like we were a couple of anatomically correct dolls that a shrink would use in a post trauma meeting with kids. You know, when he was asking them where the bad man had touched them.

Didn't even have my gun on me. Some cop, huh?

I didn't remember getting shot either. Dave had to tell me about my death and all the rest of the shit the killer did to us *after* I woke up. If I had a stomach I would've puked.

Some kid came in to drop off flowers, but still no Dingo Dan, Dan number two, Willie Chacha, or Nature. I could understand the rest of my friends not coming by to pay their respects—I wasn't as tight with them—but not Dingo Dan. We'd been best buds since public school and I didn't think a little thing like me banging his new girlfriend or dying naked in the arms of a federal agent would seem any worse than some of the shit we'd done growing up together.

Guess that shows how much I knew. Know. Whatever. The point is: This sucks big, hairy, supernatural ass.

My parents were already dead, so I wasn't expecting them. And my ex-girlfriend definitely wouldn't be coming, strict catholic upbringing and all...but nobody? No police burial? No partner? No captain? Aunts? Uncles? Or cousins—not even the ones I kissed? Outrageous. And do you know what I could do about it?

Uh huh. Not a god damned thing.

And just when I didn't think I could feel any lower, Sarah finally decided to speak to me.

She said: "Take me home".

I said "It's not like a date, Sarah. I can't. I'm sorry." I wasn't really sorry, but I thought that if I played nice with her she might stop being a bitch.

"A bitch?! Well fuck you, mister-I'm-so-suave-I-can-fuck-anybody-I-please-and-get-away-with-it-because-I-have-a-beautiful-ass. I didn't sign up to become some human taxi cab for you, let alone go running off like James Bond to stop some demon terrorists."

Apparently, she could read my thoughts. I did not know that. But more importantly, she said I had a nice ass. Maybe there was hope for us after all this was over. But then I thought that I shouldn't have thought that. Oh well. "Say, Sarah, I was thinking..."

"Yeah, right! Like I wanna have a boyfriend that I'd have to keep in the freezer so he didn't stink up the apartment. You're dead, Shakespeare. Deal with it."

I was shocked. Rejection wasn't something I'd ever had to deal with. It was something that happened to other people— ugly people, losers—but I was quickly coming to terms with the fact that, although the graveyard was a place where I'd gotten laid in the past, I probably wouldn't be dating much after my body was six feet south. So I humbly decided to not push the issue of a second romp, at least with her. There was always her sister, though. She was a minx.

"Drop dead."

Oh, yeah. "Sorry. I was kidding."

"Is that all guys do? Think about sex? That has got to be exhausting."

"You have no idea."

"Well, yeah. I think I do. You're in my head, you jerk."

Just then, I saw that my fears that no one was coming to my funeral could cease. The double doors of the viewing room opened and in filed a large crowd of men. Some carried signs, some held candles, but, all wore the same ribbon pinned to their shirts. And on those ribbons there was a rainbow, e-i-e-i-o.

It seemed that the local gay community had come out to pay their respects to what they thought to be one of their own, brutally murdered by the fascist regime. I was touched. Their sense of unity overwhelmed me. Since nobody would be able to tell it was really me doing it, I cried right then—cried like baby.

To Sarah, I said "Let's go."

"What's stopping you, big boy?"

My control over her must have been slipping. While I was distracted by the crowd gathering around the coffin, Sarah had been busy trying to get the attention of one of the men nearest the coffin.

"You're stopping me, Sarah. Let go of that person's testicles and stop singing *Swing Low Sweet Chariot*. That might do it."

She let go of the mildly confused man's johnson, but continued to sing until I/we were out the door and around the corner. I guess she figured it was the only power she had left. This was good, because I was beginning to get a little sick of the constant war over her arms and legs.

I really had to sit down somewhere and read the manual that Dave gave me after shoving my soul into her body. The next bench we passed, I grabbed onto it and lowered us into a sitting position. Sarah, having her own ideas, tried to make a run for it, but I held tight to the bench and told her that if she didn't stop fighting I was going to step in front of the next car. I wasn't kidding, either. What was gonna happen? I'd die again. So fucking what. That was probably why she stopped; because I was done pissing around.

Confused?

Of course you are. You don't know about Sarah being a medium, or my murder at the hands of a demon assassin...or even about Dave, the grossly obese undead guy.

Sorry. I'm just a little agitated.

You know, being dead and all.

First off, have you ever been to a séance? Seen a ghost—
Elvis or otherwise? Not like it makes any difference. I just
thought it might help us connect a little better if you had.

Let me explain. In the beginning, there was nothing...

2

One week earlier. Movie night.

"Yeah, nothing," Nature said. "I seen all this shit before, uh huh. Whose pick is it this week, anyway?"

"Dingo's," I told him, stepping out of the "adults only" room after finding nothing I hadn't seen before either. "You had your pick last week, dude."

And what a pick that was. Nature chose *Driving Miss Daisy* 'cause he thought it was a mis-shelved porno. Hell, I was kinda curious myself, but nothing, zilcho poonage—not even a little old lady tit.

And even after finding out it wasn't a skin flick, we at least thought that having Morgan Freeman in it would be enough to make the movie halfway enjoyable—he's been in some pretty sweet movies and his voice was cool as shit—but no. Not even the voice of God himself could fuck start that turkey. All he did was exactly what the title said: Drive Miss Daisy's grumpy ass around.

After all the crap movies he's put us through over the years, I don't even know why we let Nature take a turn on Movie Night.

Just between you and me, Nature's not exactly on Mensa's mailing list if you know what I mean. And we just let him hang with us because he's the only one we know who doesn't drink—great guy to have around on bar night—saves a shitload on cab fares.

"Speaking of turns," I said. "Where's Dingo? I wanna make sure he doesn't pick something out that tries to touch my inner lesbian."

I followed Nature's grinning nod to the front of the video store. Then he said, "I don't even know why he gets a pick this week. He's taking off at nine anyway. Got a date or something. Meeting up with this new chick he's been seeing, uh huh."

The "Uh huh" thing used to get on my nerves, but then I came to realize it was kind of like his own personal punctuation mark; his way of ending a sentence, you know? Now, I don't even notice it...mostly.

"New chick," I said. "He never said nothing to me about any new chick. What's her name?"

"Sarah, I think He said she was some kind of gypsy or something."

Boing! It was then that I understood why Dingo hadn't told me about his new girl. Being my best friend, Dingo would know I'd think that her being a gypsy was just about the hottest thing ever. God bless the black-hearted bastard, he wasn't wrong.

I didn't want to seem too interested, so I picked up a movie jacket and pretended to peruse some chick flick. "Really? So, what does she look like?"

"Never seen her, but Dan number two says she's a real honey."

Recalling some of Dan number two's past conquests, what Nature said meant nothing. Dan number two's taste in women leaned toward whatever was left after last call at a bar, when the lights came up.

I left Nature to do whatever it was he did when we weren t there to tell him to do it, and went to the front of the store to continue my investigation into Dingo's new tang. It seemed Dingo and I had some trust issues to work out that had been hanging between us since back in school.

He thought I cock blocked him on a girl he was trying to get with. Lingering on a perceived past injustice like that was only gonna constipate him again. (Dingo gorged on bricks of cheese when he brooded.)

What? You looking at me 'cause you think I know why? It's his thing. Move on.

Besides, that girl back in college was a lifetime ago—not to mention the fact that she wasn't really his girlfriend, anyway. She said so right before I threw her into my patented "Bus driver" position. Couldn't even remember what she looked like. As I said: ancient history.

I stepped up behind Dingo and waited for him to finish with the piss-poor job he was doing at flirting with the girl at the counter. Chick couldn't have been more than eighteen.

When he saw me, he held up the disc he'd picked out and shrugged. "I heard it was a flop, but thought I'd get it anyway. Can't be any worse than that Killer Clown snuff movie Dan number two picked out that one time. Remember that? Big Top Chop?"

I chuckled. "Actually, I kind of got a kick out of that one. Say, listen: I heard you got yourself a date tonight. That you were gonna take off at nine. Were you planning on partying without me, amigo? How are you gonna have any fun without the Bard there to bring the good word to the masses?"

After so many years of being friends Dingo knew exactly what I was saying.

"She's special, Shakespeare. I really like this girl and don't want you guys to fuck it up for me." He brandished his movie choice, *Waterworld*, and said, "Besides, it's movie night and you know how much Nature hates change.

"Yeah, sure," I brushed his misplaced concern off like it was dandruff. "No biggie. Go shine on, you crazy diamond."

What a dick. Last time I play co-pilot for him.

Who needs to guzzle beer and party? Who needs to ogle hot gypsies while tossing back shooters of tequila? Who needs to forget that he'd been dumped for the very first time in his fucking life by a girl who he thought might be the one to make him burn his booty call book?

To answer all three I needed only to single out one man. Me, Shakespeare, that's who. Then I began thinking about her again and how she dumped me.

Fucking Sheila...for some dude named Cary, of all people! How could she leave me for a guy with a chick's name? Who names their little baby boy Cary?

Could be he's British.

Even Dutch, maybe.

Meet the crew. You already know about Nature and Dingo Dan, but I haven't told you very much about Dan number two and Willie Chacha. They were pulling double duty tonight, all of them. It was movie night, but they were also there to lend whatever moral support they could to yours truly; being two weeks since my girlfriend had left me, I was still reeling from the alien feeling of being the dumpee for a switch.

They tried. I could see they were trying, but they sucked at the Dr. Phil thing.

In the midst of stuffing a fistful of popcorn into his mouth, Dan number two said, "You're a cop. Why don't you stake her out or some shit, follow her around and see where she goes."

I didn't want to tell him I already did and it took me exactly nowhere. All I got for my trouble was her father punching me in the gut when he caught me under one of their windows at three am, and Sheila meeting some chick at a restaurant.

Nature's contribution to the healing of my bruised ego was just plain sad.

He said, "I wouldn't let it bug you, Shakes. It ain't so bad getting dumped, uh huh. At least you got us, right?"

I tried not to look constipated while he spoke, but sometimes listening to him was about as painful as taking a baby-sized shit.

The boys went on for a while—even looked like they were being sincere—but I don't think one of them could've understood what I was going through. Shakespeare Poole didn't get dumped. Not ever.

What I needed was distraction, and not some "Welcome to the Sissy Club" hug-fest. I needed noise and plenty of tail to sniff at; I needed the tang the astronauts wished they brought with them into deep space. There was nowhere better to find those things than in a bar full of drunk women.

Dingo and his new chick would be there, and it's not like I was planning nothing. I just wanted to see what kind of gypsy chick would be attracted to a fella like Dingo.

Right after Dingo left for his date, I said, "You pussies wanna sit around here stroking each other and watching this piece of shit, or do you want to do what Dingo's gonna be doing by the end of the night?"

Nature gave me a look like he was answering a question on Jeopardy. "You mean barfing in the back of my Subaru?"

"Yeah, that's exactly what I meant, Nature. Shut up and watch your movie."

Always the mayor of a little village known as Obvious, Willie Chacha sat up, belched, and then said: "You want to get a look at Dingo's new squeeze, don't you?"

I lied to him and said no, that I wanted to blow off some steam, but he wasn't stupid. "Nature, get your keys. We're going out."

As we were getting ready to leave, who do you suppose strolled in to stick a pin in my half-inflated erection?

Uh huh. the ex. You'll notice I didn't capitalize the "the" there. See? Just goes to show how upset I was with her.

"William, Jason, Daniel," she said to the boys, not so much friendly as, say, acknowledging their right to call themselves hominids. She didn't say "hi" to me, but since she *did* enter my apartment, I imagined it was implied.

I never really thought about it 'til right then how she called the crew by their real names. None of them seemed to mind, so it shouldn't bother me like it did...but it did. Fuck, I didn't even know how she knew Nature's given name was Jason. It's not like I told her.

When she turned her eyes towards me I froze like a twelve-year-old caught masturbating.

It was a dark and stormy stare, one that had held me in its Medusa-like grip during—but mostly after—many a boozy night. No words, just the laser beam of death.

That's Sheila for you. But don't blame her. I brought it on myself.

You'll see. Apparently, it's in my nature to bring out the worst in women, to make them hate everything about themselves and cause them to wallow in the filth and mental stagnation that is Shakespeare Poole—her words, not mine. I, myself, didn't get it; the mental stagnation part. What did a scummy pond have to do with a relationship? It was just like her to try and confuse me.

She knew it was movie night, sure she did. Why show up then, when she knew goddamn well that the crew would be there? I was all ears, hoping she'd enlighten me. But unless she was transmitting at a level only another bitch could hear, or through the tractor beam she had locked onto my face, I wasn't getting it.

Just when the silence became so uncomfortable that the boys began to shuffle their feet and gaze around the room at my Bud Girl posters, Sheila dropped the stun gun stare and did one of those head wobbles that usually end with a finger being pointed.

Never one to disappoint, there was the finger.

She said: "There was a parking ticket on my car this morning, and I was pulled over twice today; once on the way to work, and once on the way to my friend's place. You wouldn't have had anything to do with that, now, would you, Tinyspeare? Because, if that's the case, you can stop right now. I'm done with you and I'm done trying to turn you into a human being. You got that?"

Huh. I was only kidding when I was talking to some of the boys down at the station about her, but I guess they thought I wasn't. Goes to show, though. Cops take care of their own. I was touched.

Kinda funny, though, right?

The "Tinyspeare" thing was a pretty low blow, but I knew she didn't mean anything by it. I had videotapes that proved otherwise.

I made a mental note to send her dad one of our tapes. Then I smiled instead of answering for the stops by the cops.

Sheila yelled at me one more time, gave the boys an obviously well rehearsed recap of the many reasons she'd left me, and then she slammed the door on her way out.

I could tell right away that she'd upset the fellas. They

milled around, looking anywhere but at me.

I pointed at Nature, and said, "Boy," and clapped my hands twice. "Bring forth the bong. We need to purge some guilt."

As we stood around my coffee, sharing the sweet leaf, I couldn't help but think about Sheila and the real reason she stopped by. She could've called the answering machine to bitch me out about the speeding tickets. Maybe she thought I should've been sitting in the dark, listening to *The Cure* while I cut myself with a sharpened spoon.

When I reached into the closet for my jacket, Willie Chacha plucked a baseball bat from the top shelf and ran his thumb along the myriad of dents along the body. He poked me with the business end, almost driving me into the closet, and then swung the bat in a wide arc, missing Nature's head by a, well, a hair. "Mailbox baseball, anyone?"

In a very un-Nature-like way, Nature forcefully yanked the bat away from Willie and squeezed it like he wanted to swing it himself. "Nuh uh, man. You assholes still owe me reparations for the last six times, uh huh."

Dan number two grabbed the bat from him and tossed it into the closet. "Yeah, doofus, but we let you hang with us, don't we? Ain't that enough?"

As they bickered I realized just how traumatized they were by the deviation caused by the ex, and also knew that I had to put a stop to the insults before Nature took his car and went home. Why pay for a cab when you don't need to?

When Dingo Dan's not around, I call Dan number two, just plain Dan, so I said: "Shut up, Dan. First off, he can't be a doofus. Got a driver's license, doesn't he?" I knew that Dan would understand the implied statement, and he nodded, backing off.

Then he voiced what I, myself, was already thinking.

Dan jabbed his thumb over his shoulder as he dropped his jacket on a chair. "Maybe we should hit that bong one more time before we go."

3

Sarah

Me and the boys had never been out to the bar on our Monday Movie night, so I had no idea that it was gonna be so packed – and the line going in didn't look to be moving too fast. The bouncer at the door was some beady eyed albino gorilla I'd never seen before, wearing a t-shirt he must've snatched out of a five-year-olds closet; the seams along his biceps looked about ready to fissure if he sneezed. Maybe he'd eaten the regular bouncer – who's to say?

Whatever. The fact remained that the line stretched around the corner and I wasn't Paris Hilton. I wasn't about to palm the dude any cash, and Shakespeare Poole didn't wait in line for nothing, so I reached for the only weapons in my arsenal: a big, sloppy, shovelful of bullshit and my badge.

I flashed my shield and tossed the giant a story about the most dastardly criminal I could think of on such short notice – a crazed serial monogamist who'd been terrorizing local nightclubs, and was last spotted in the area wearing nothing but a dog collar and a pink sweater.

The bouncer seemed sceptical. I might've crossed the line with the pink sweater. He looked at me, looked at my badge, looked past me at the crew, and thrust his chin in the direction of the boys. "Those mutherfuckers cops too?"

The crew bobbed their heads and grinned, which more or less killed the sense of imminent danger that any one of the hundreds of patrons might be faced with if confronted with a serial monogamist.

I stepped in front of the boys, and said, long and slow, "You betcha." Then I jabbed a thumb over my shoulder at Nature. "And if you'd like, I could leave one of the officers out here to keep you safe while the rest of us take a look inside."

The big man's eyes, which I didn't believe could get any beadier – if that's even a word – pulled together so tight they met at the bridge of his nose. I got the impression he didn't believe I was exactly truthful with him, but he shrugged and dropped the velvet rope.

Once the door closed behind us, Nature caught up to me and grabbed me by the elbow. "What the hell were you thinking telling him we was cops? And offering to leave me out there with him? You could get in a lot of shit for that, uh huh."

That's what I loved about Nature. He was just so goddamned practical, so innocent. I tousled his hair and slapped him on the ass. Over the music, I yelled, "Go get your dick wet and don't worry so much, Nature. Besides, I think we coulda took him."

I was pretty sure Nature was a virgin, but it wasn't because he was ugly. It was his mouth. Every time he came close to scoring, some idiot imp would take possession of his brain and out would come some of stupidest shit you ever heard come out of the mouth of a man looking to get laid.

You know, thinking back, the rest of us should have pooled together and paid a hooker to plug him into the wild side. Maybe after a taste of the good stuff, he might not have acted like such a dweeb.

Dingo must have been expecting us to come out, even though I promised we wouldn't. Instead of being propped up by his elbows at the bar like usual, double fisting Buds, him and his new girl were hunkered down in a booth near the back of the club. Dingo had his hand out, palm up, and his girl was holding it by the fingers. They were both leaned over his hand, staring at it, like they were watching a flea doing somersaults between his thumb and fuck-you finger.

When we stepped up to the booth, Sarah saw us first and smiled, not knowing who the hell we were, probably, but smiling anyway. When I first saw her up close, my heart stuttered twice and stopped. For most men there was either Mary Anne or Ginger – either/or, that's it – but she was both and then some.

I spent a lifetime in those eyes...and by the time she looked questioningly down at Dingo, I'd already mentally taken her in every position known to man – and some practiced only by the spider monkeys of western Asia. I was in lust.

Dingo knew what he'd find even before he turned to see what she was looking at. Before he was all the way around, he was already telling her our names.

She said, just how I imagined she would, "Nice to meet you all. Dan has told me so much about you."

She said it like she was saying it to all of us, but she was looking at me the whole time.

Then, sticking her hand out to me, she said, "I hear you're a cop. I just love cops."

I think we shared something in that handshake; I could feel a sort of connection, you know?

Maybe Dingo saw what I saw too, because he scooted over 'til he was almost sitting on her and said, "Since you're here."

I didn't hear him add "you might as well join us," but I'm sure he meant to.

I looked at his drink, not his normal pair of Bud, and asked, "What's with the drink? You drinking rum?"

When he shook his head, then darted his eyes at the rest of the boys and mumbled "Pepsi," I did a double take.

No wonder he didn't want us around. Next thing he was gonna tell us was that salmon wasn't a bad colour for some guys as long as it matched their eye shadow.

I did the only thing a best buddy could do during such a crisis. I flagged down a waitress and said, "Twelve Tequila, ten Bud." I paused, raising my eyebrows to Sarah.

She said, just as sexy as I thought she would, "Bud sounds good."

What an angel.

To the waitress, I said, "Okay, instead of ten, make that twelve Bud. Stat, lady. Go. I think I have a friend here in danger of falling victim to that serial monogamist who's been running around causing pandemonium and infecting innocent bar-goers."

The waitress steadied her full tray of empties and leaned down with a look of shock on her face. "You know, I heard of him. They were talking about him outside just now. I hope they get that sick bastard."

I glanced hurriedly at Dingo, who had his hands wrapped around the glass of Pepsi in a white knuckled chokehold. "Quick, lady, we're running out of time. And don't forget the tequila."

Dingo wasn't too happy with us at first, crashing his date and all, but after six or seven beers, he was almost back to his old self. We found out that Sarah was not only a Gypsy by birth, but that she was also a medium. Looked more like a petite to me, and I said so too, but then she laughed and explained what being a medium was all about.

Believing she was fucking with us, I said, "Aw, come on. You're just yanking my chain. You telling me you talk to the dead?"

She nodded while taking a long slug from her bottle. "Sometimes."

I said: "So, what, you learned from your mom? From being a Gypsy?"

"No. My sister and I trained with a woman we met at a nudists retreat."

When my eyebrows rose, and I leaned forward in my chair, Dingo Dan shot me a hard look. You know what, though? Hard as that look was, it wasn't nowhere near as hard as I was right then.

Willie Chacha, who was just circling back to the table to drop off his empty and grab a full bottle from the cluster in the middle, said, "Hey, why don't we have a séance and see if we can find out where Bobby Slow-Mo kept his cash. You know he still owed us money before he died, right?"

Hoping I was wrong, I said, loud enough for everyone to hear, "Oh, she doesn't want to do that kind of stuff tonight, Willie. Besides, you know there's no such thing." Plus, just in case it wasn't crap, I didn't want to tell him that I already collected the money from Bobby's widow, but then lost it all playing cards with her. I think she cheated.

Sarah stood and planted her hands on her hips. If I'm not

mistaken, she also shot me the Evil Eye. Then she said, "Ah, ho. Nonbeliever, eh?"

"No, It's nothing like that," I said, raising my hands to ward off whatever magic might be behind the 'Eye'. "I just thought you'd rather have fun than work."

She squinted at me. "I think I'm going to enjoy proving you wrong, mister Shakespeare. Besides, being a medium isn't work, it's a calling."

"Shakes," I said. "But feel free to call me anything you want."

"Before this night is through, you'll believe," she said, and bent down and placed her palms flat on the table, effectively opening her top for me to see—hell, for everybody there, with the exception of Dingo—that she wasn't wearing a bra. If I didn't know better, it even seemed like she was daring us to look away.

I gulped. "I, for one, would believe anything that came out of your mouth." I'm pretty sure my opinion was unanimous, but it was kind of hard to tell with Dingo. He was way past shit faced, sitting there with his lids half closed and his face greener than the envy I felt for him over bagging such an awesome girl.

Sarah, suddenly way more mysterious than she'd been before the wardrobe malfunction, was still staring at me. "Well?"

I couldn't speak for the rest of the crew, but I didn't remember the conversation well enough to know exactly what the "well" question was for, so I asked.

She said that we could have a séance for that guy Willie mentioned.

"I know just the place," I said, and winked. I downed the rest of my beer and slammed the bottle on the table. "Nature! Let's roll."

Nature knew. He was already swinging his keys on his finger. Or maybe he was there all the time, following me around like my own boy-Friday and I only noticed when I need him.

Right then, right there, I was happy. Things were gonna

change, I could feel it.

As for Sarah, I'd fallen in lust with her even before she spoke.

This, my friends, was the girl who innocently started the whole ball of snow tumbling down the mountain...at least for me.

Apologies. I'm getting a little ahead of myself again. My point is this: She was hot, had a clothing optional attitude, and seemed as airy as a carload of fog farts. I guess that's all I'm trying to say. Oh, and best of all she really, really, loved cops. Shakespeare Poole was in luck, and Dingo Dan was apparently not. That's because Shakespeare was a cop. That's me.

While we waited for Dingo and Dan number two to finish theirs beers, I leaned across and asked Sarah what she did when she wasn't raising the dead or staring at hands.

She eyed me suspiciously for a second or two before answering. "I do legal piecework for The Wildlife Federation."

Okay, so maybe you can forget what I said about the fog farts, but she was still my kind of gal.

☺

On the way out of the bar a hand the size of a pancake skillet slapped my chest, stopping me in my tracks. "I thought you were coming back out if you didn't find that crazy serial monogamist?"

I pushed the bouncer's hand away and stepped past him. "We did," I said, pointing back at Dingo Dan, who was half stumbling, half being carried out between Willie Chacha and Dan number two. "That's him there. Had to stun him, too. We regret any inconvenience we may have caused. You're safe now. Carry on."

"It's all good," the bouncer said, nodding at our job well done. "I'm just glad you got him. I couldn't imagine what would happen if somebody like him was allowed to roam free."

I could tell that the beady eyed muscle head was dying for his shift to end so he could sprint home, dust off a dictionary, and look up a word or two. Behind his rapidly blinking eyes, I imagined long unused gears spinning fast enough to cause smoke.

Sarah laughed all the way to the car. We all did—well, everybody 'cept Dingo Dan. He was looking pretty green. I flashed back to Nature's earlier words about what Dingo would be doing by the end of the night. He'd said Dingo would be puking in the back of his Subaru. Fuck, maybe Nature was a prophet.

"Shotgun," I said, before anyone got a chance to beat me to it. If Dingo was gonna puke, he sure wasn't gonna be puking on me.

Sarah was still giggling when we pulled out of the parking lot, headed for my place. This may seem pretty limp, but I remember thinking at the time that it sounded just about what I imagined an angel's laugh would be like.

Not like I beat myself up about it—you live, you die, that's it—but I sometimes wonder what would've happened if I hadn't met her that night. If not, then maybe that demon wouldn't have put a bullet through my skull, and you wouldn't be reading about a cool motherfucker named Shakespeare.

Who's dead.

Please look for the remainder of *Shakespeare's Dead: A Tragedy in III Acts!* this coming summer.

Be good to each other. If you can't, have a good alibi, two rolls of duct tape, extra clothes (and rubber boots), a shovel (spade), a hacksaw, an axe, several disposable towels, a 40 pack of industrial strength garbage bags (triple bag everything!), several plastic tarps, neoprene gloves (carry extras – wear extras), a jug of bleach, a can of gasoline, and about five bags of lye. Or own a pig farm. Another option is to, you know, let it slide. Life's too short to be an asshole. For those too insane to know the difference, the above was a joke.

Peace/out, kiddies. Also, but by no means lesser for being second, thanks for reading my little tale about a girl of worth. Zoe'll be back, along with a few of her friends, in the sequel.

Cheers

Gerald Johnston,
Corunna, Ontario
Oct/21/12

**Why are you looking here. Go buy another book.
This one's done.** ☺